A CARTOON NETWORK ORIGINAL

ADVENTURE TIME™

THUNDER ROAD

ROSS RICHIE CEO & Founder
MATT GAGNON Editor-in-Chief
FILIP SABLIK President of Publishing & Marketing
STEPHEN CHRISTY President of Development
LANCE KREITER VP of Licensing & Merchandising
PHIL BARBARO VP of Finance
ARUNE SINGH VP of Marketing
BRYCE CARLSON Managing Editor
SCOTT NEWMAN Production Design Manager
KATE HENNING Operations Manager
SIERRA HAHN Senior Editor
DAFNA PLEBAN Editor, Talent Development
SHANNON WATTERS Editor
ERIC HARBURN Editor
WHITNEY LEOPARD Editor
CAMERON CHITTOCK Editor
CHRIS ROSA Associate Editor
MATTHEW LEVINE Associate Editor
SOPHIE PHILIPS-ROBERTS Assistant Editor
GAVIN GRONENTHAL Assistant Editor

MICHAEL MOCCIO Assistant Editor
AMANDA LaFRANCO Executive Assistant
KATALINA HOLLAND Editorial Administrative Assistant
JILLIAN CRAB Design Coordinator
MICHELLE ANKLEY Design Coordinator
KARA LEOPARD Production Designer
MARIE KRUPINA Production Designer
GRACE PARK Production Design Assistant
CHELSEA ROBERTS Production Design Assistant
ELIZABETH LOUGHRIDGE Accounting Coordinator
STEPHANIE HOCUTT Social Media Coordinator
JOSÉ MEZA Event Coordinator
HOLLY AITCHISON Operations Assistant
MEGAN CHRISTOPHER Operations Assistant
RODRIGO HERNANDEZ Mailroom Assistant
MORGAN PERRY Direct Market Representative
CAT O'GRADY Marketing Assistant
LIZ ALMENDAREZ Accounting Administrative Assistant
CORNELIA TZANA Administrative Assistant

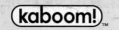

Created by Pendleton Ward

Written by **Jeremy Sorese**
Illustrated by **Zachary Sterling**
Colors by **Laura Langston**
Letters by **Mike Fiorentino**

Cover by **Jonathan Cantero**

Designer **Kara Leopard**
Assistant Editor **Michael Moccio**
Editor **Whitney Leopard**

With Special Thanks to Marisa Marionakis, Janet No, Curtis Lelash, Conrad Montgomery, Kelly Crews, Scott Malchus, Adam Muto and the wonderful folks at Cartoon Network.

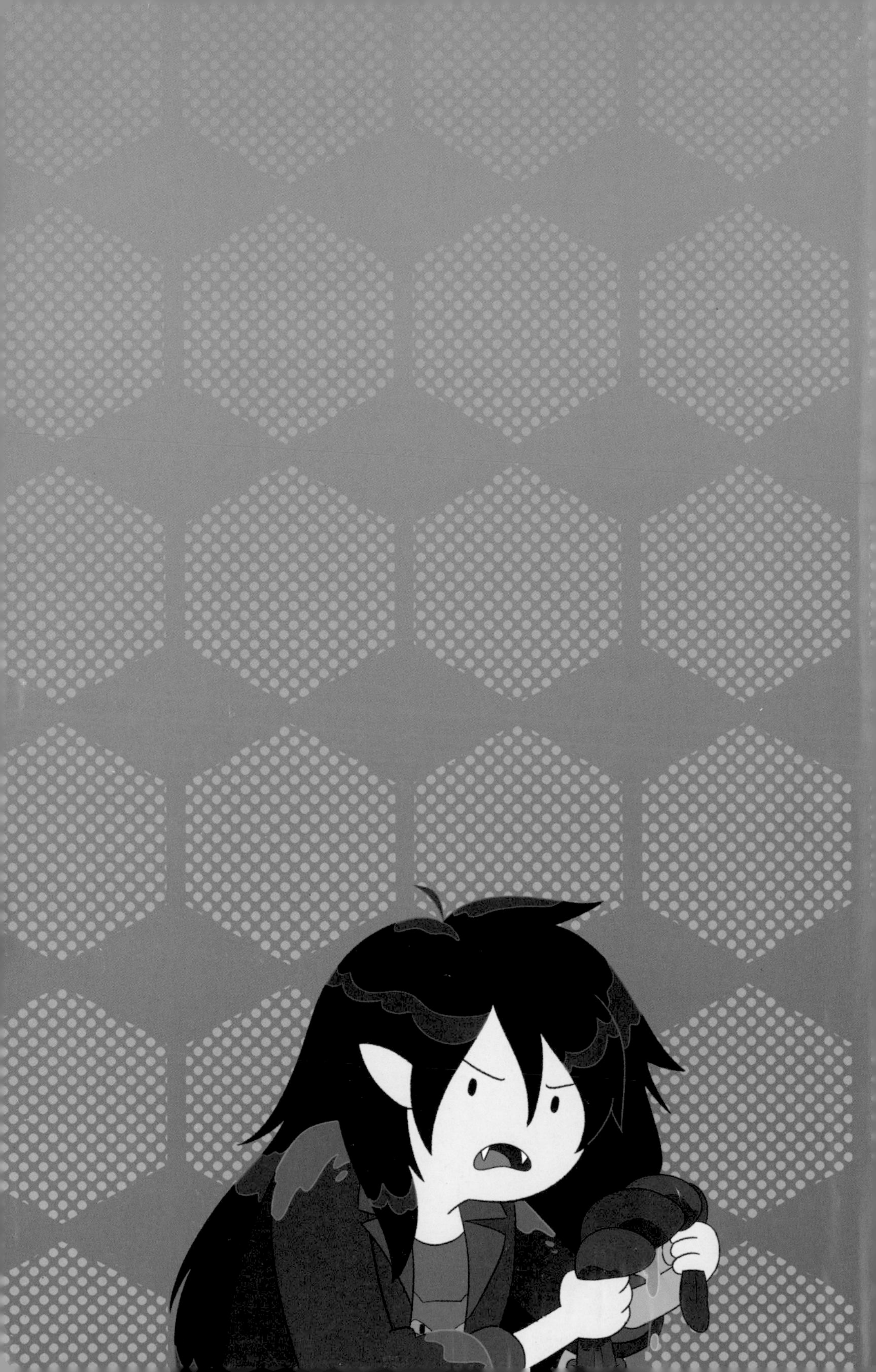

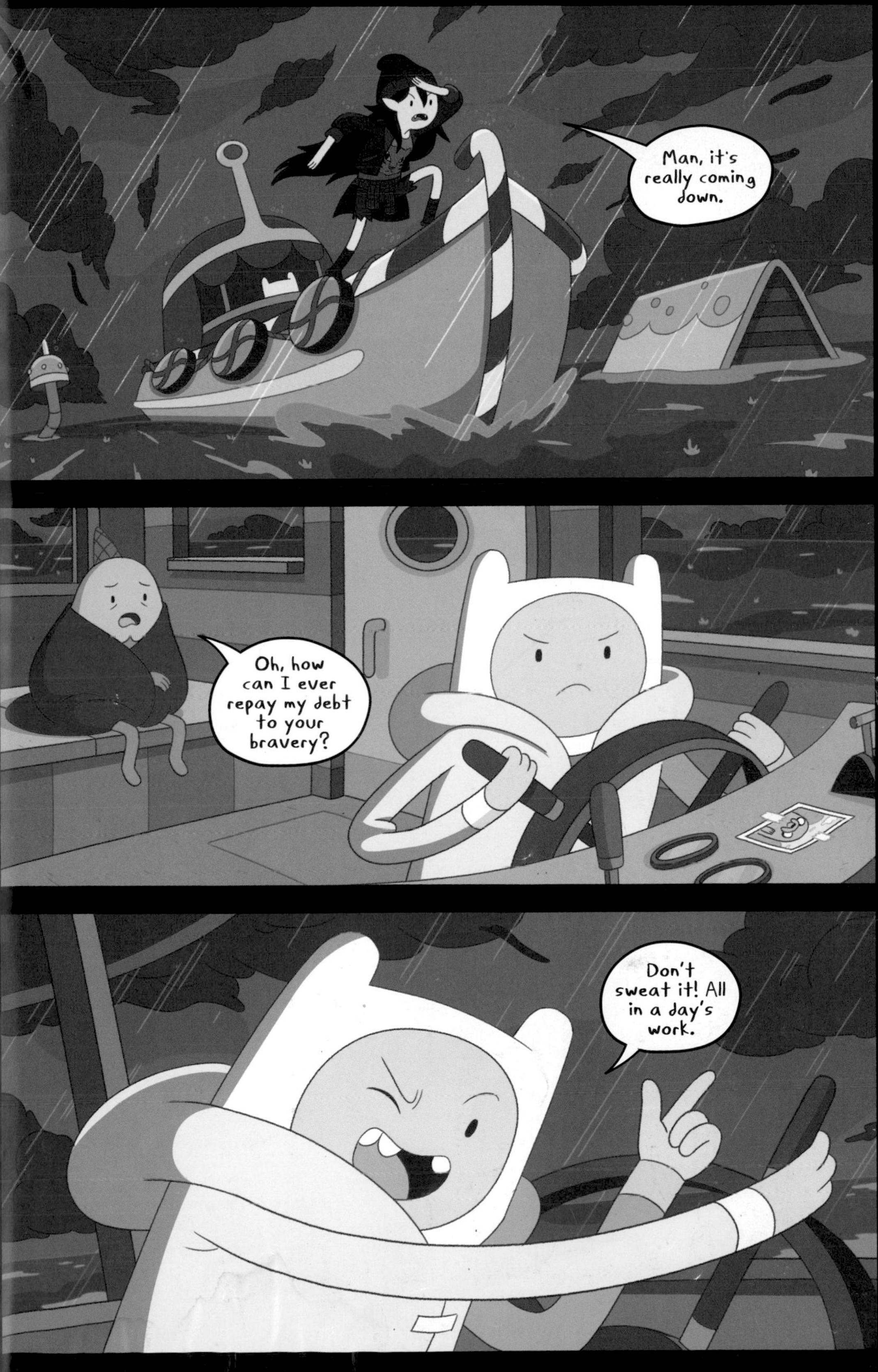
Man, it's really coming down.
Oh, how can I ever repay my debt to your bravery?
Don't sweat it! All in a day's work.

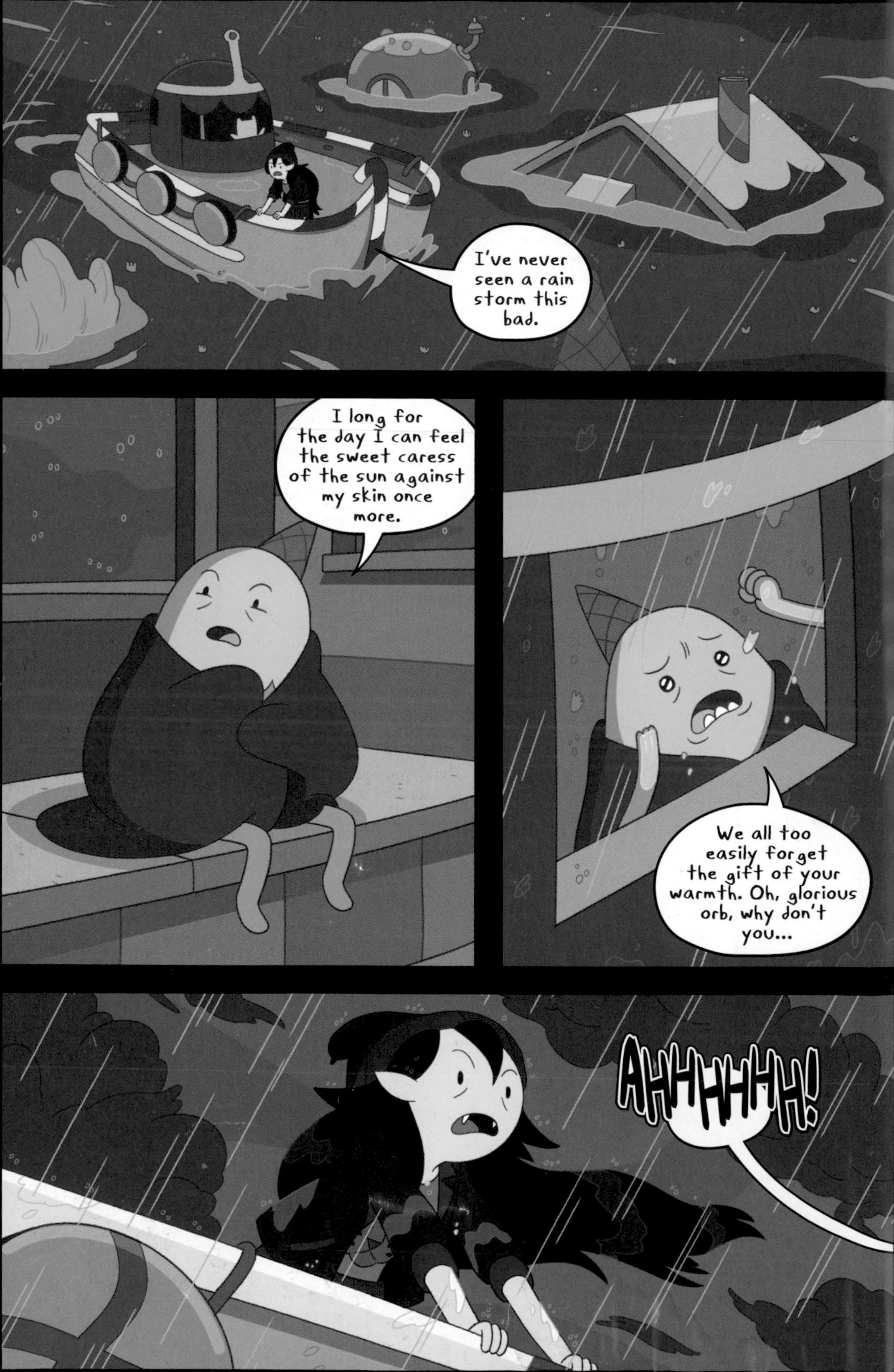
I've never seen a rain storm this bad.
I long for the day I can feel the sweet caress of the sun against my skin once more.
We all too easily forget the gift of your warmth. Oh, glorious orb, why don't you...
AHHHHHH!

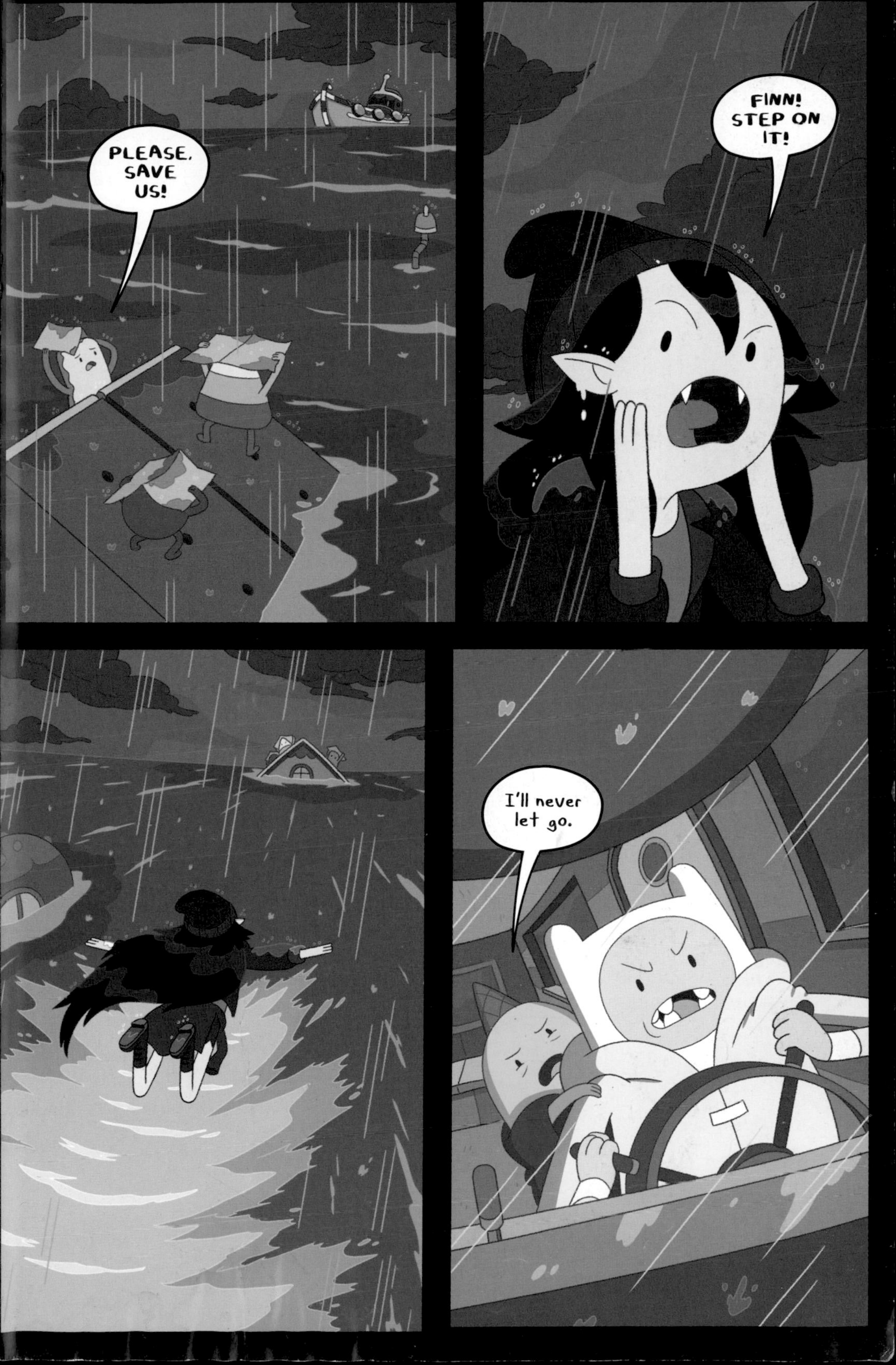
PLEASE, SAVE US!
FINN! STEP ON IT!
I'll never let go.

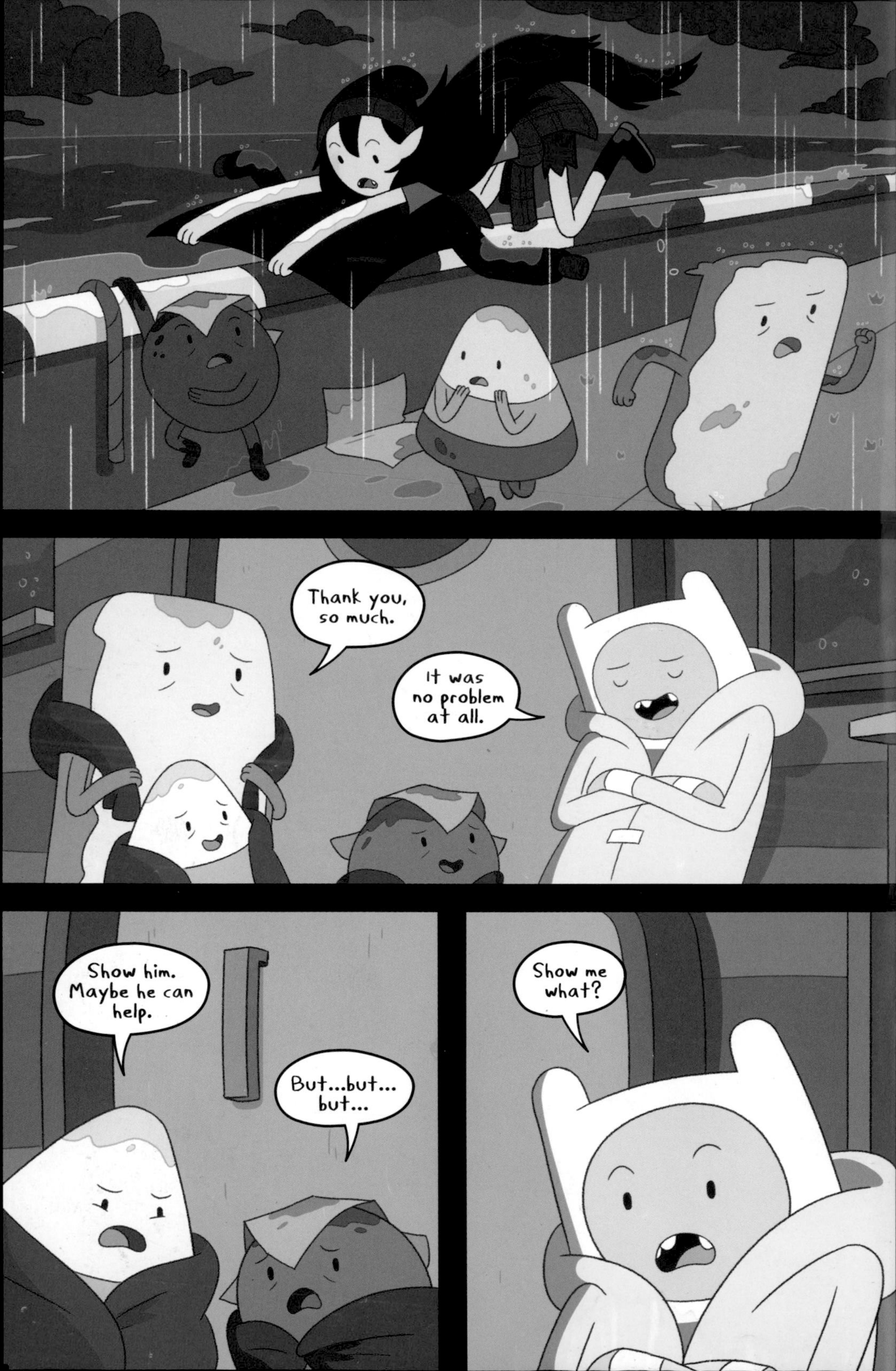
Thank you, so much.
It was no problem at all.
Show him. Maybe he can help.
But...but... but...
Show me what?

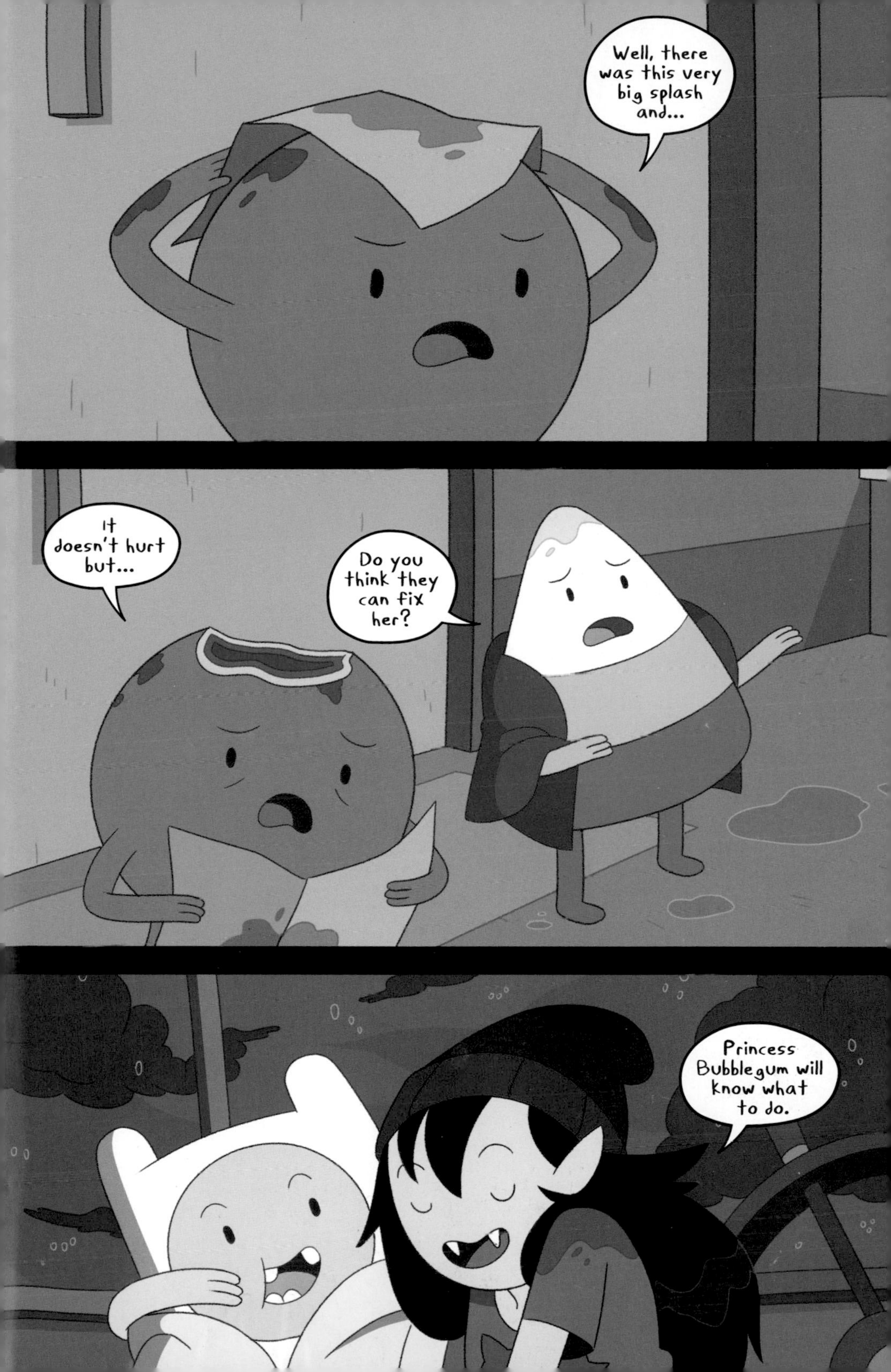
Well, there was this very big splash and...
It doesn't hurt but...
Do you think they can fix her?
Princess Bubblegum will know what to do.

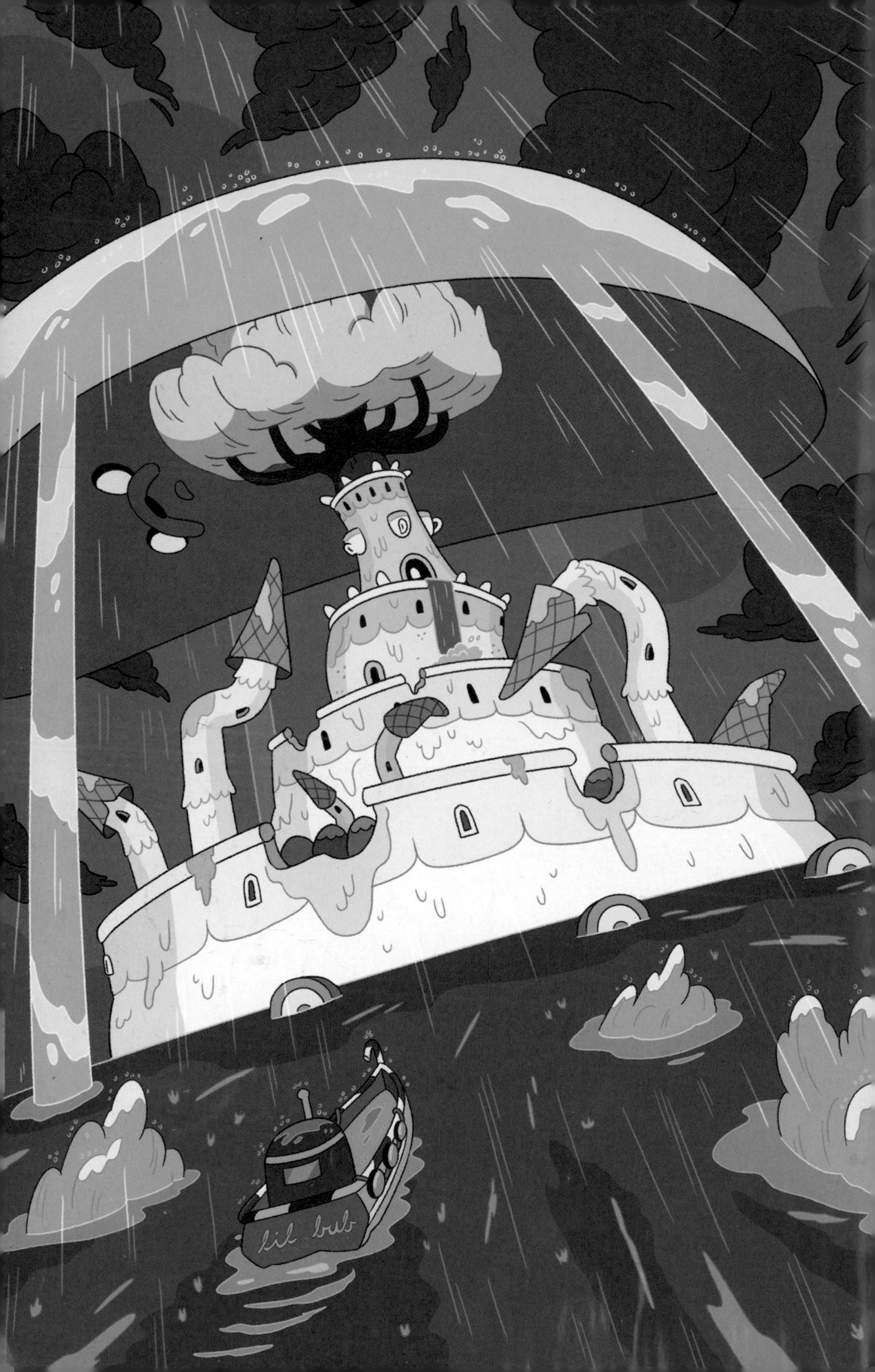
lil bub

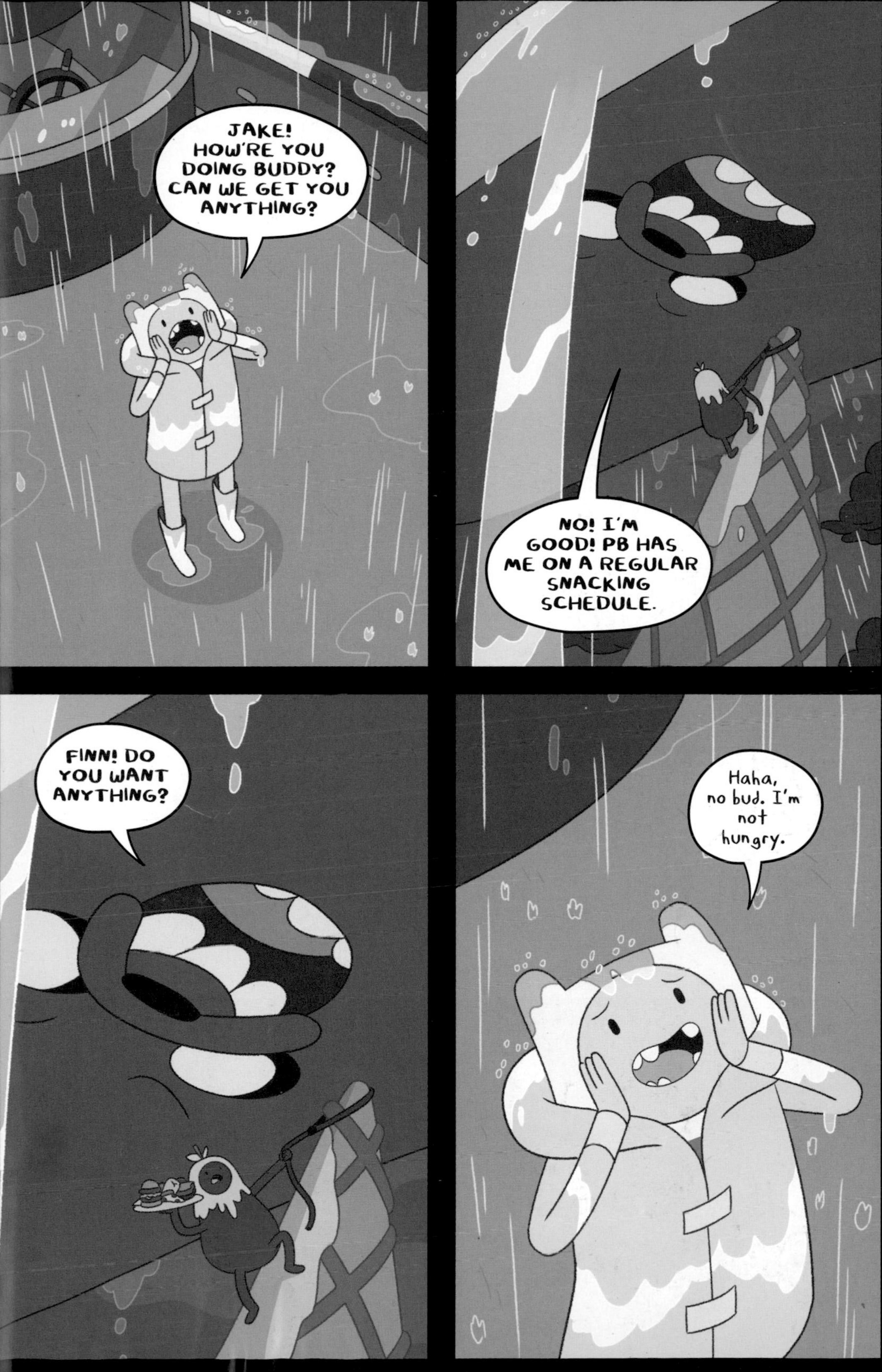
JAKE! HOW'RE YOU DOING BUDDY? CAN WE GET YOU ANYTHING?
NO! I'M GOOD! PB HAS ME ON A REGULAR SNACKING SCHEDULE.
FINN! DO YOU WANT ANYTHING?
Haha, no bud. I'm not hungry.

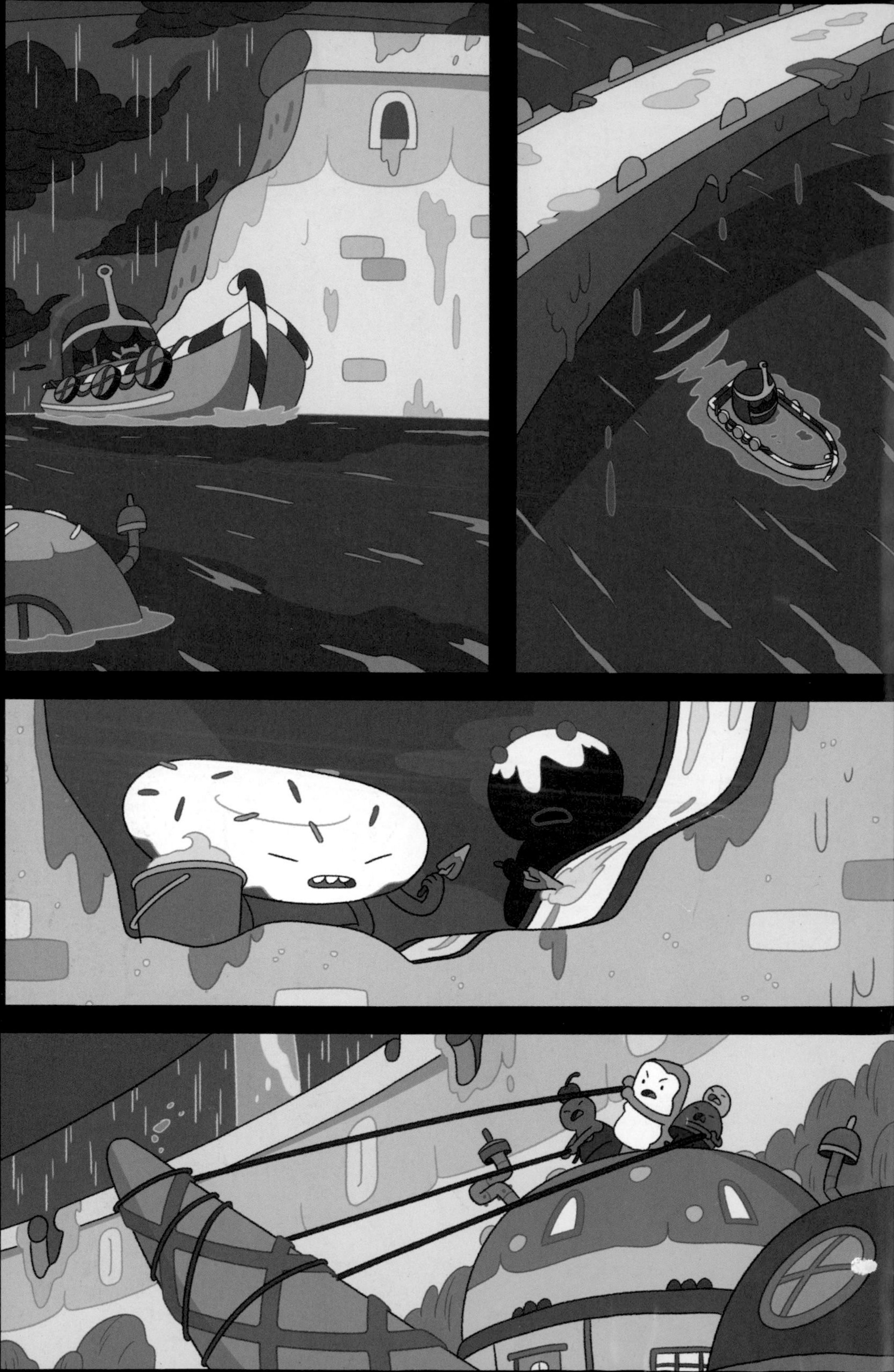

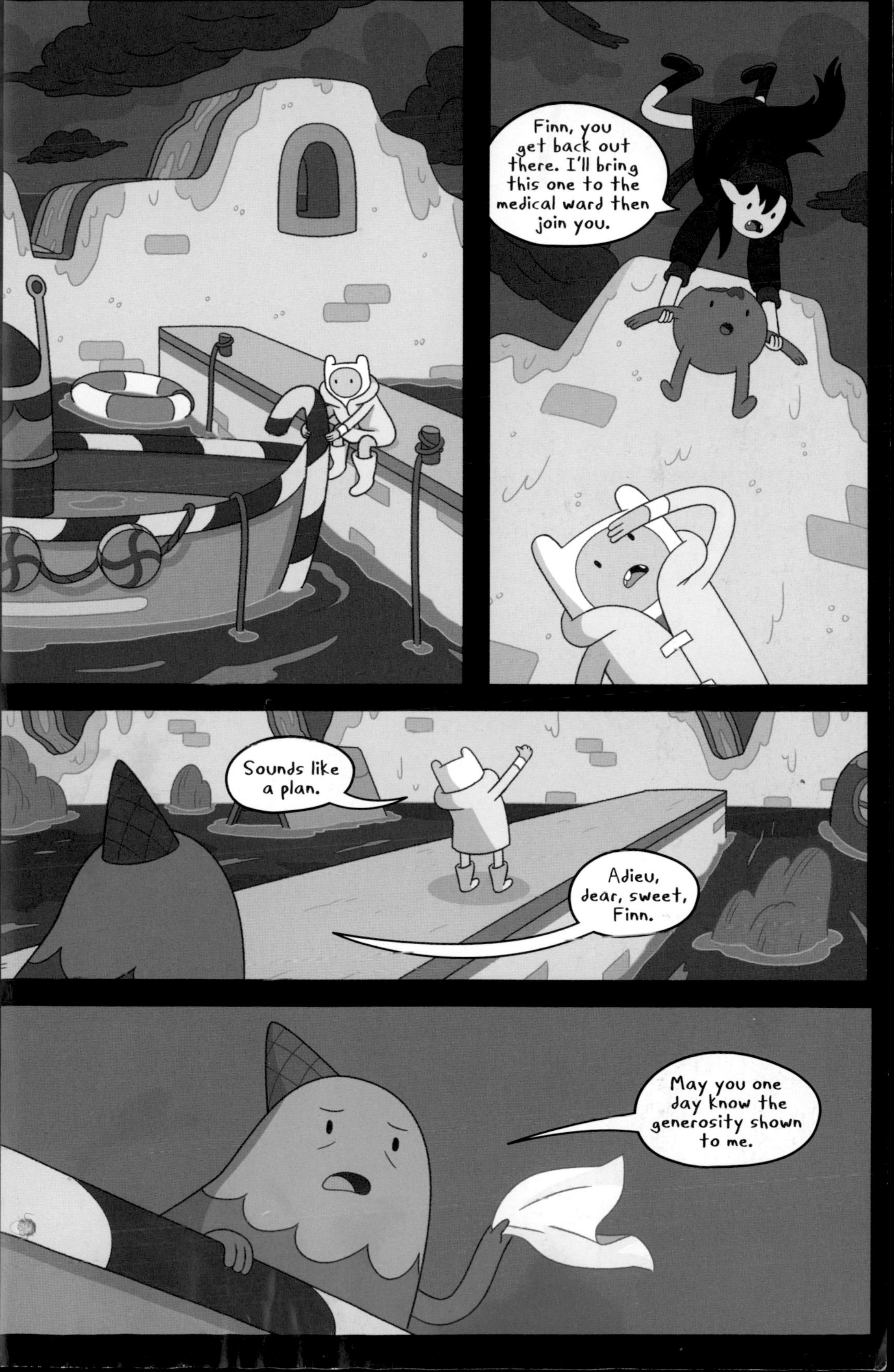
Finn, you get back out there. I'll bring this one to the medical ward then join you.
Sounds like a plan.
Adieu, dear, sweet, Finn.
May you one day know the generosity shown to me.

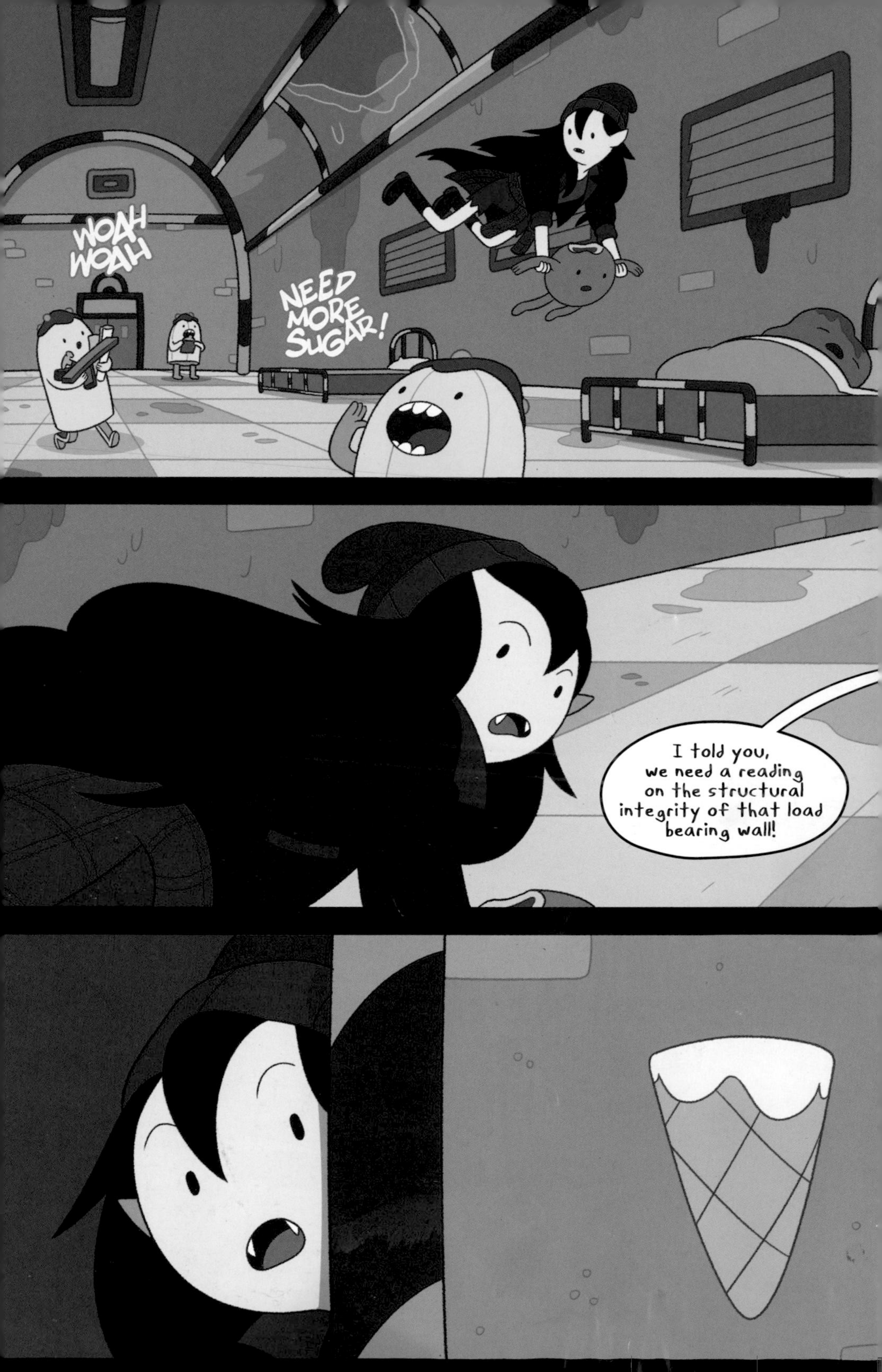

WOAH WOAH
NEED MORE SUGAR!
I told you, we need a reading on the structural integrity of that load bearing wall!

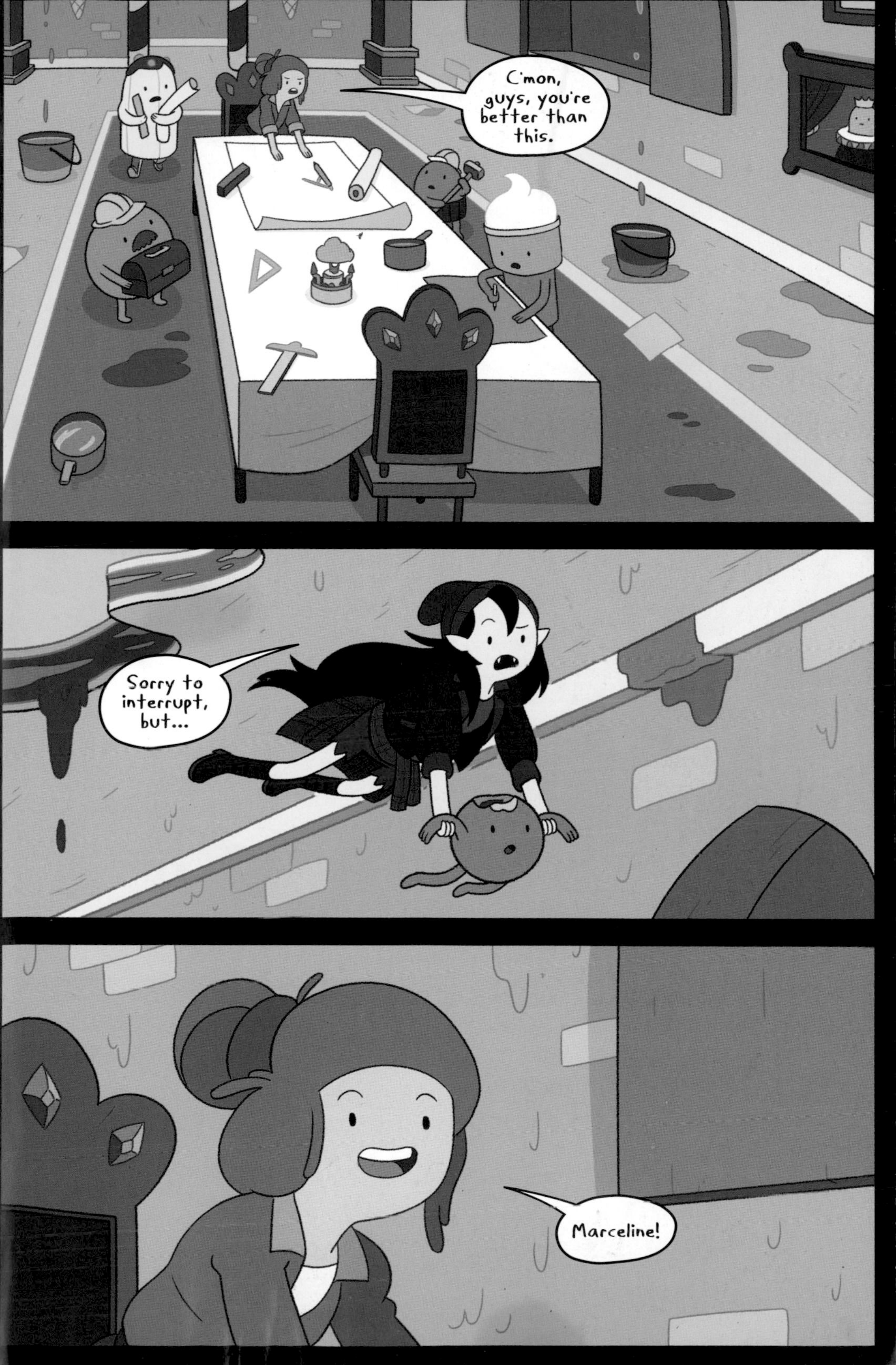
C'mon, guys, you're better than this.
Sorry to interrupt, but...
Marceline!

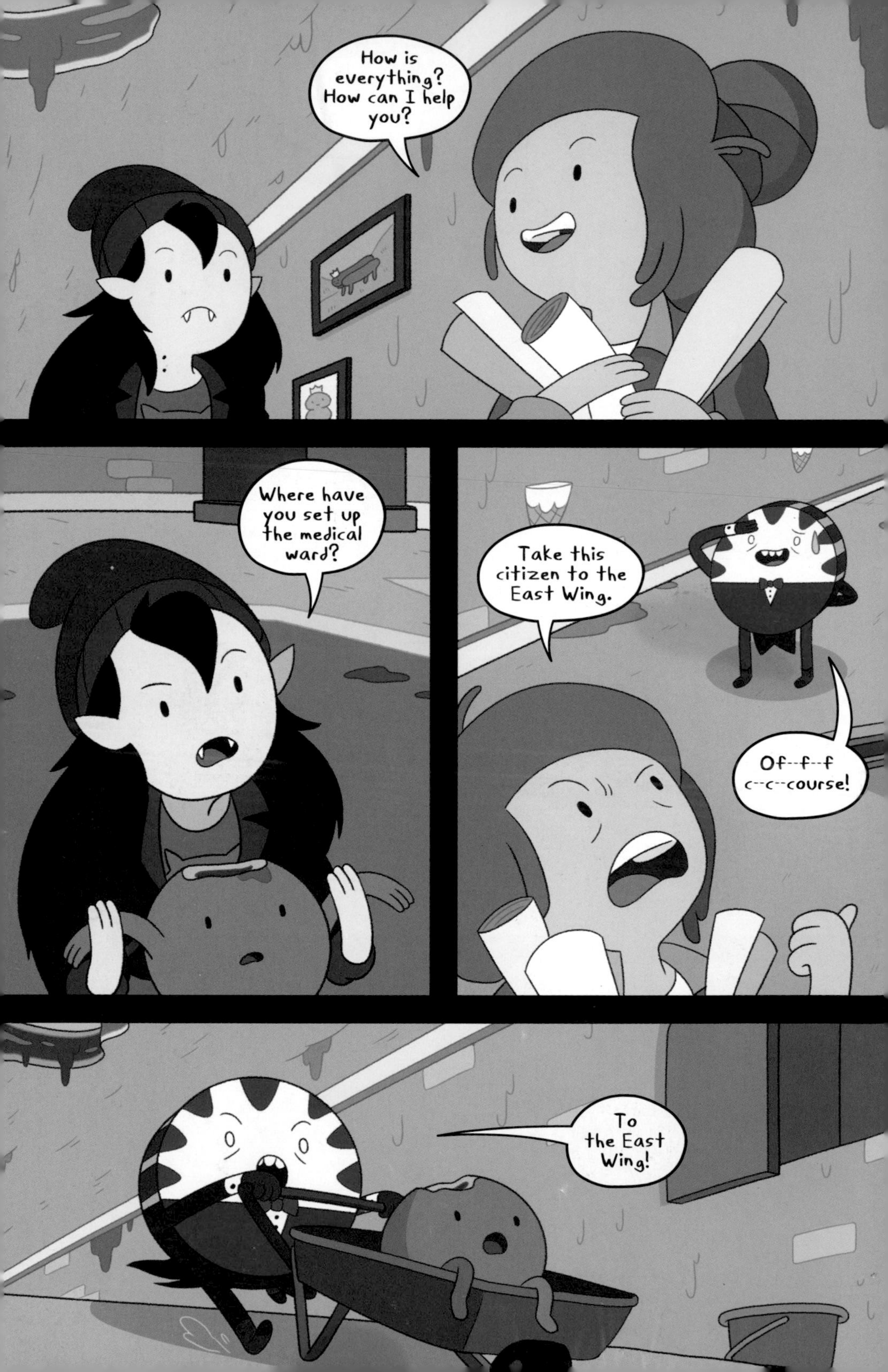
How is everything? How can I help you?
Where have you set up the medical ward?
Take this citizen to the East Wing.
Of--f--f c--c--course!
To the East Wing!

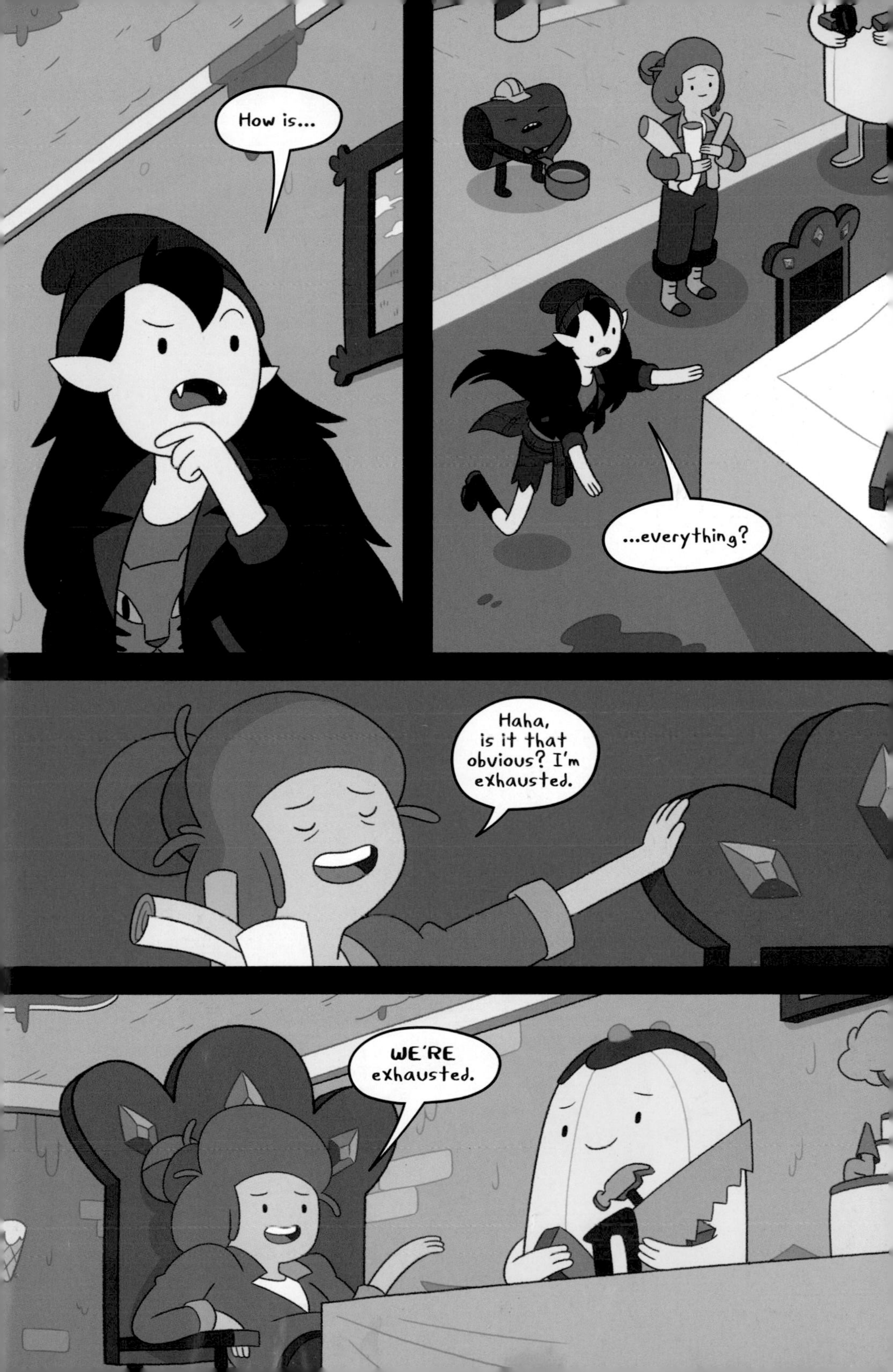
How is...
...everything?
Haha, is it that obvious? I'm exhausted.
WE'RE exhausted.

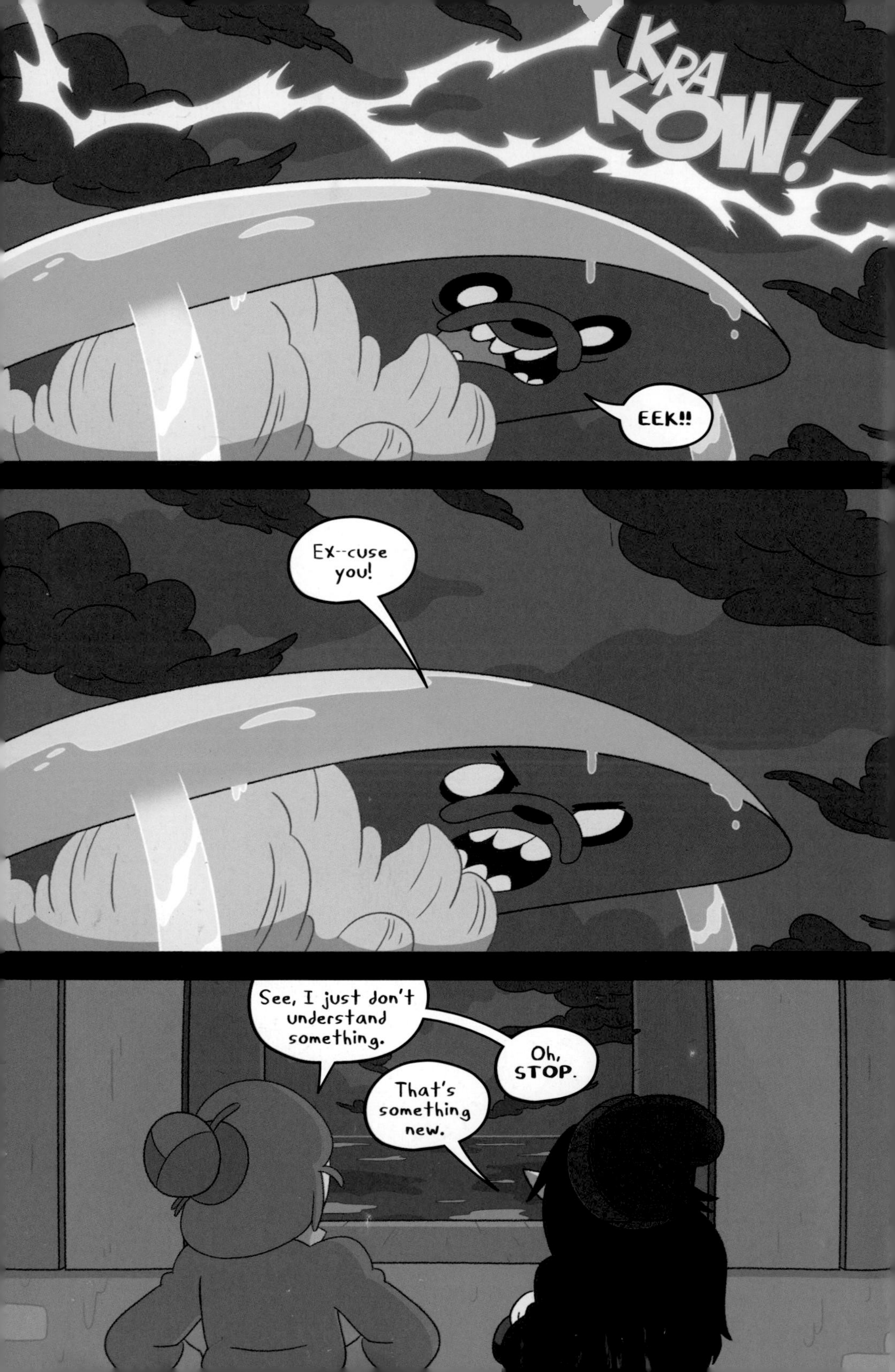
KRA KOW!
EEK!!
Ex--cuse you!
See, I just don't understand something.
Oh, STOP.
That's something new.

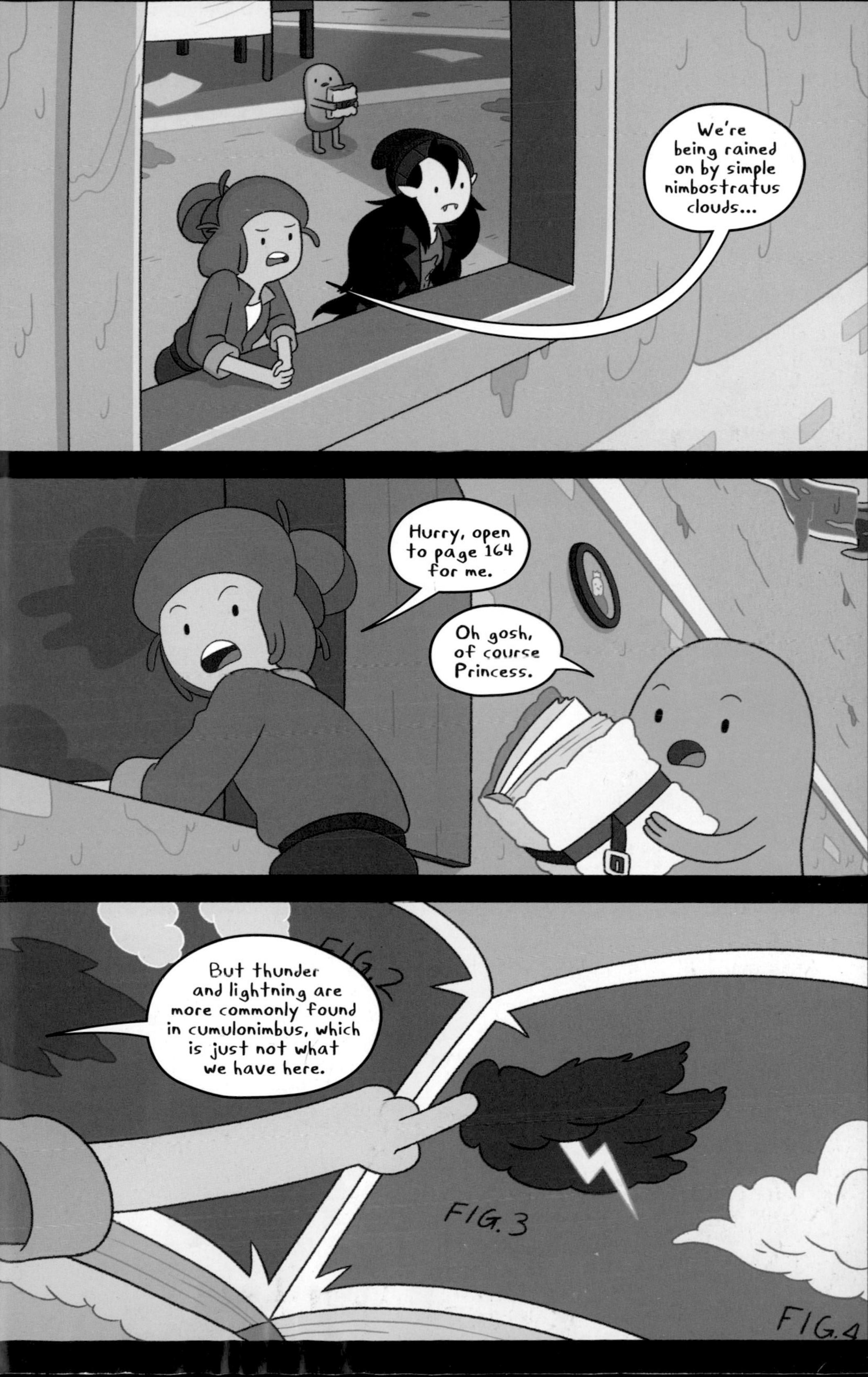
We're being rained on by simple nimbostratus clouds...
Hurry, open to page 164 for me.
Oh gosh, of course Princess.
FIG. 2
But thunder and lightning are more commonly found in cumulonimbus, which is just not what we have here.
FIG. 3
FIG. 4

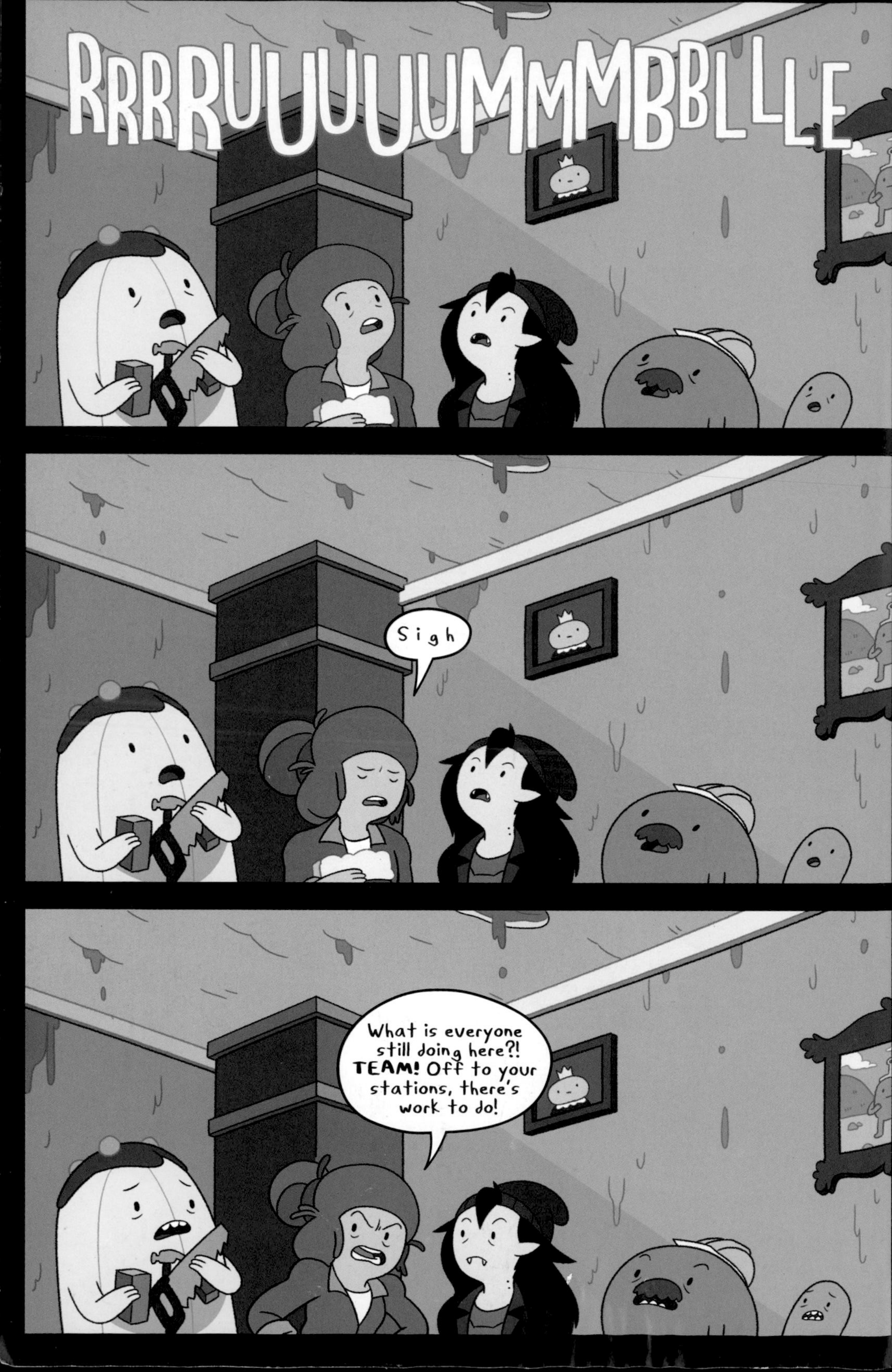
RRRRUUUUUMMMBBLLLE
Sigh
What is everyone still doing here?! **TEAM!** Off to your stations, there's work to do!

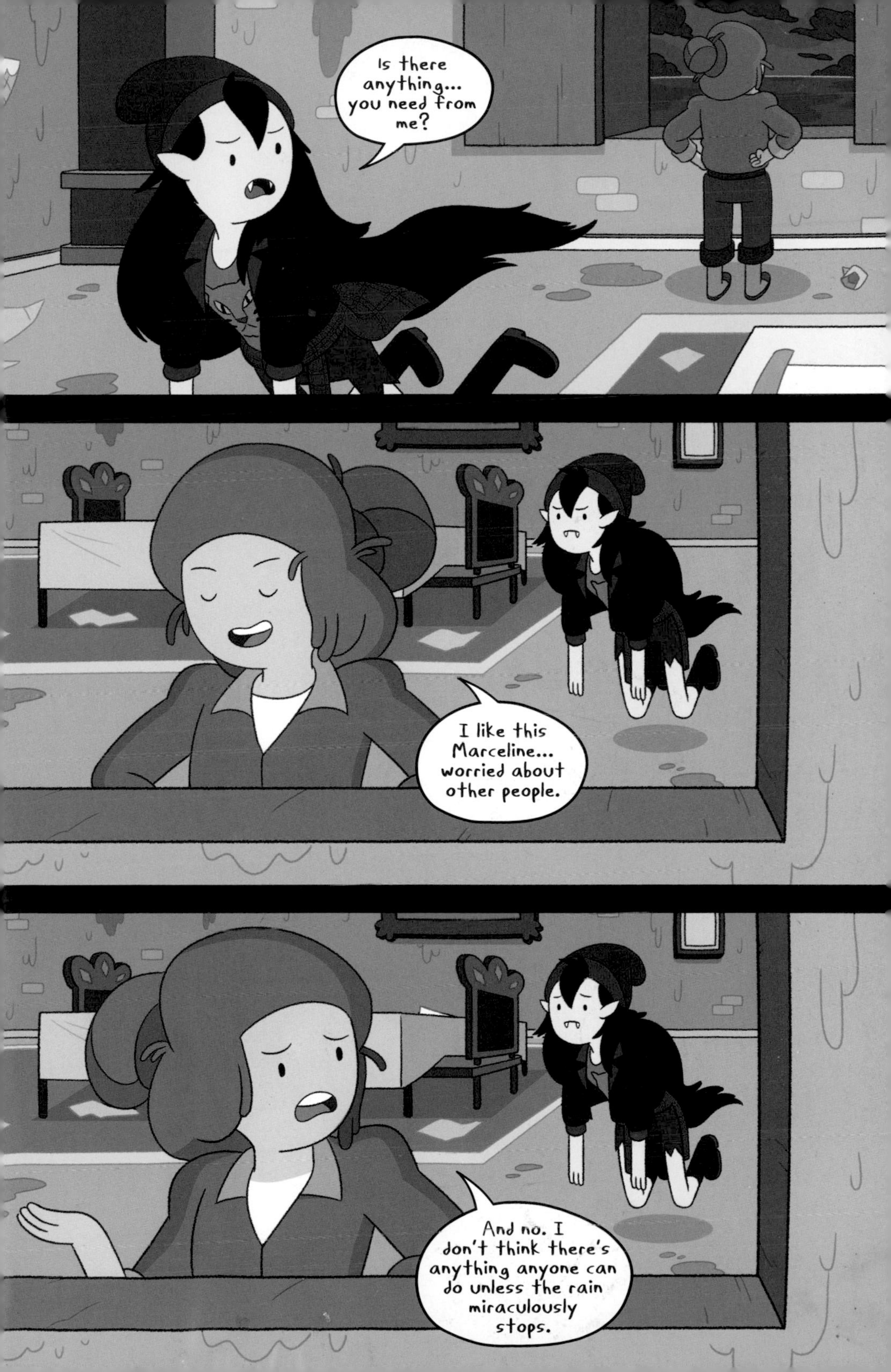
Is there anything... you need from me?
I like this Marceline... worried about other people.
And no. I don't think there's anything anyone can do unless the rain miraculously stops.

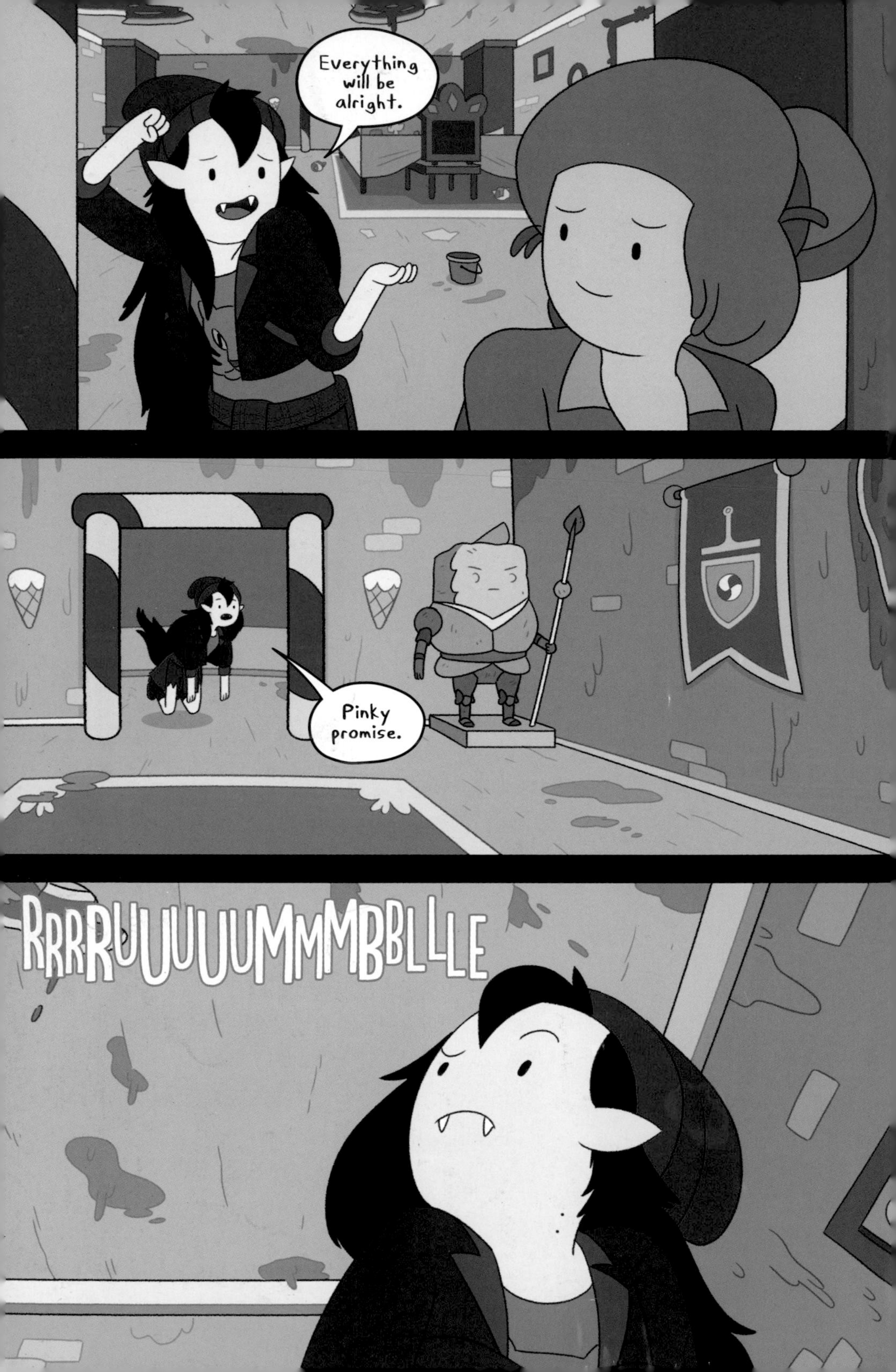
Everything will be alright.
Pinky promise.
RRRRUUUUUMMMBBLLLE

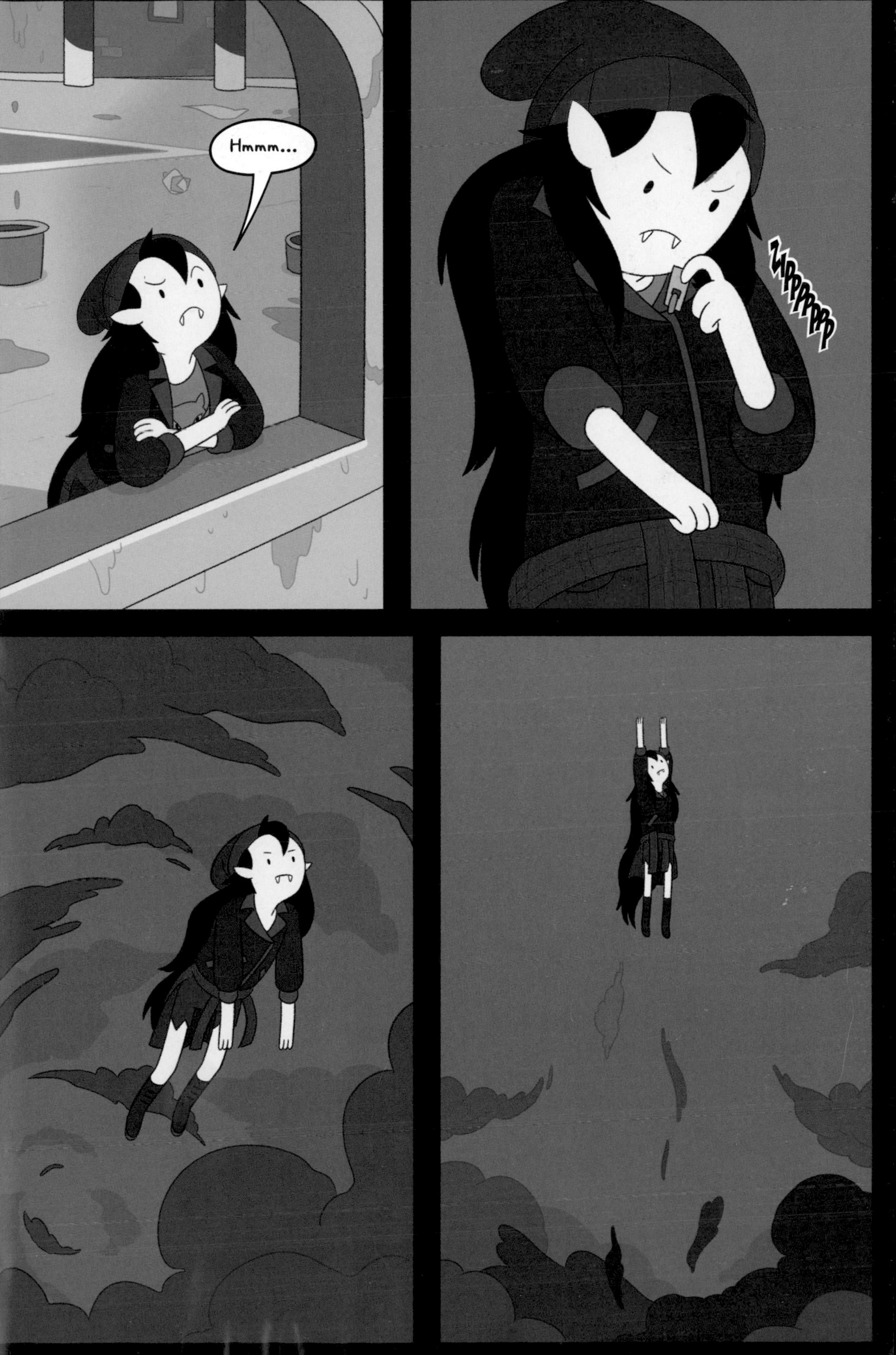
Hmmm...
ZIPPPPPPP

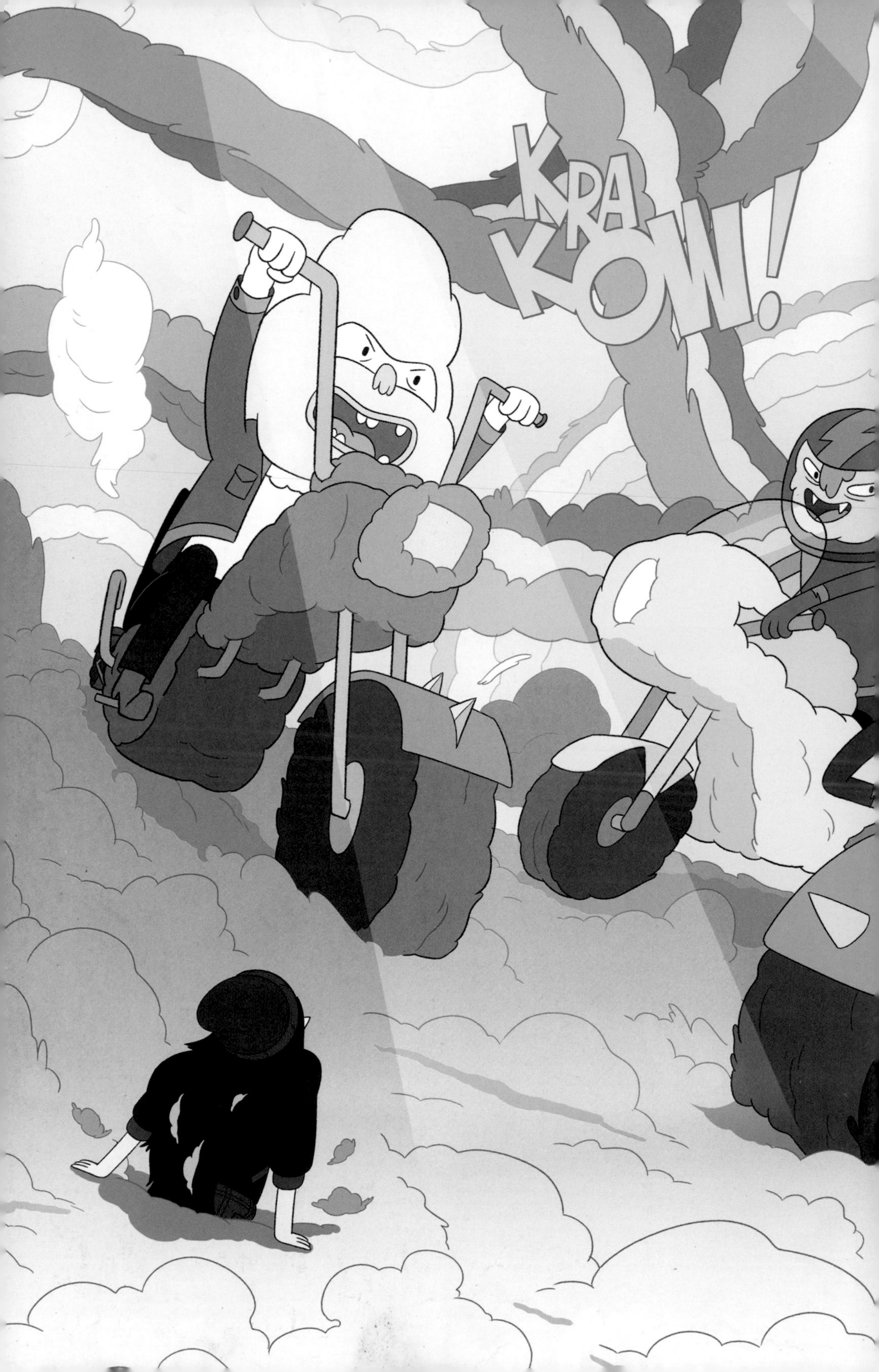
KRA
KOW!

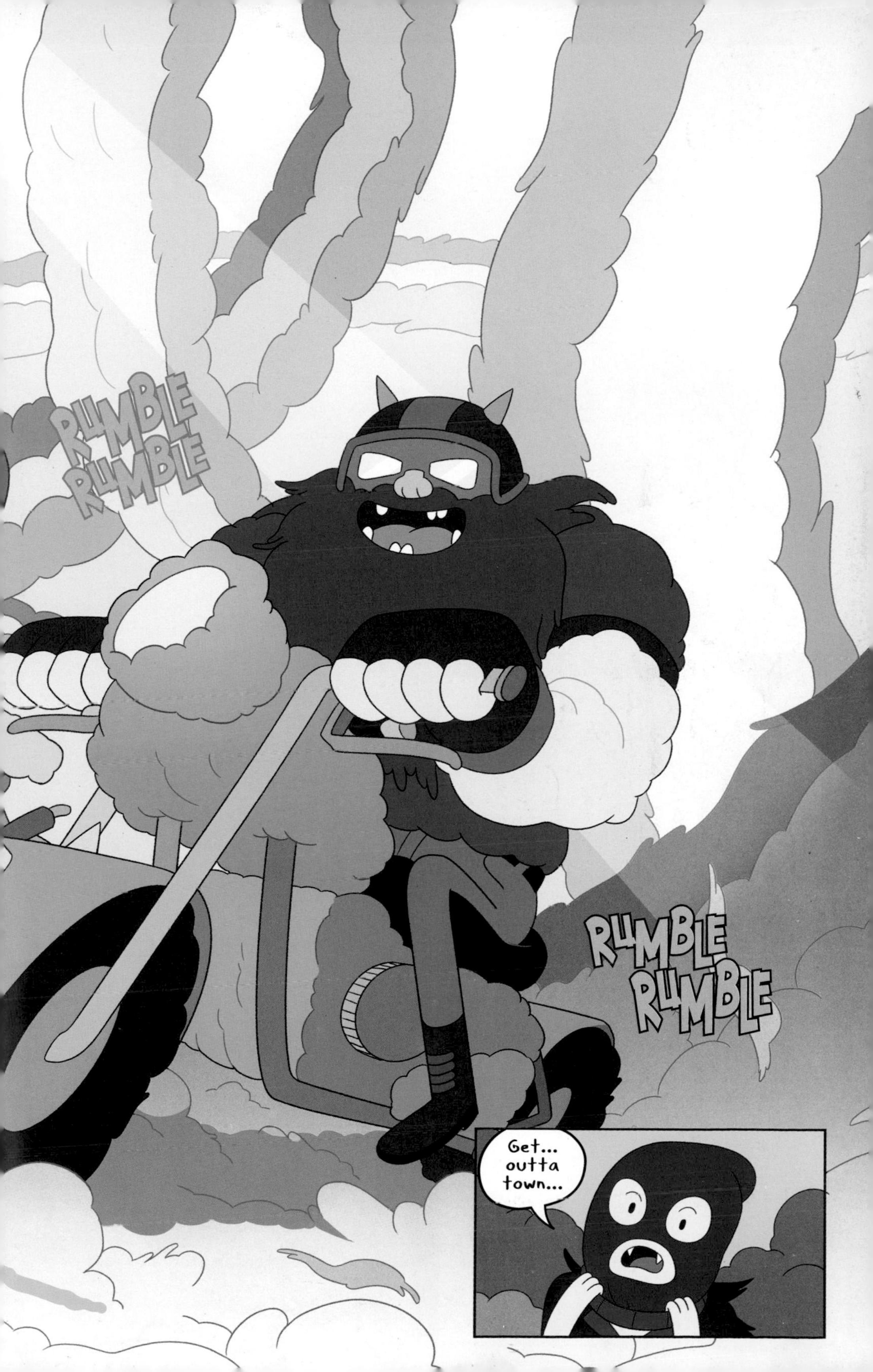
RUMBLE
RUMBLE
RUMBLE
RUMBLE
Get... outta town...

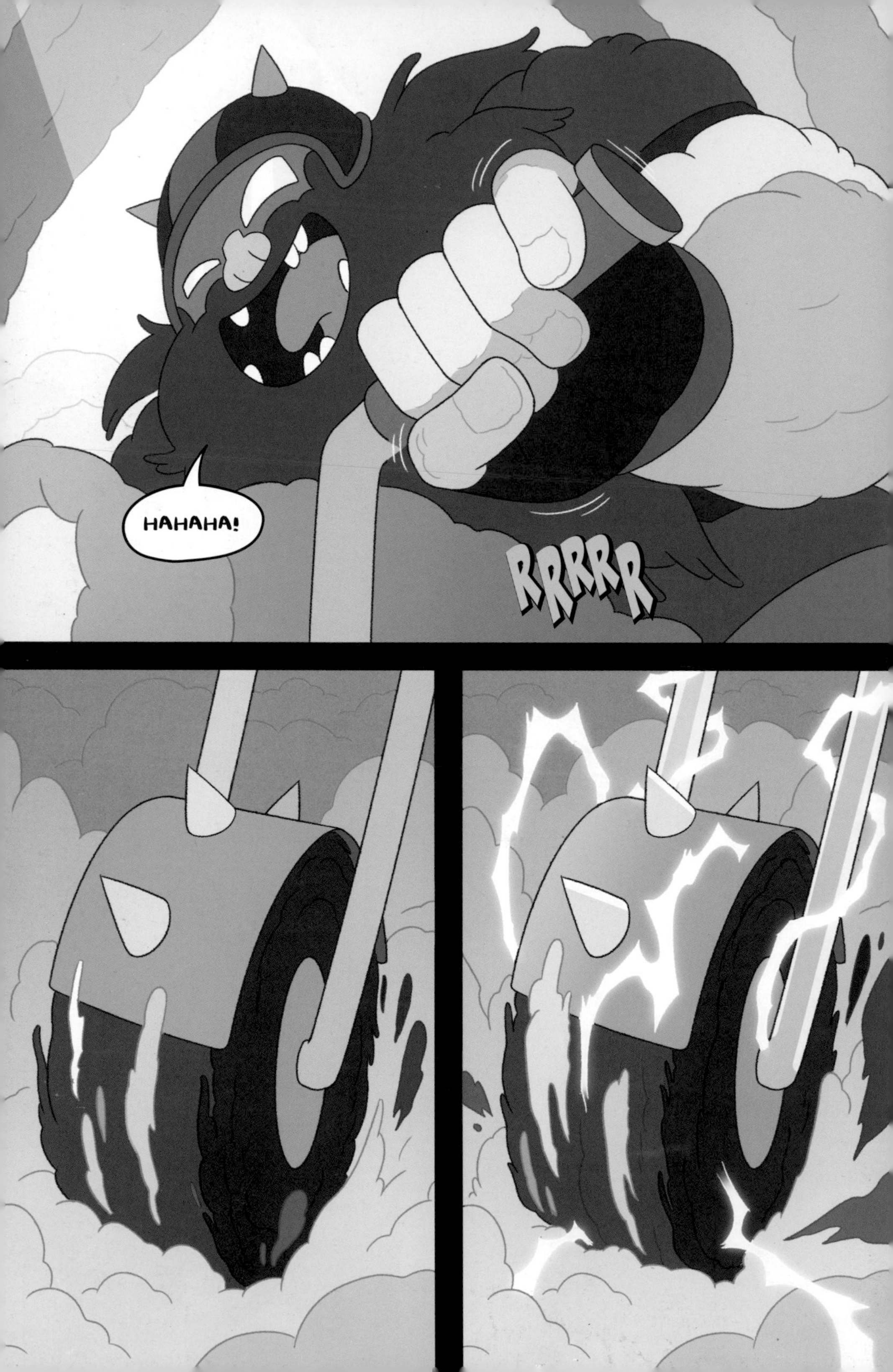
HAHAHA!
RRRRR

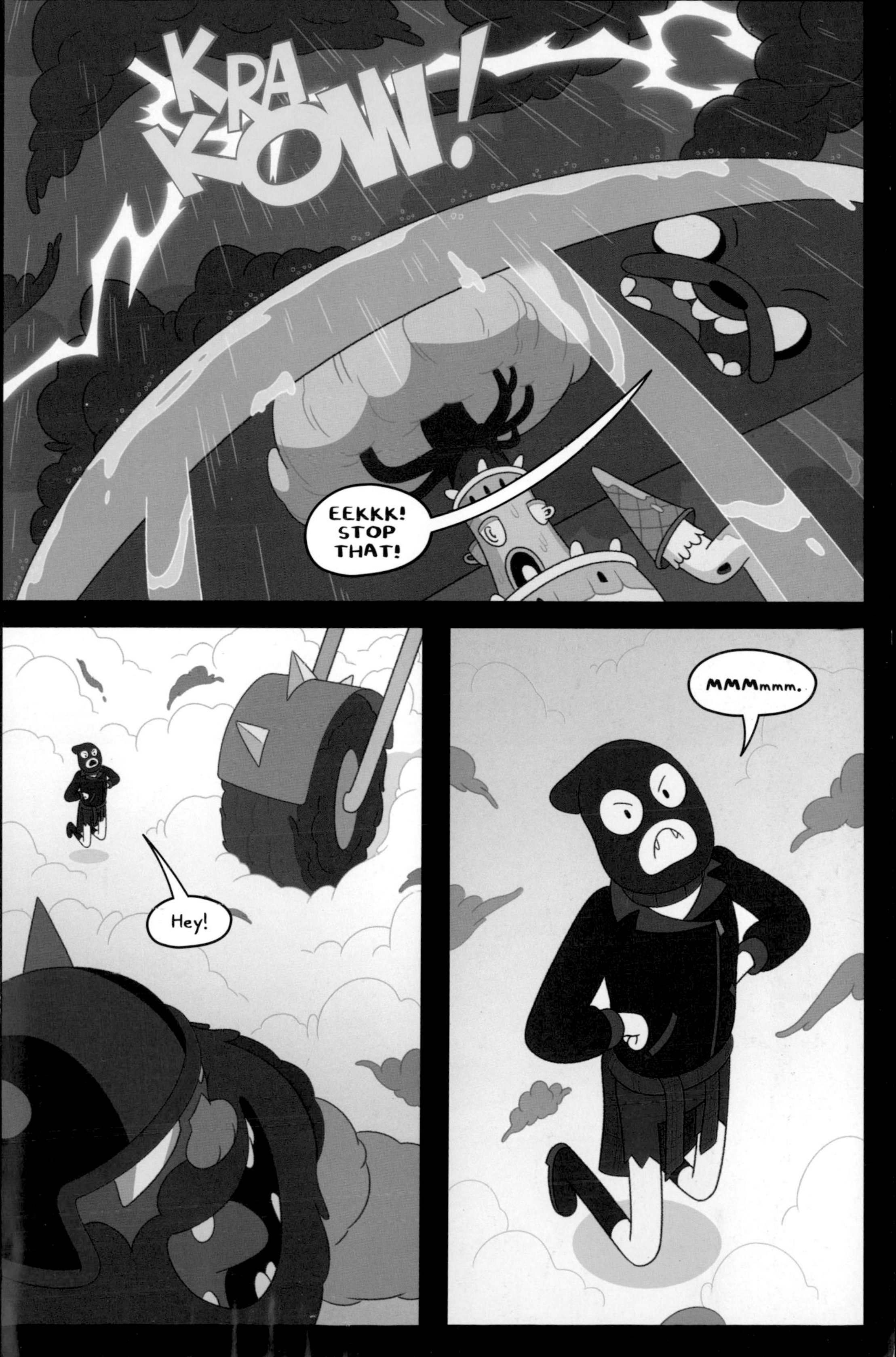
KRA-KOW!
EEKKK! STOP THAT!
Hey!
MMMmmm.

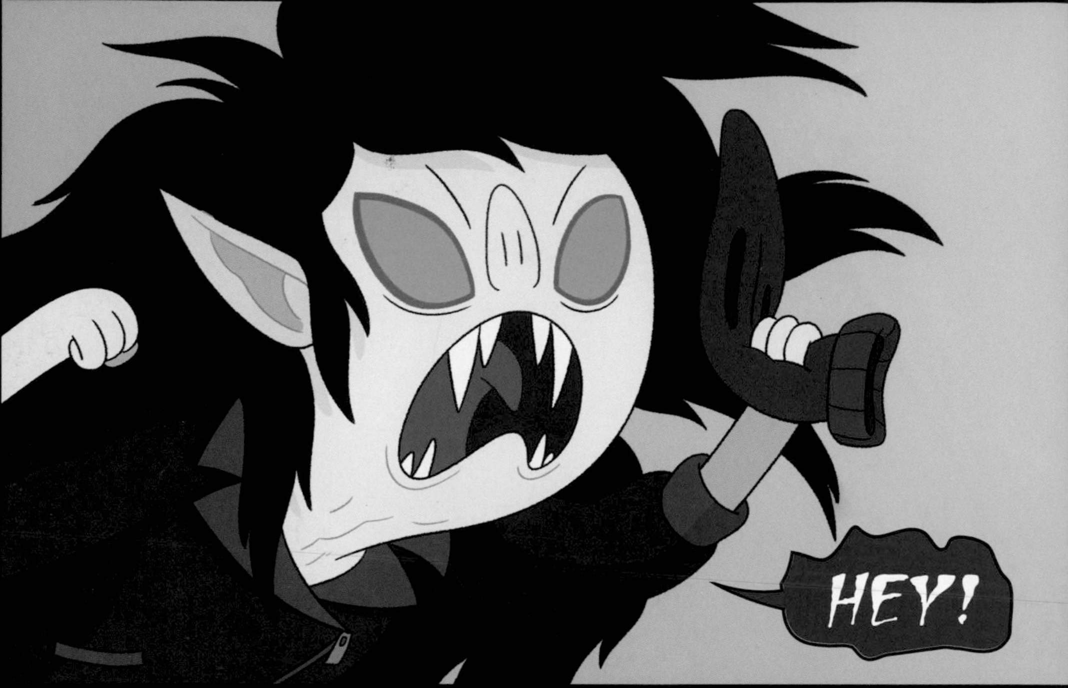
HEY!

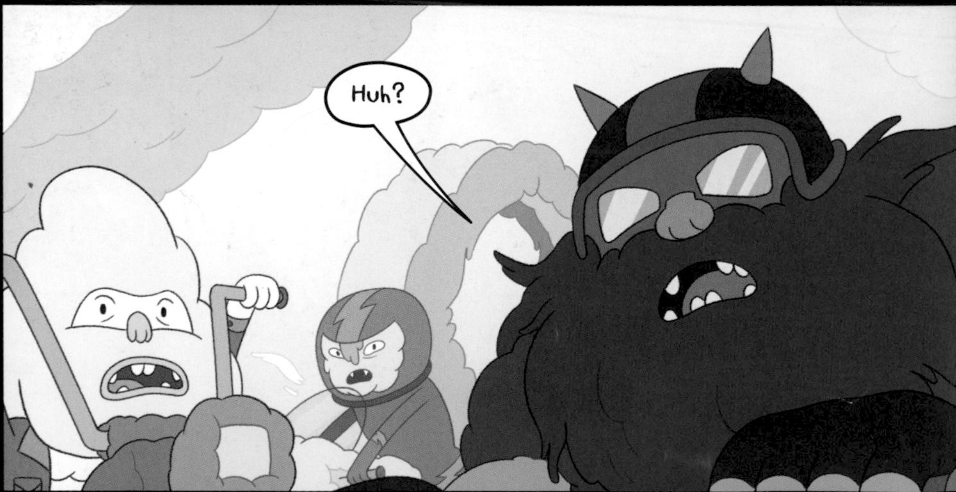
Huh?

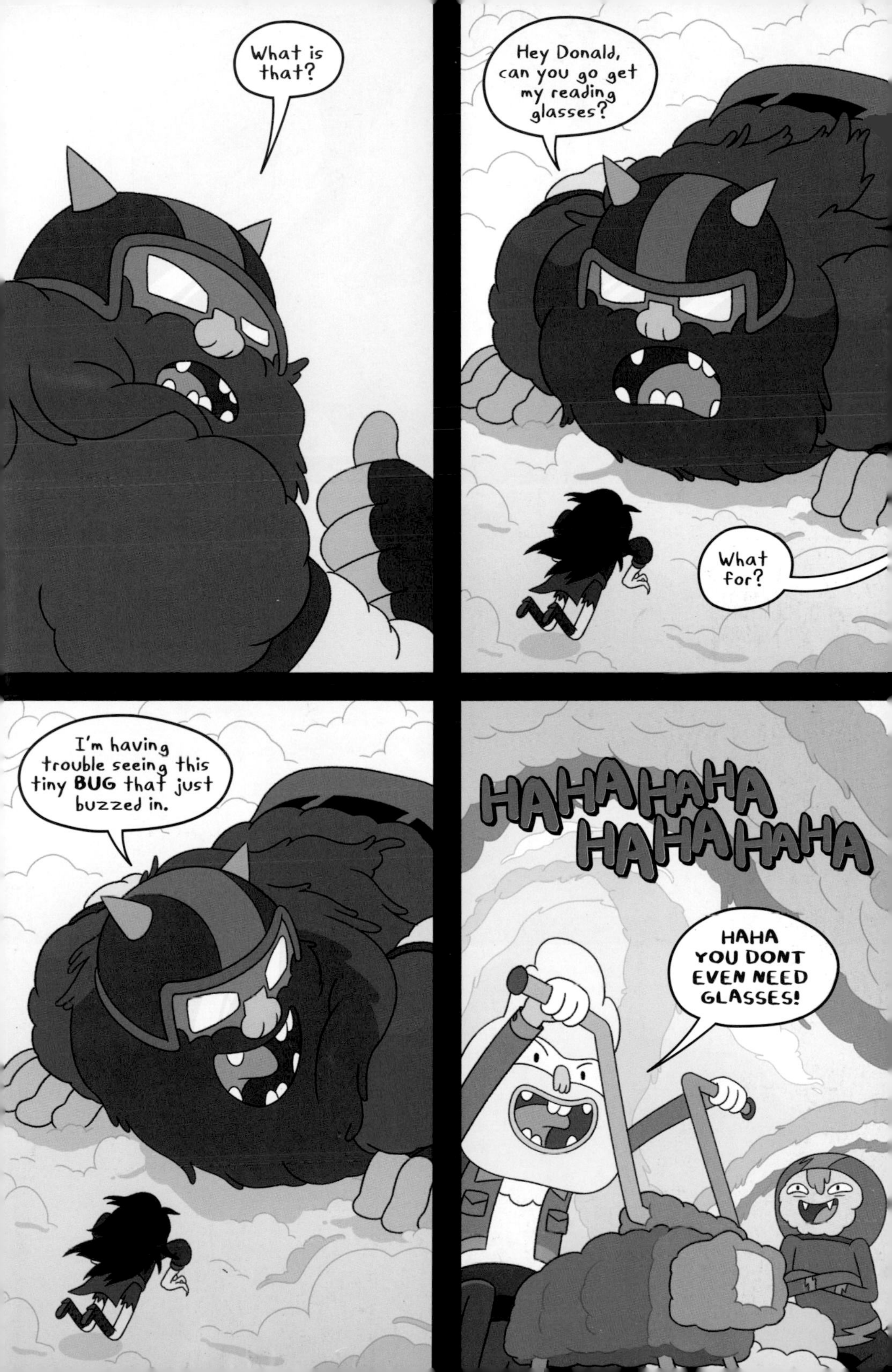
What is that?
Hey Donald, can you go get my reading glasses?
What for?
I'm having trouble seeing this tiny BUG that just buzzed in.
HAHAHAHA HAHAHAHA
HAHA YOU DONT EVEN NEED GLASSES!

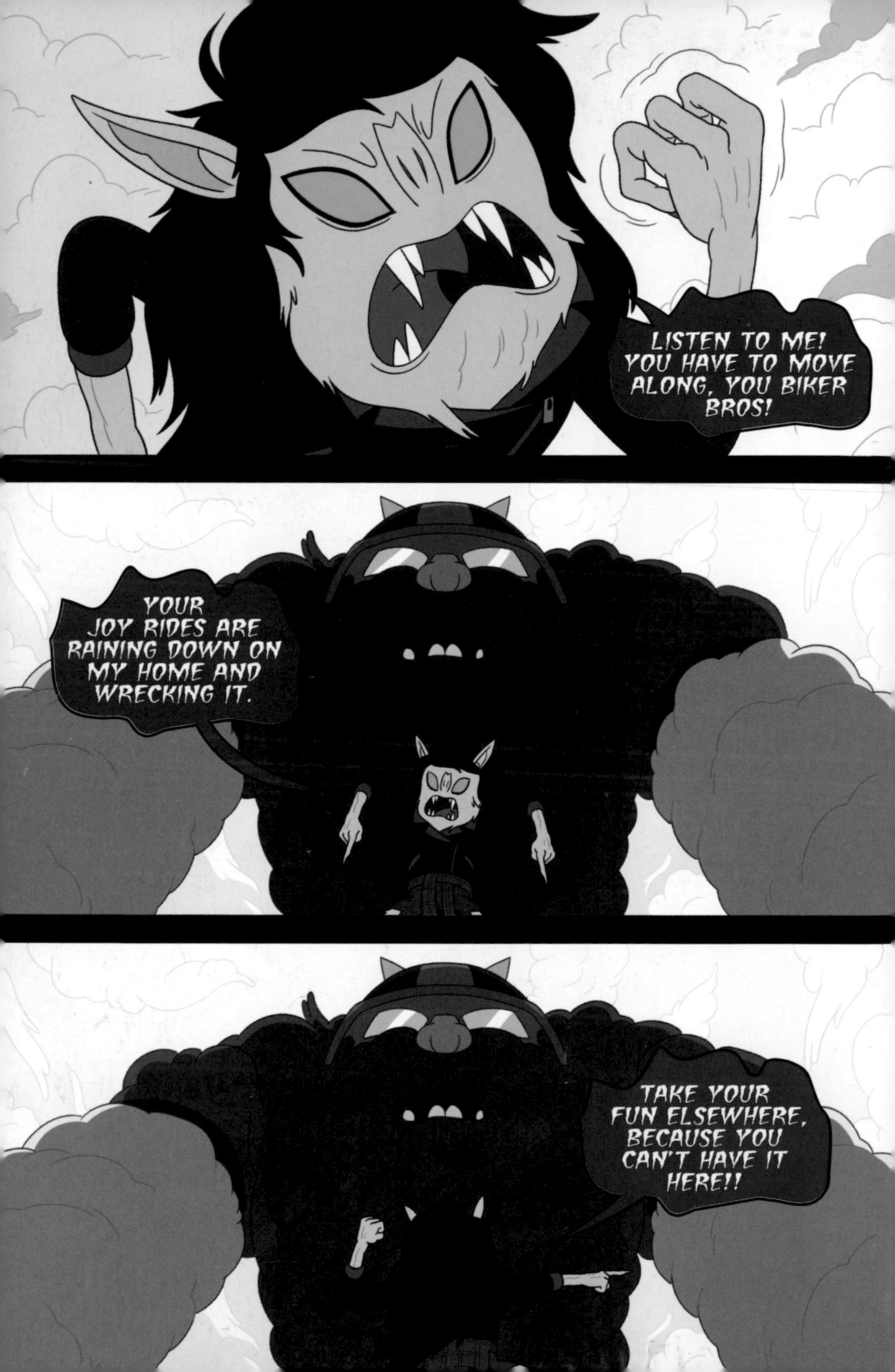
LISTEN TO ME! YOU HAVE TO MOVE ALONG, YOU BIKER BROS!
YOUR JOY RIDES ARE RAINING DOWN ON MY HOME AND WRECKING IT.
TAKE YOUR FUN ELSEWHERE, BECAUSE YOU CAN'T HAVE IT HERE!!

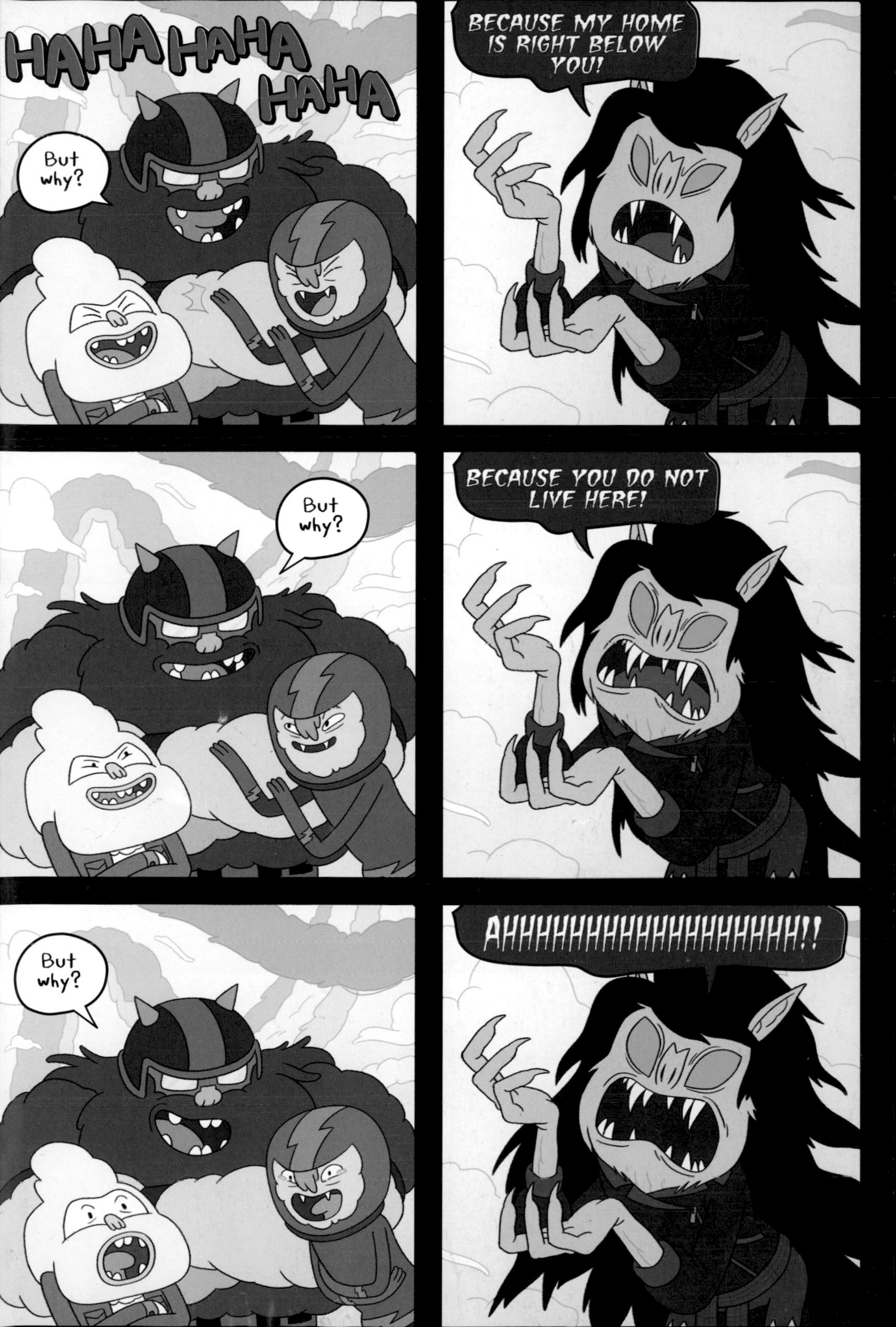
HAHA HAHA HAHA
But why?
BECAUSE MY HOME IS RIGHT BELOW YOU!
But why?
BECAUSE YOU DO NOT LIVE HERE!
But why?
AHHHHHHHHHHHHHHHHHHH!!

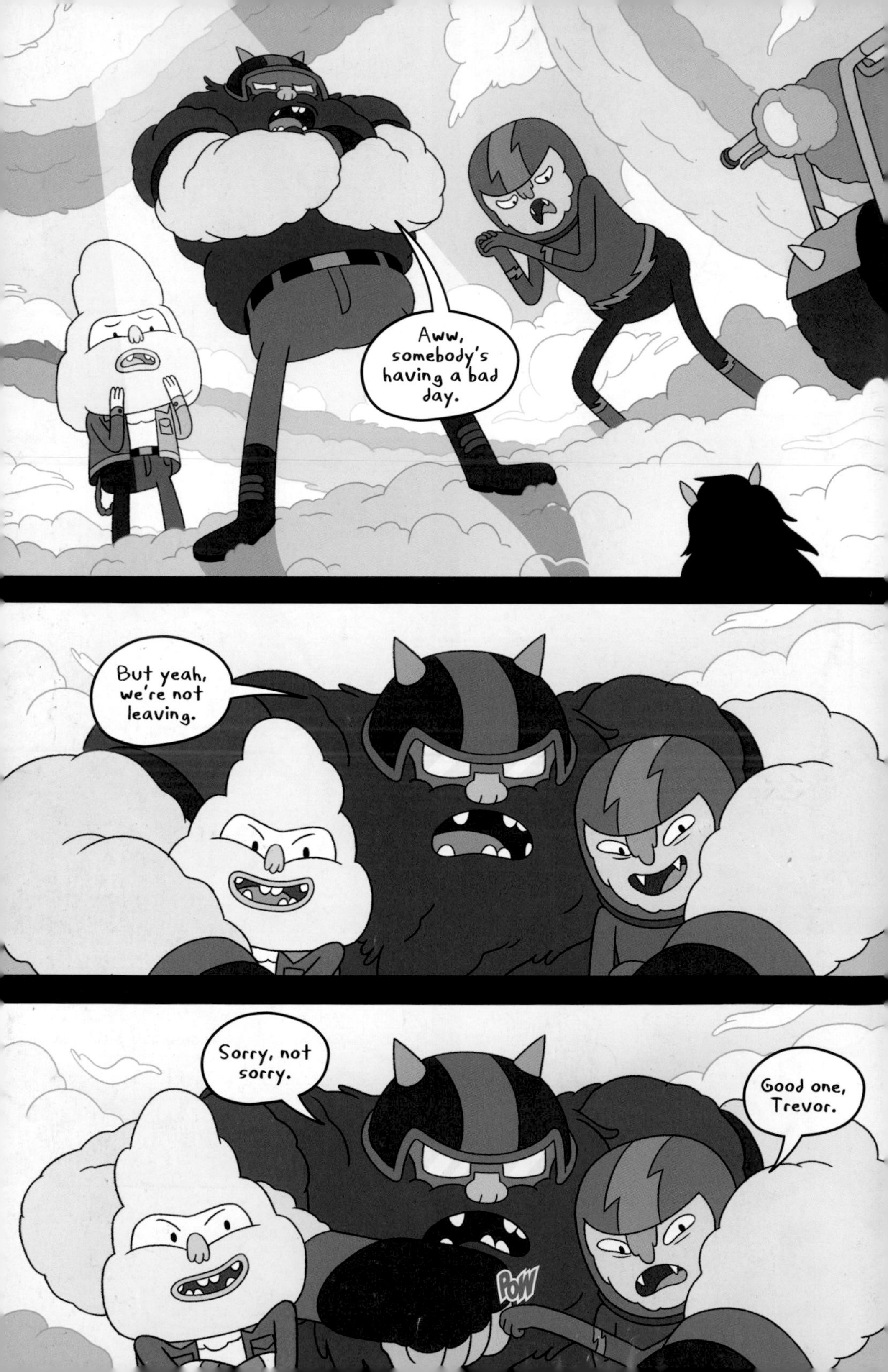
Aww, somebody's having a bad day.
But yeah, we're not leaving.
Sorry, not sorry.
Good one, Trevor.
POW

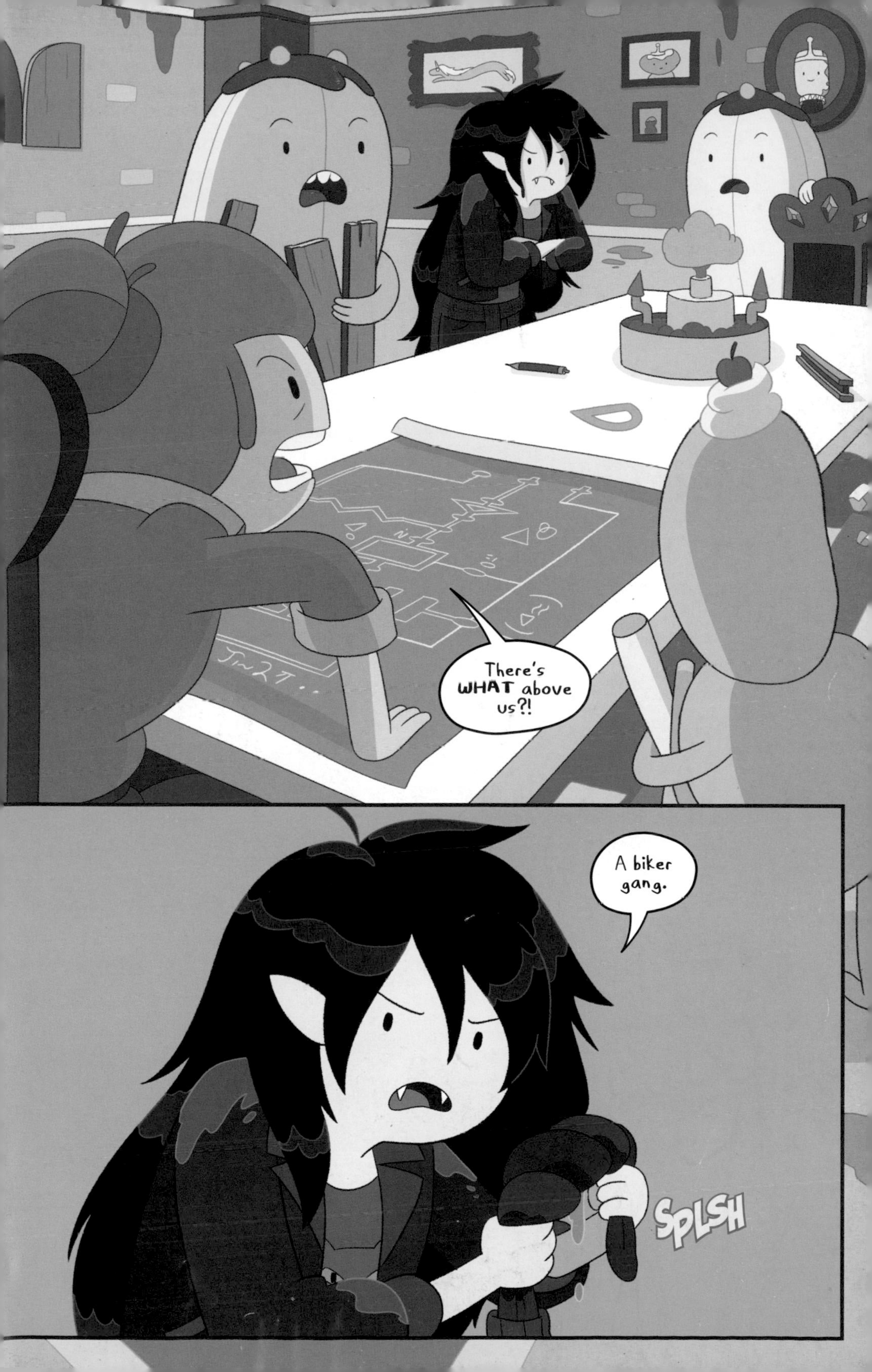
There's **WHAT** above us?!
A biker gang.
SPLSH

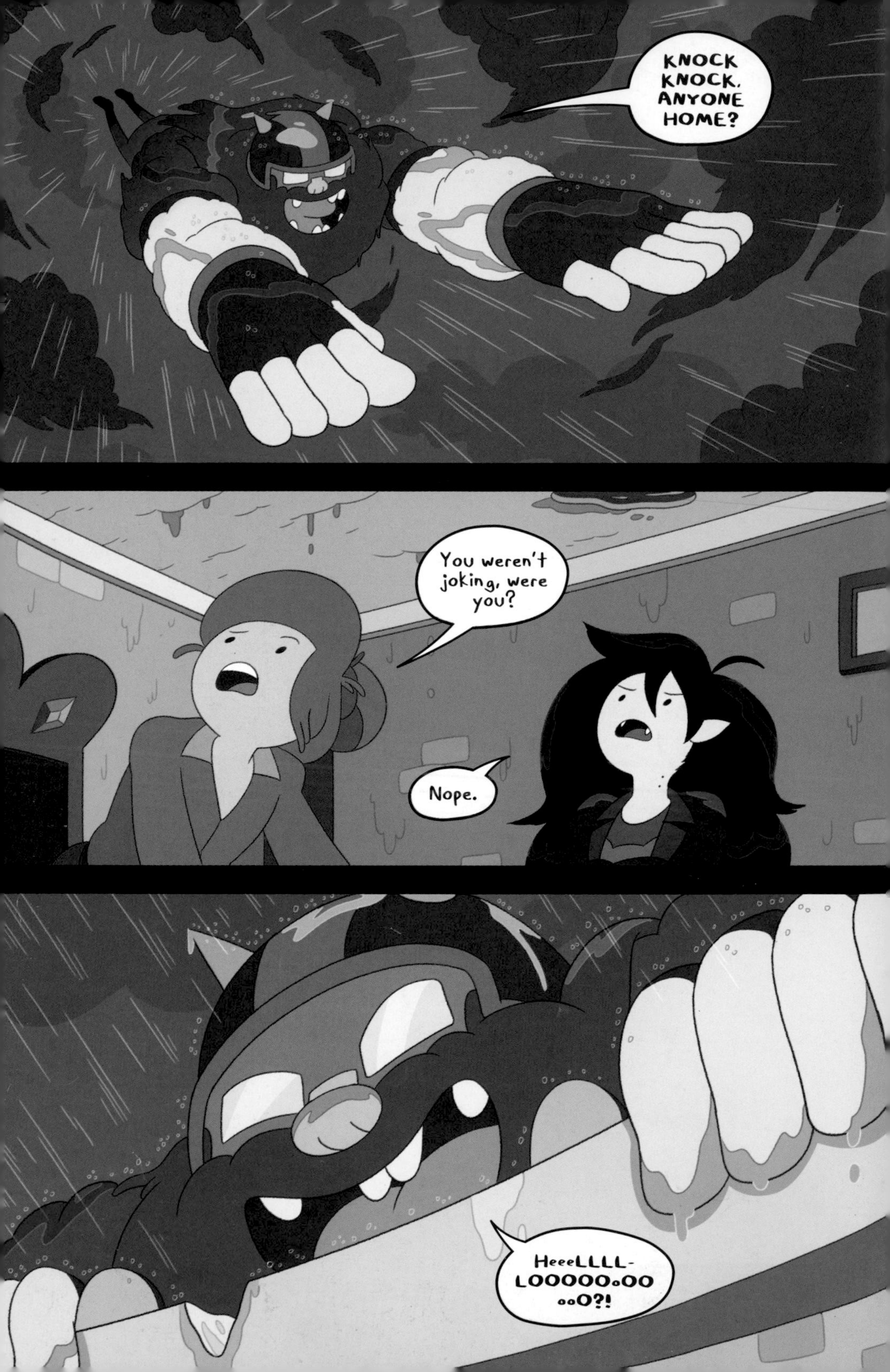
KNOCK KNOCK. ANYONE HOME?
You weren't joking, were you?
Nope.
HeeeLLLL-LOOOOO₀OO ₀₀O?!

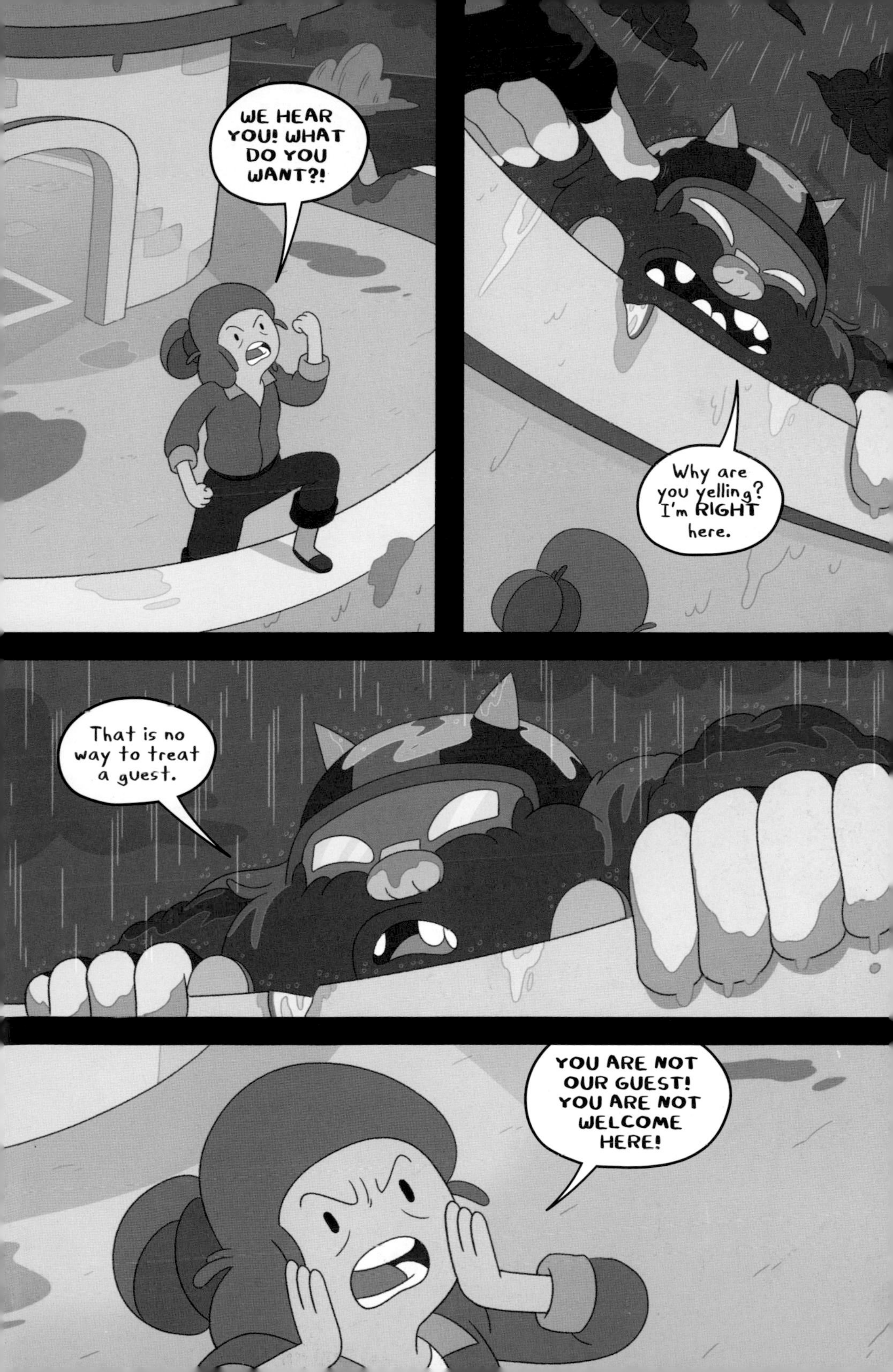
WE HEAR YOU! WHAT DO YOU WANT?!
Why are you yelling? I'm RIGHT here.
That is no way to treat a guest.
YOU ARE NOT OUR GUEST! YOU ARE NOT WELCOME HERE!

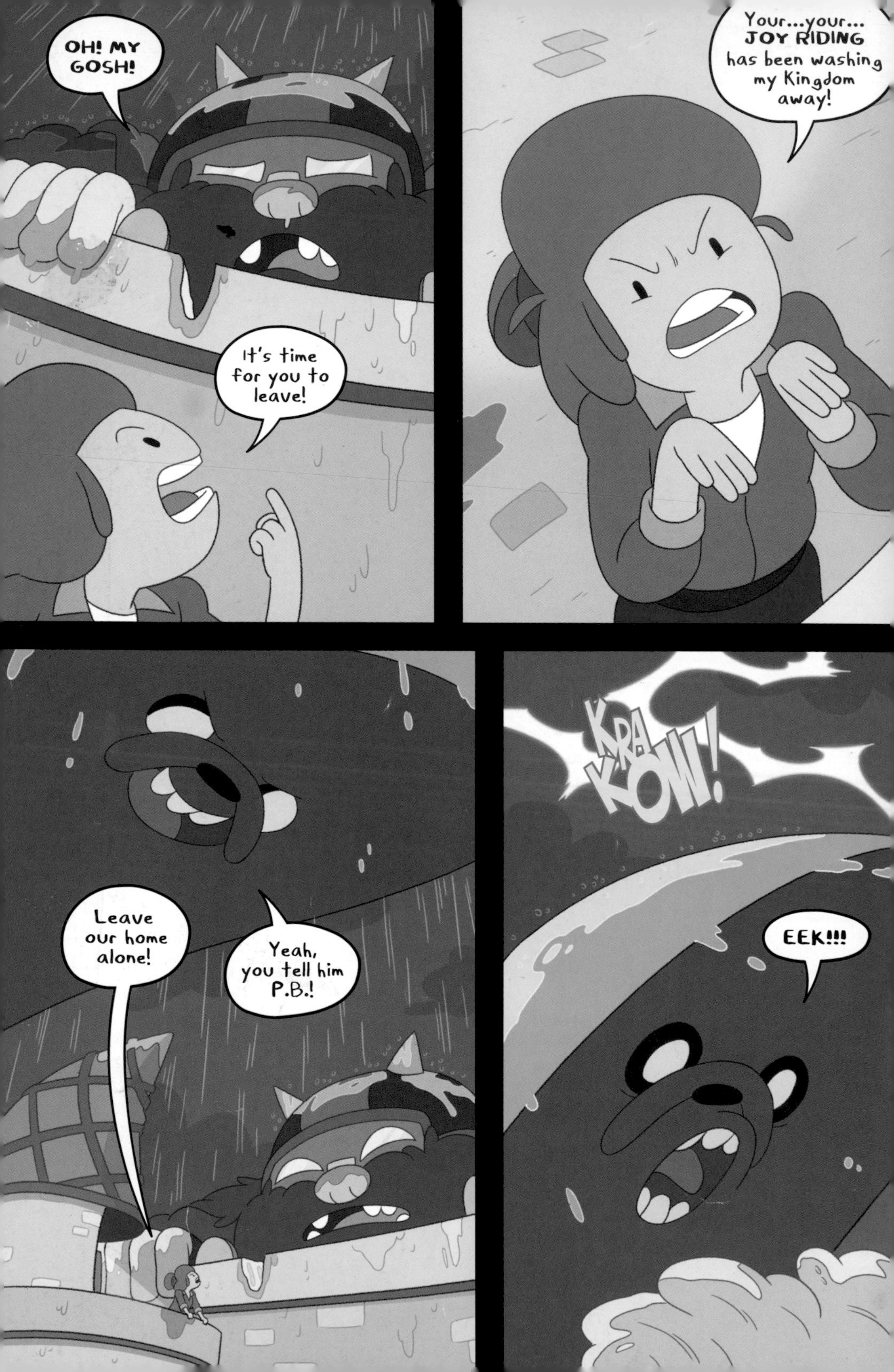
OH! MY GOSH!
It's time for you to leave!
Your...your... JOY RIDING has been washing my Kingdom away!
Leave our home alone!
Yeah, you tell him P.B.!
KRA KOW!
EEK!!!

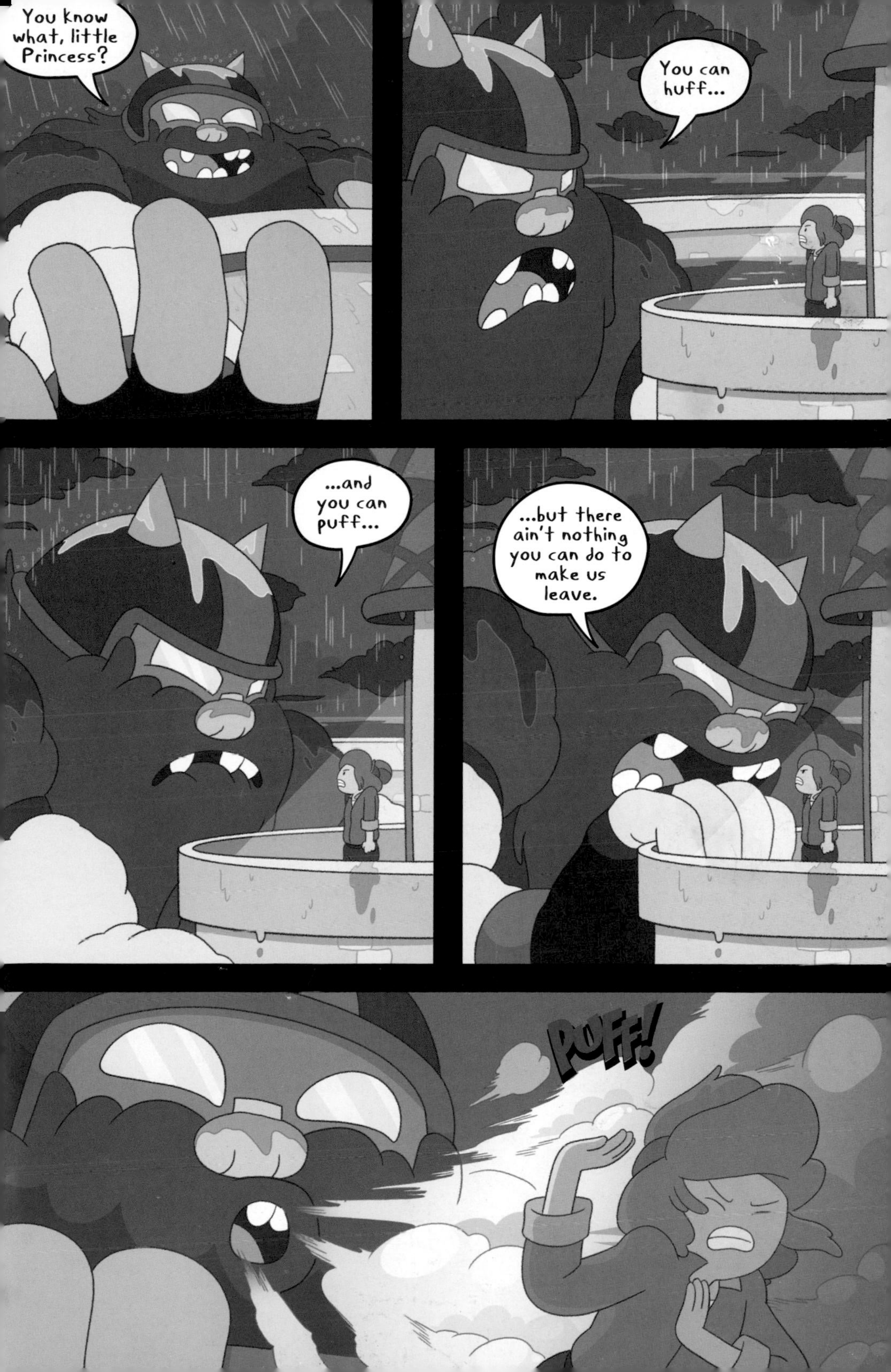
You know what, little Princess?
You can huff...
...and you can puff...
...but there ain't nothing you can do to make us leave.
POFF!

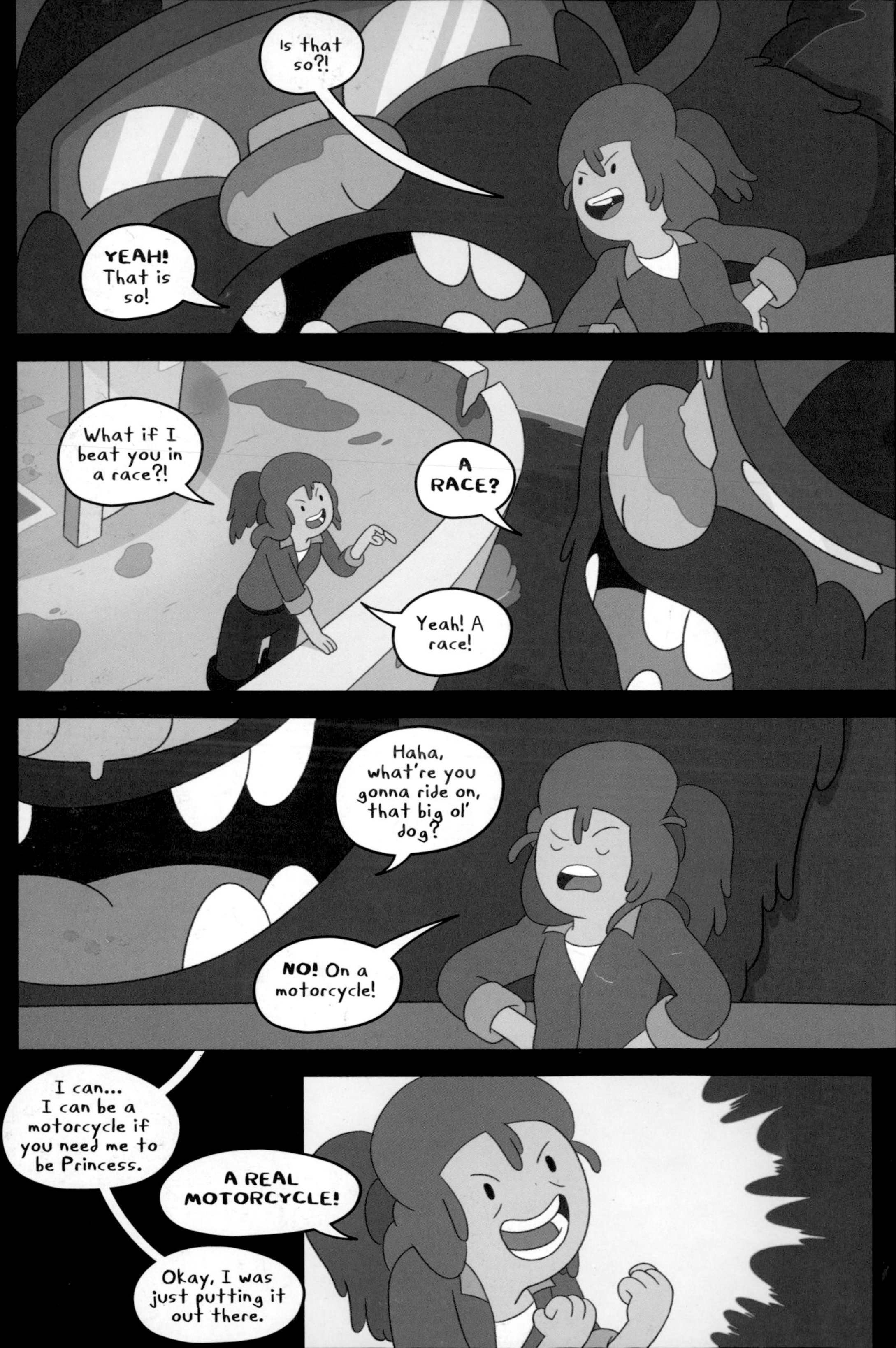

Is that so?!
YEAH! That is so!
What if I beat you in a race?!
A RACE?
Yeah! A race!
Haha, what're you gonna ride on, that big ol' dog?
NO! On a motorcycle!
I can... I can be a motorcycle if you need me to be Princess.
A REAL MOTORCYCLE!
Okay, I was just putting it out there.

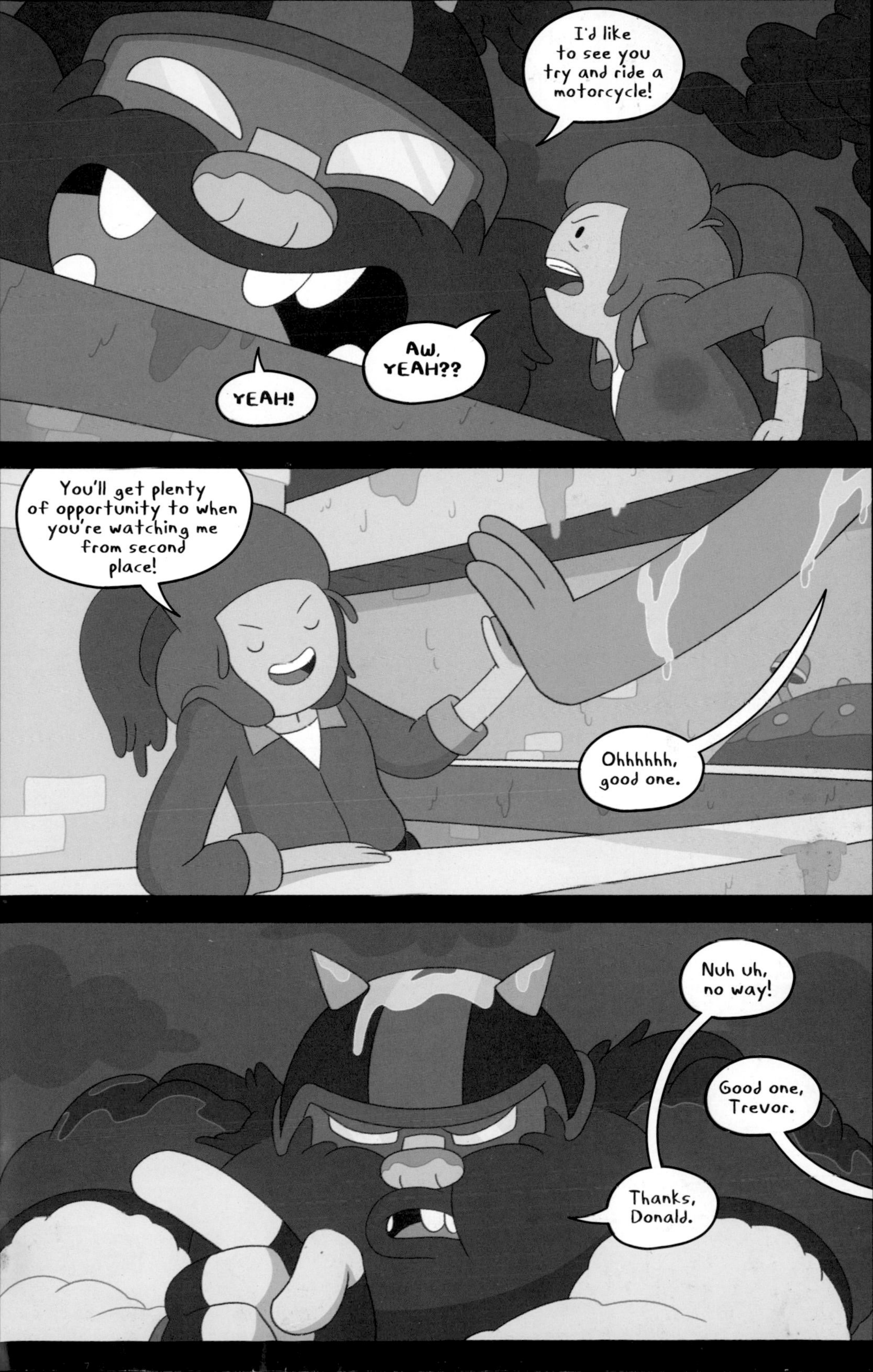
I'd like to see you try and ride a motorcycle!
AW, YEAH??
YEAH!
You'll get plenty of opportunity to when you're watching me from second place!
Ohhhhhh, good one.
Nuh uh, no way!
Good one, Trevor.
Thanks, Donald.

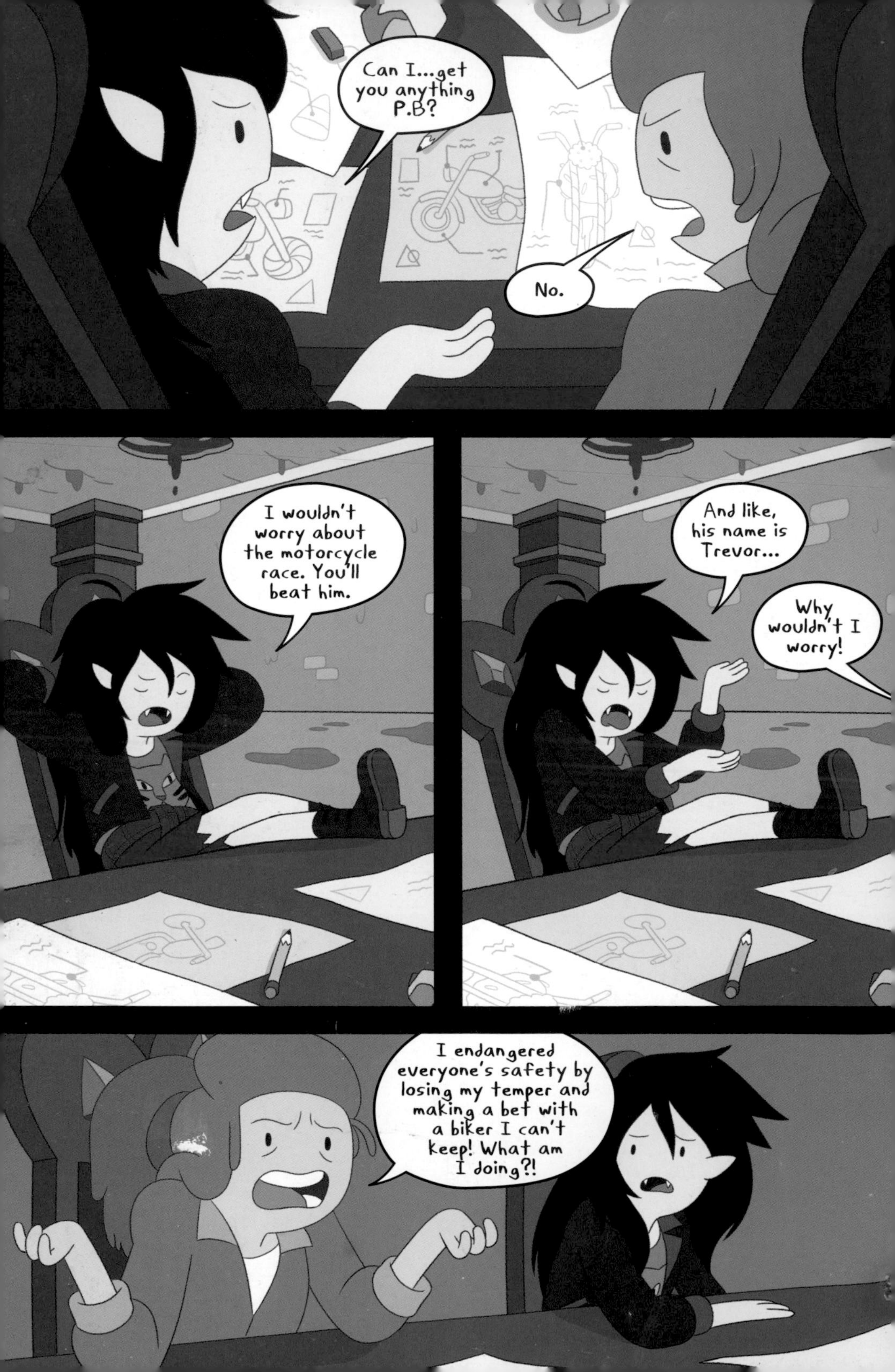
Can I...get you anything P.B?
No.
I wouldn't worry about the motorcycle race. You'll beat him.
And like, his name is Trevor...
Why wouldn't I worry!
I endangered everyone's safety by losing my temper and making a bet with a biker I can't keep! What am I doing?!

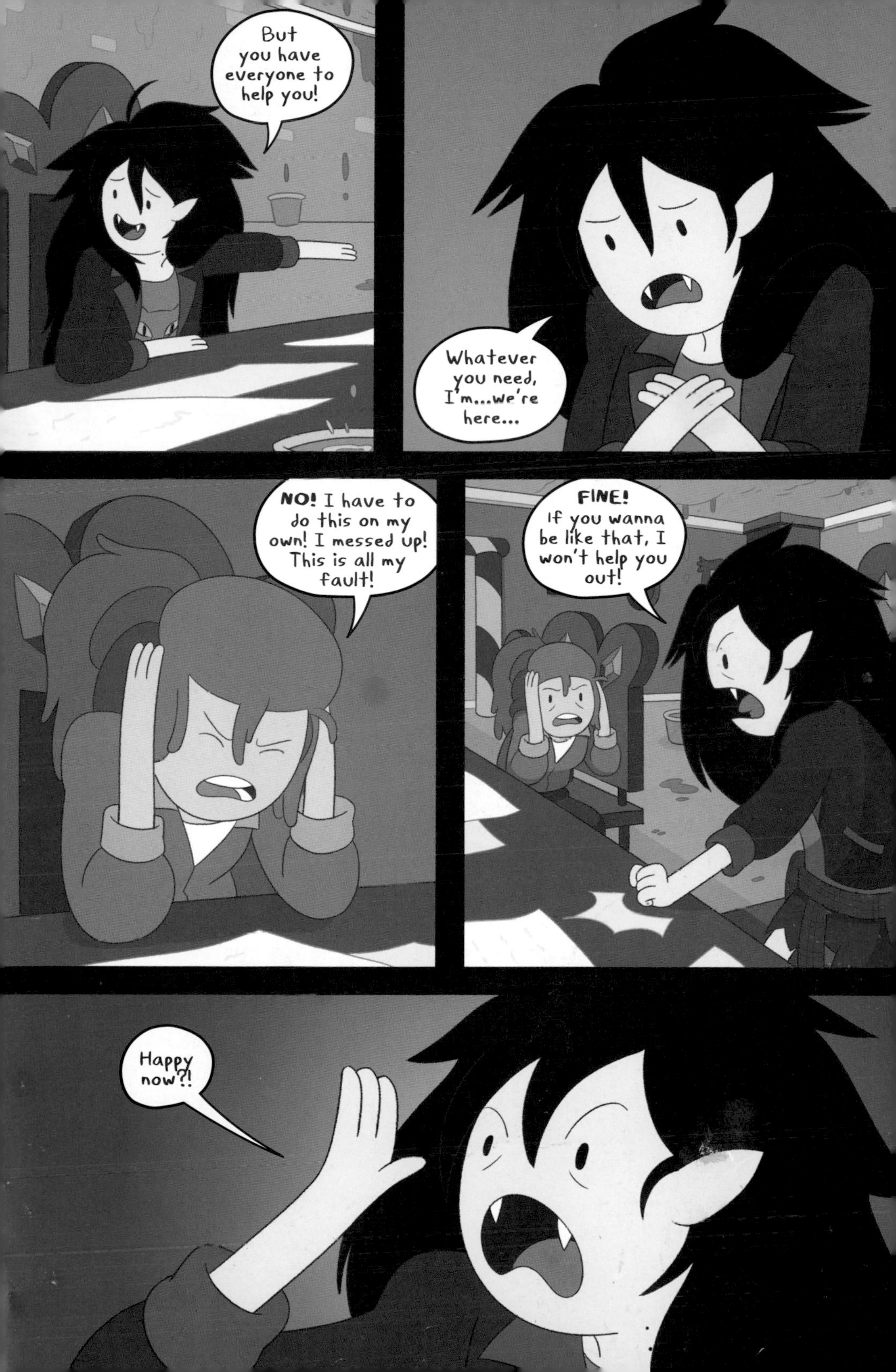
But you have everyone to help you!
Whatever you need, I'm...we're here...
NO! I have to do this on my own! I messed up! This is all my fault!
FINE! If you wanna be like that, I won't help you out!
Happy now?!

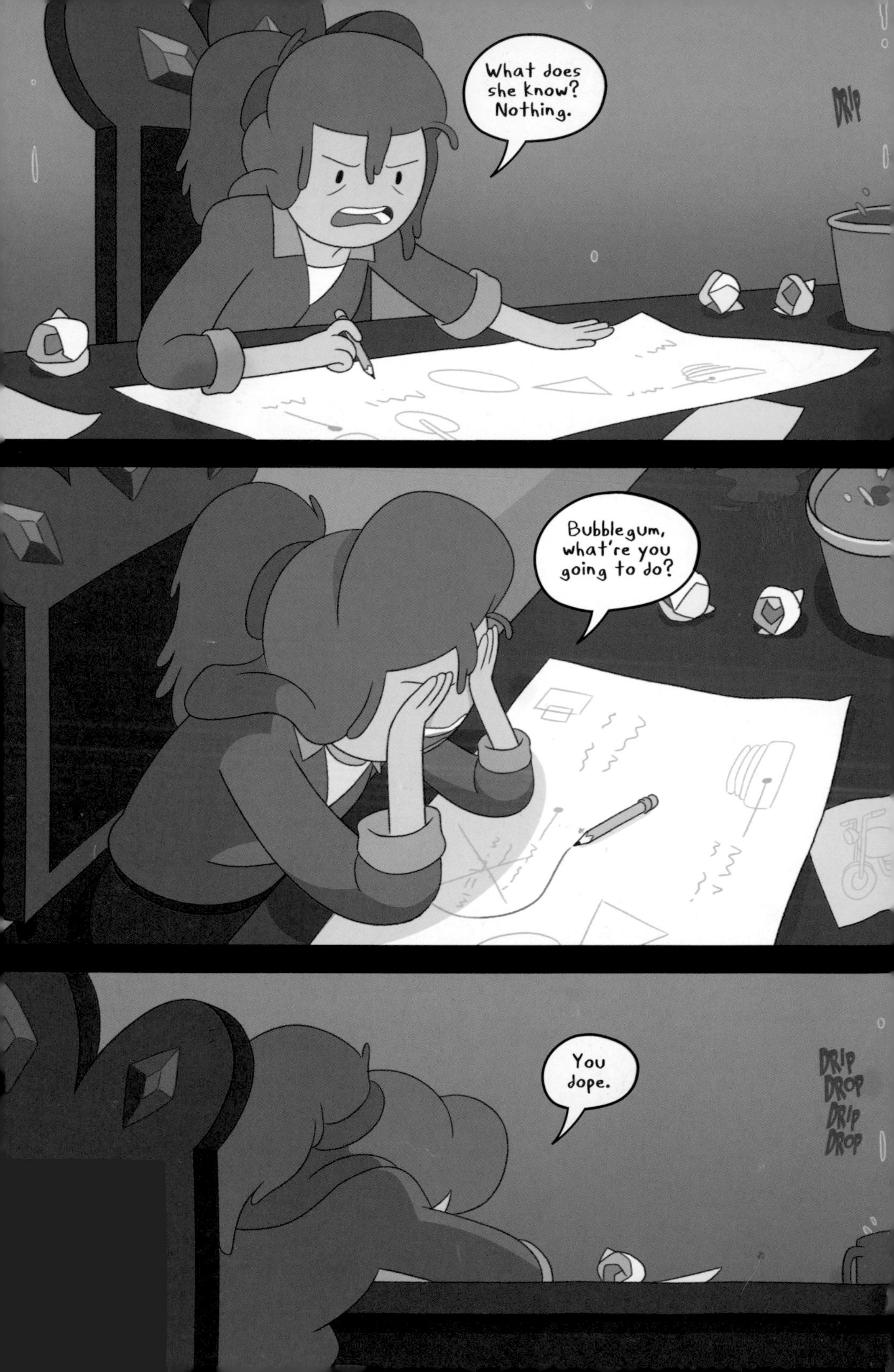
What does she know? Nothing.
DRIP
Bubblegum, what're you going to do?
You dope.
DRIP DROP DRIP DROP

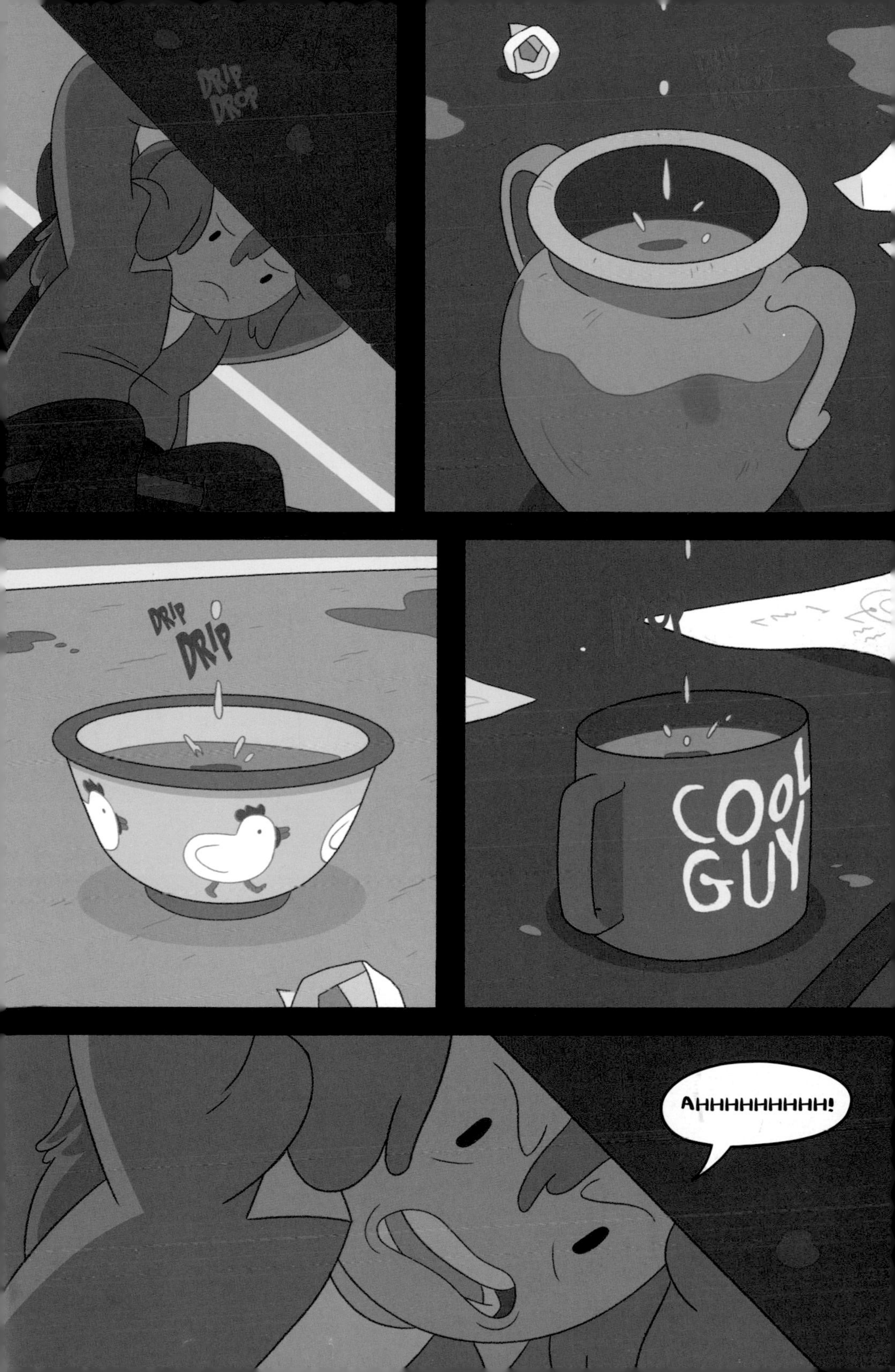
DRIP
DROP
DRIP
DRIP
COOL
GUY
AHHHHHHHHH!

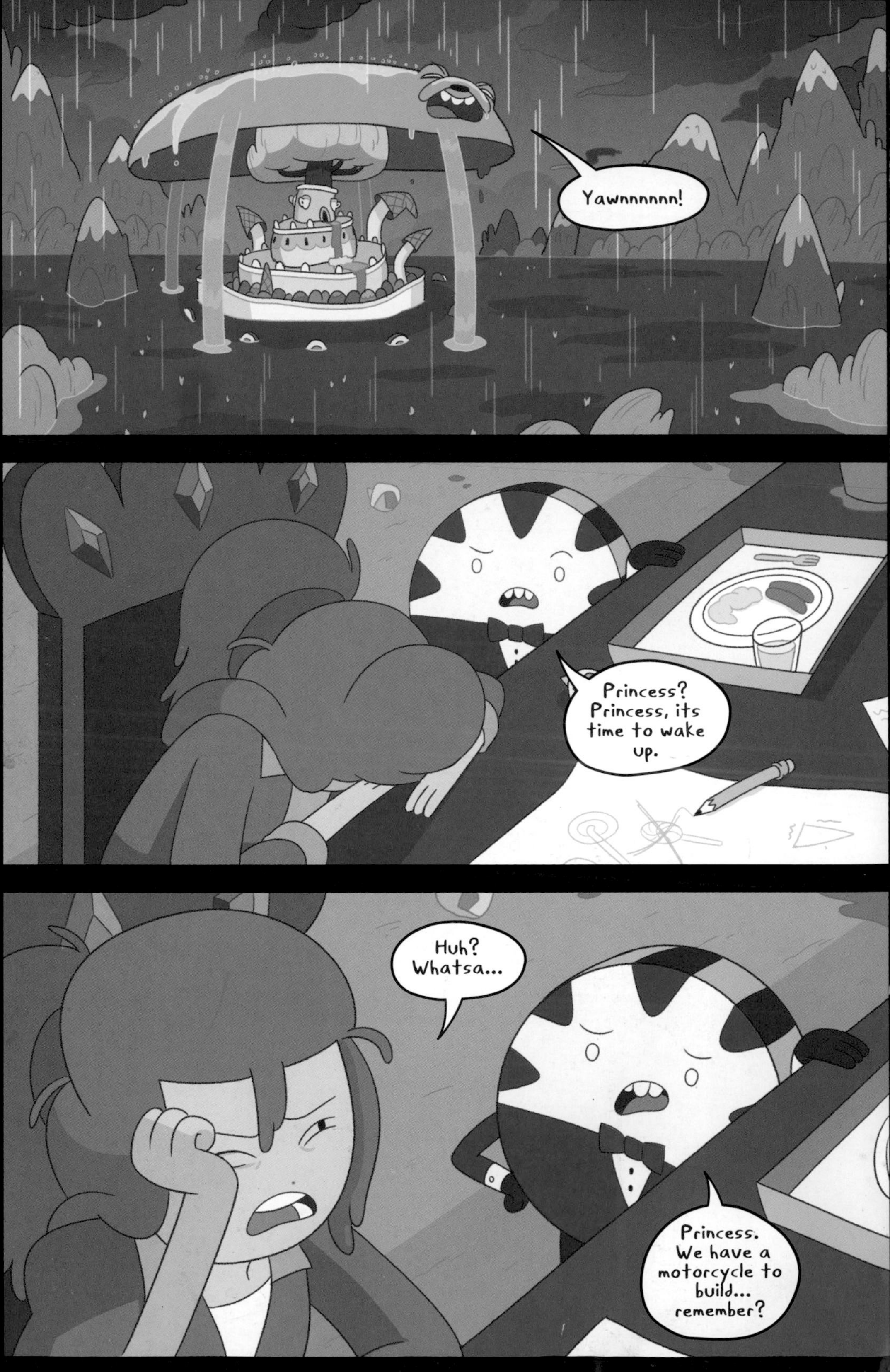
Yawnnnnnn!
Princess? Princess, its time to wake up.
Huh? Whatsa...
Princess. We have a motorcycle to build... remember?

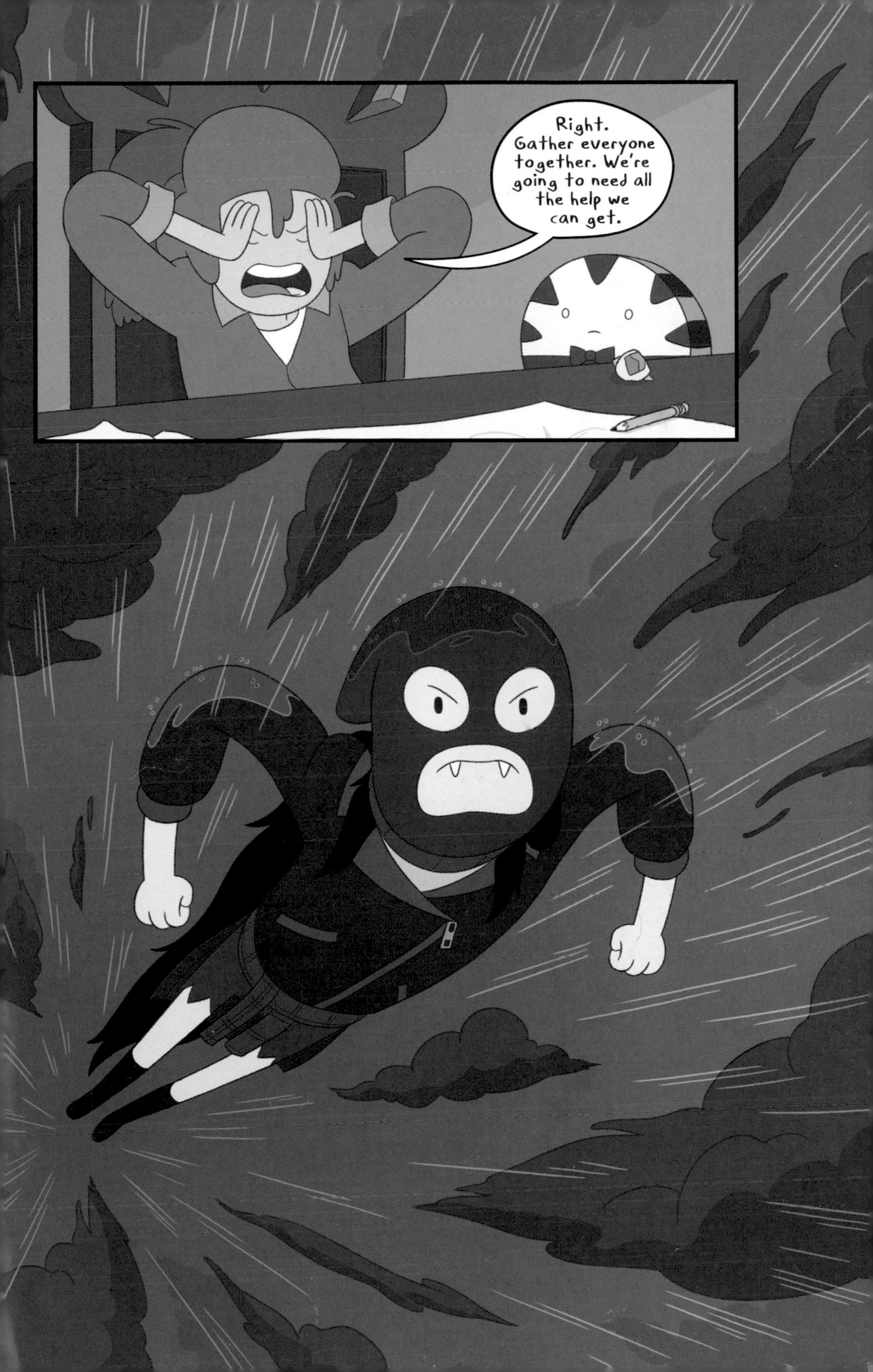
Right. Gather everyone together. We're going to need all the help we can get.

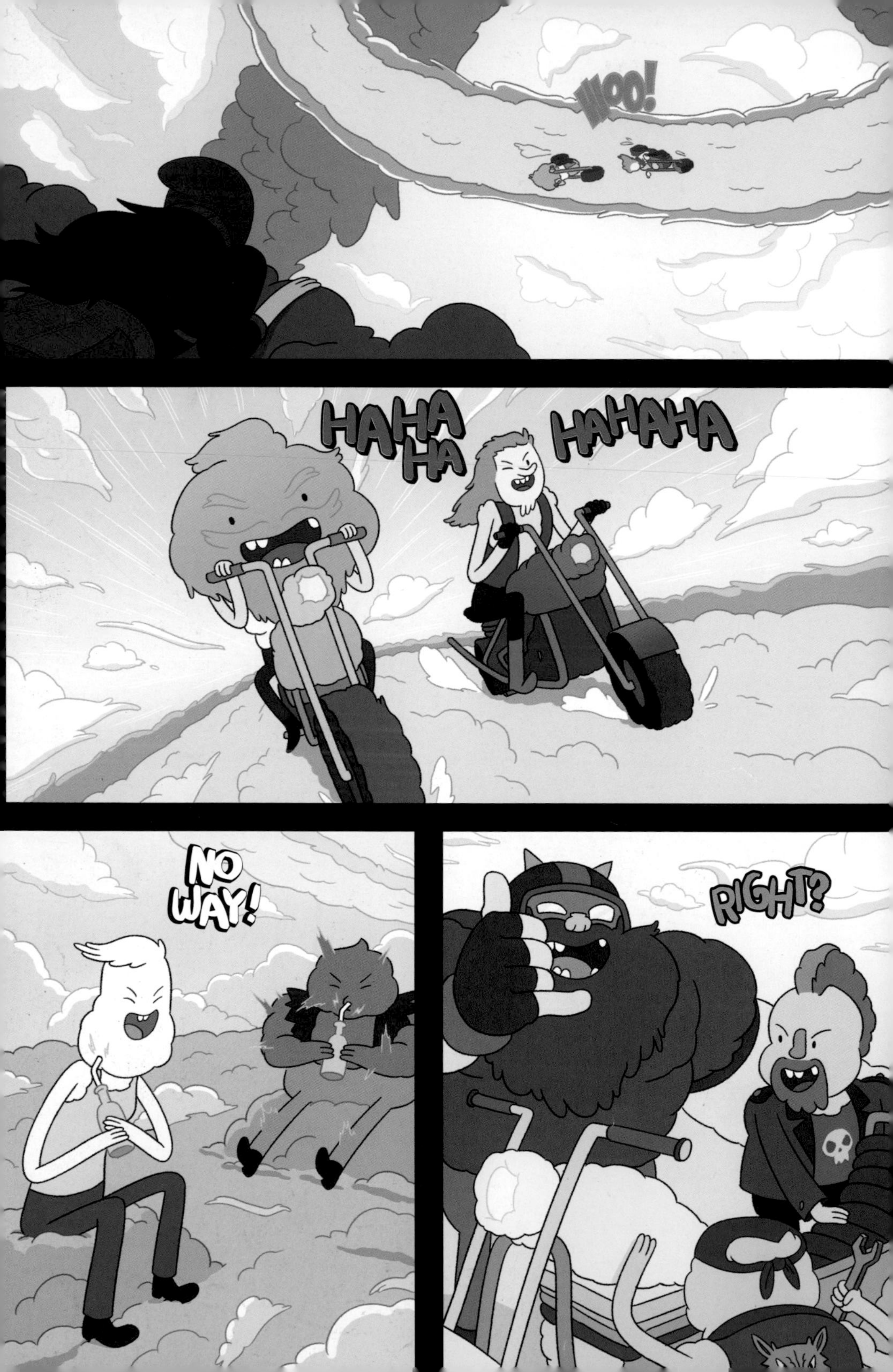
WOO!
HAHA HA
HAHAHA
NO WAY!
RIGHT?

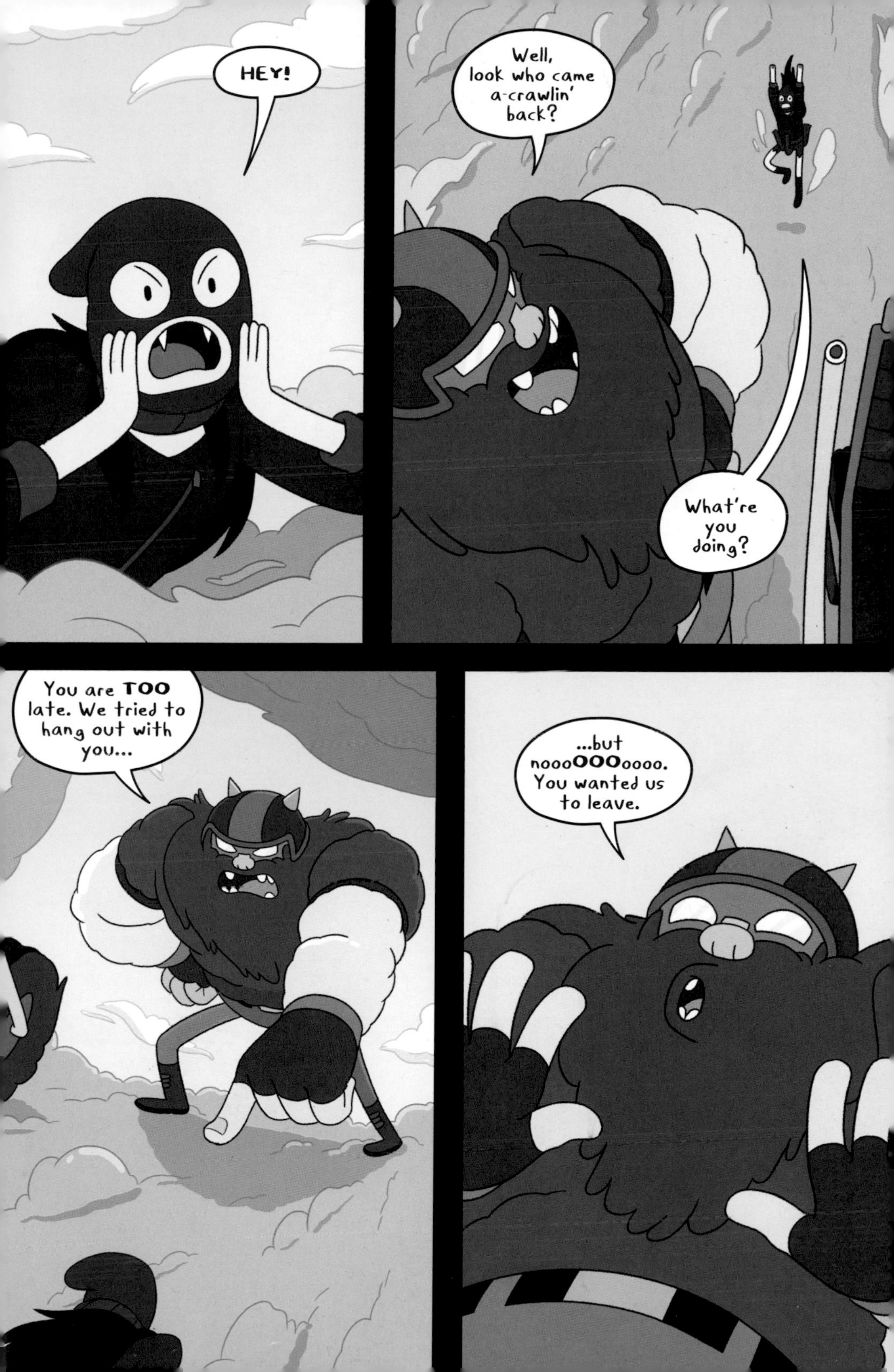
HEY!
Well, look who came a-crawlin' back?
What're you doing?
You are TOO late. We tried to hang out with you...
...but noooOOOoooo. You wanted us to leave.

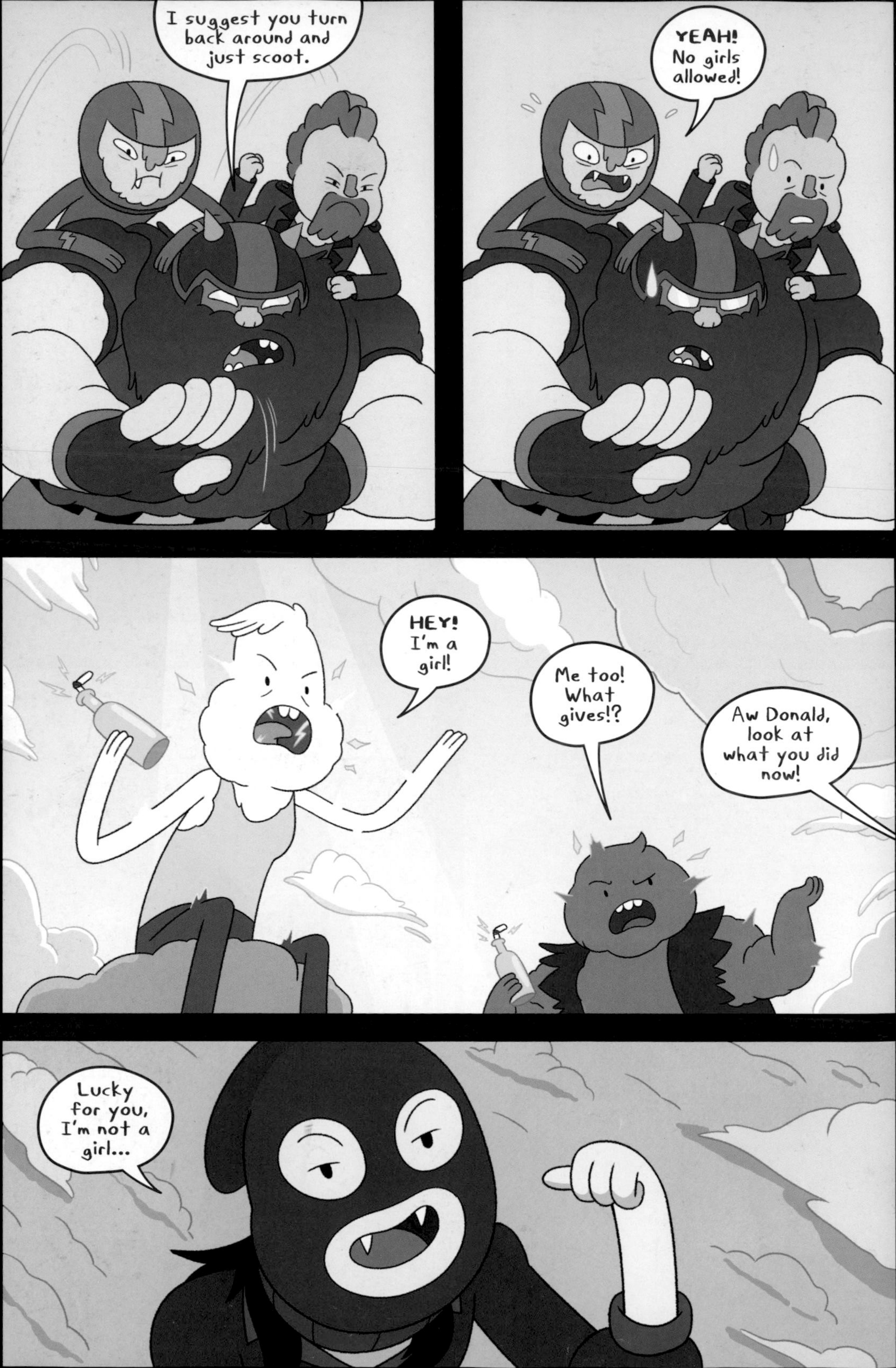
I suggest you turn back around and just scoot.
YEAH! No girls allowed!
HEY! I'm a girl!
Me too! What gives!?
Aw Donald, look at what you did now!
Lucky for you, I'm not a girl...

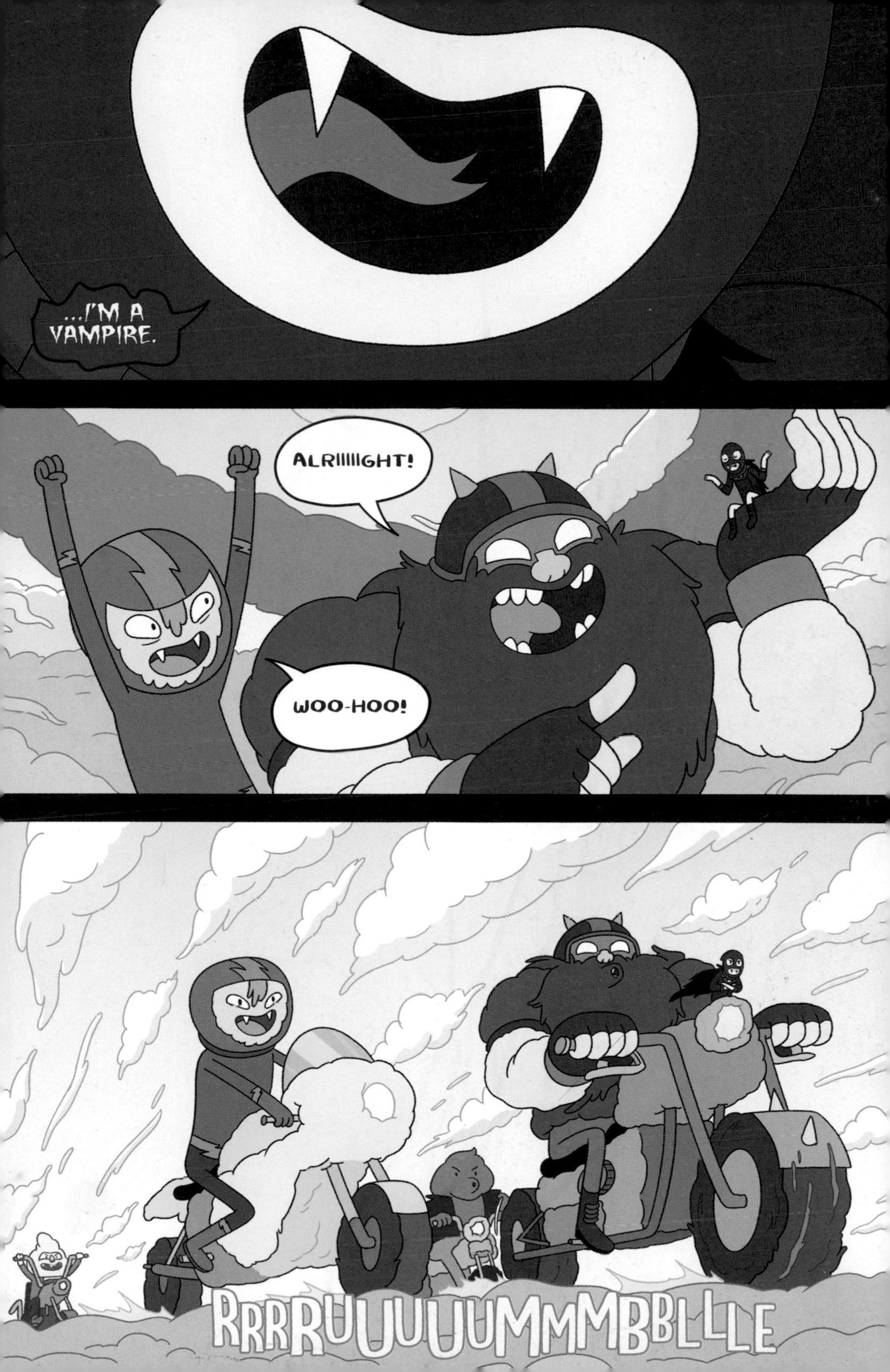
...I'M A VAMPIRE.
ALRIIIIIGHT!
WOO-HOO!
RRRRUUUUUMMMBBLLLE

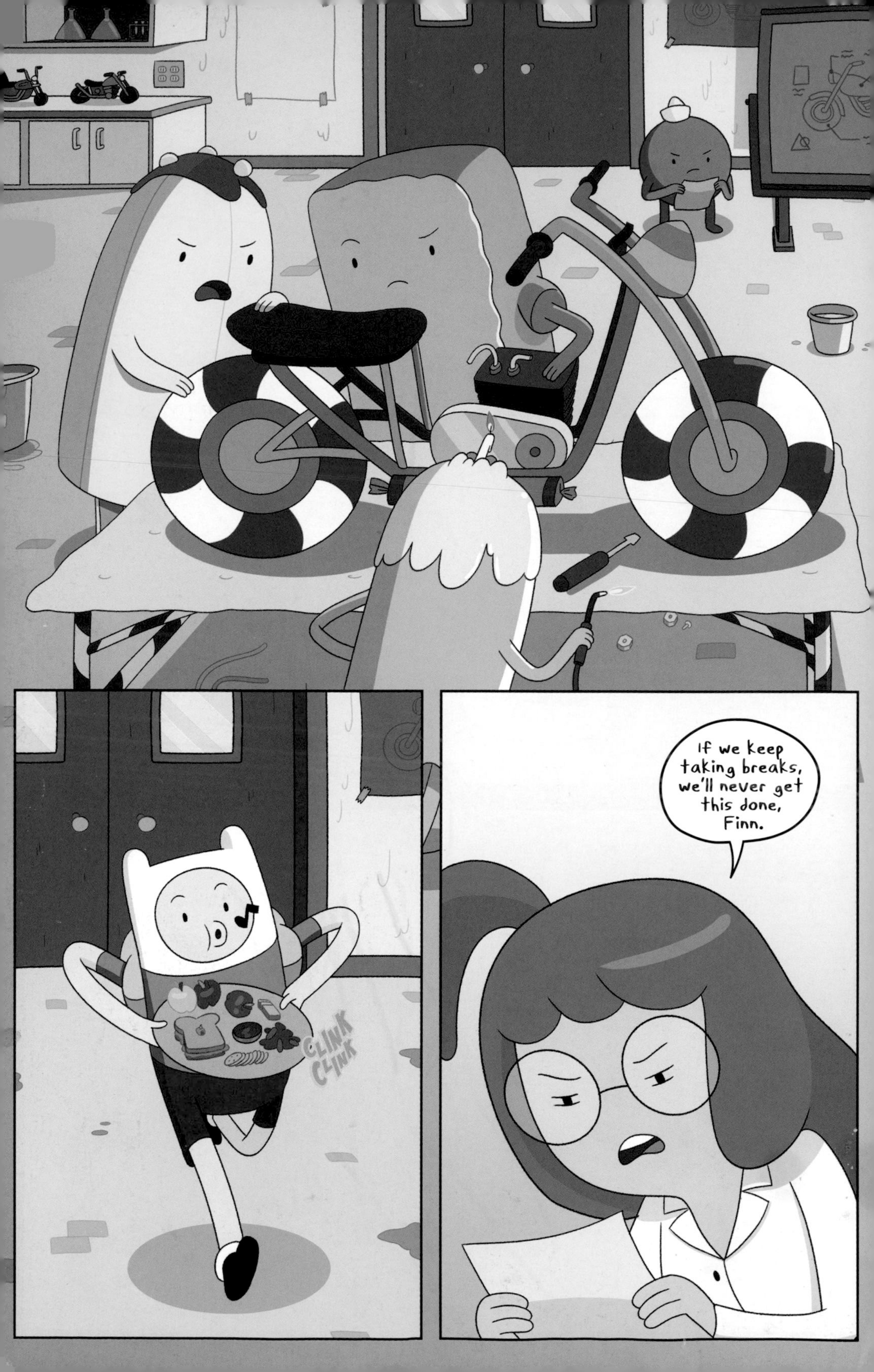
CLINK CLINK
If we keep taking breaks, we'll never get this done, Finn.

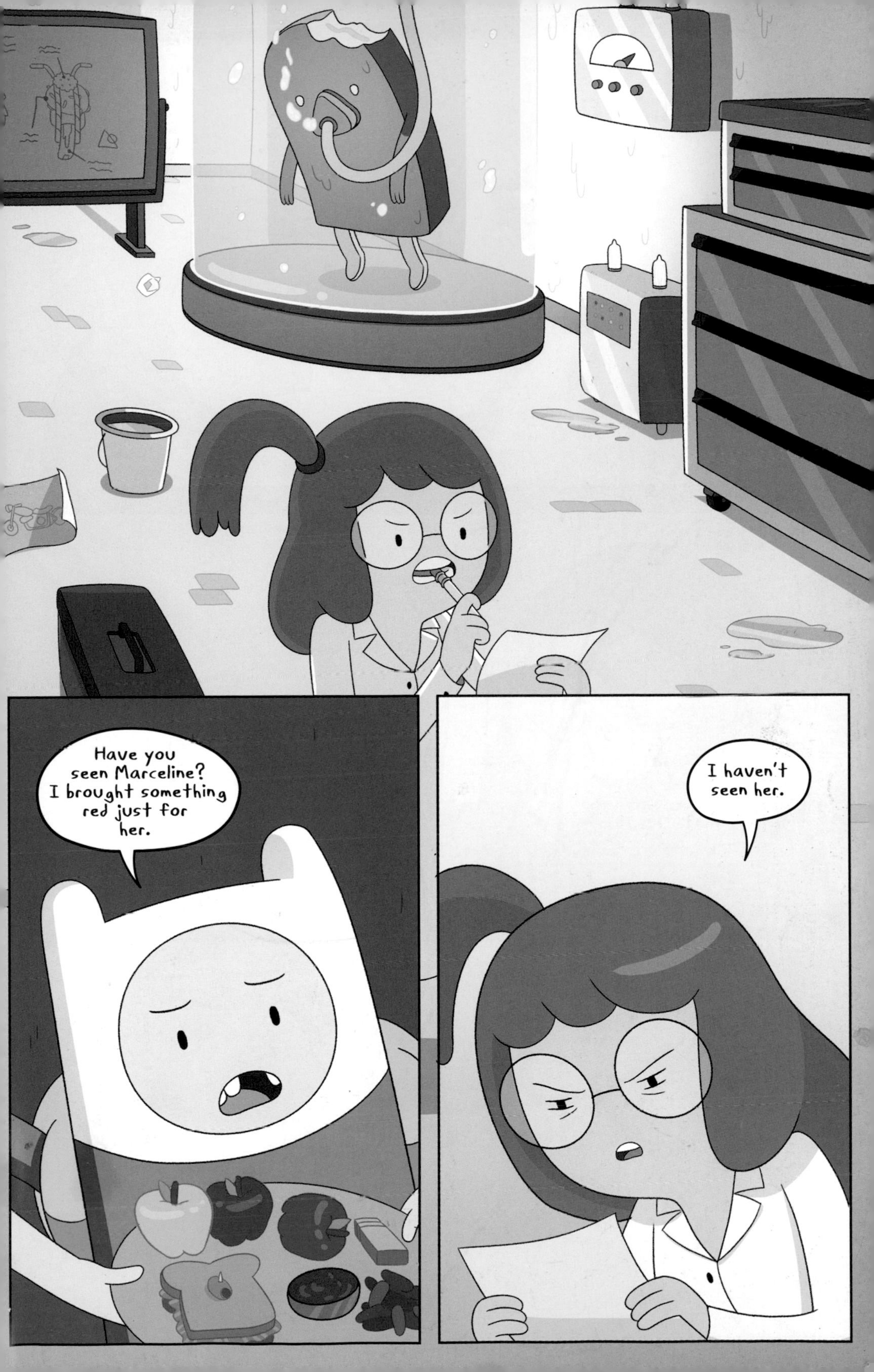
Have you seen Marceline? I brought something red just for her.
I haven't seen her.

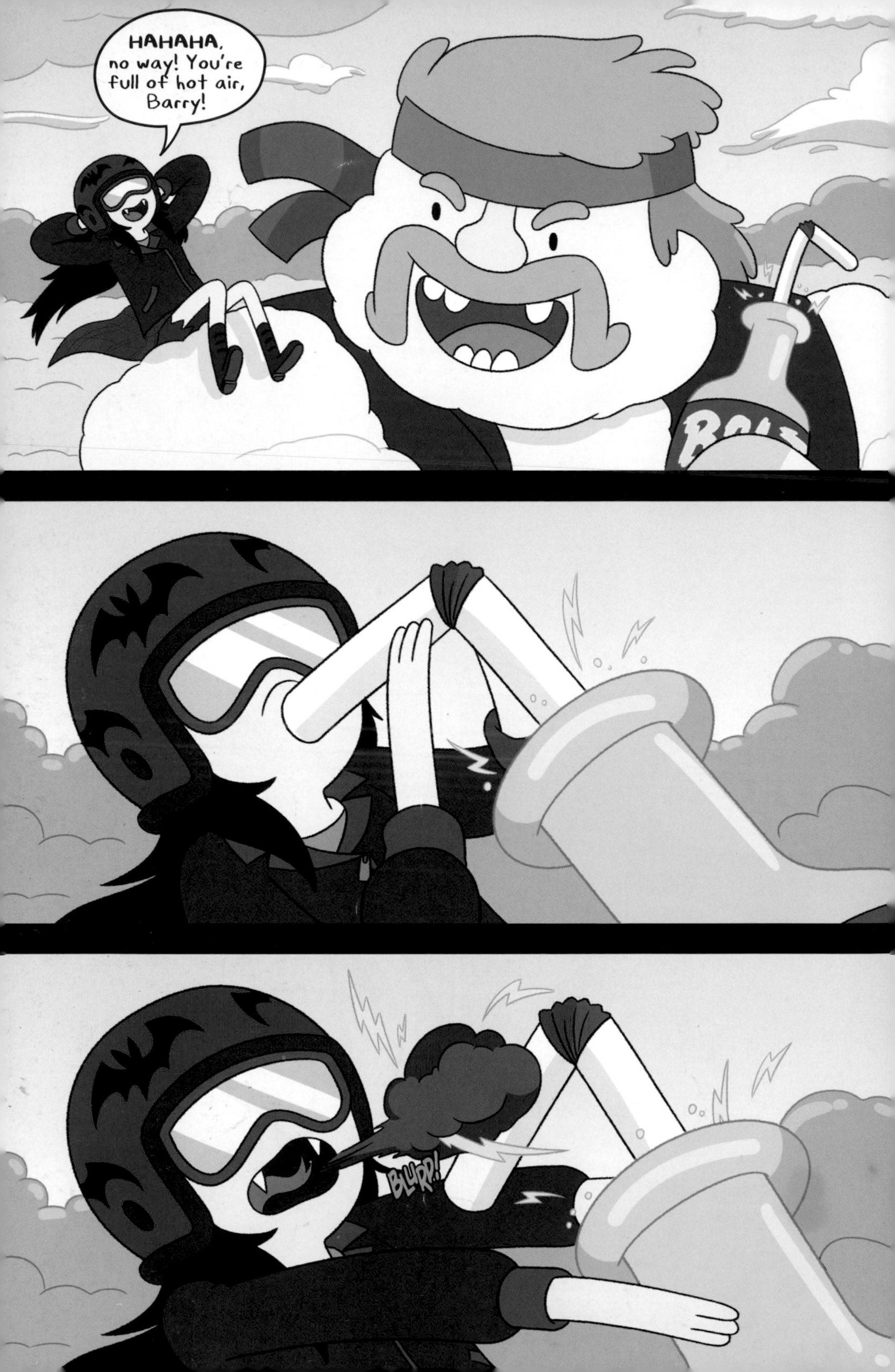
HAHAHA, no way! You're full of hot air, Barry!
BLURP!

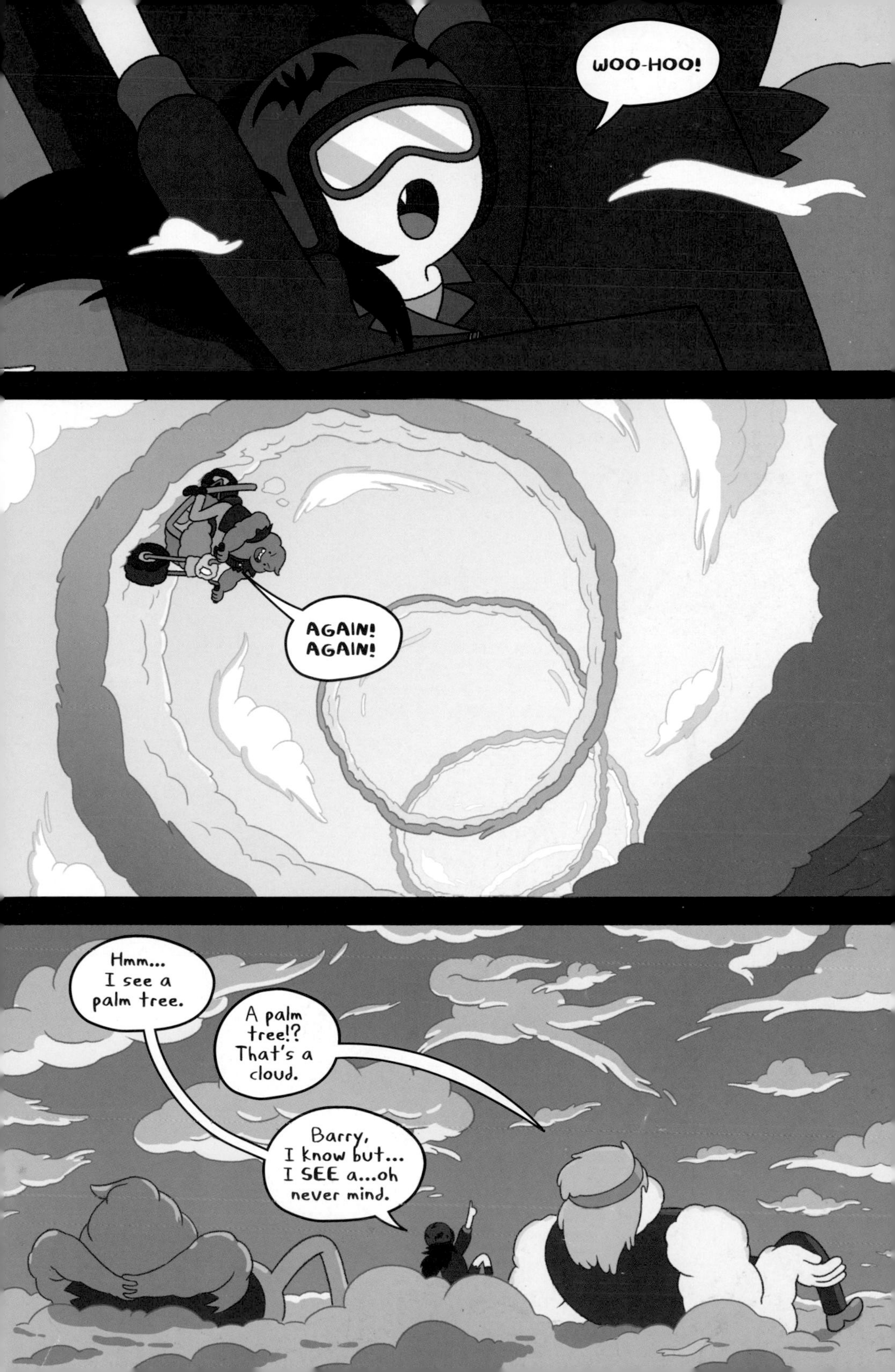
WOO-HOO!
AGAIN! AGAIN!
Hmm... I see a palm tree.
A palm tree!? That's a cloud.
Barry, I know but... I SEE a...oh never mind.

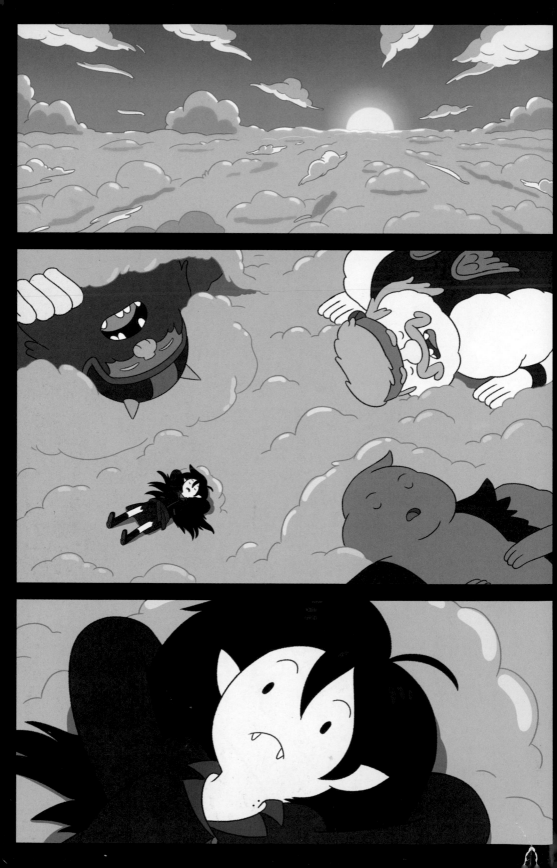

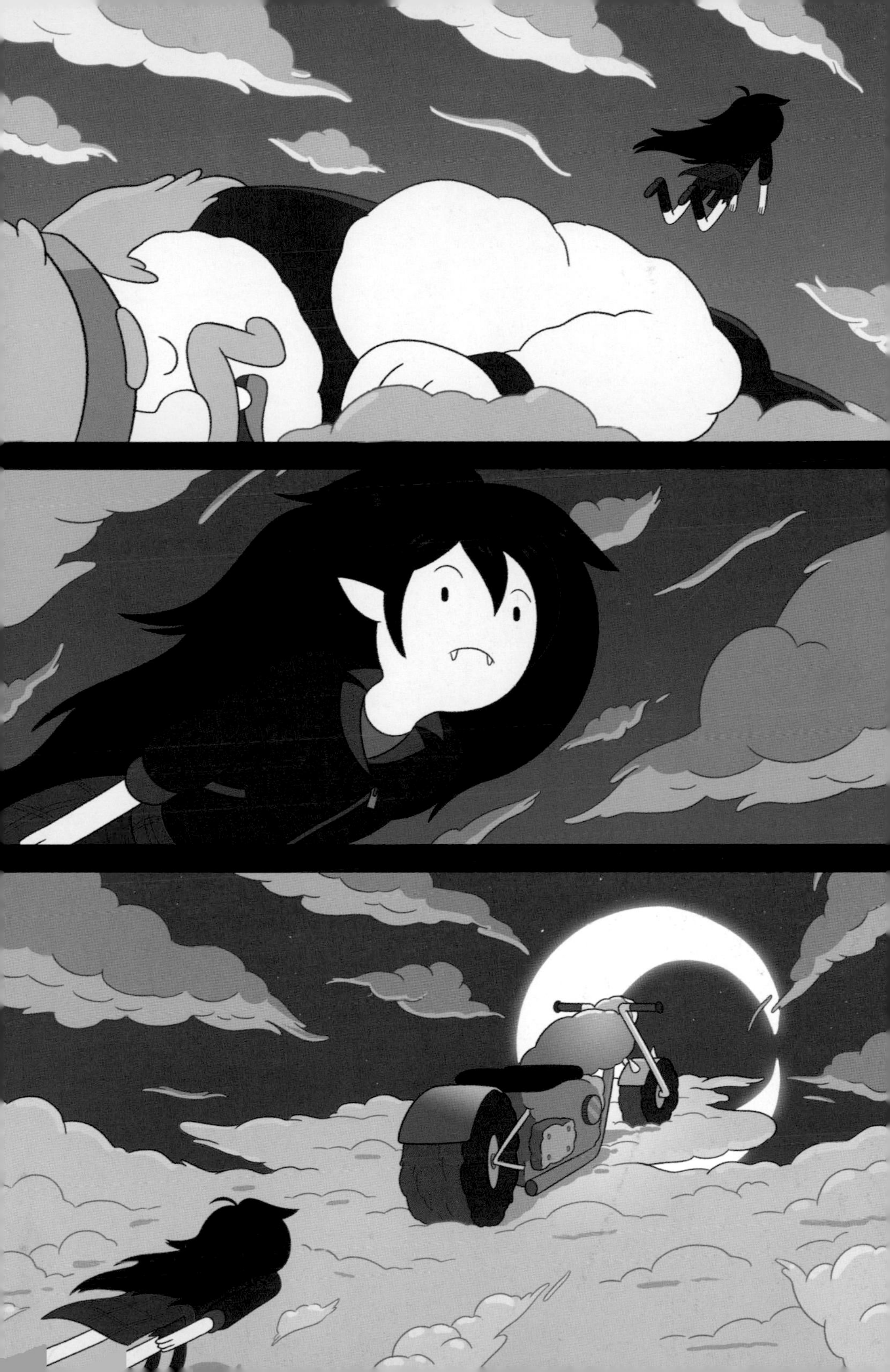

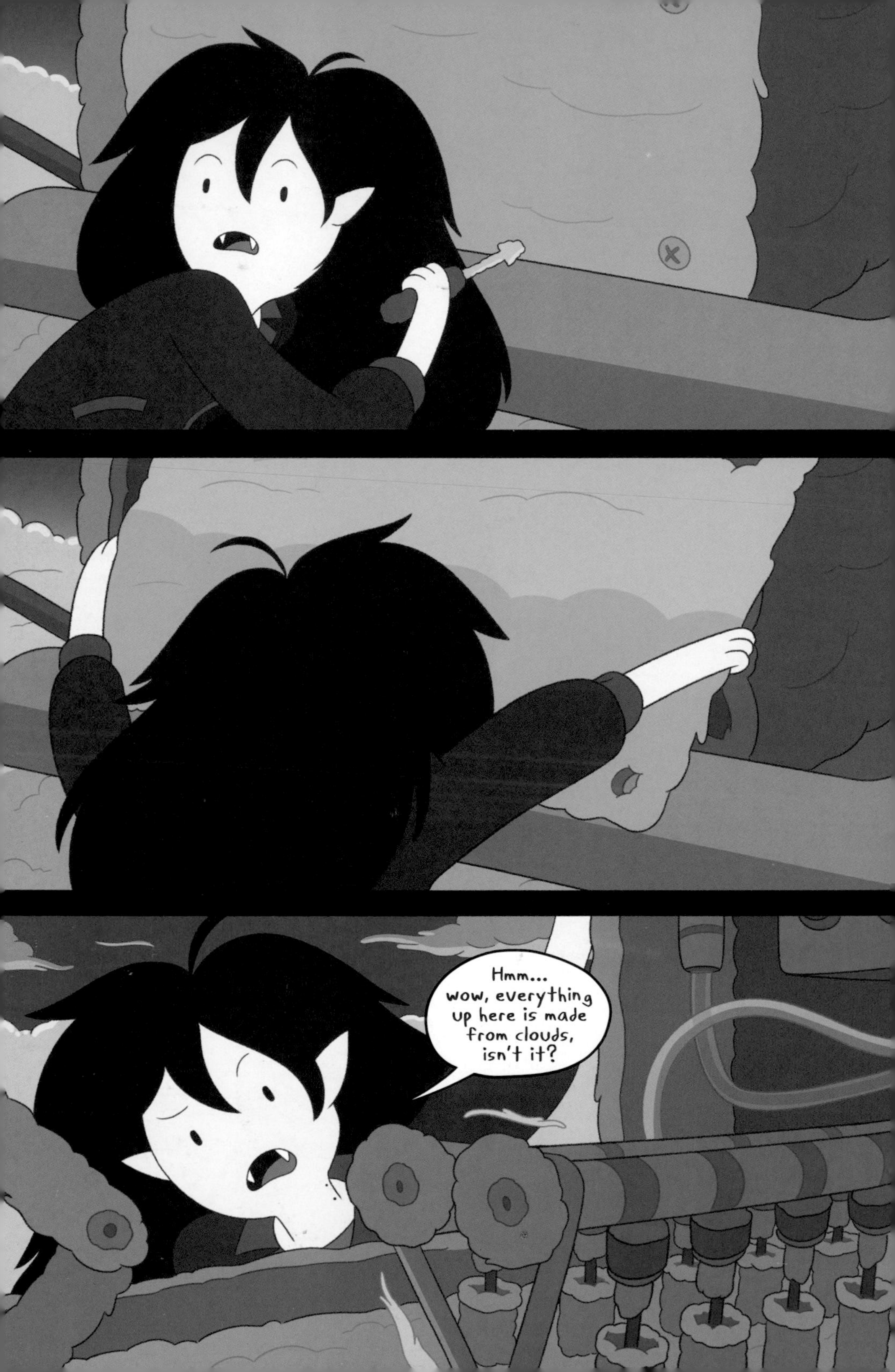
Hmm... wow, everything up here is made from clouds, isn't it?

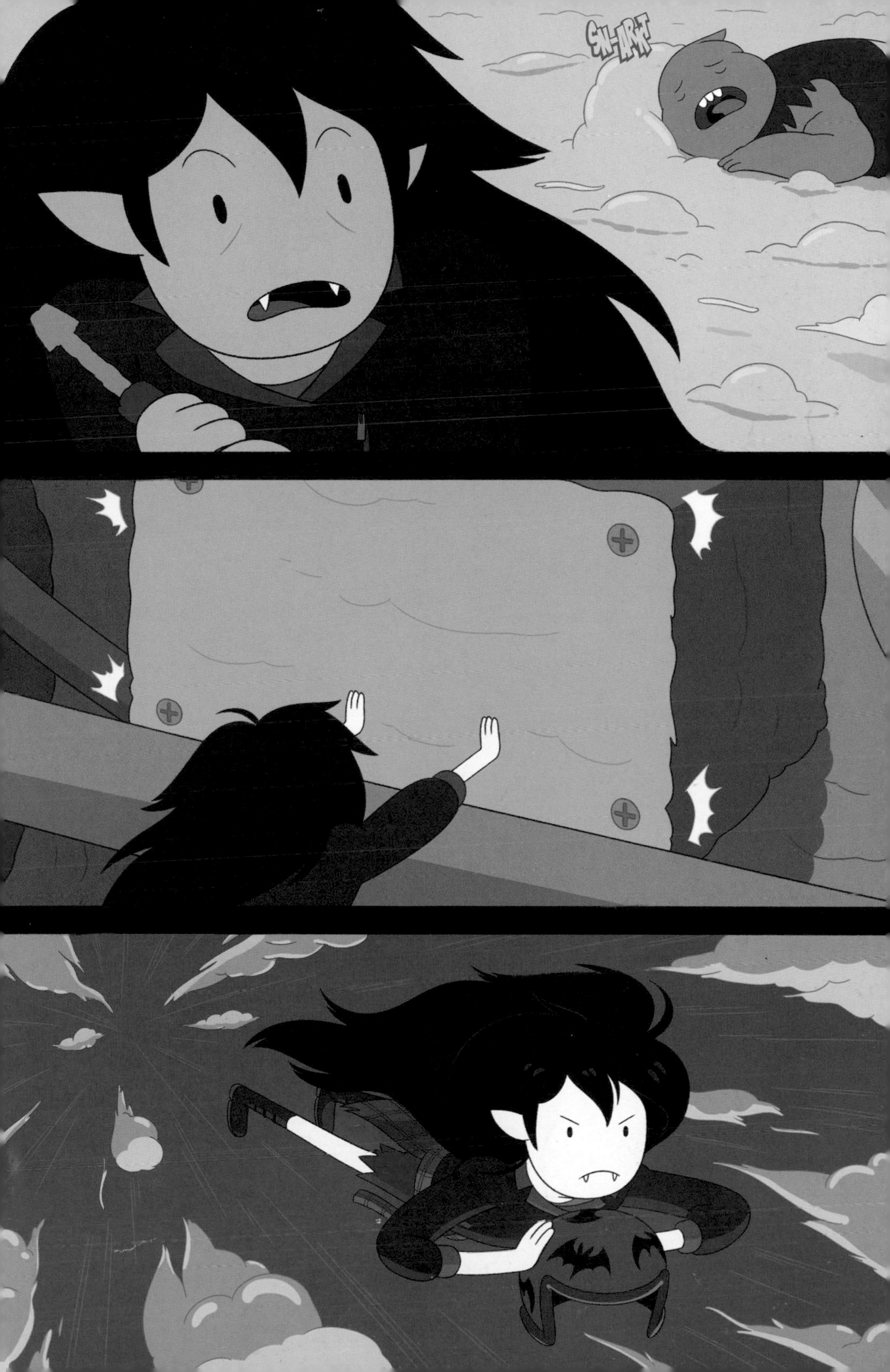
SN-ARKT

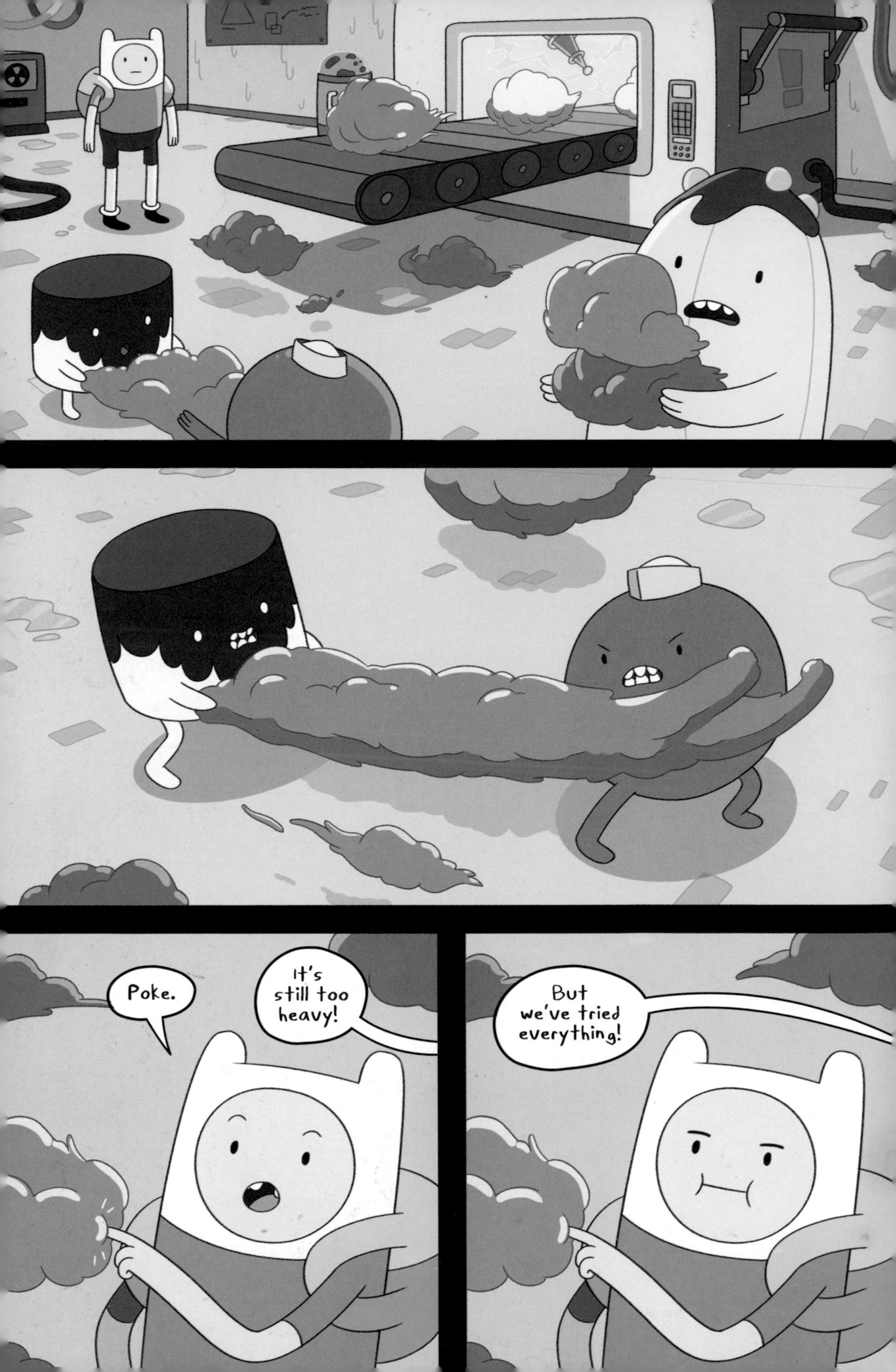
Poke.
It's still too heavy!
But we've tried everything!

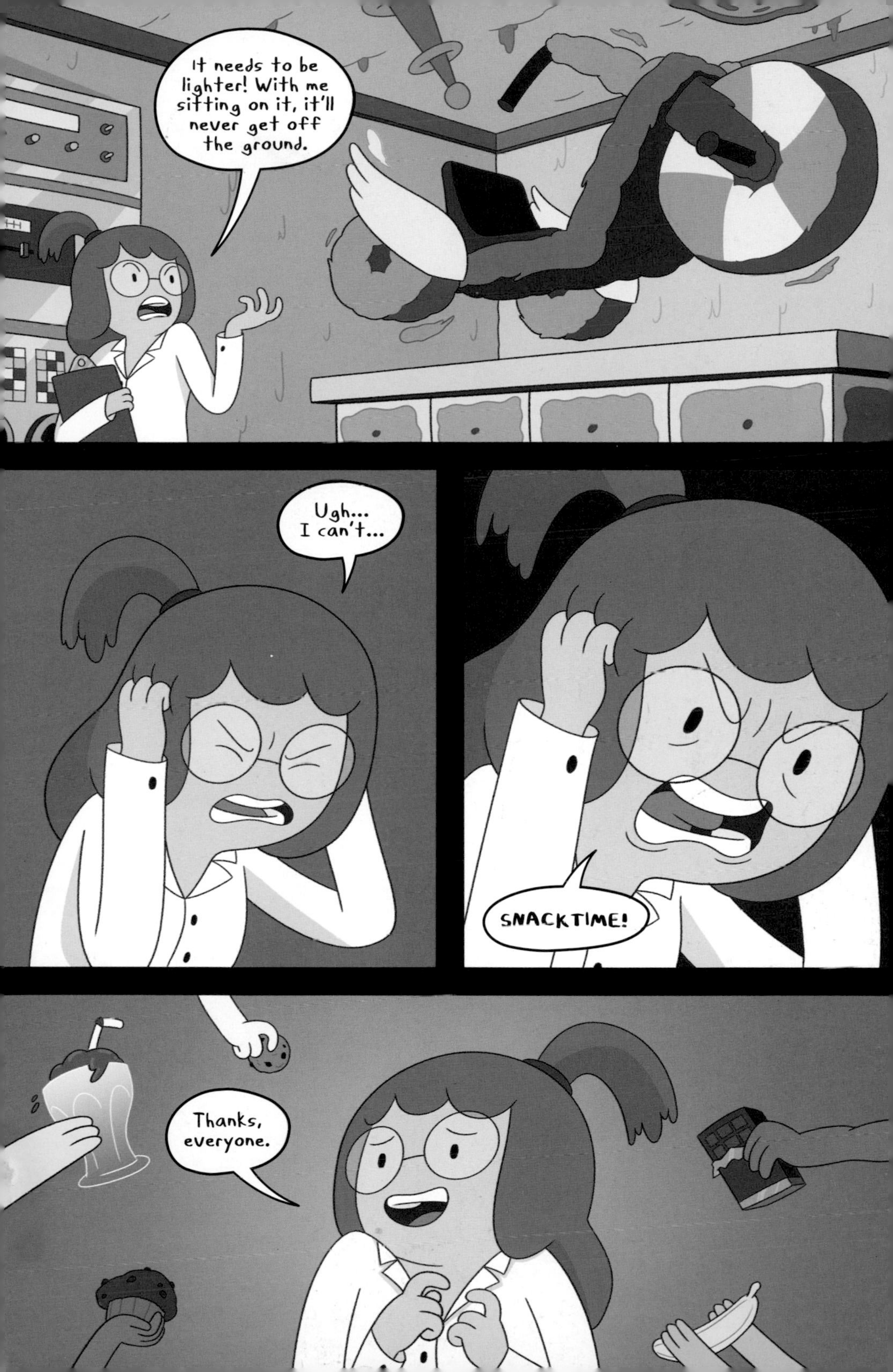
It needs to be lighter! With me sitting on it, it'll never get off the ground.
Ugh... I can't...
SNACKTIME!
Thanks, everyone.

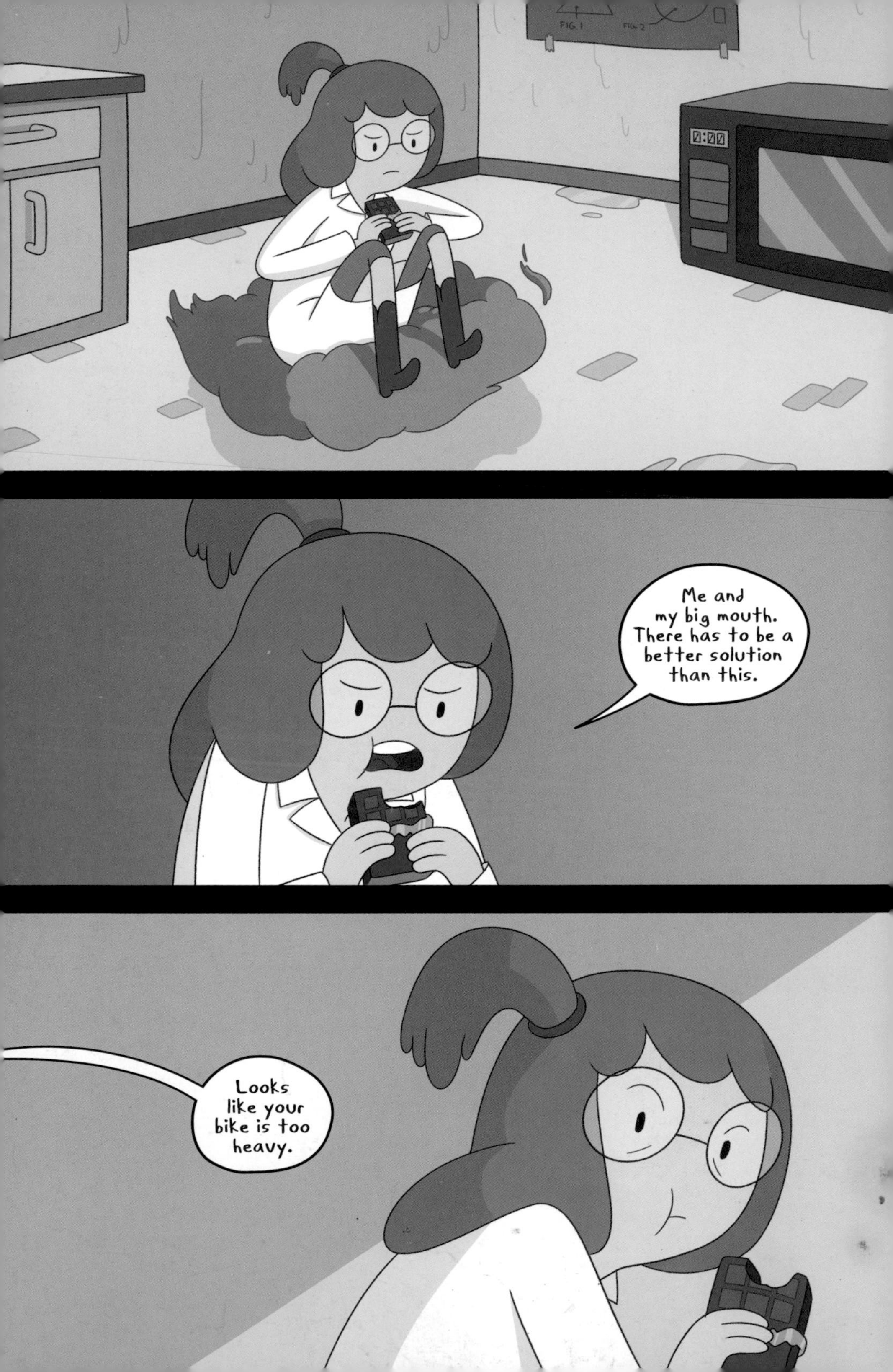
FIG. 1
FIG. 2
0:00
Me and my big mouth. There has to be a better solution than this.
Looks like your bike is too heavy.

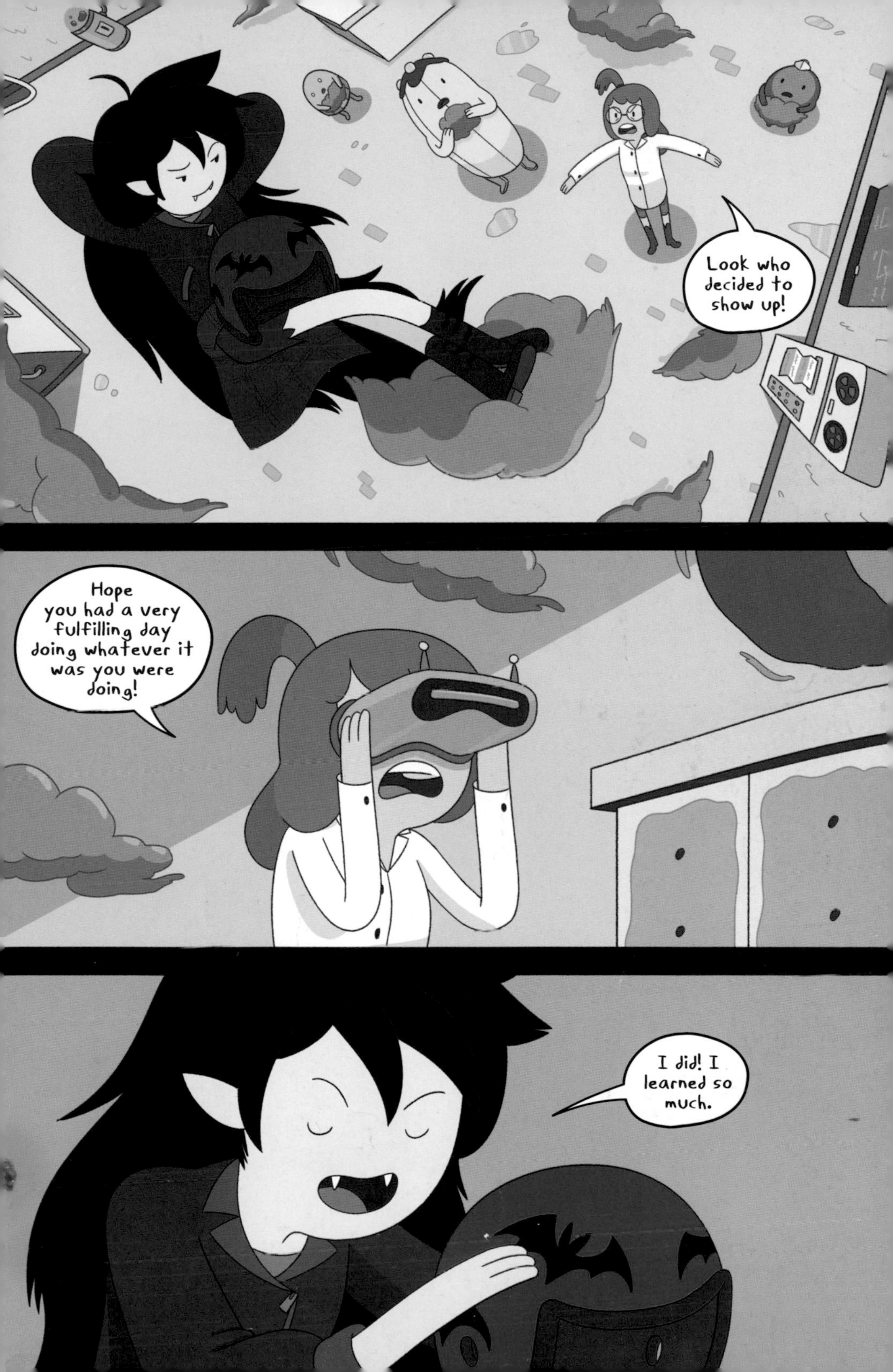
Look who decided to show up!
Hope you had a very fulfilling day doing whatever it was you were doing!
I did! I learned so much.

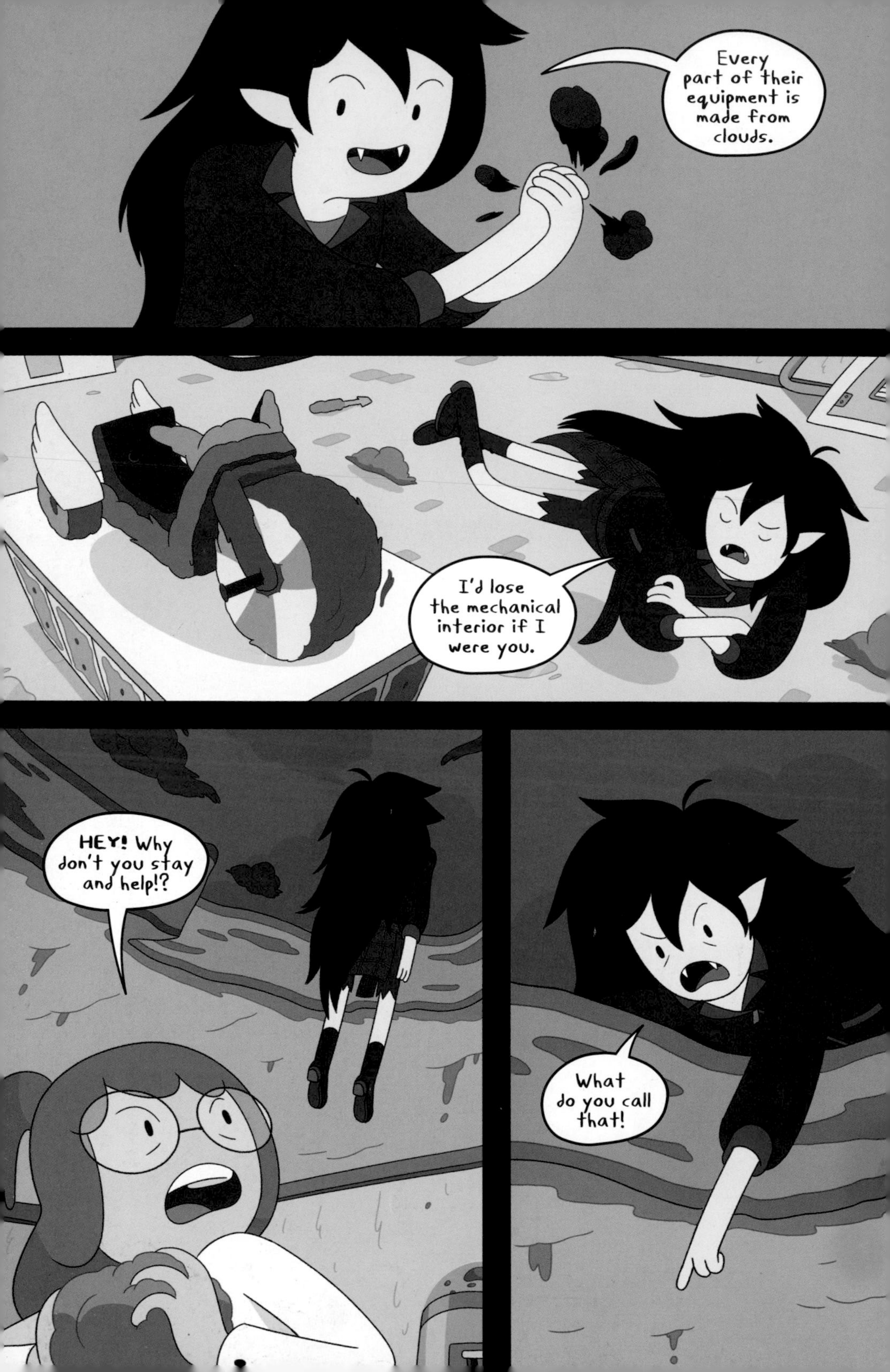
Every part of their equipment is made from clouds.
I'd lose the mechanical interior if I were you.
HEY! Why don't you stay and help!?
What do you call that!

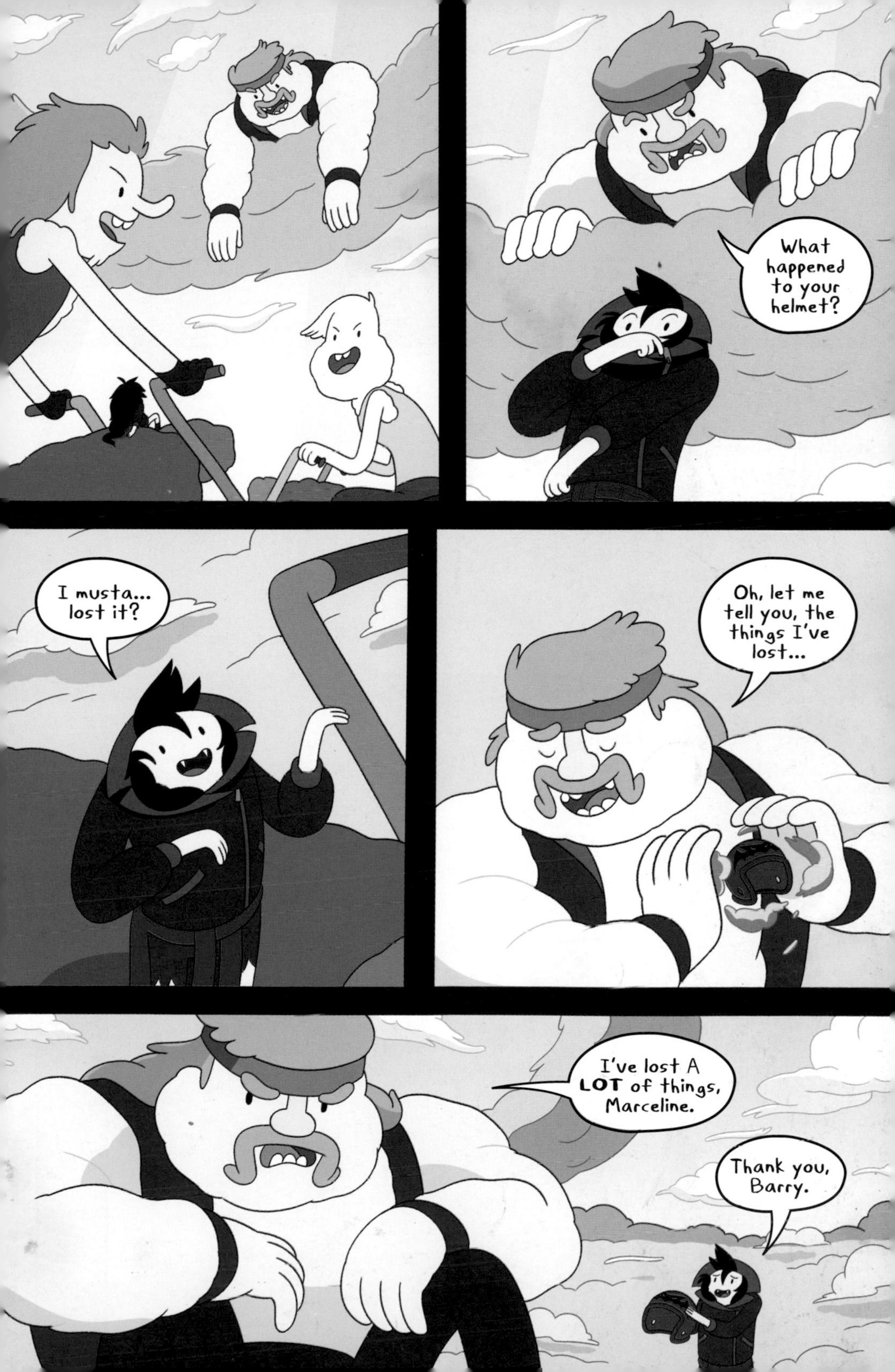
What happened to your helmet?
I musta... lost it?
Oh, let me tell you, the things I've lost...
I've lost A **LOT** of things, Marceline.
Thank you, Barry.

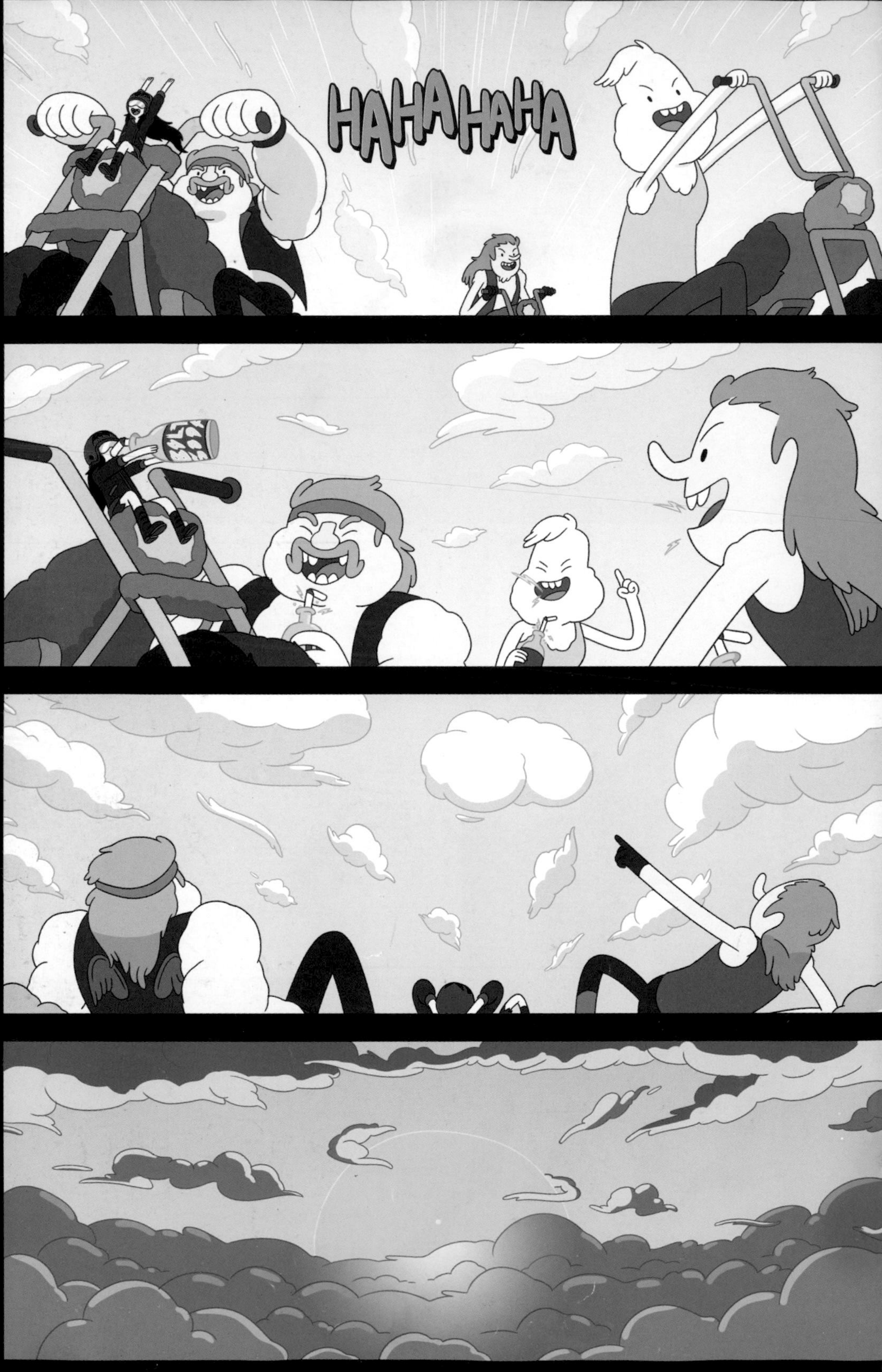
HAHAHAHA

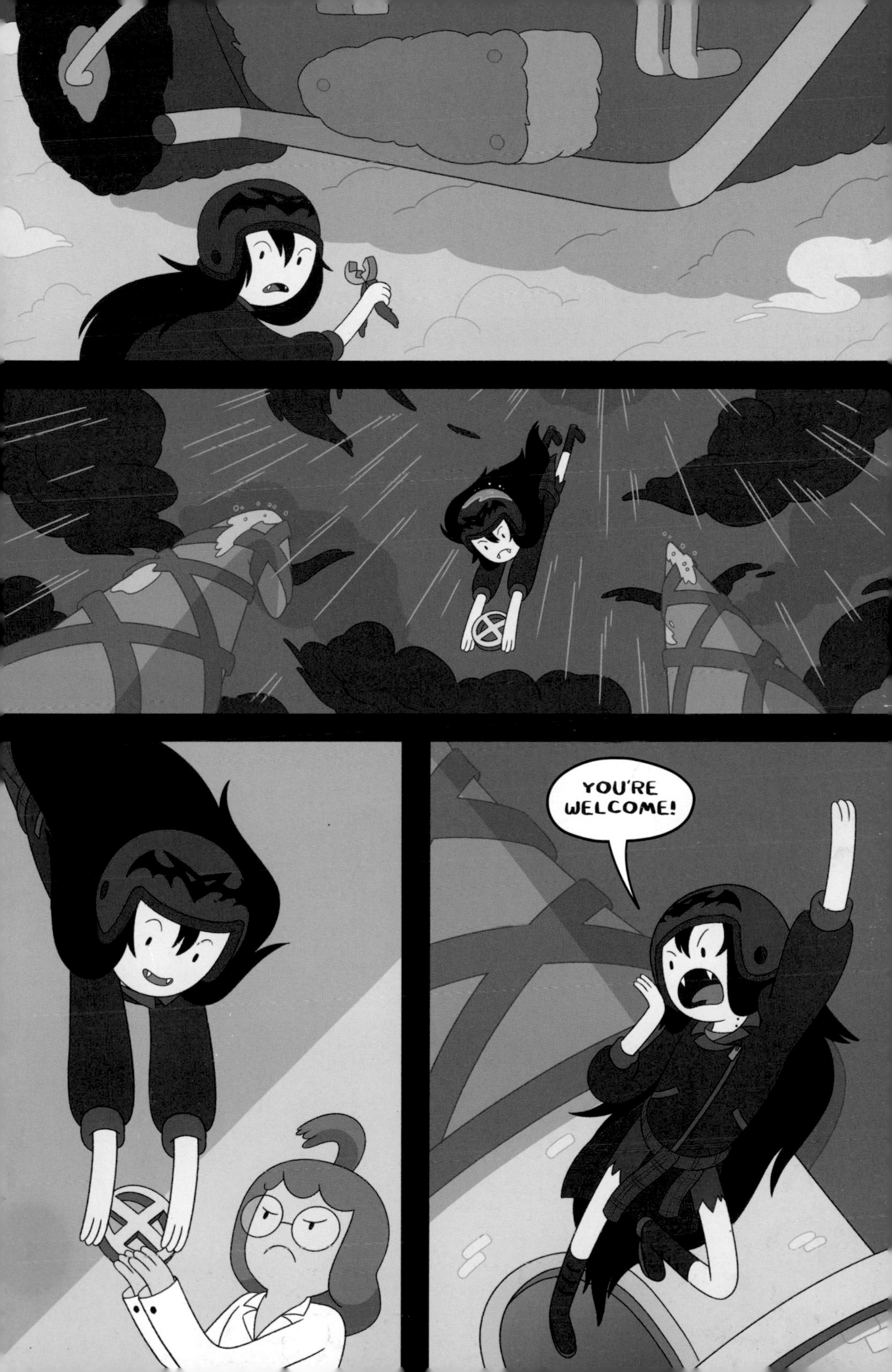
YOU'RE WELCOME!

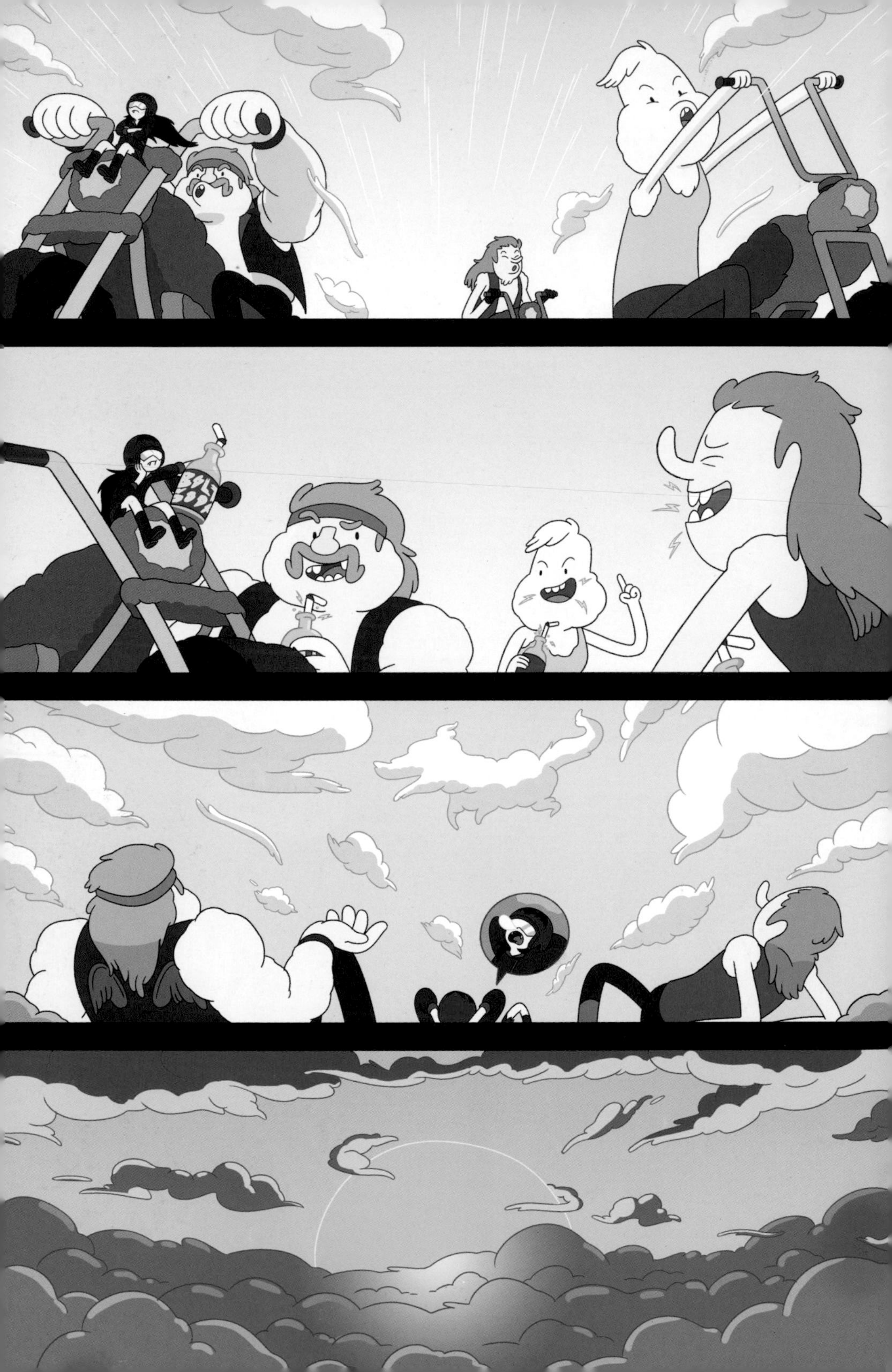
BOLT
SODA

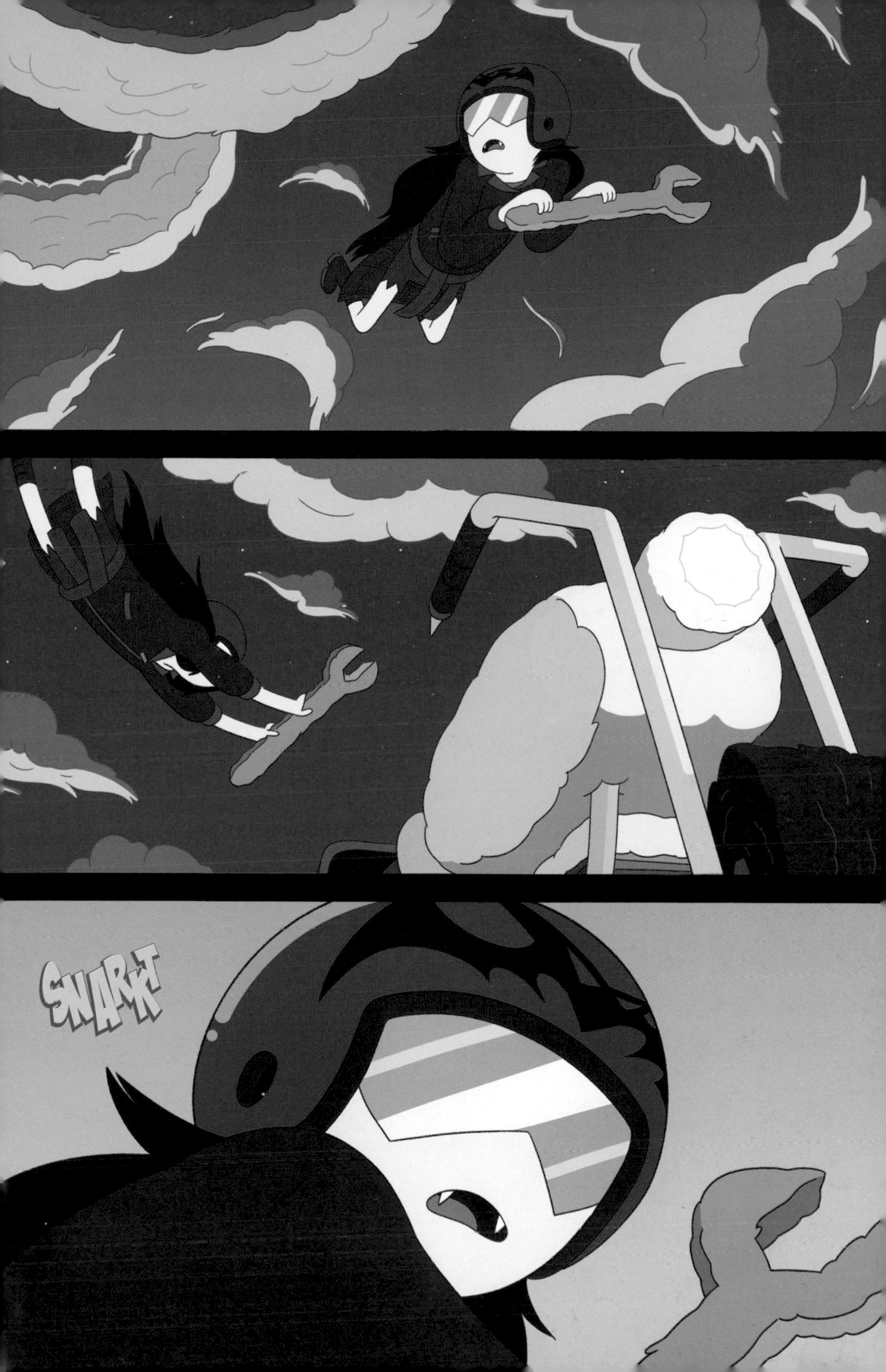
SNARKT

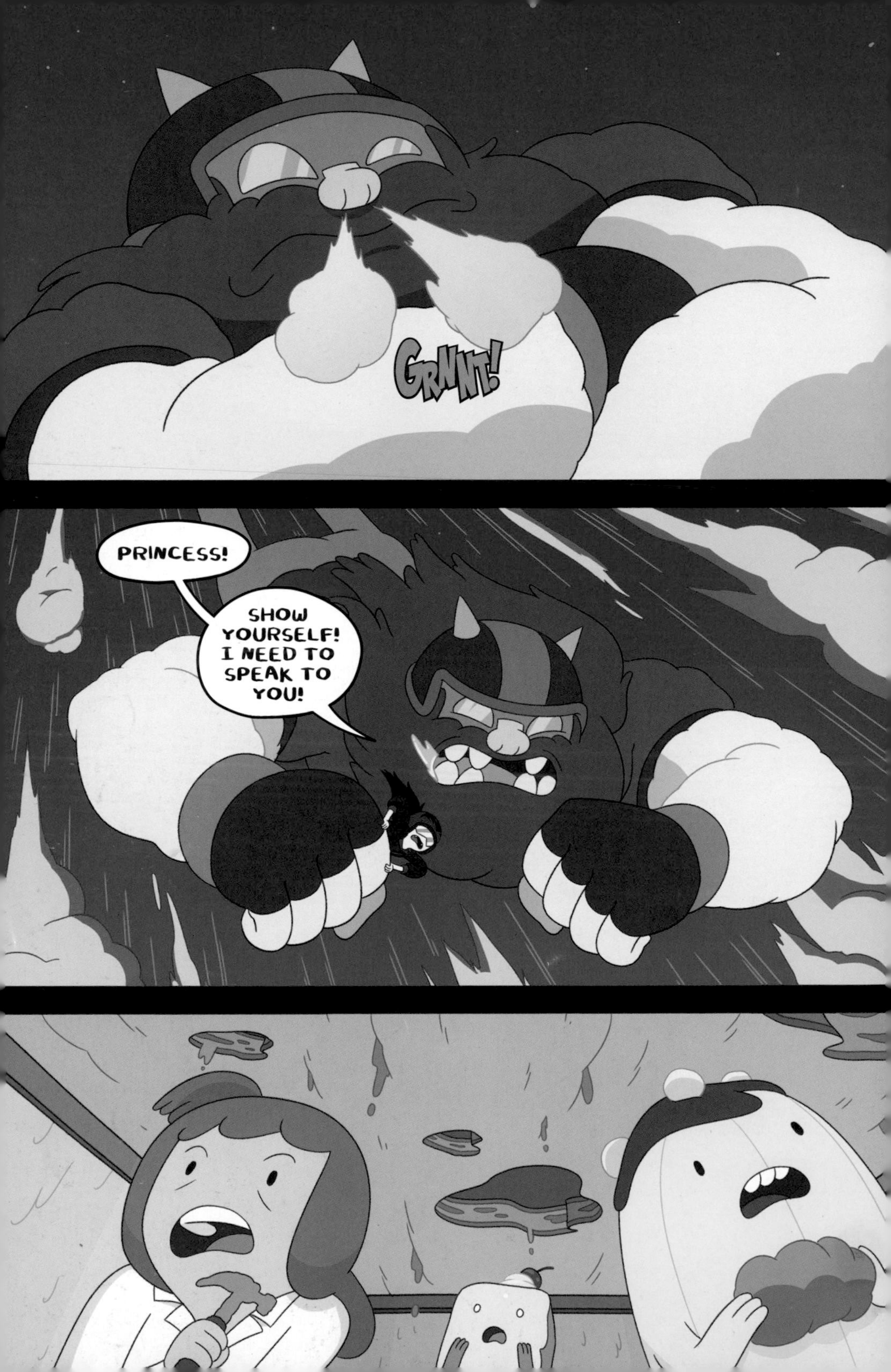
GRNNT!
PRINCESS!
SHOW YOURSELF! I NEED TO SPEAK TO YOU!

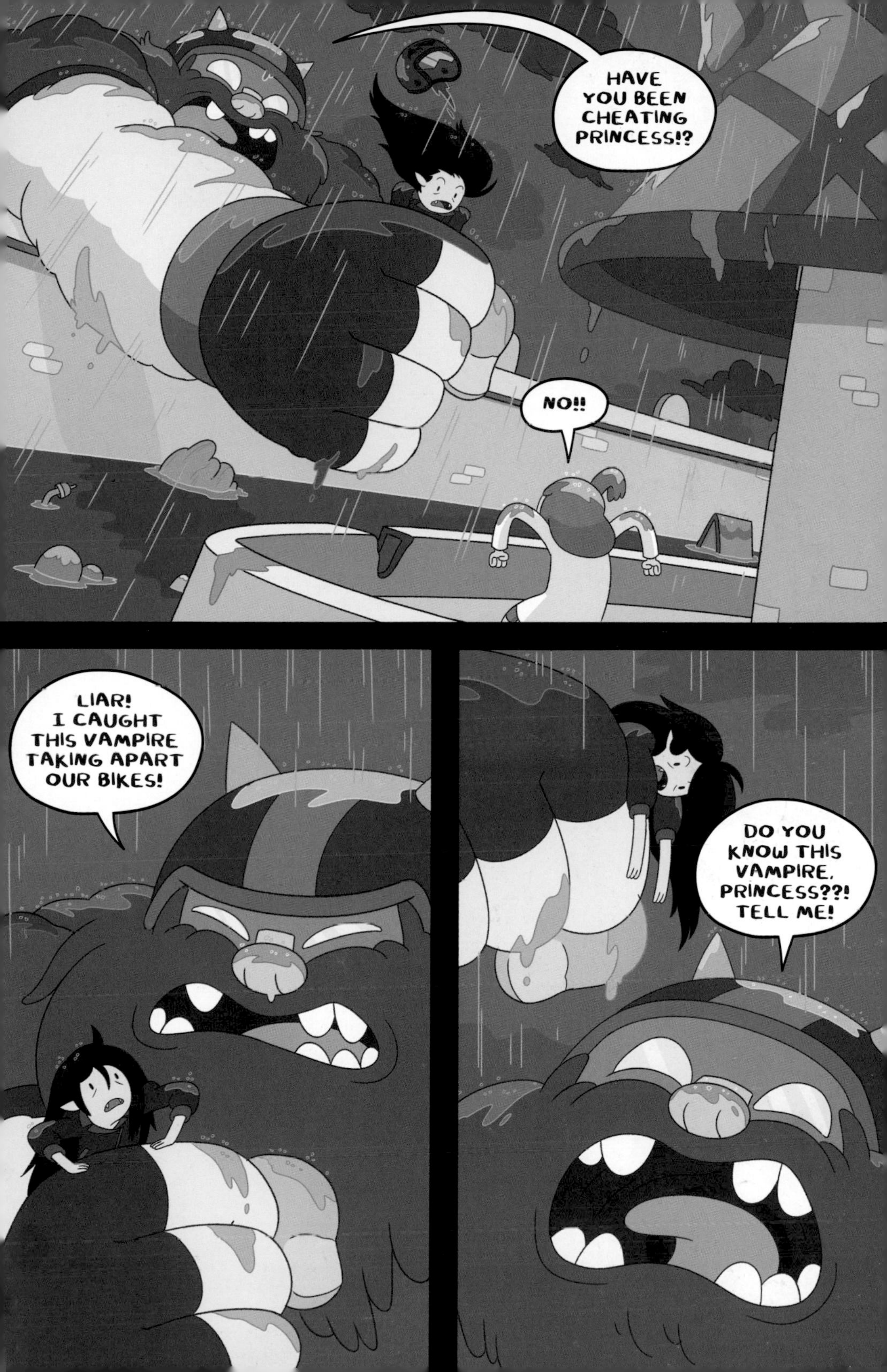
HAVE YOU BEEN CHEATING PRINCESS!?
NO!!
LIAR! I CAUGHT THIS VAMPIRE TAKING APART OUR BIKES!
DO YOU KNOW THIS VAMPIRE, PRINCESS??! TELL ME!

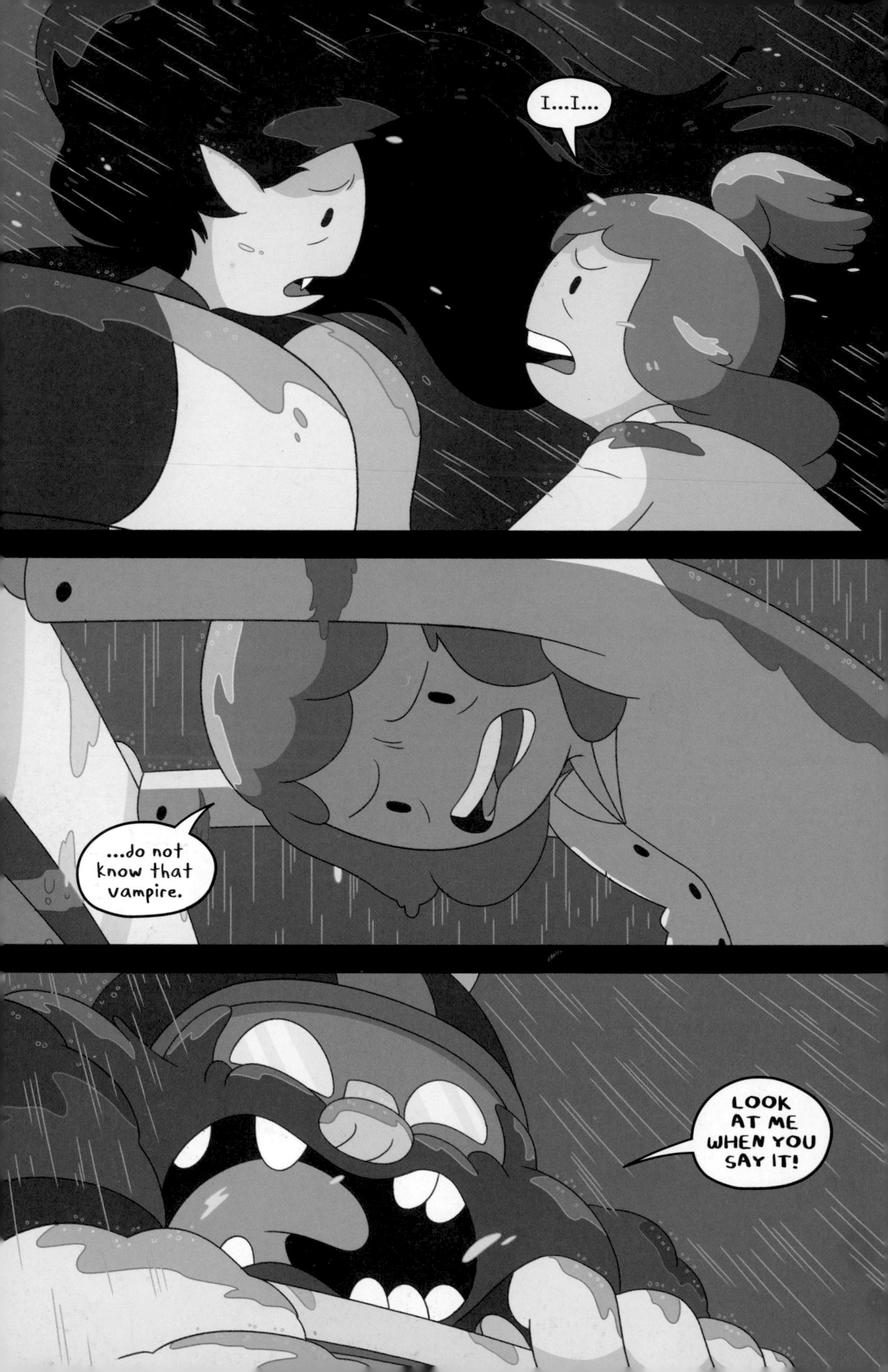
I...I...
...do not know that vampire.
LOOK AT ME WHEN YOU SAY IT!

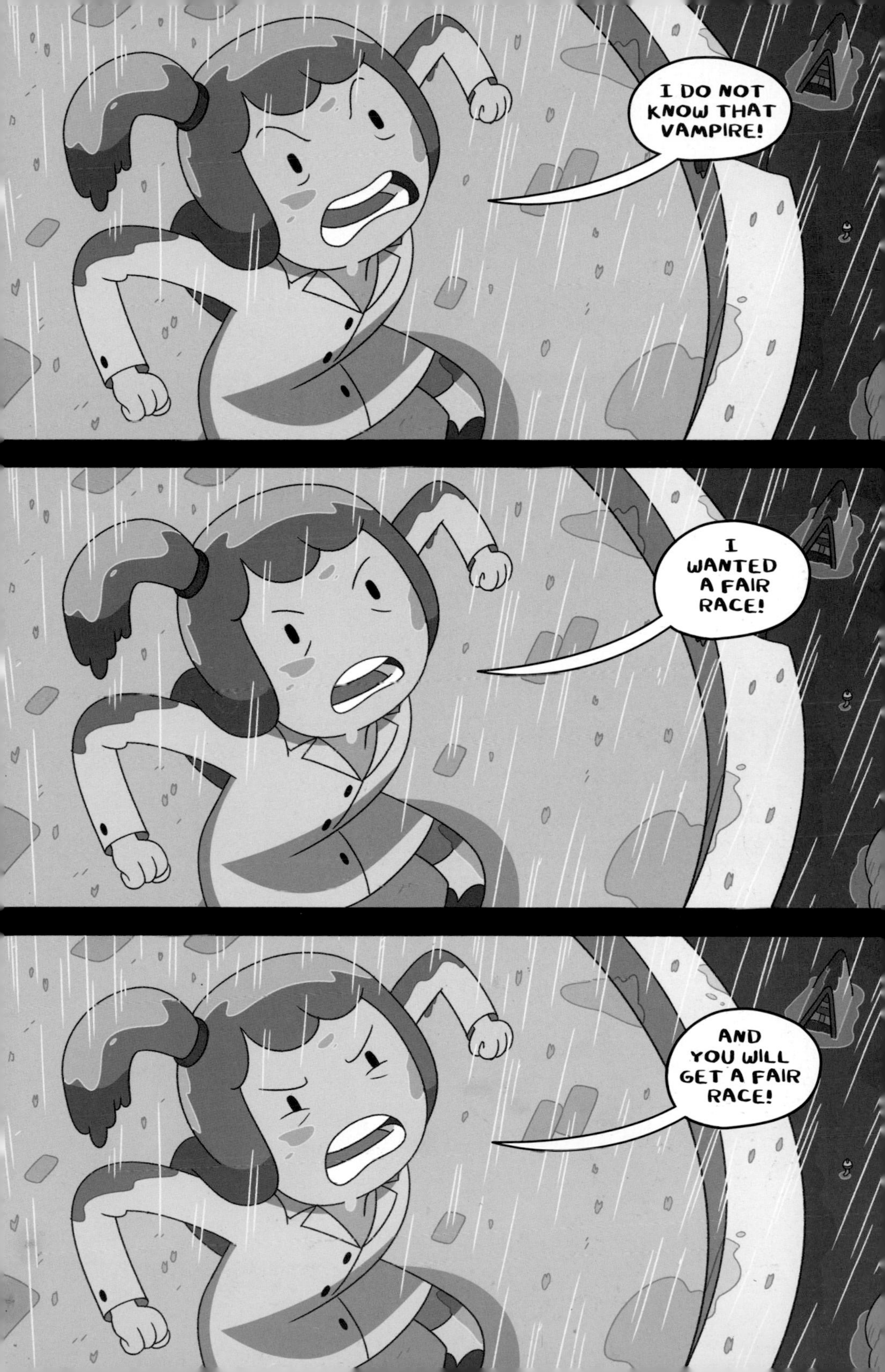
I DO NOT KNOW THAT VAMPIRE!
I WANTED A FAIR RACE!
AND YOU WILL GET A FAIR RACE!

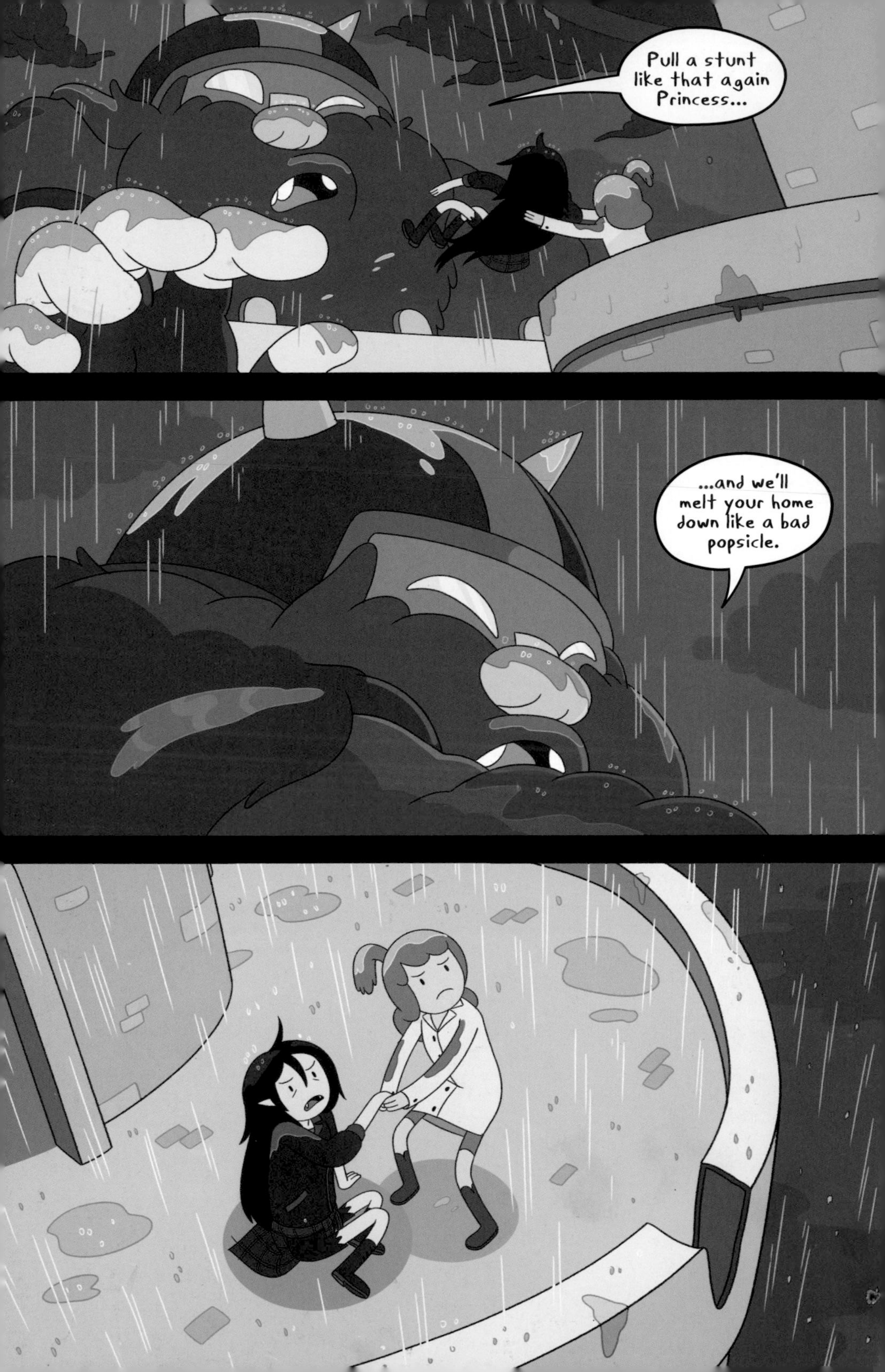
Pull a stunt like that again Princess...
...and we'll melt your home down like a bad popsicle.

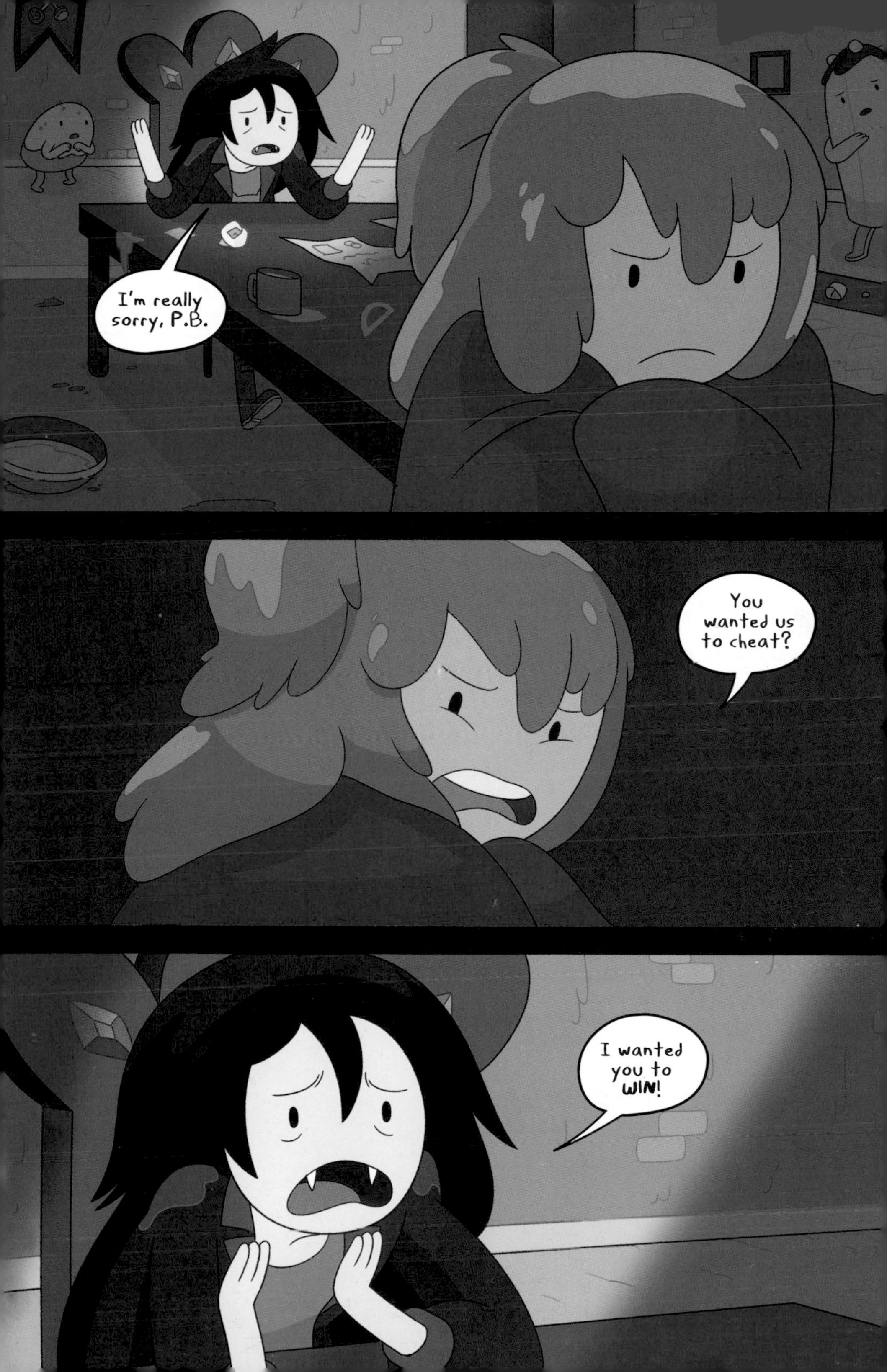
I'm really sorry, P.B.
You wanted us to cheat?
I wanted you to WIN!

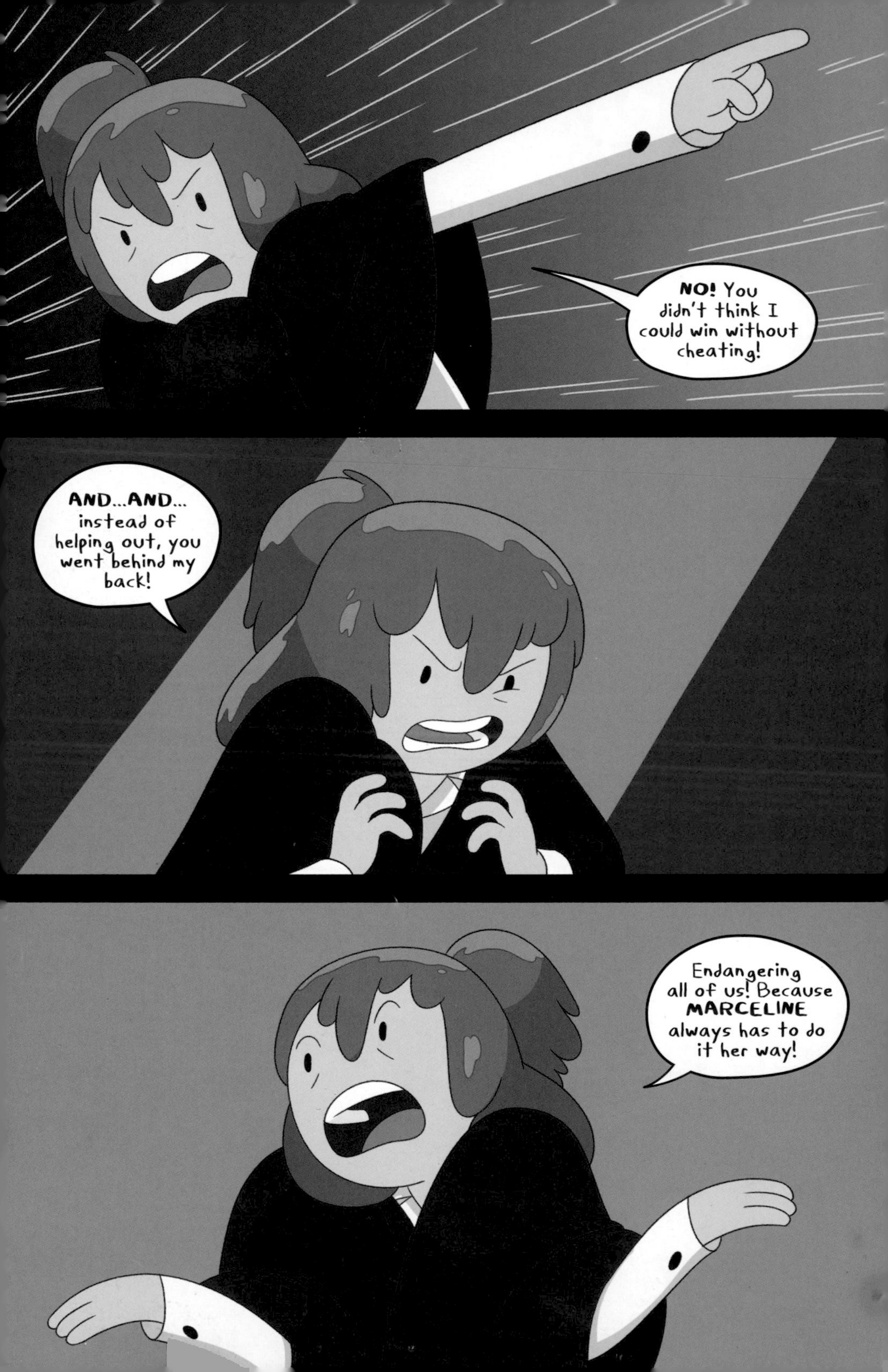
NO! You didn't think I could win without cheating!
AND...AND... instead of helping out, you went behind my back!
Endangering all of us! Because MARCELINE always has to do it her way!

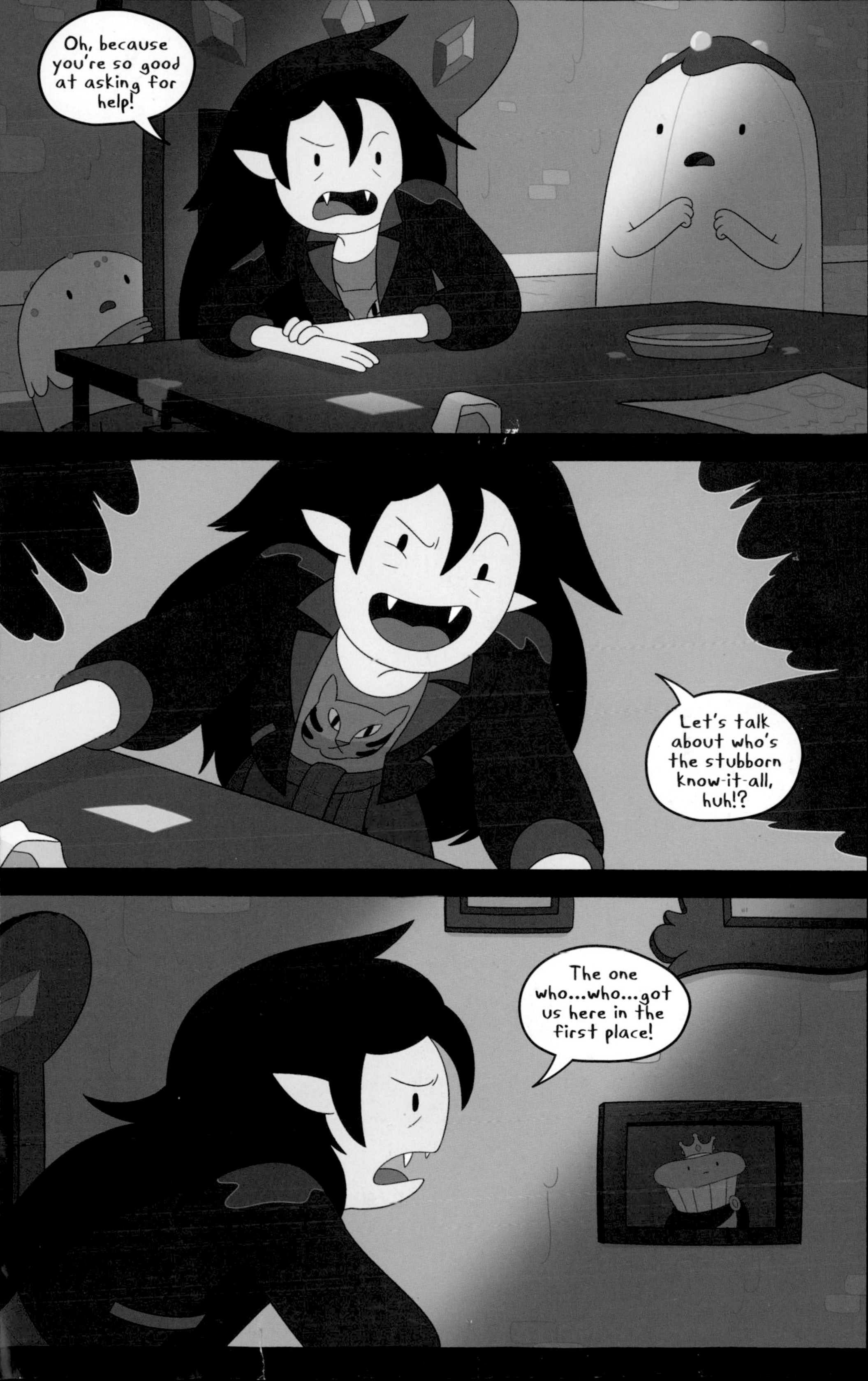
Oh, because you're so good at asking for help!
Let's talk about who's the stubborn know-it-all, huh!?
The one who...who...got us here in the first place!

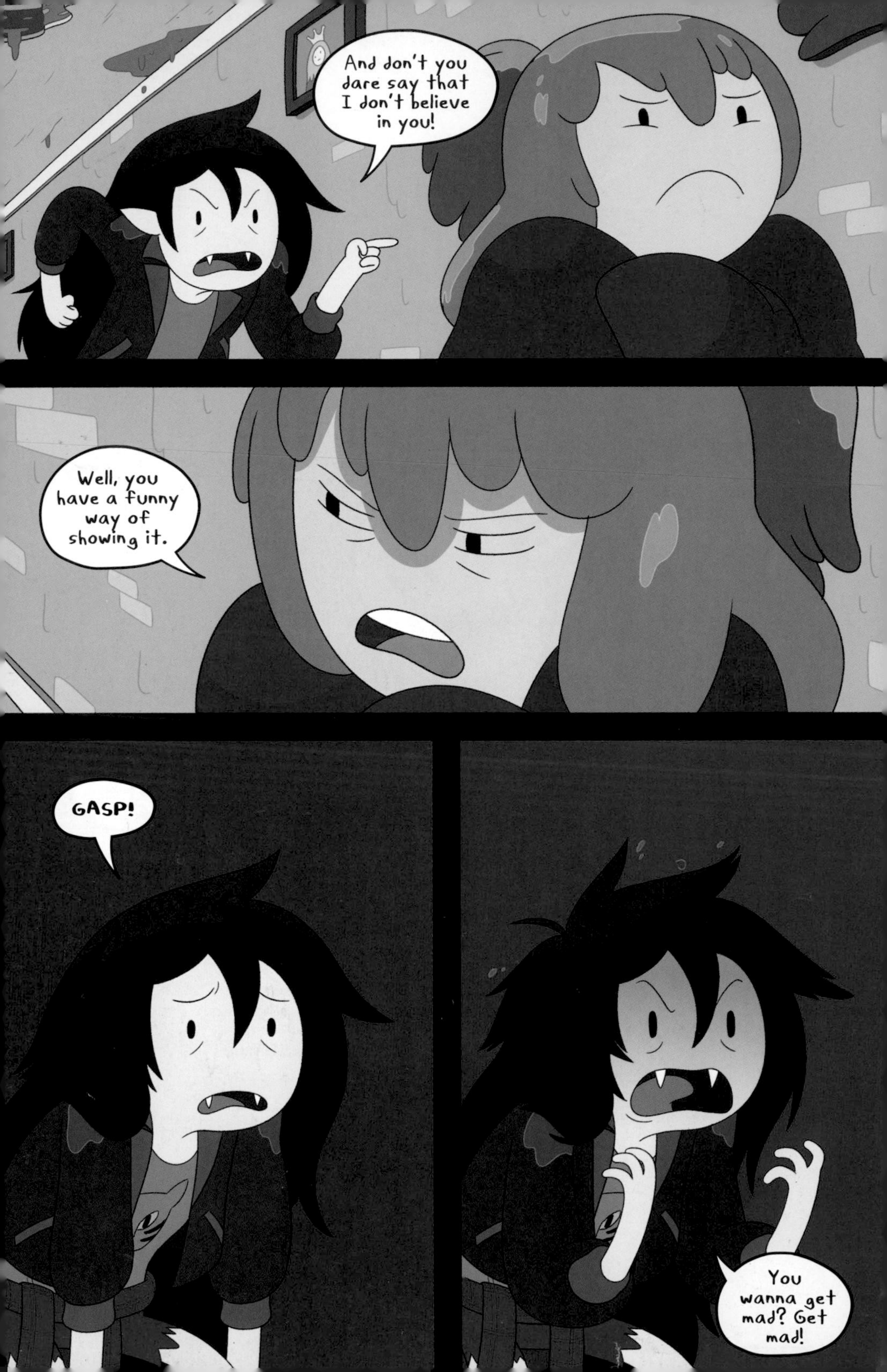
And don't you dare say that I don't believe in you!
Well, you have a funny way of showing it.
GASP!
You wanna get mad? Get mad!

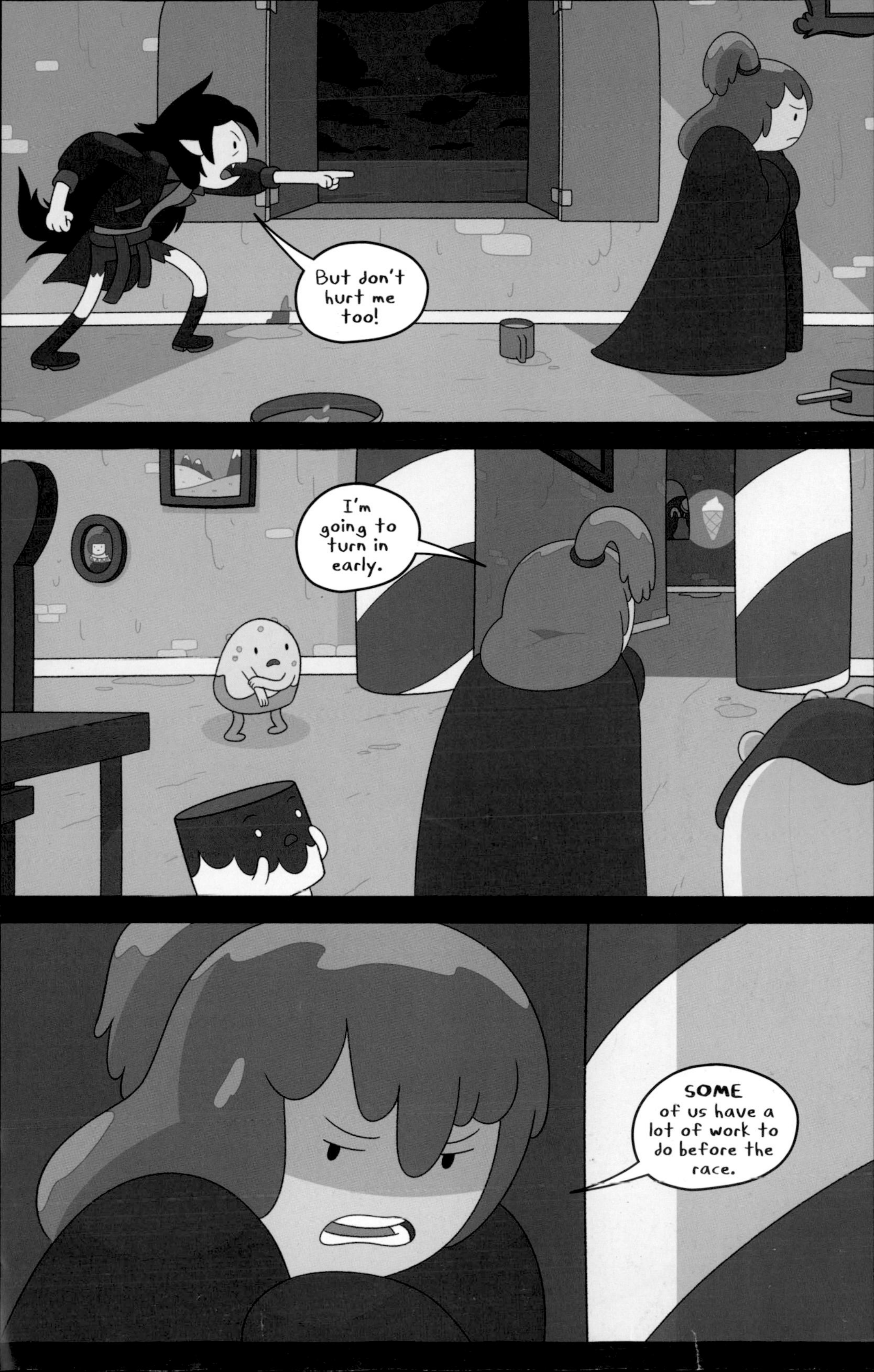
But don't hurt me too!
I'm going to turn in early.
SOME of us have a lot of work to do before the race.

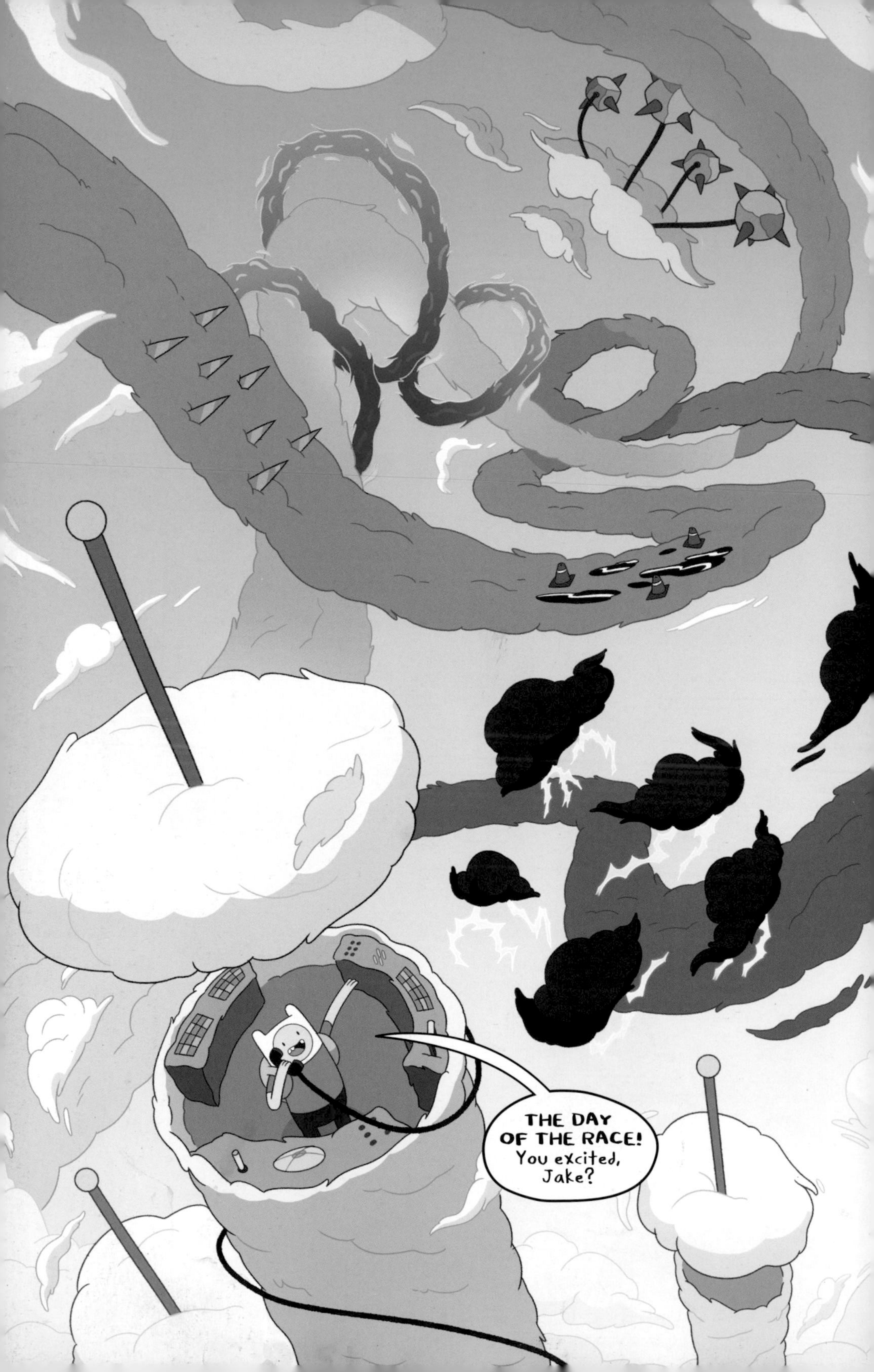
THE DAY OF THE RACE! You excited, Jake?

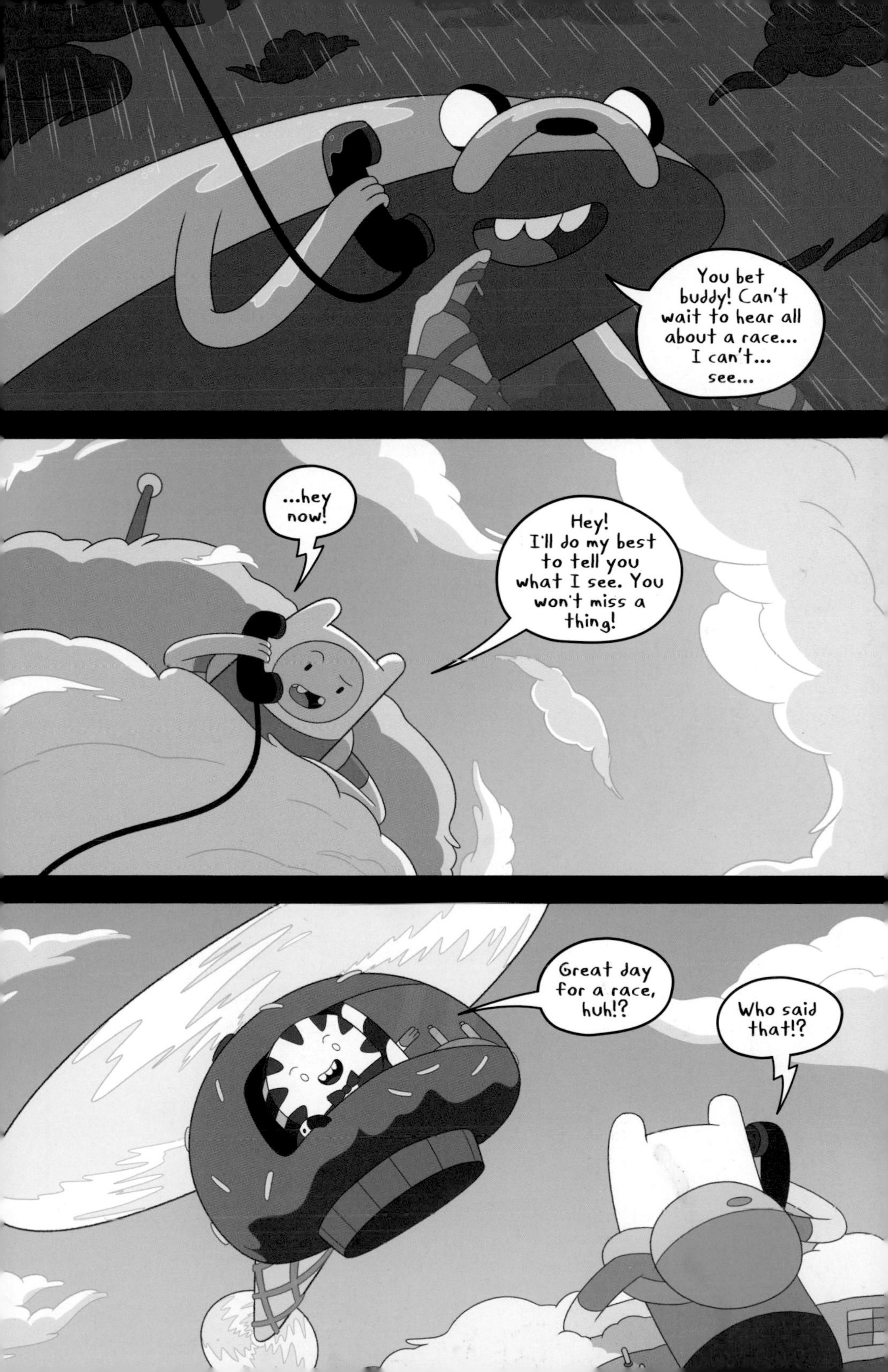

You bet buddy! Can't wait to hear all about a race... I can't... see...
...hey now!
Hey! I'll do my best to tell you what I see. You won't miss a thing!
Great day for a race, huh!?
Who said that!?

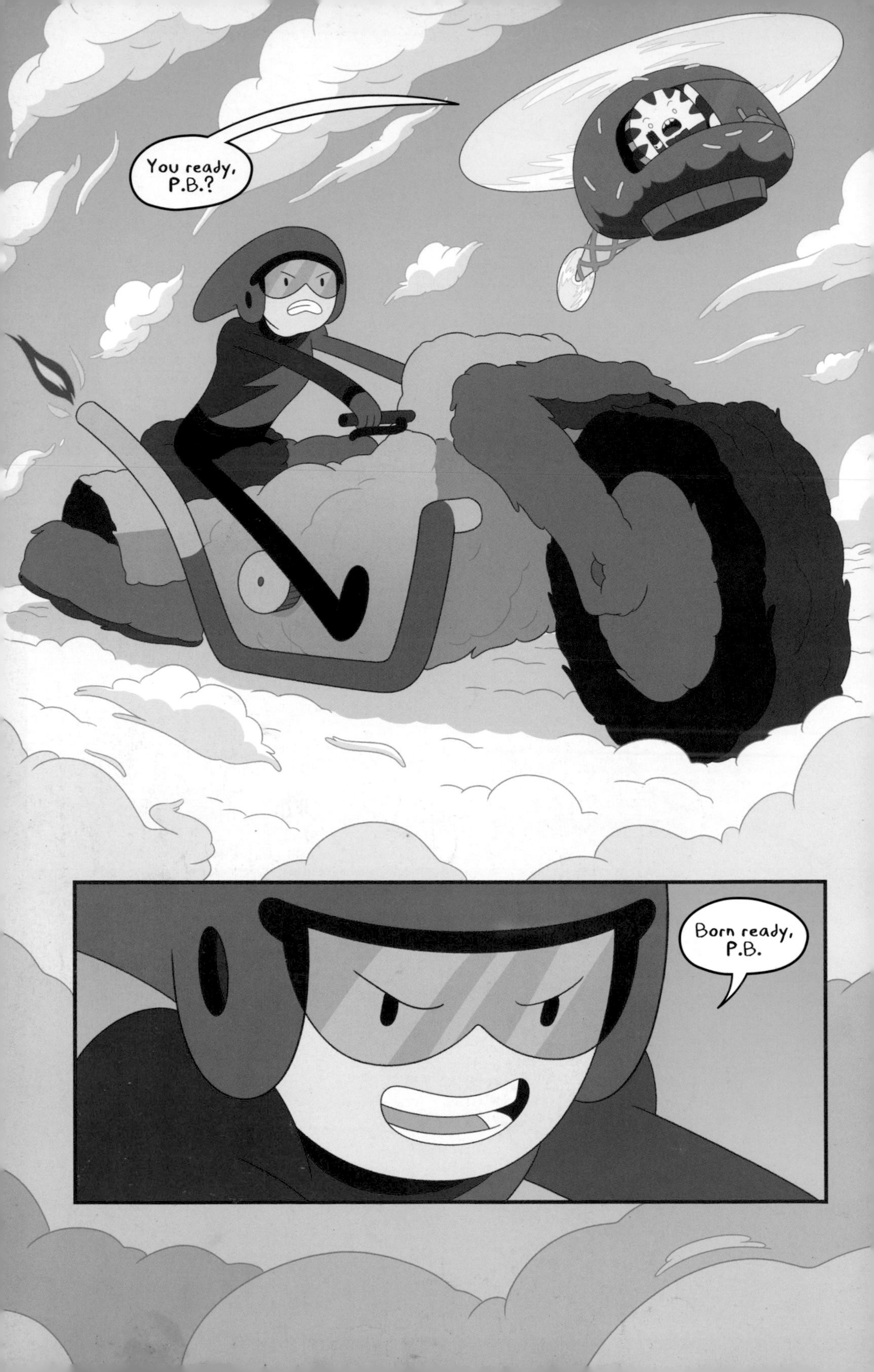
You ready, P.B.?
Born ready, P.B.

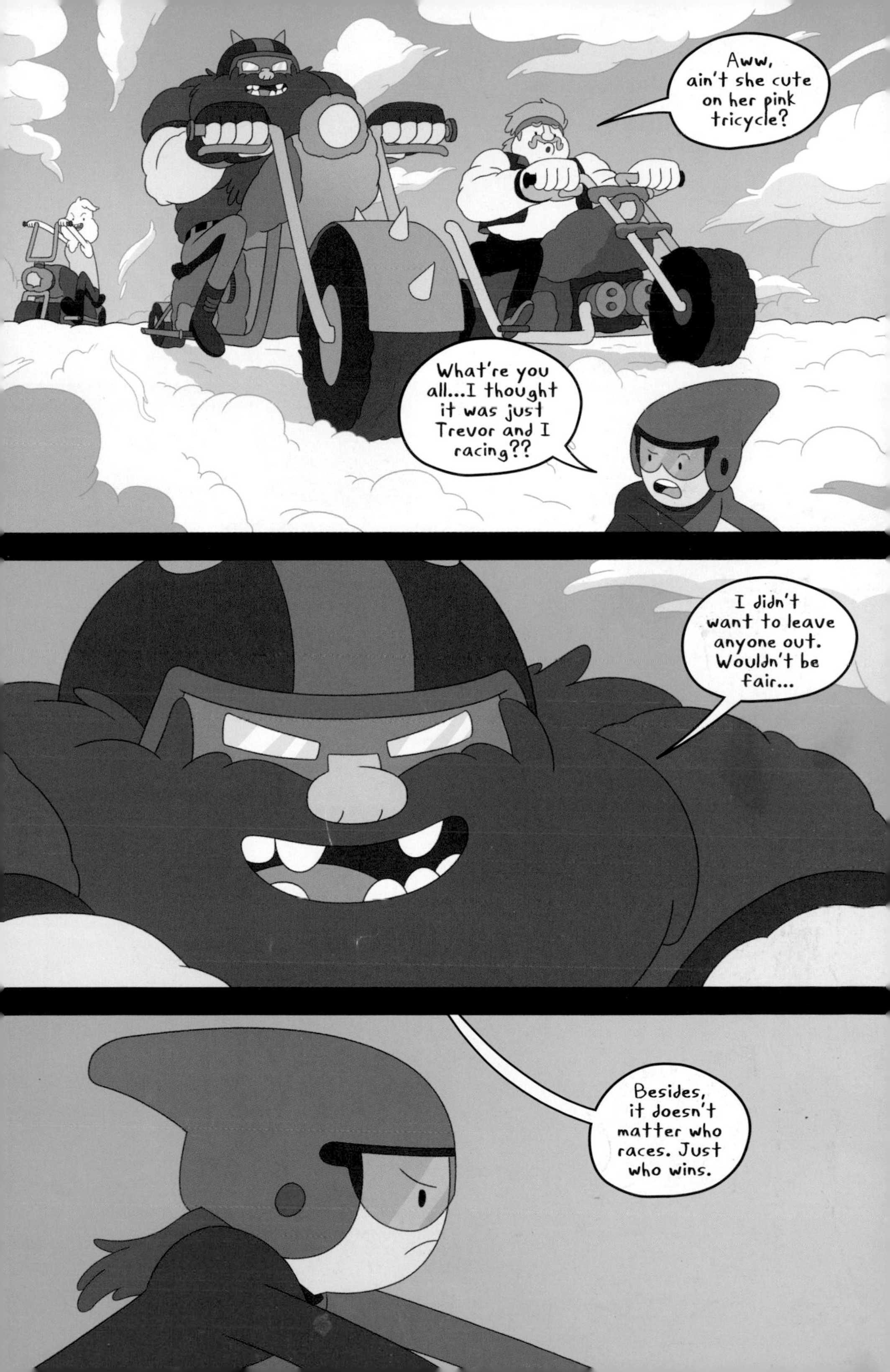
Aww, ain't she cute on her pink tricycle?
What're you all...I thought it was just Trevor and I racing??
I didn't want to leave anyone out. Wouldn't be fair...
Besides, it doesn't matter who races. Just who wins.

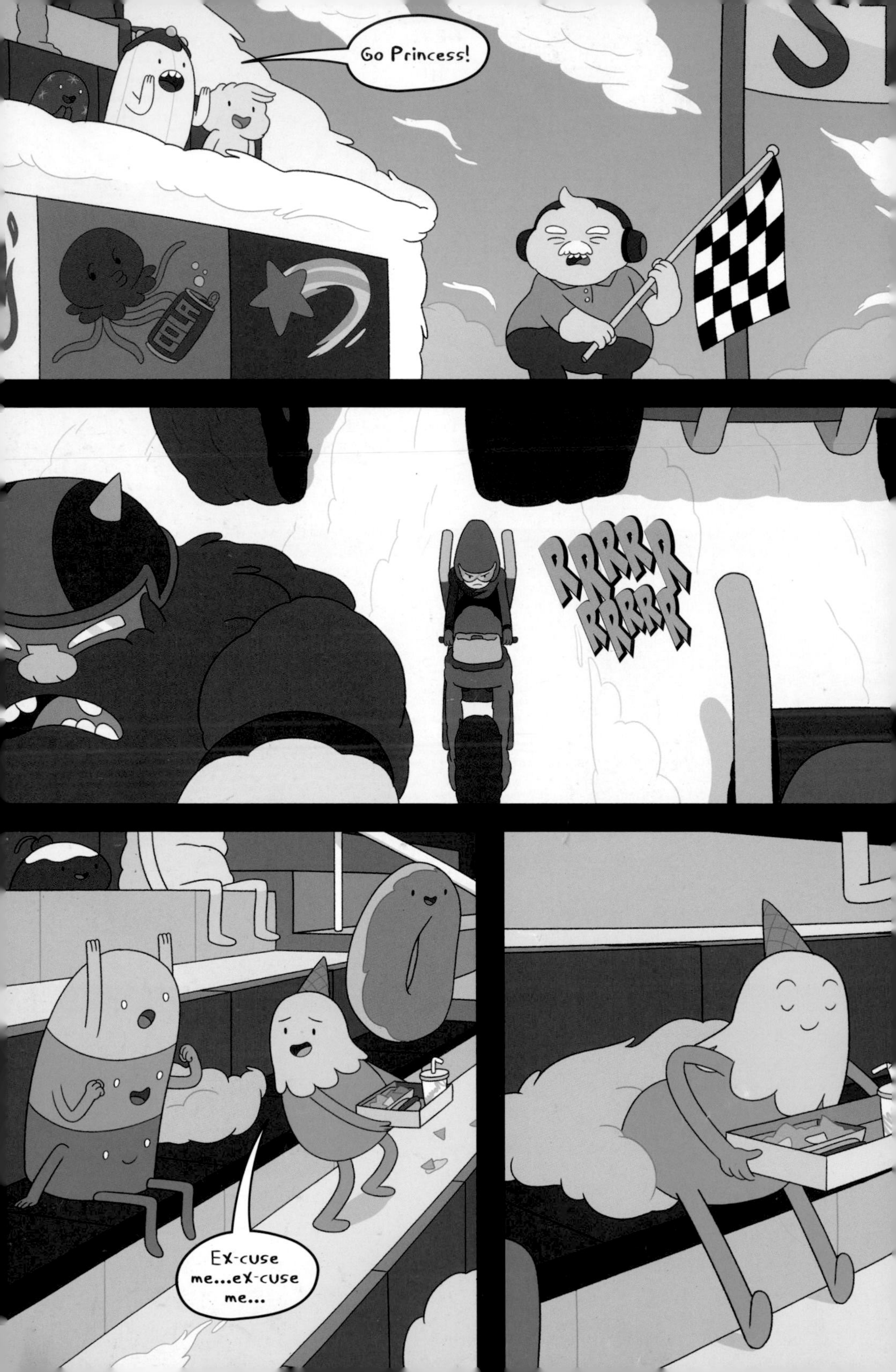
Go Princess!
COLA
RRRRR RRRRR
EX-cuse me...eX-cuse me...

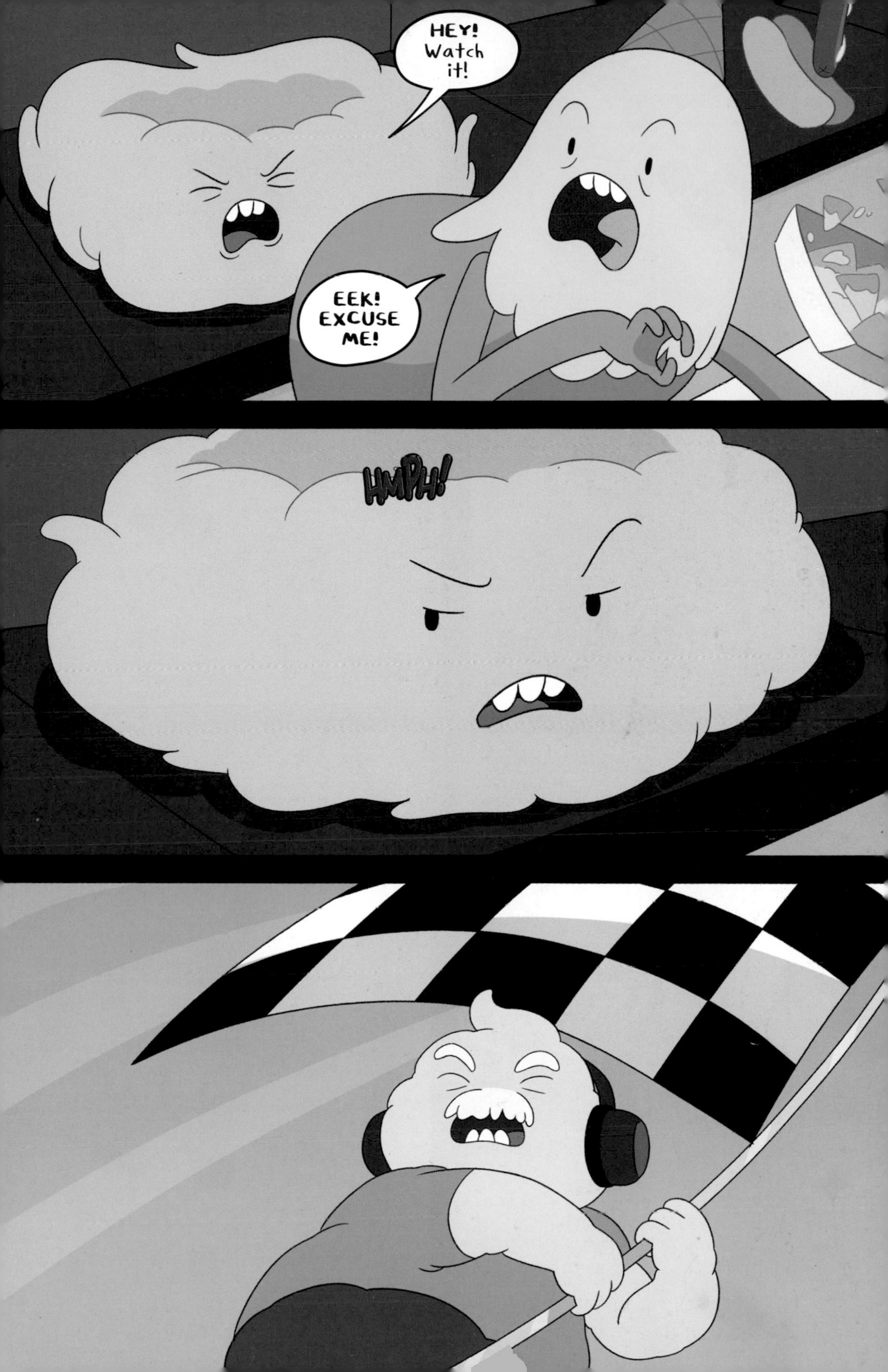
HEY! Watch it!
EEK! EXCUSE ME!
HMPH!

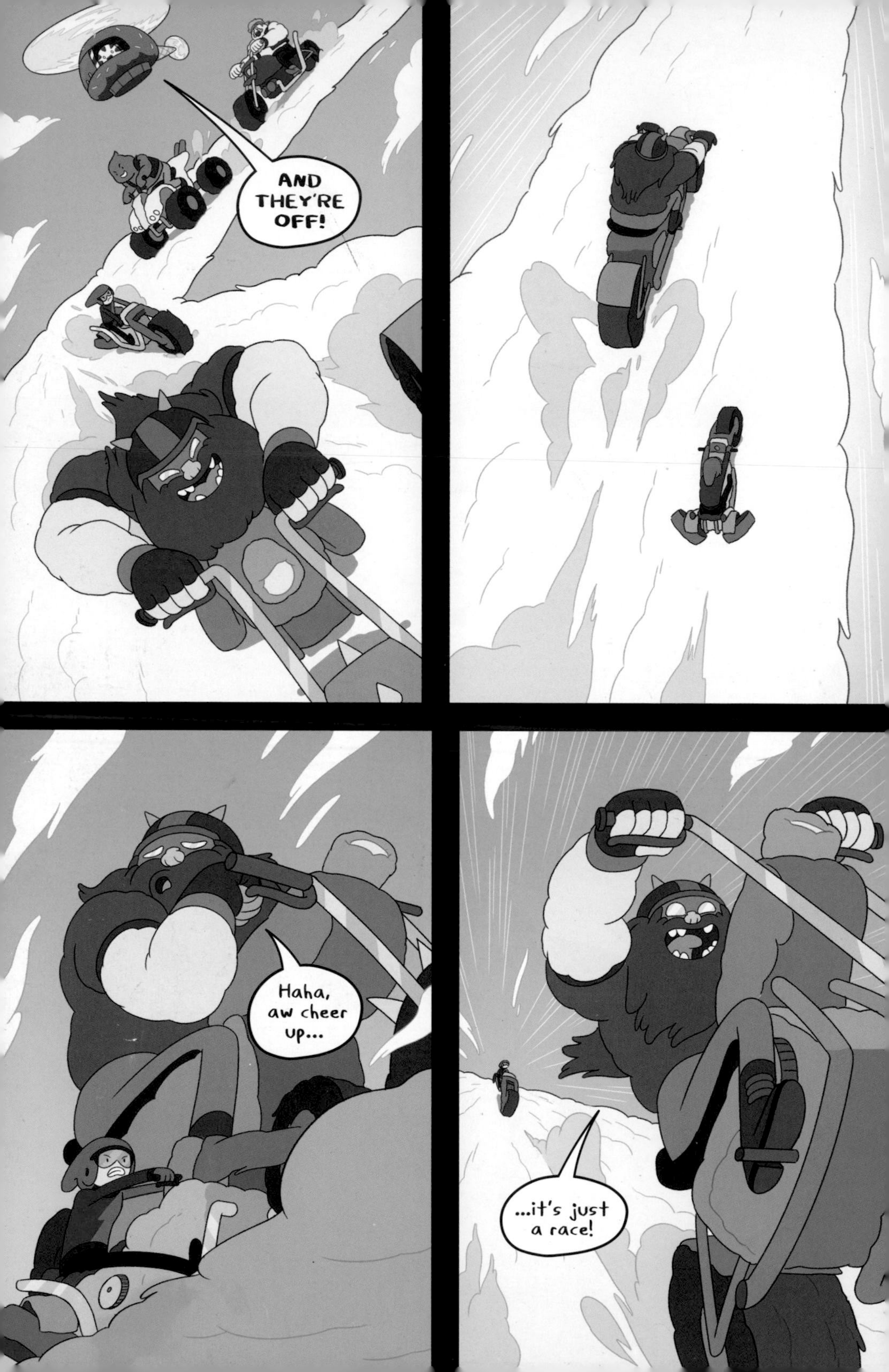
AND THEY'RE OFF!
Haha, aw cheer up...
...it's just a race!

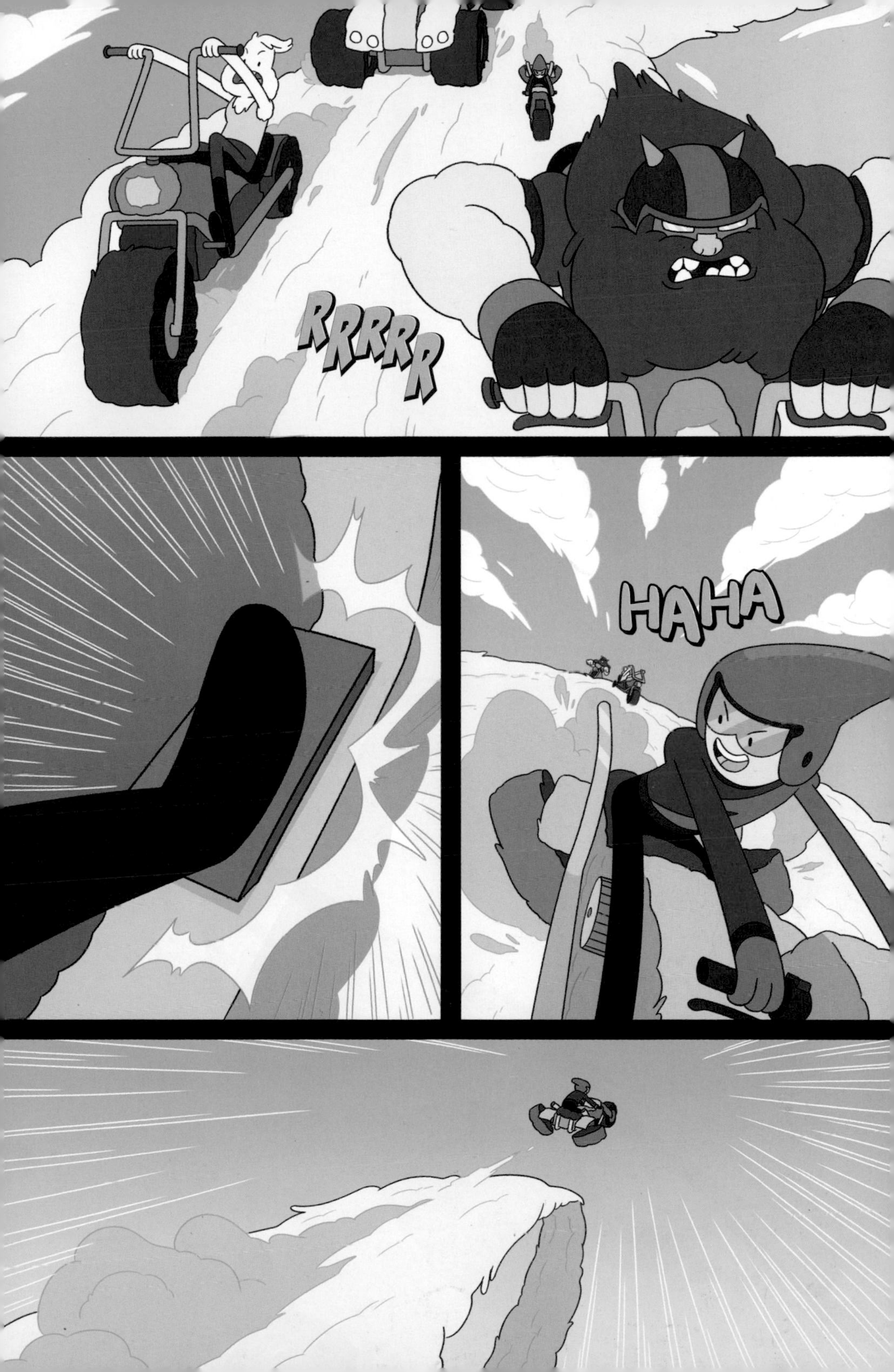
RRRRRR
HAHA

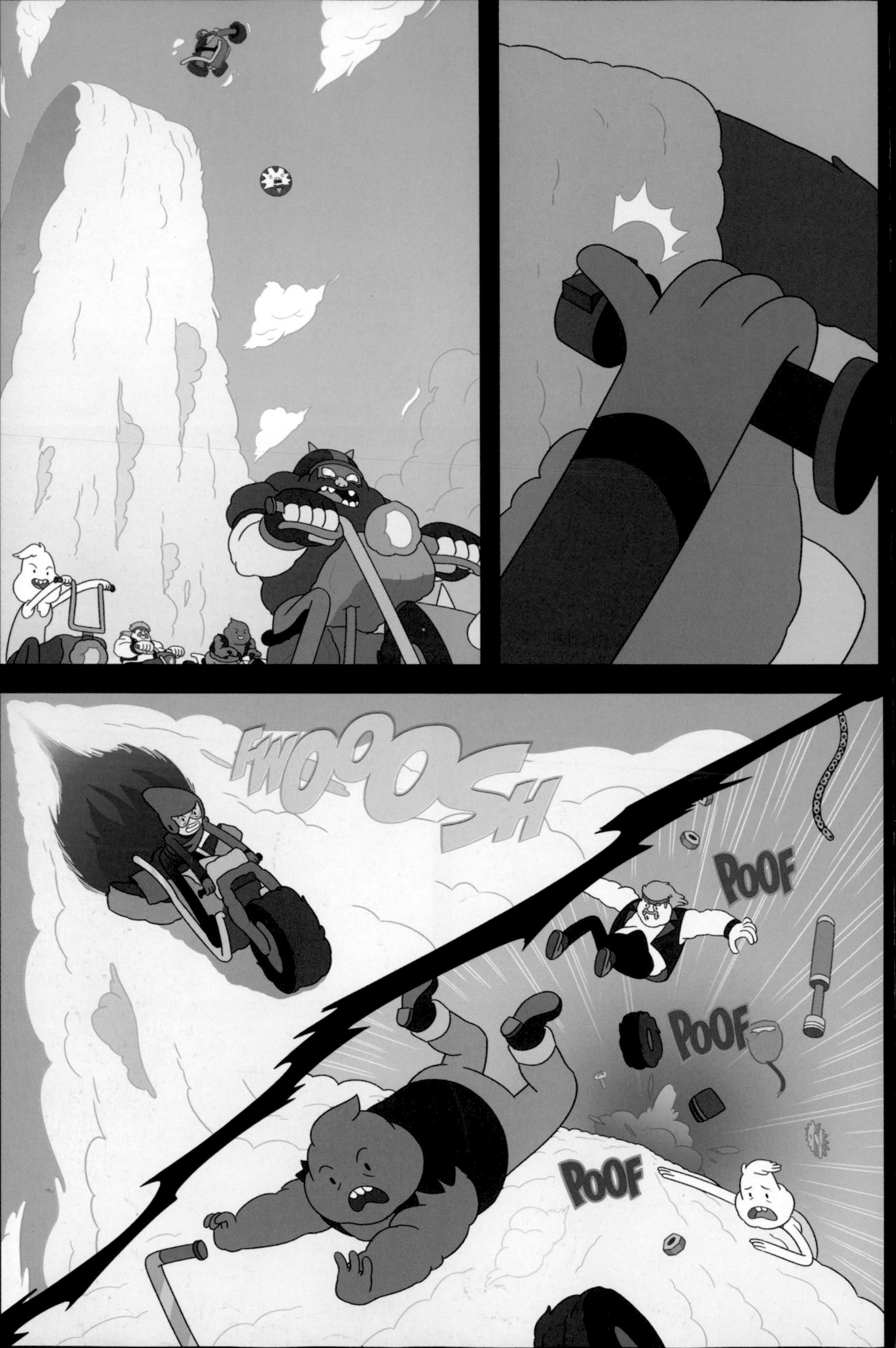
FWOOOSH
POOF
POOF
POOF

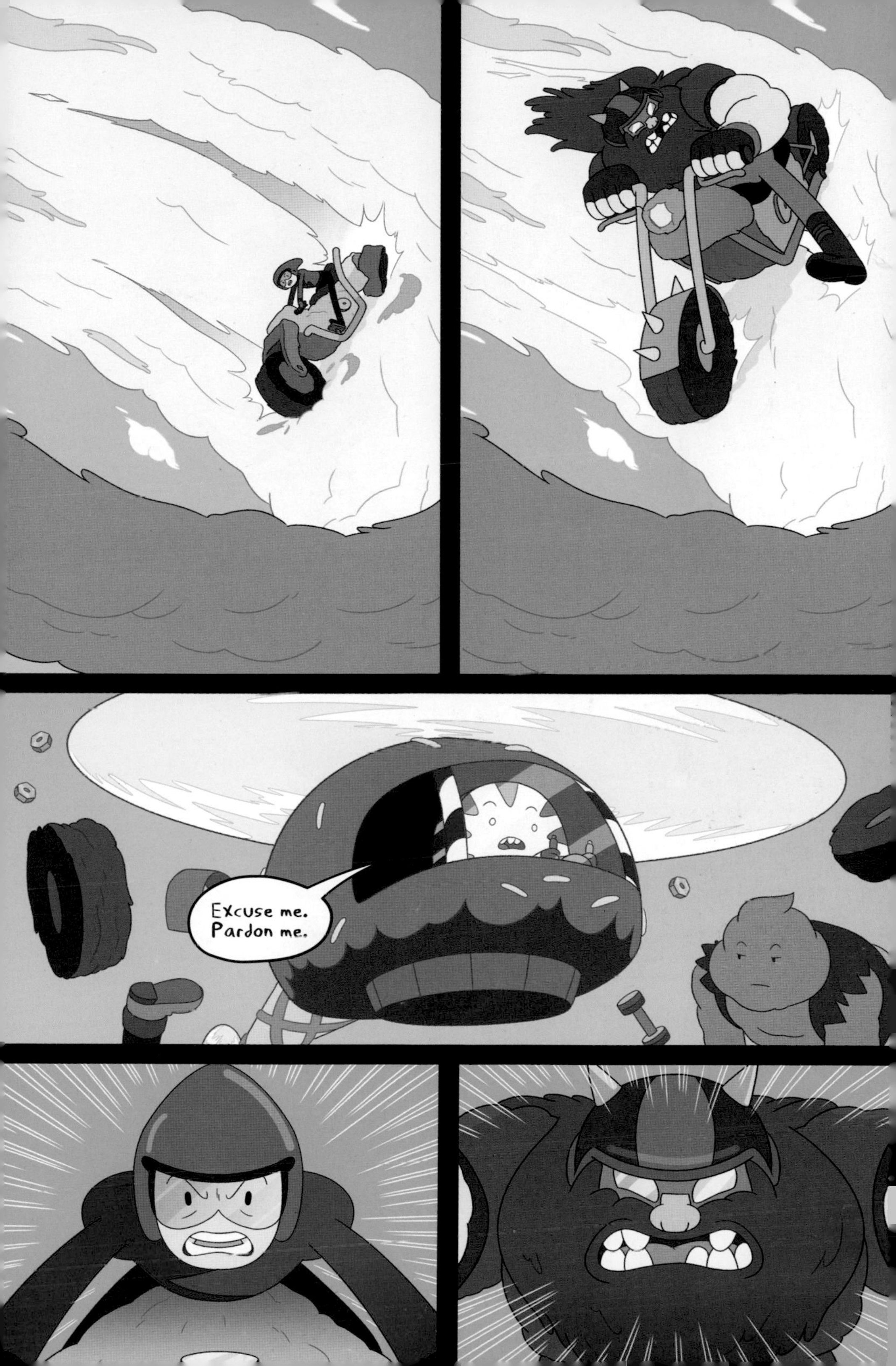
Excuse me.
Pardon me.

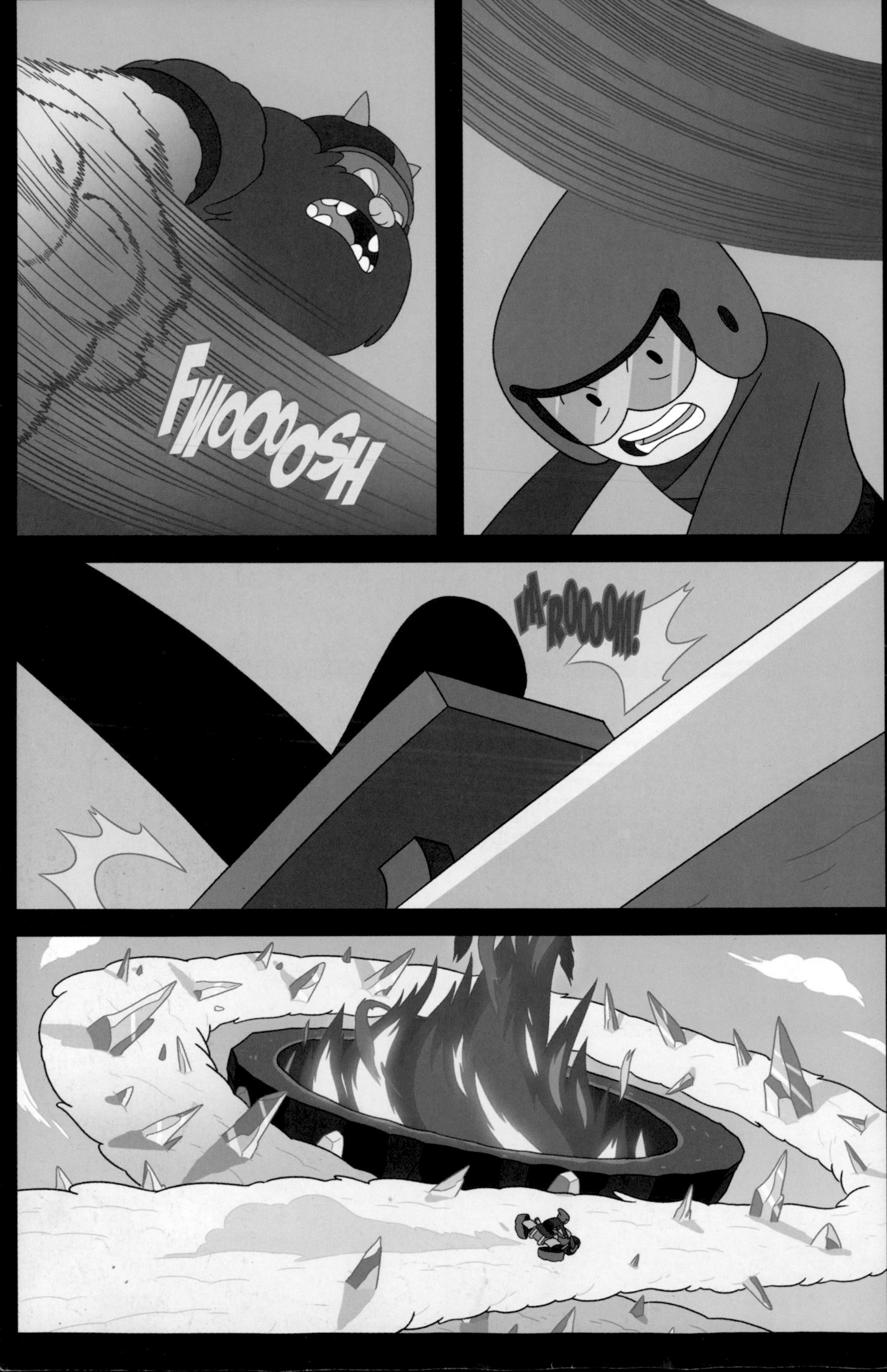
FWOOOOSH
VA-ROOOOM!

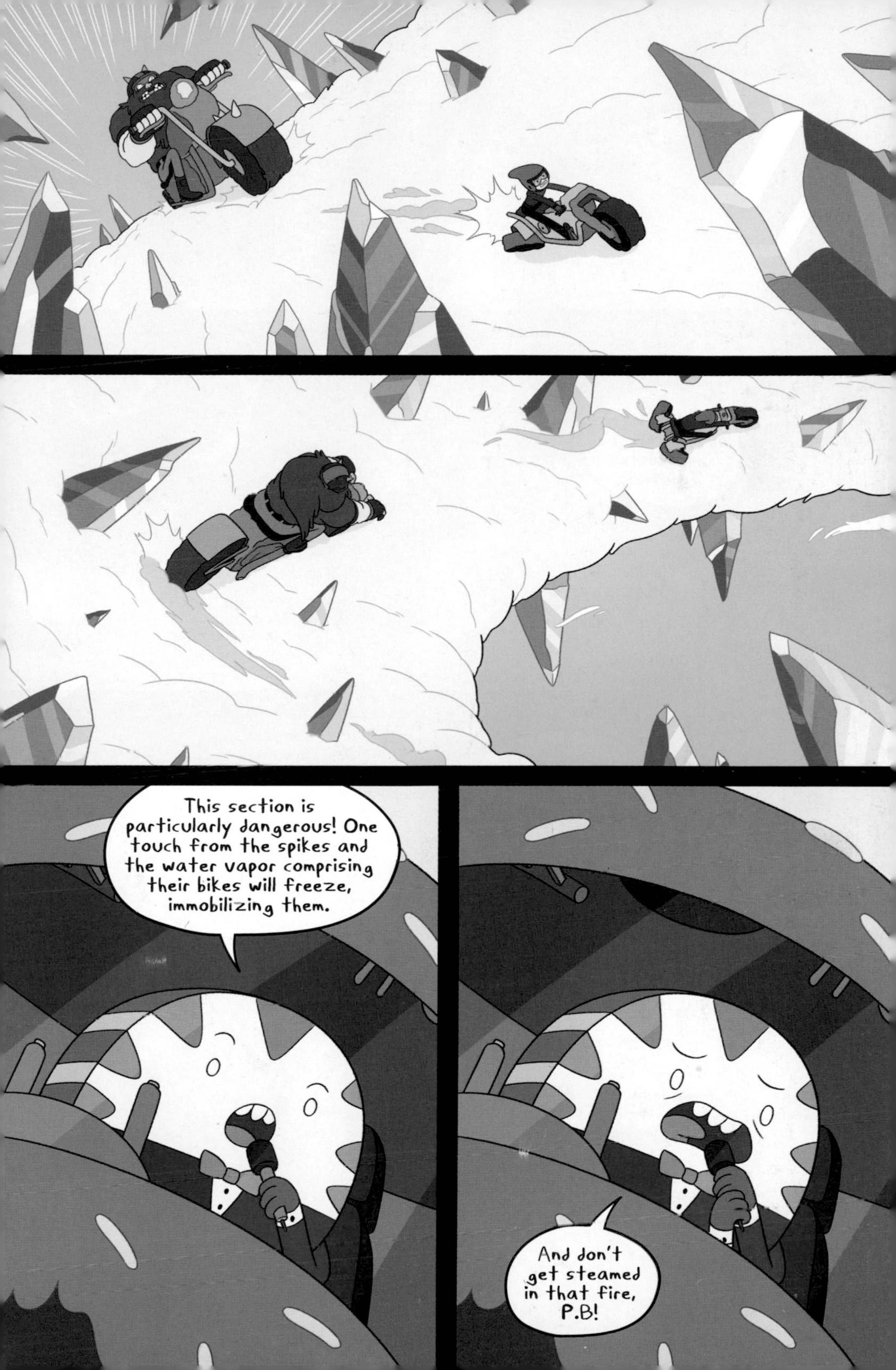
This section is particularly dangerous! One touch from the spikes and the water vapor comprising their bikes will freeze, immobilizing them.
And don't get steamed in that fire, P.B!

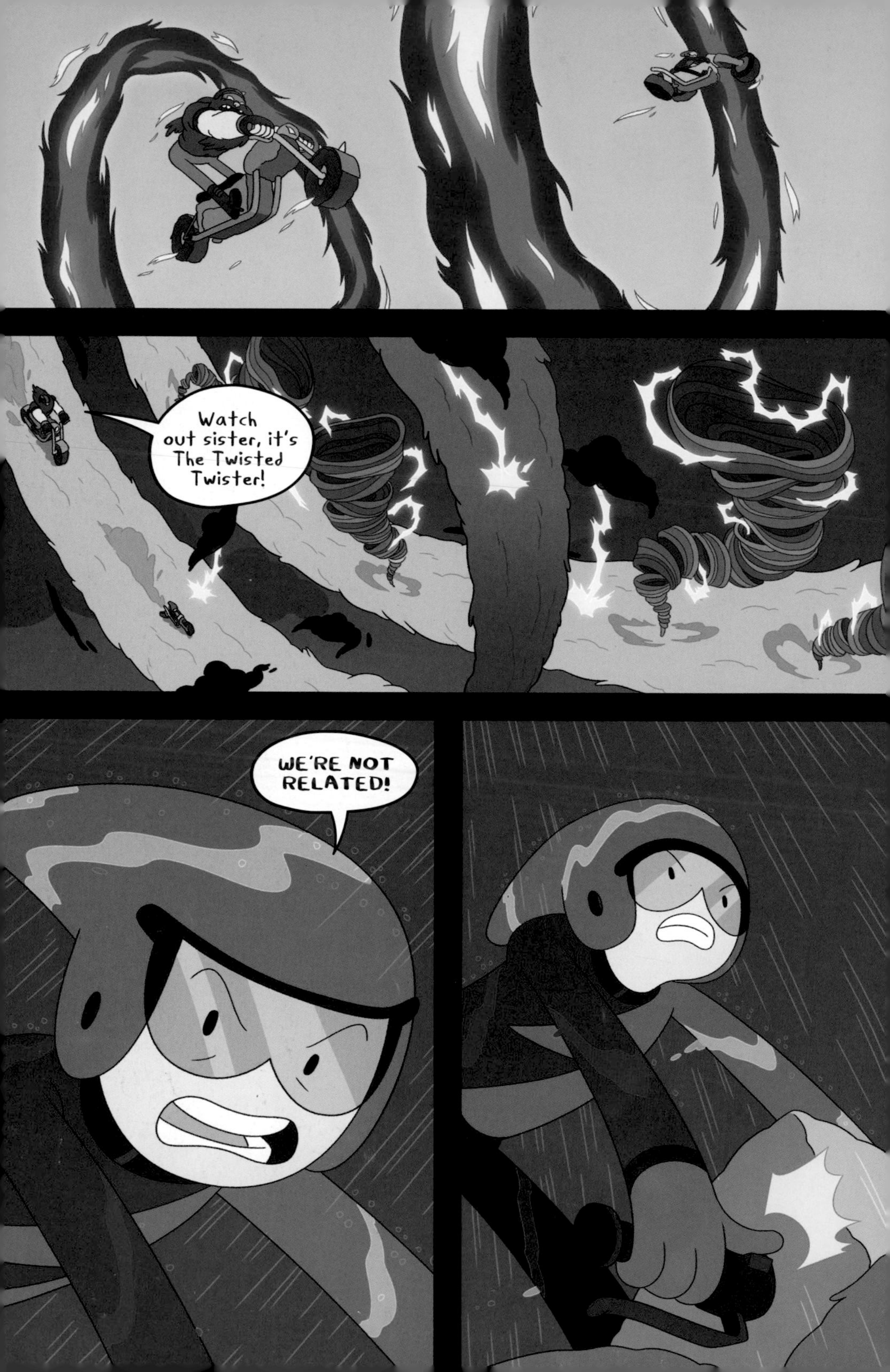
Watch out sister, it's The Twisted Twister!
WE'RE NOT RELATED!

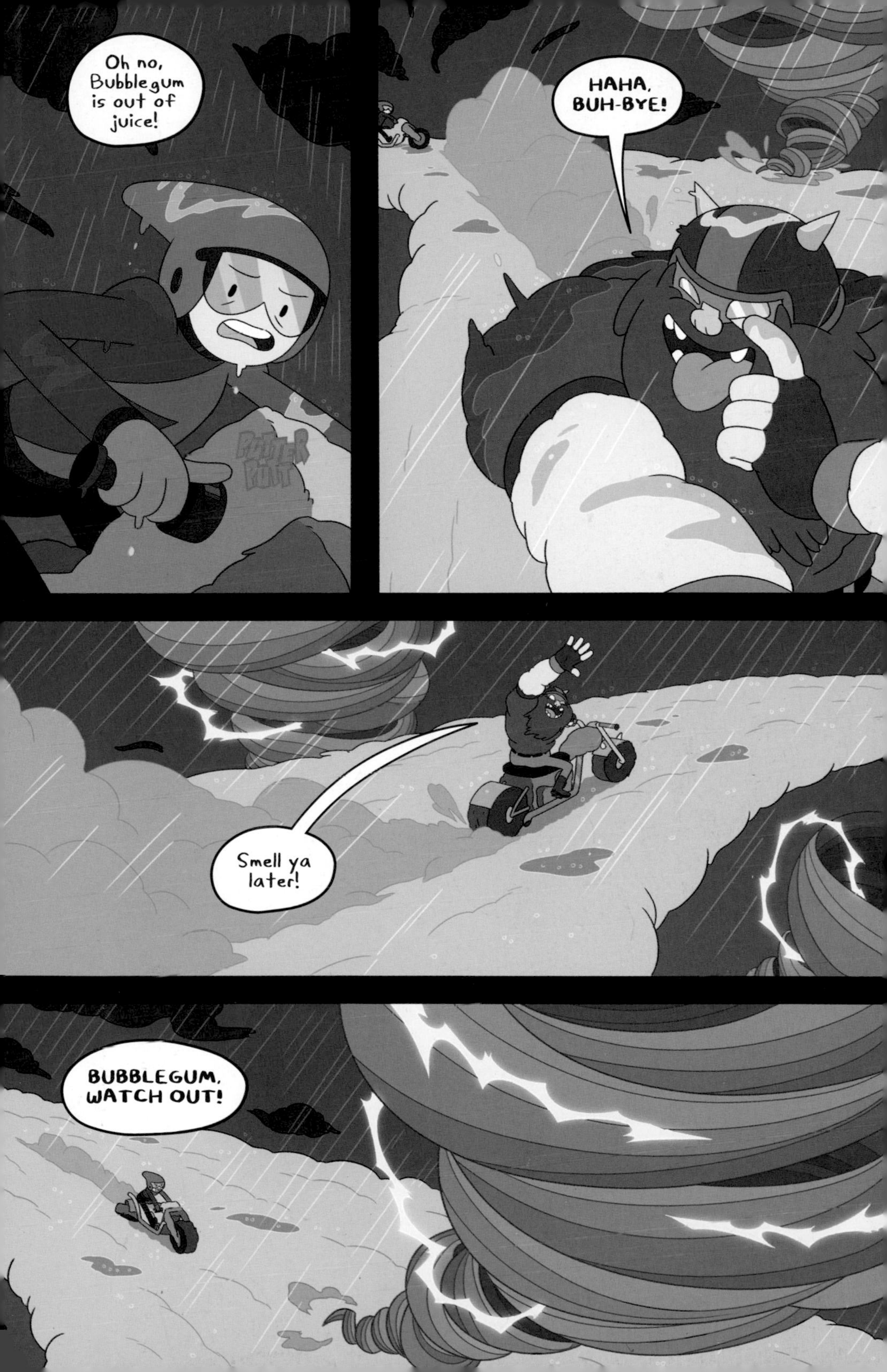
Oh no, Bubblegum is out of juice!
HAHA, BUH-BYE!
Smell ya later!
BUBBLEGUM, WATCH OUT!

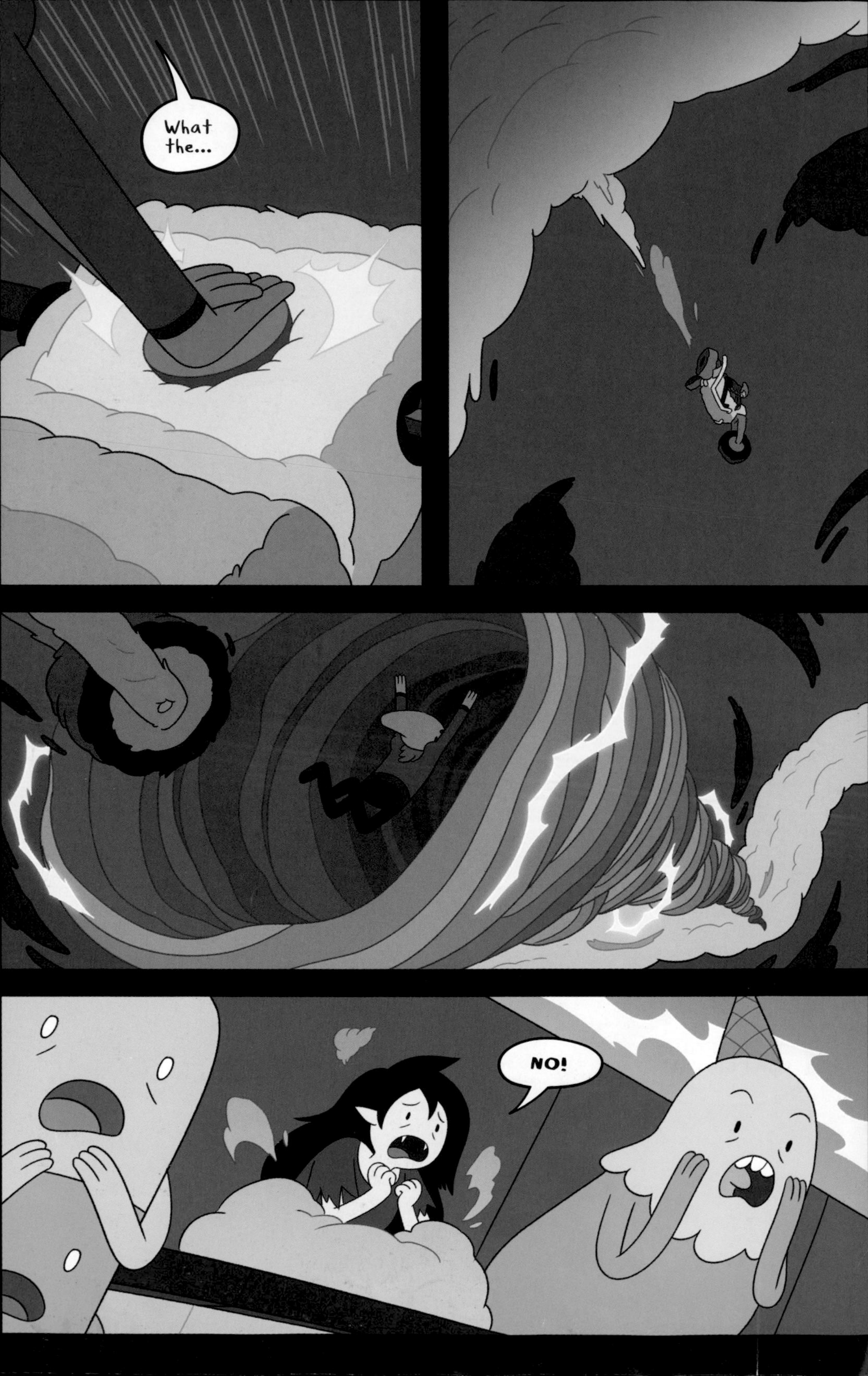
What the...
NO!

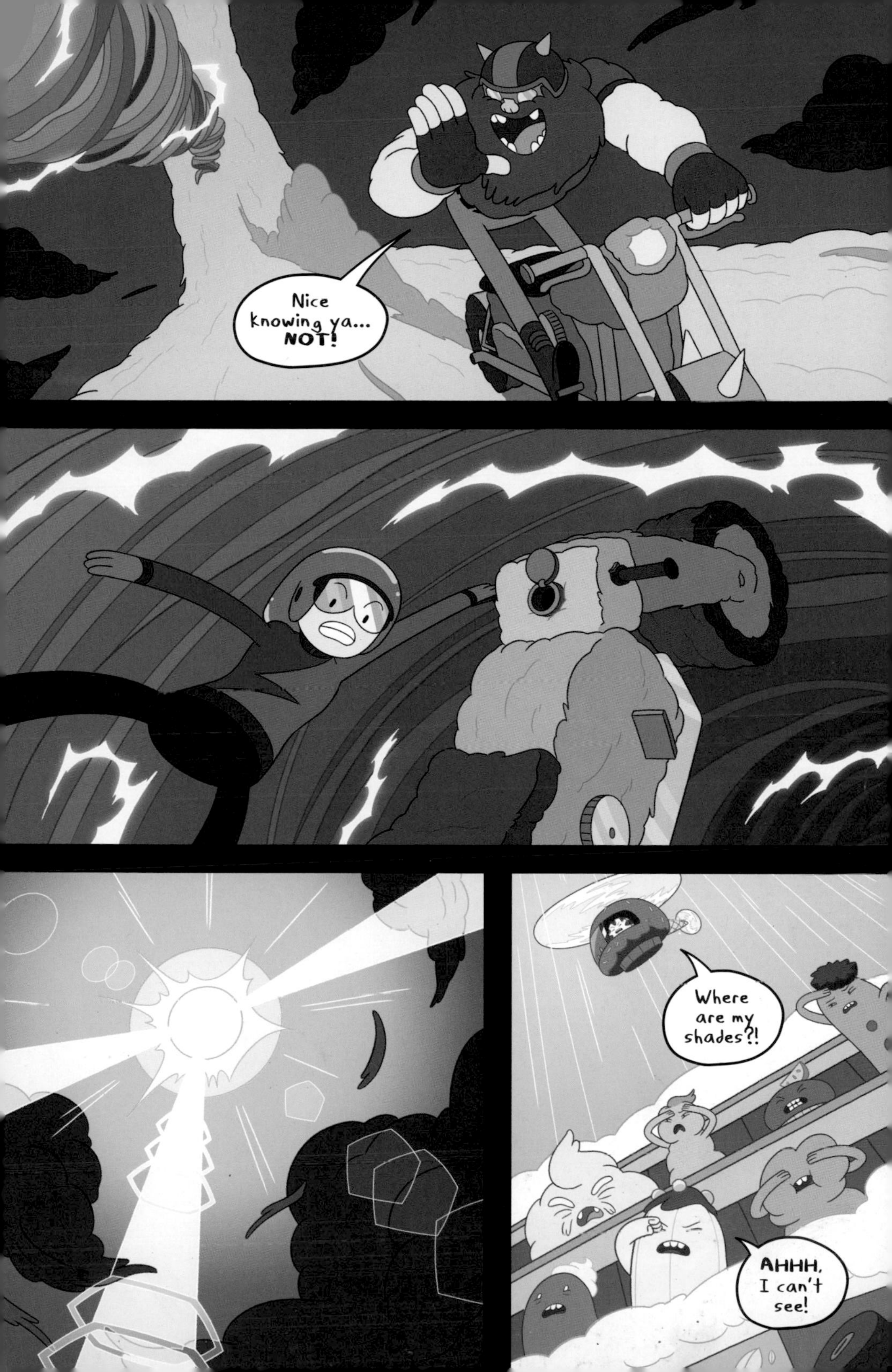
Nice knowing ya... **NOT!**
Where are my shades?!
AHHH, I can't see!

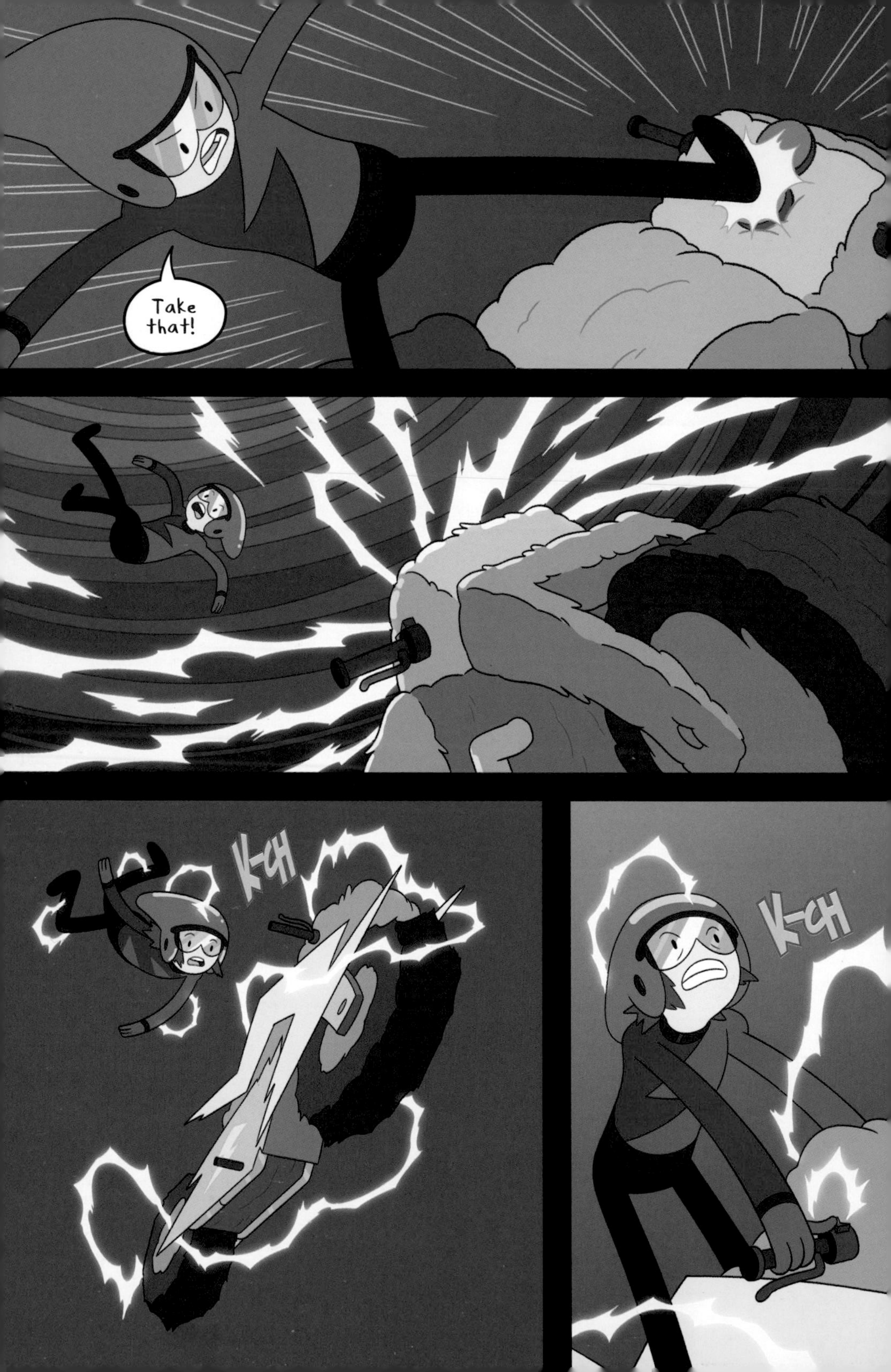
Take that!
K-CH
K-CH

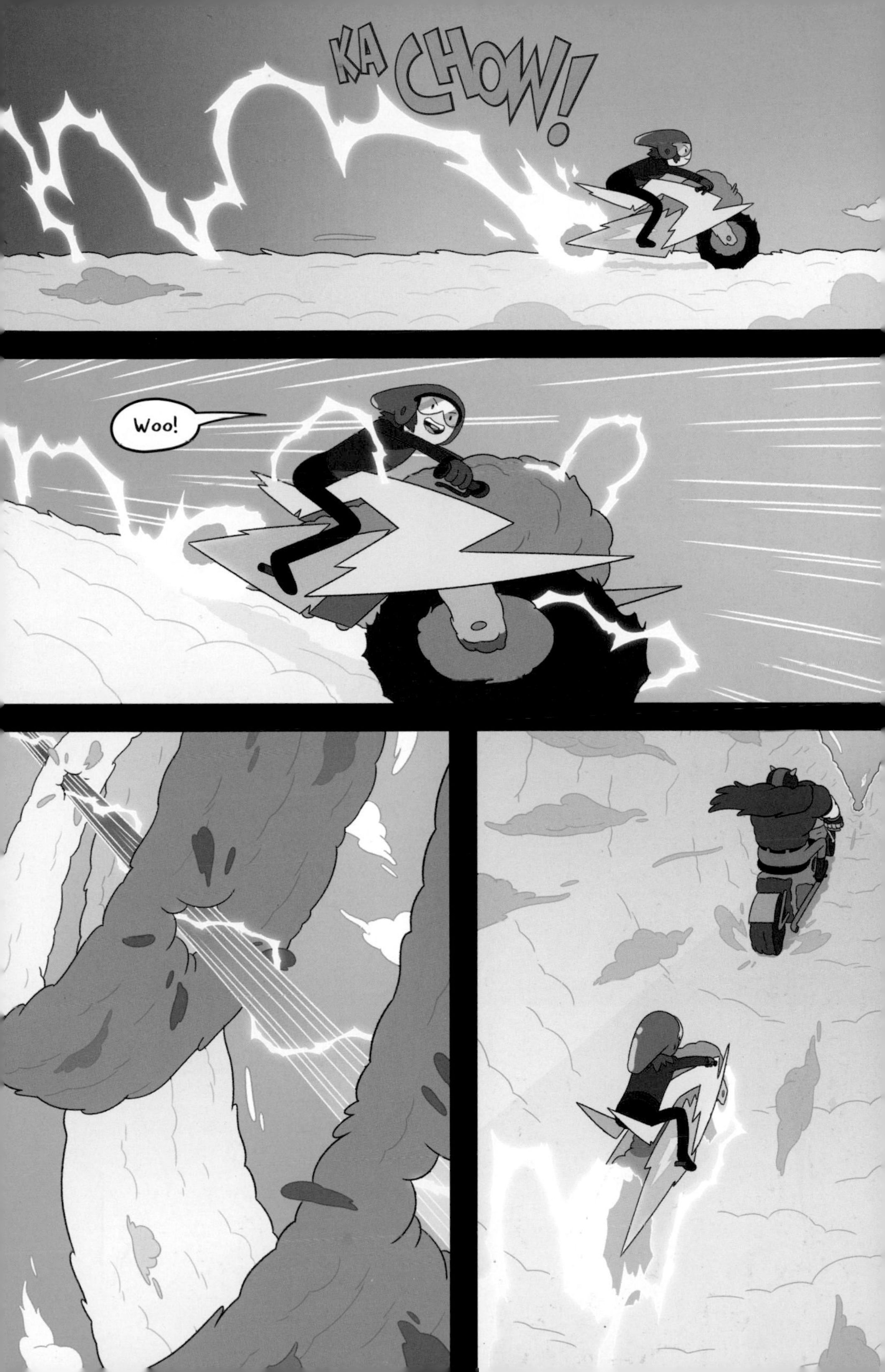
KA CHOW!
Woo!

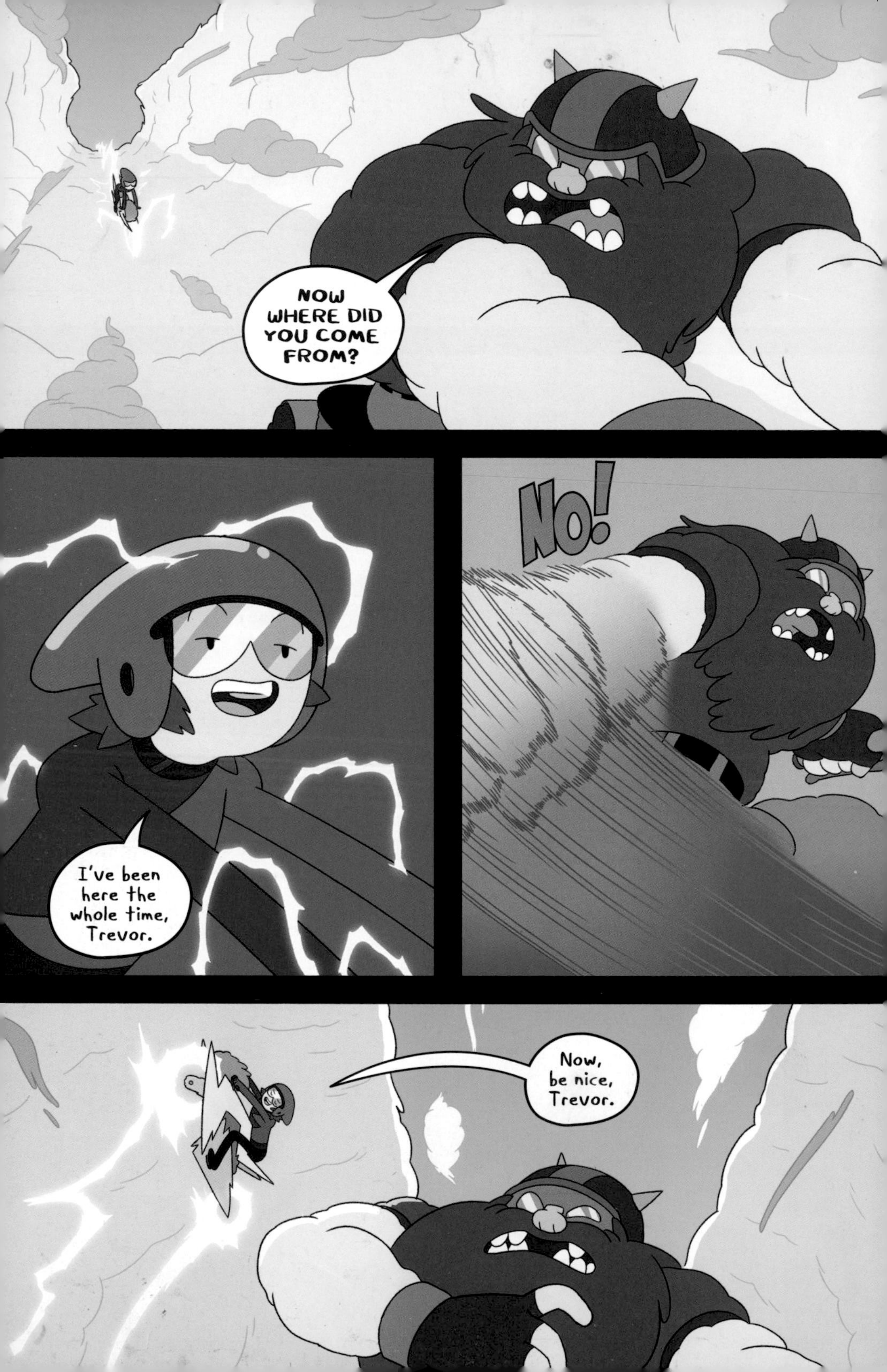
NOW WHERE DID YOU COME FROM?
I've been here the whole time, Trevor.
NO!
Now, be nice, Trevor.

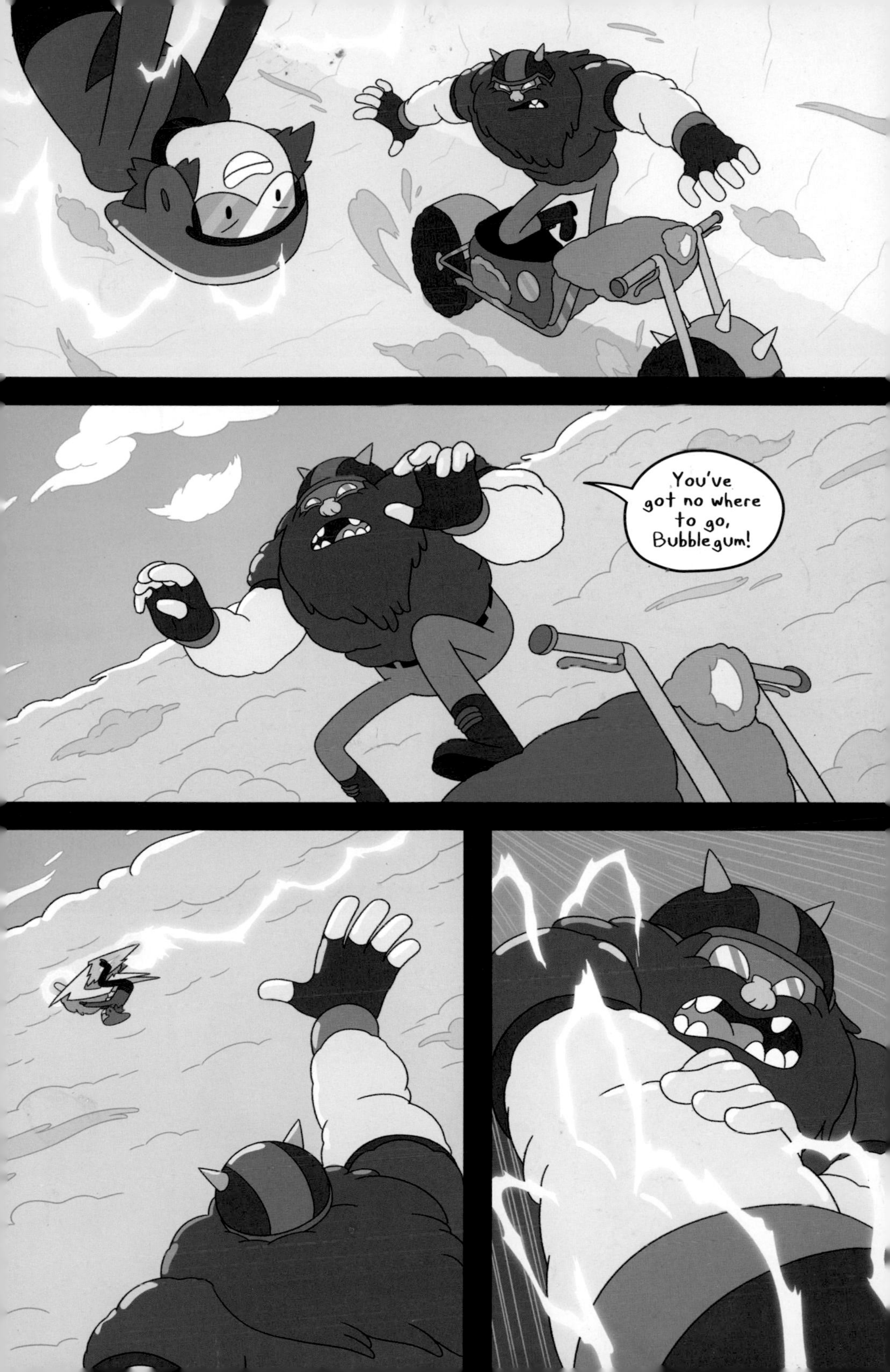
You've got no where to go, Bubblegum!

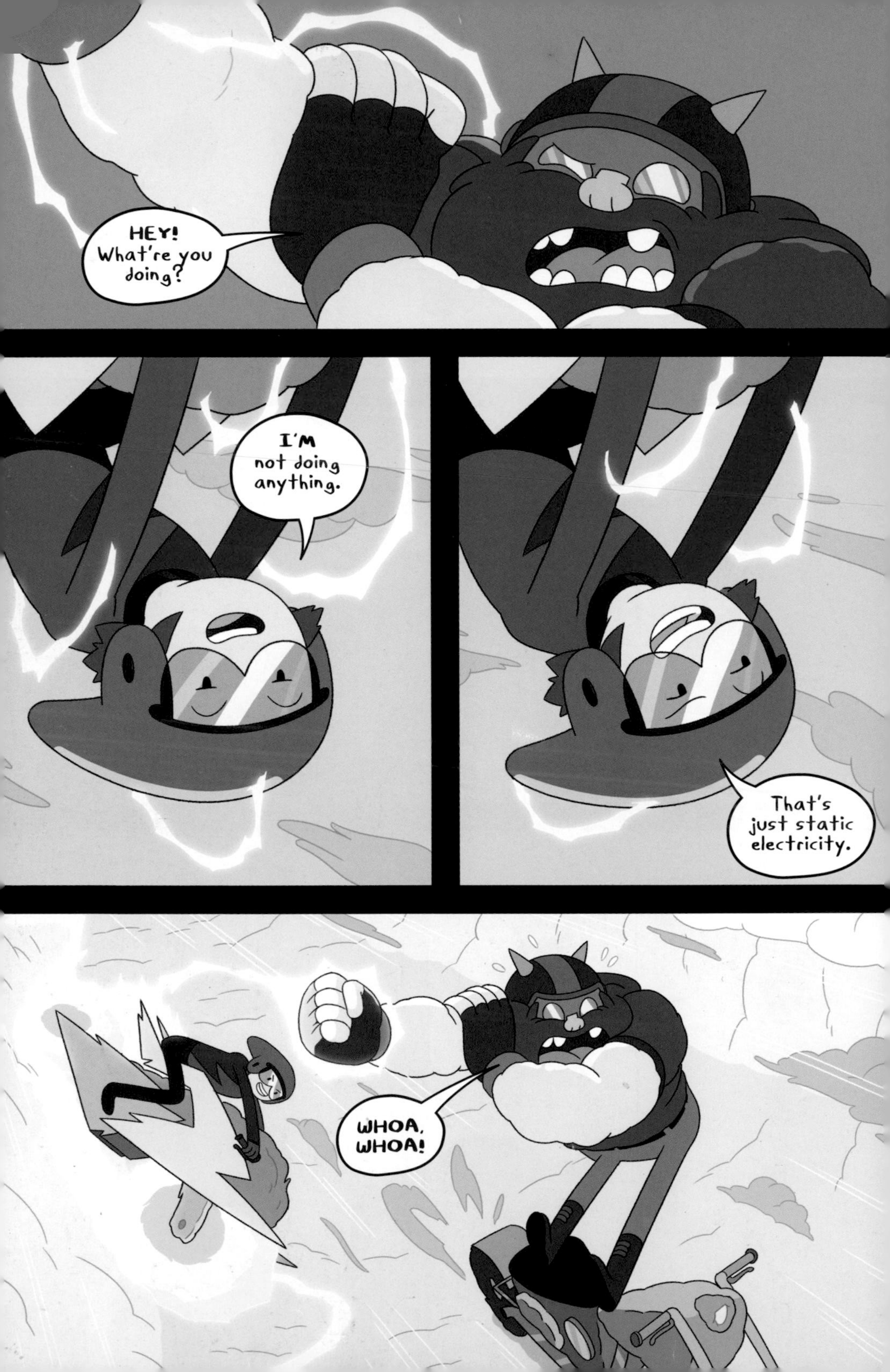
HEY! What're you doing?
I'M not doing anything.
That's just static electricity.
WHOA, WHOA!

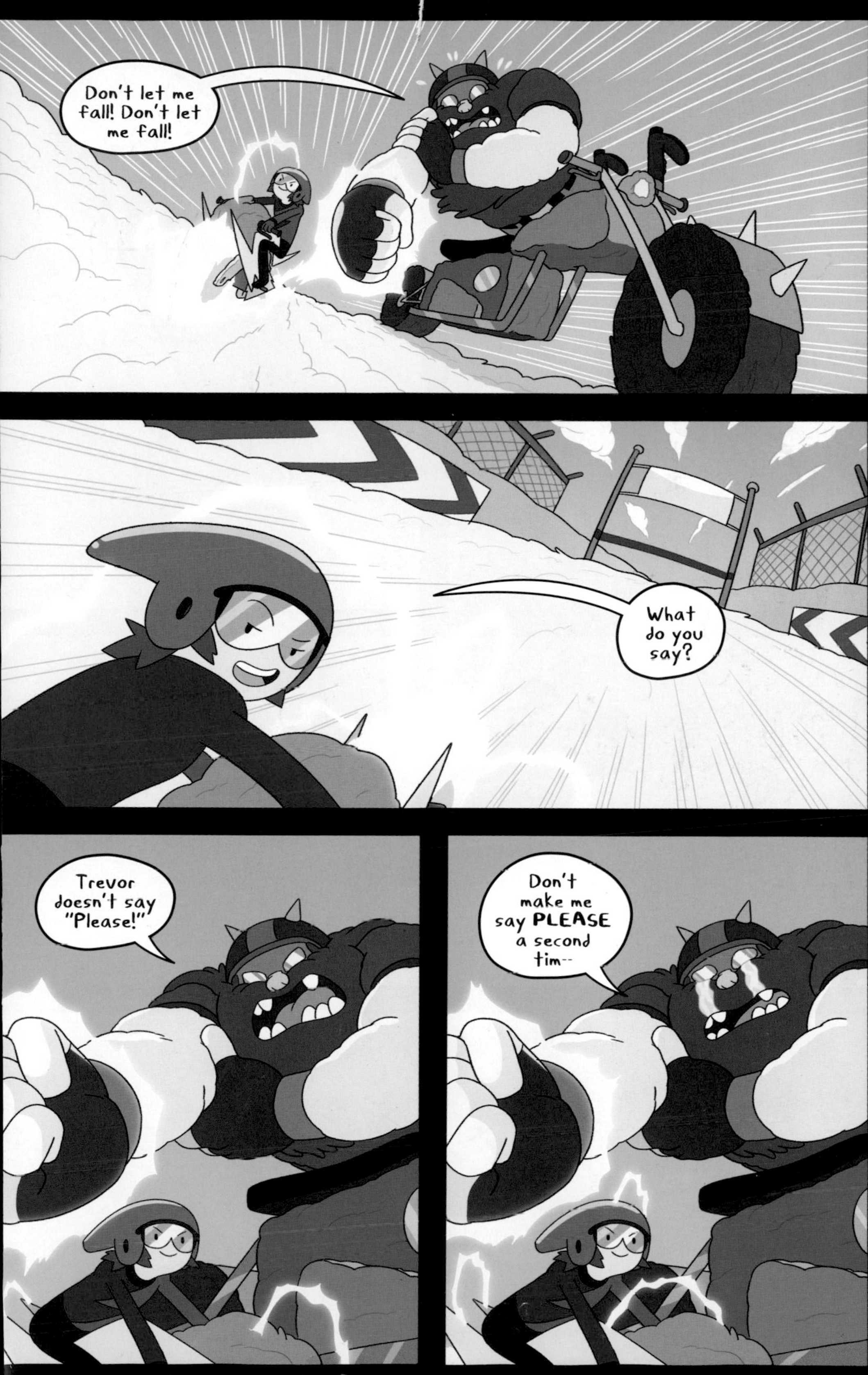
Don't let me fall! Don't let me fall!
What do you say?
Trevor doesn't say "Please!"
Don't make me say **PLEASE** a second tim--

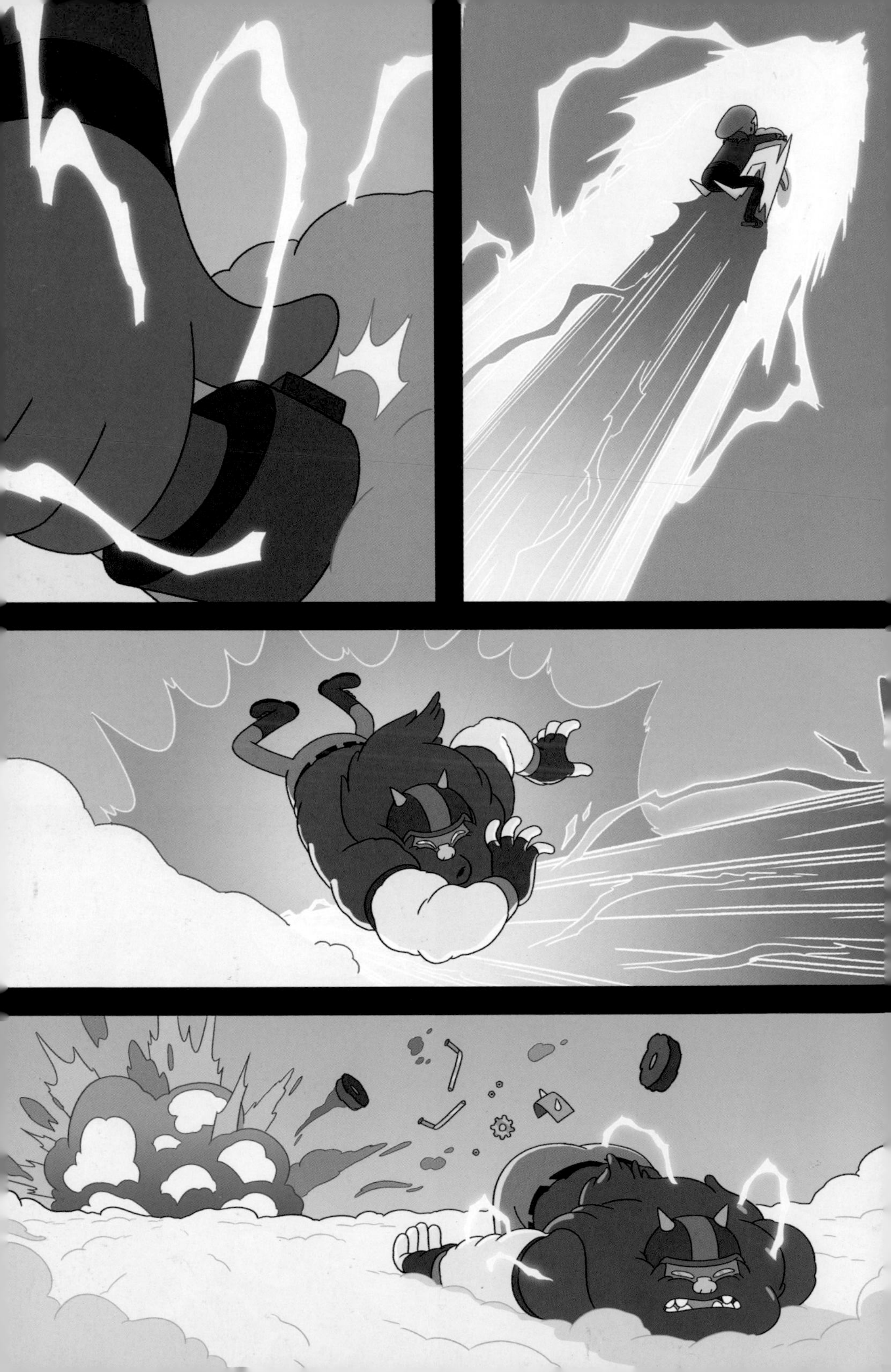

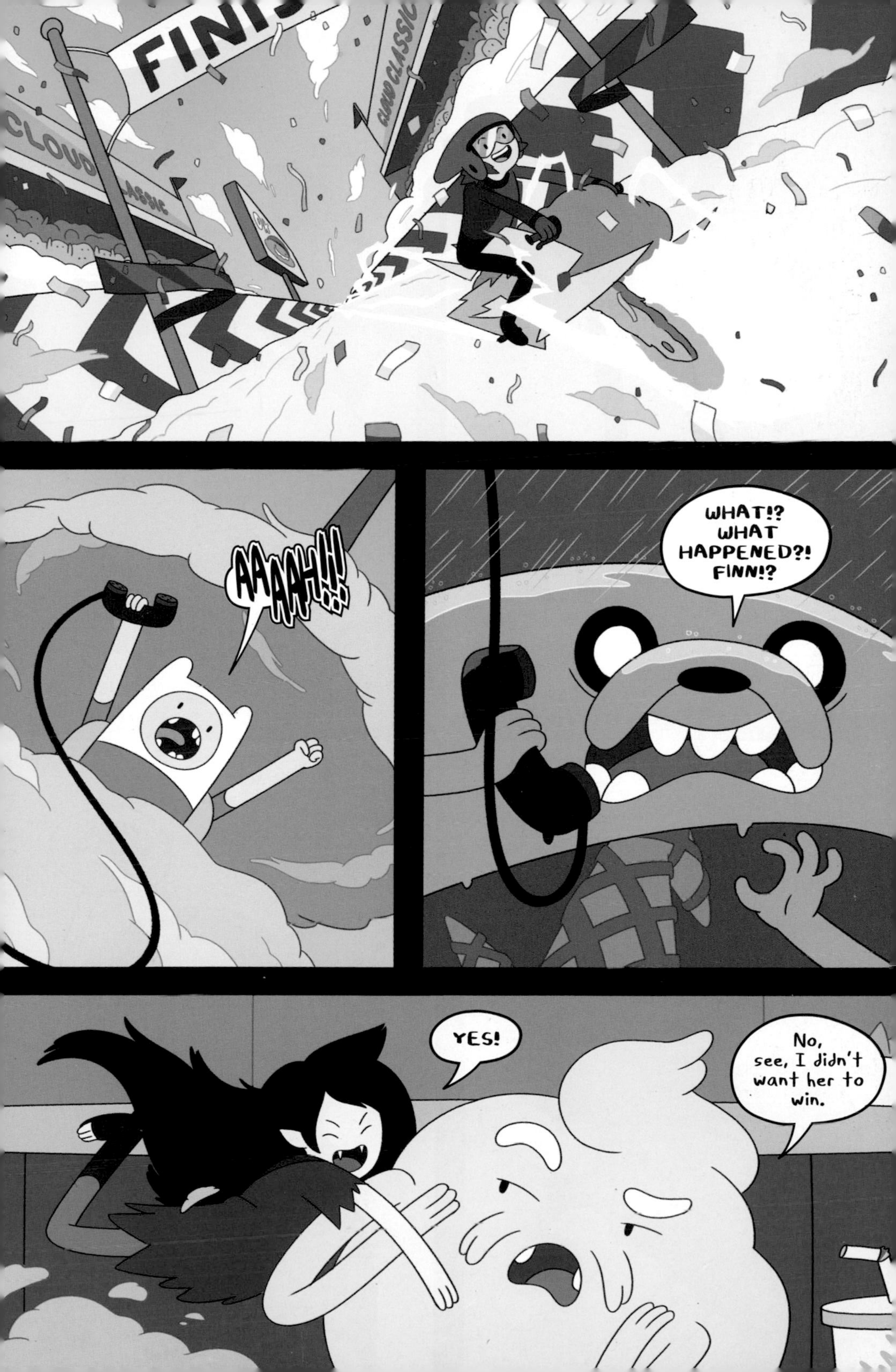
FINIS
CLOUD CLASSIC
CLOUD CLASSIC
AAAAH!!!
WHAT!? WHAT HAPPENED?! FINN!?
YES!
No, see, I didn't want her to win.

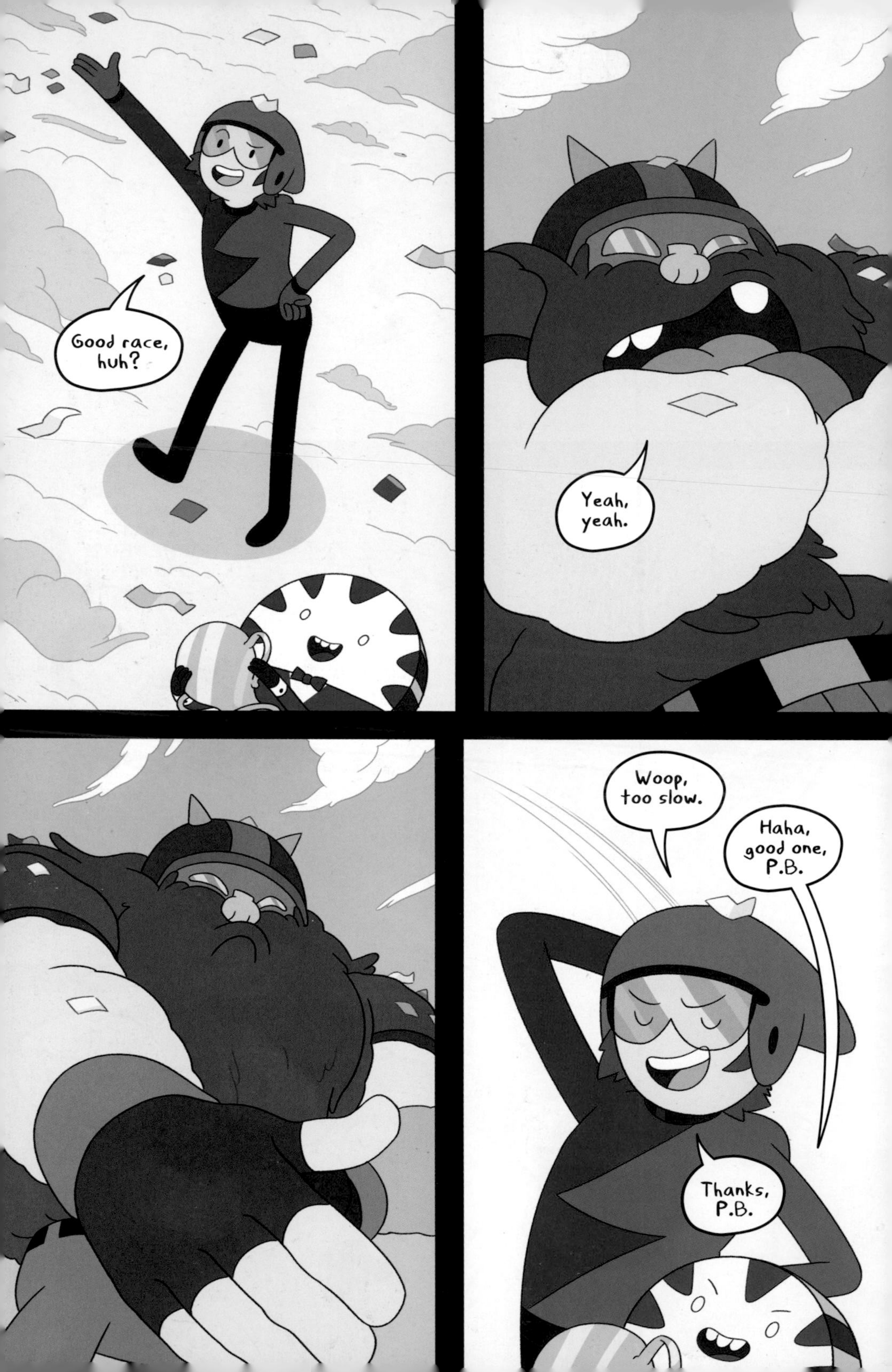
Good race, huh?
Yeah, yeah.
Woop, too slow.
Haha, good one, P.B.
Thanks, P.B.

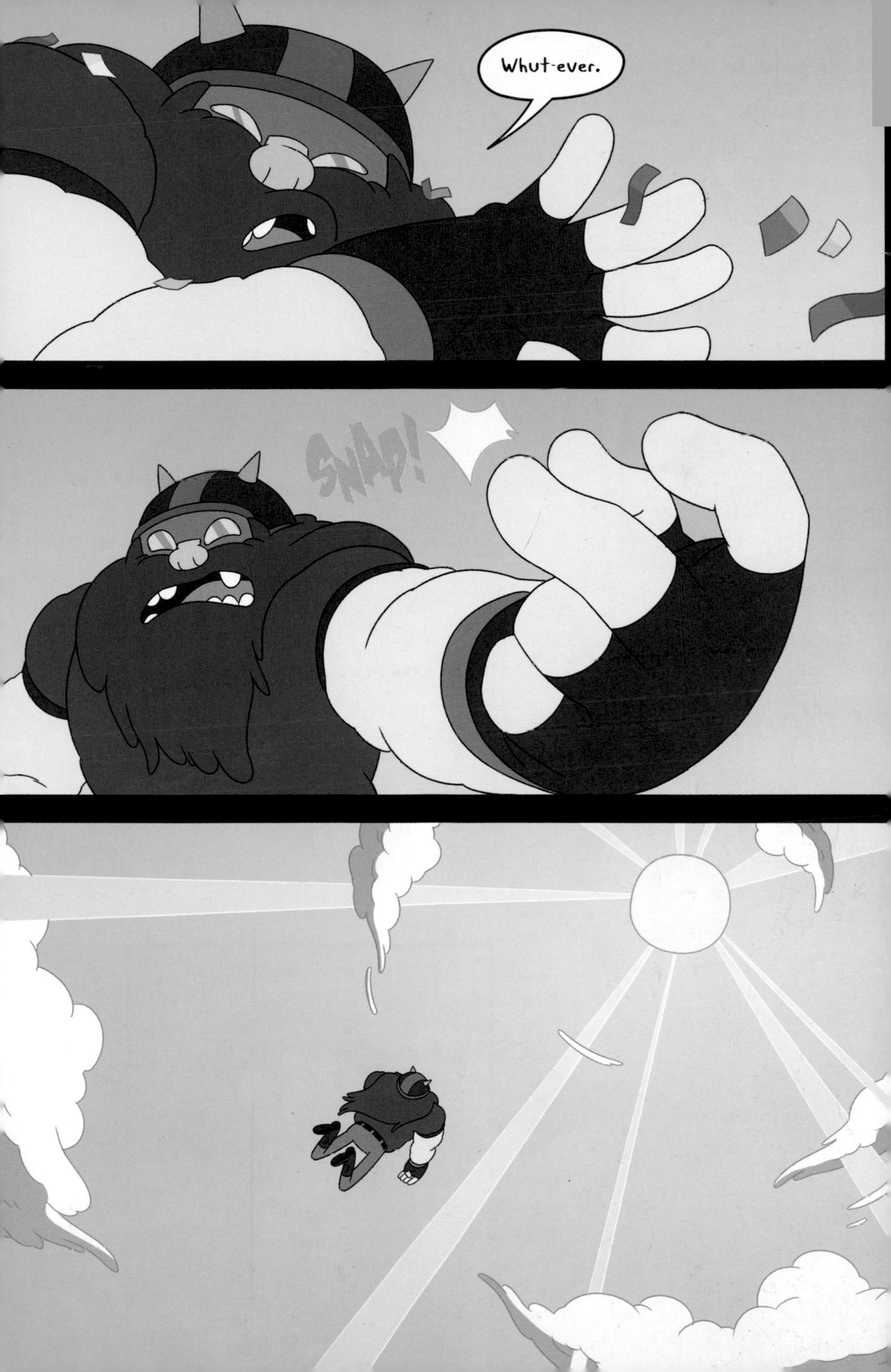
Whut-ever.
SNAP!

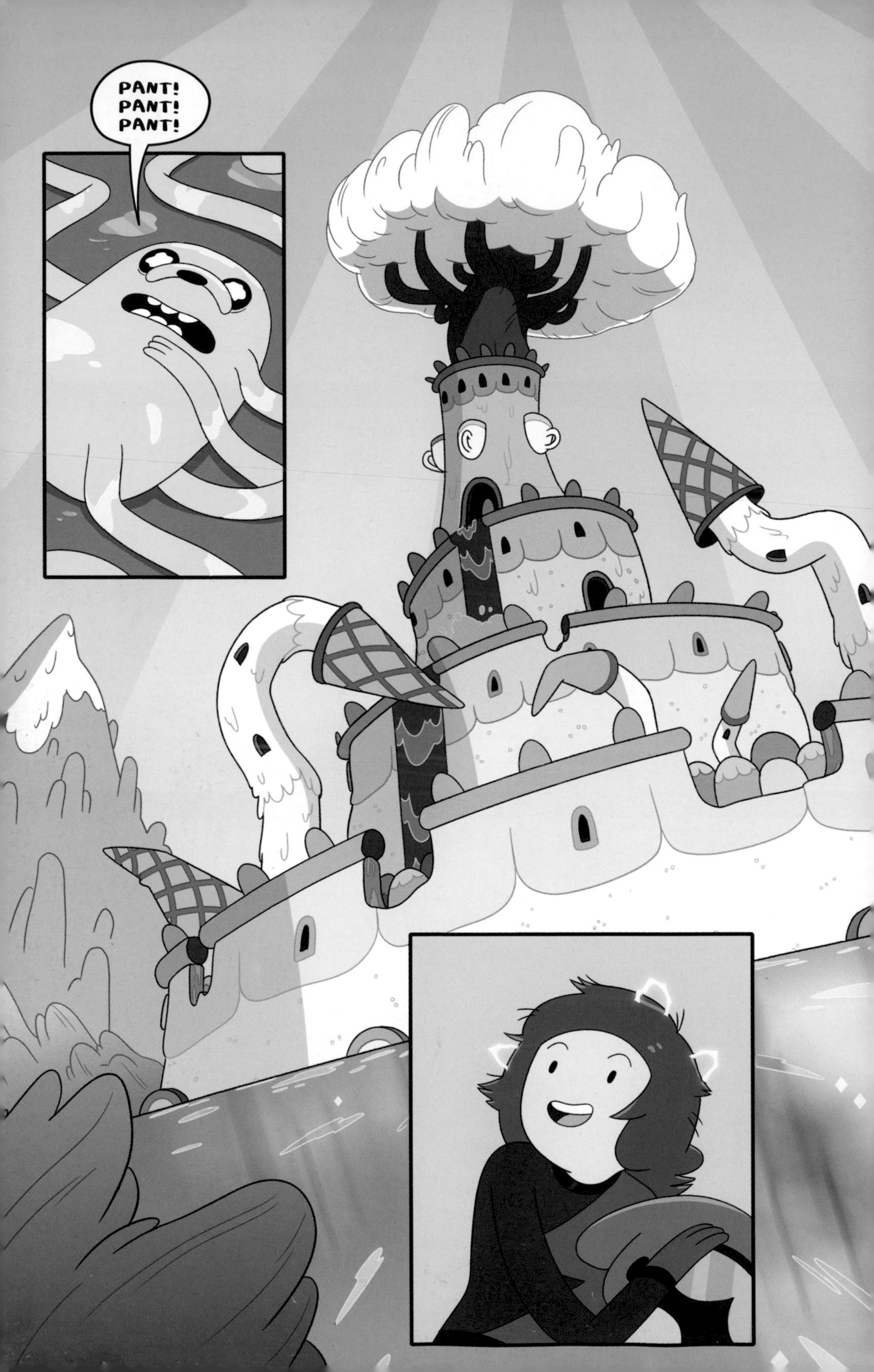
PANT! PANT! PANT!

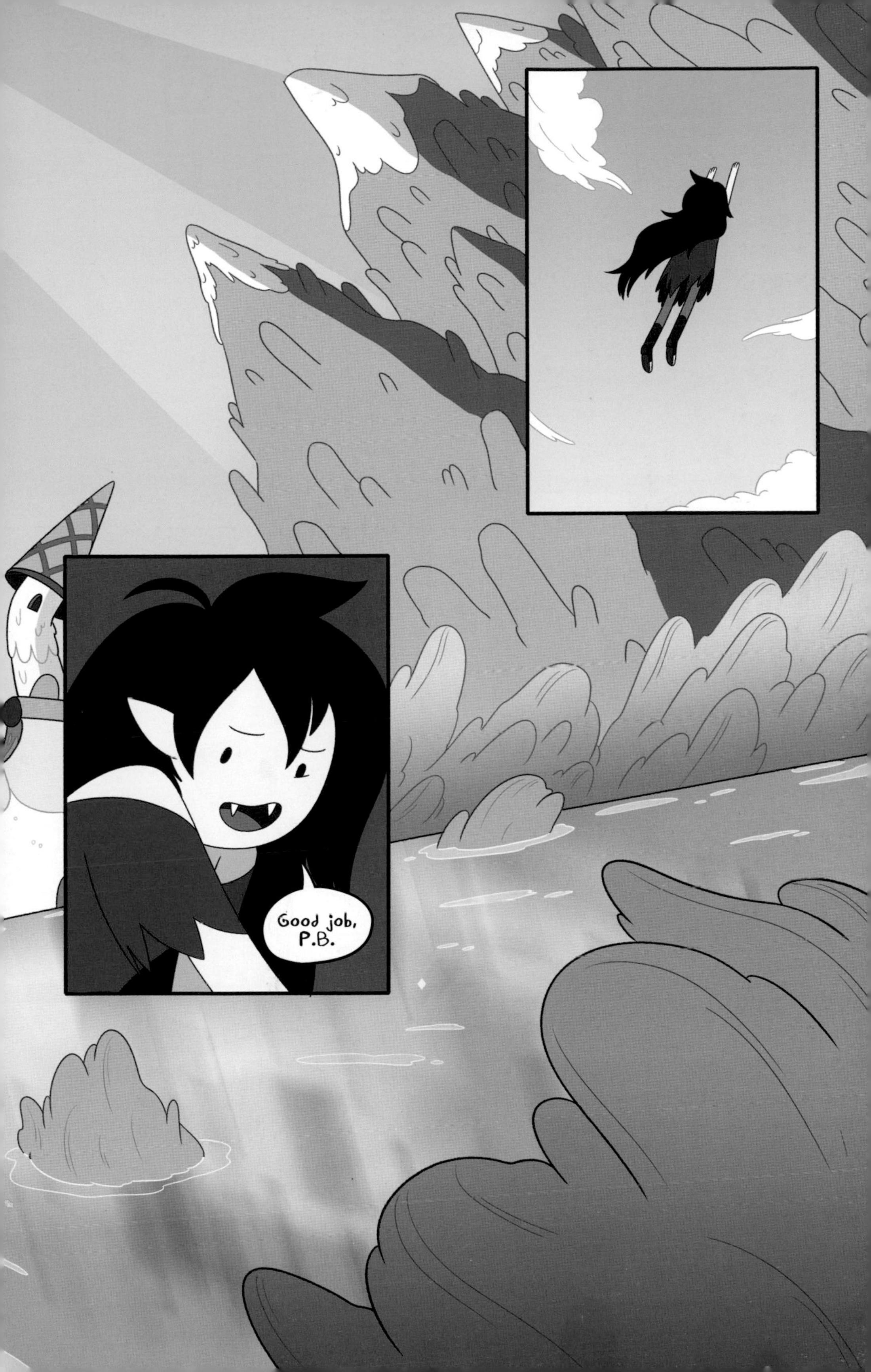
Good job, P.B.

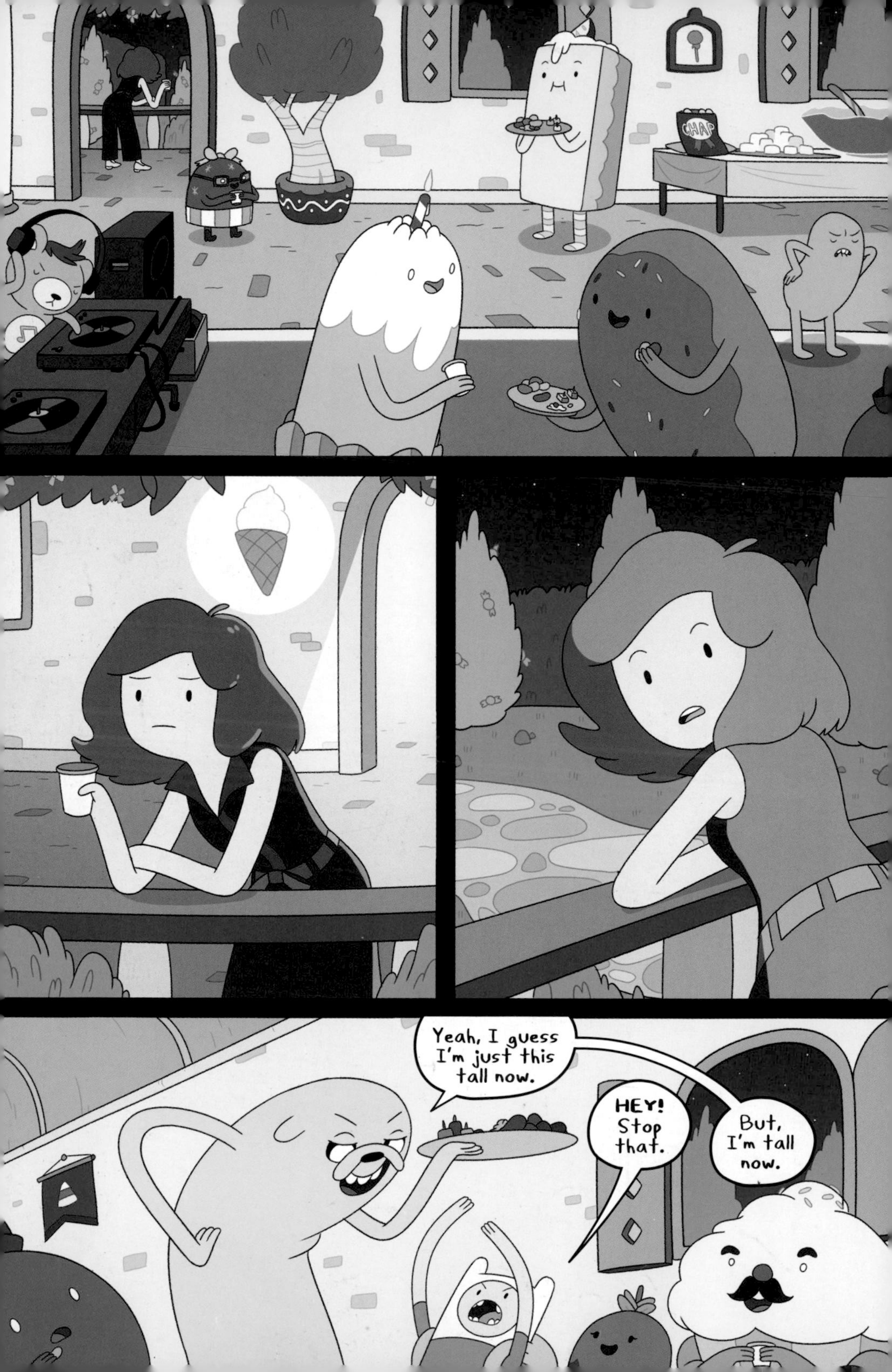

CHAP
Yeah, I guess I'm just this tall now.
HEY! Stop that.
But, I'm tall now.

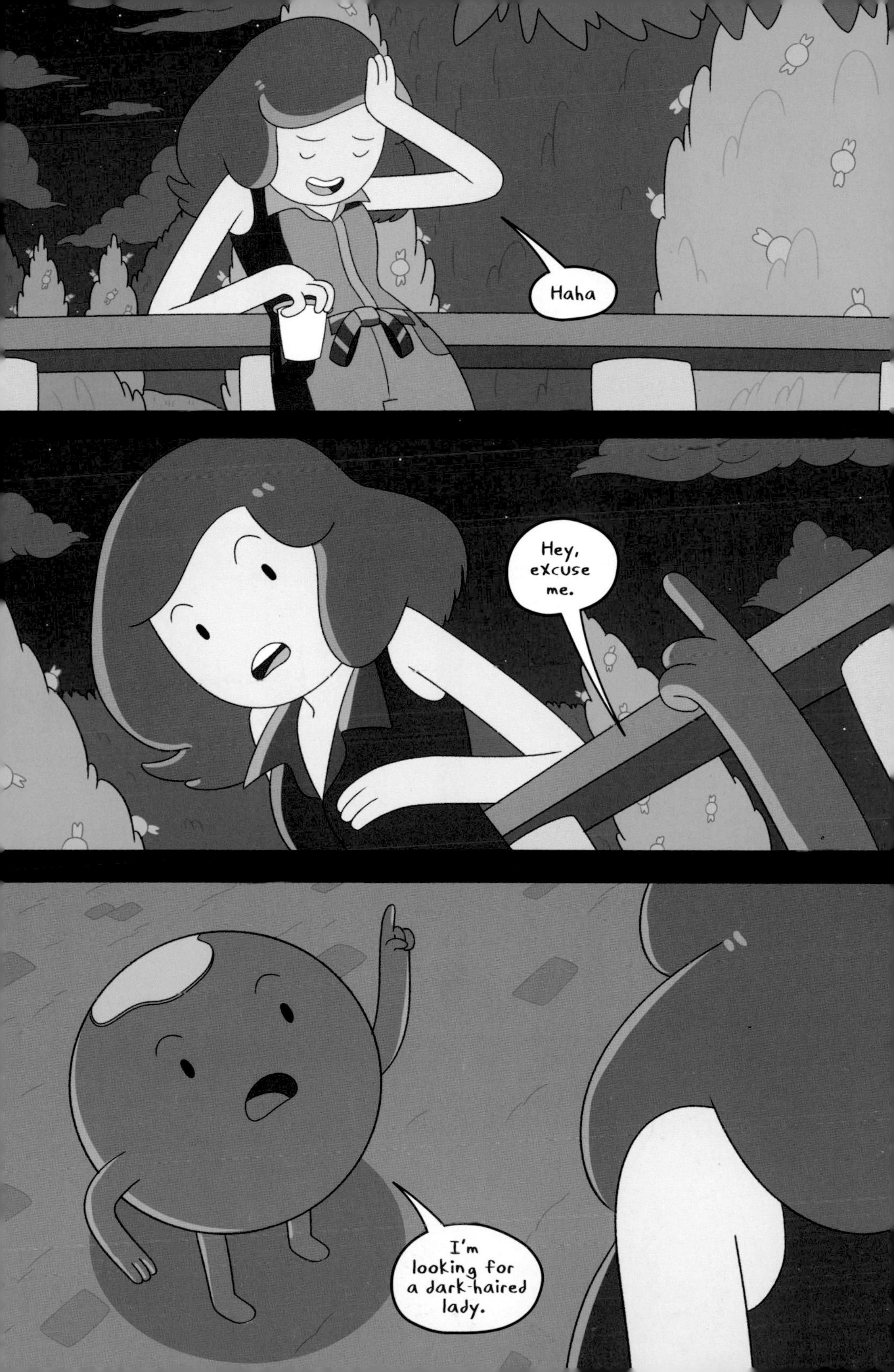
Haha
Hey, excuse me.
I'm looking for a dark-haired lady.

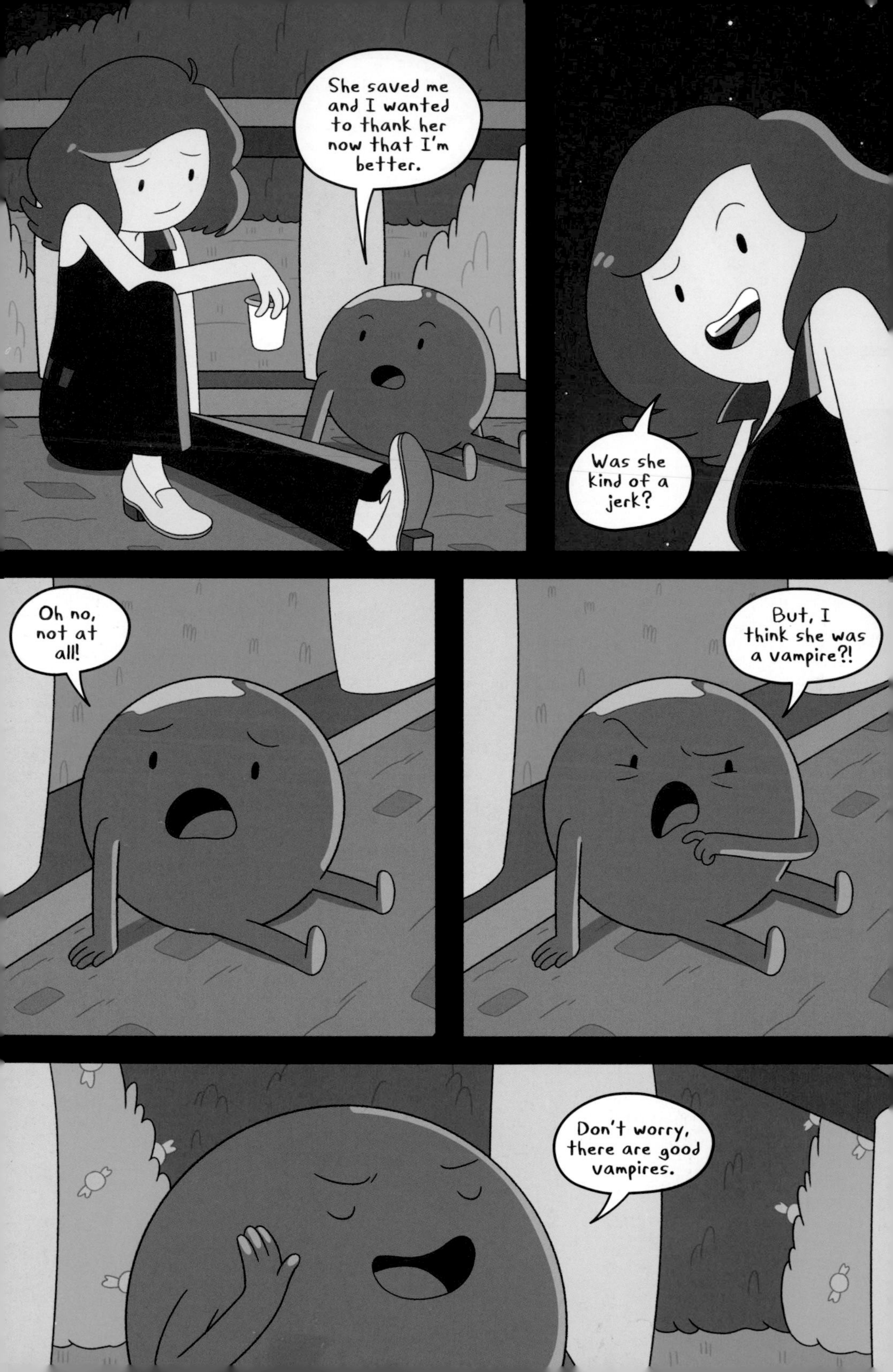
She saved me and I wanted to thank her now that I'm better.
Was she kind of a jerk?
Oh no, not at all!
But, I think she was a vampire?!
Don't worry, there are good vampires.

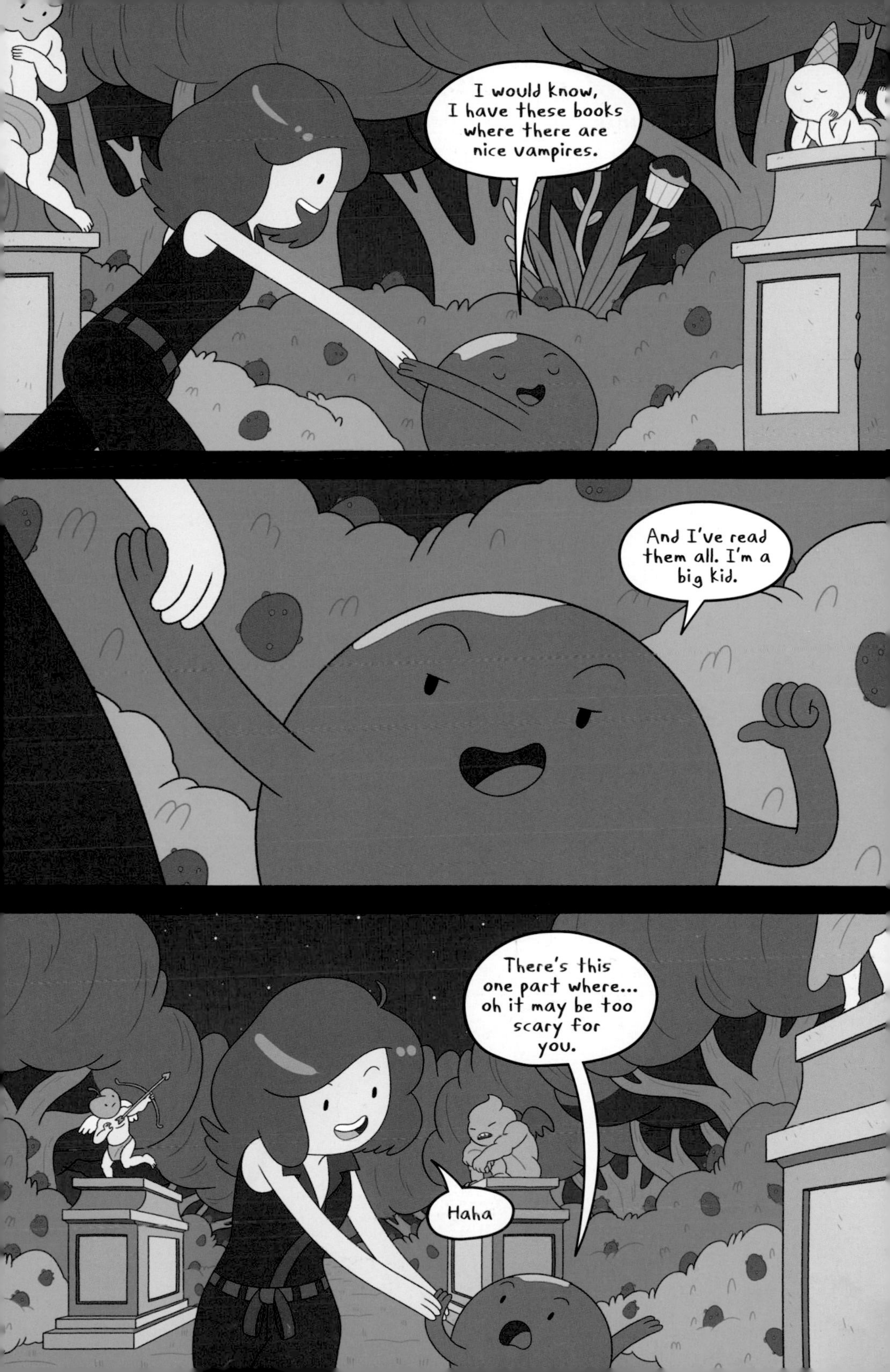
I would know, I have these books where there are nice vampires.
And I've read them all. I'm a big kid.
There's this one part where... oh it may be too scary for you.
Haha

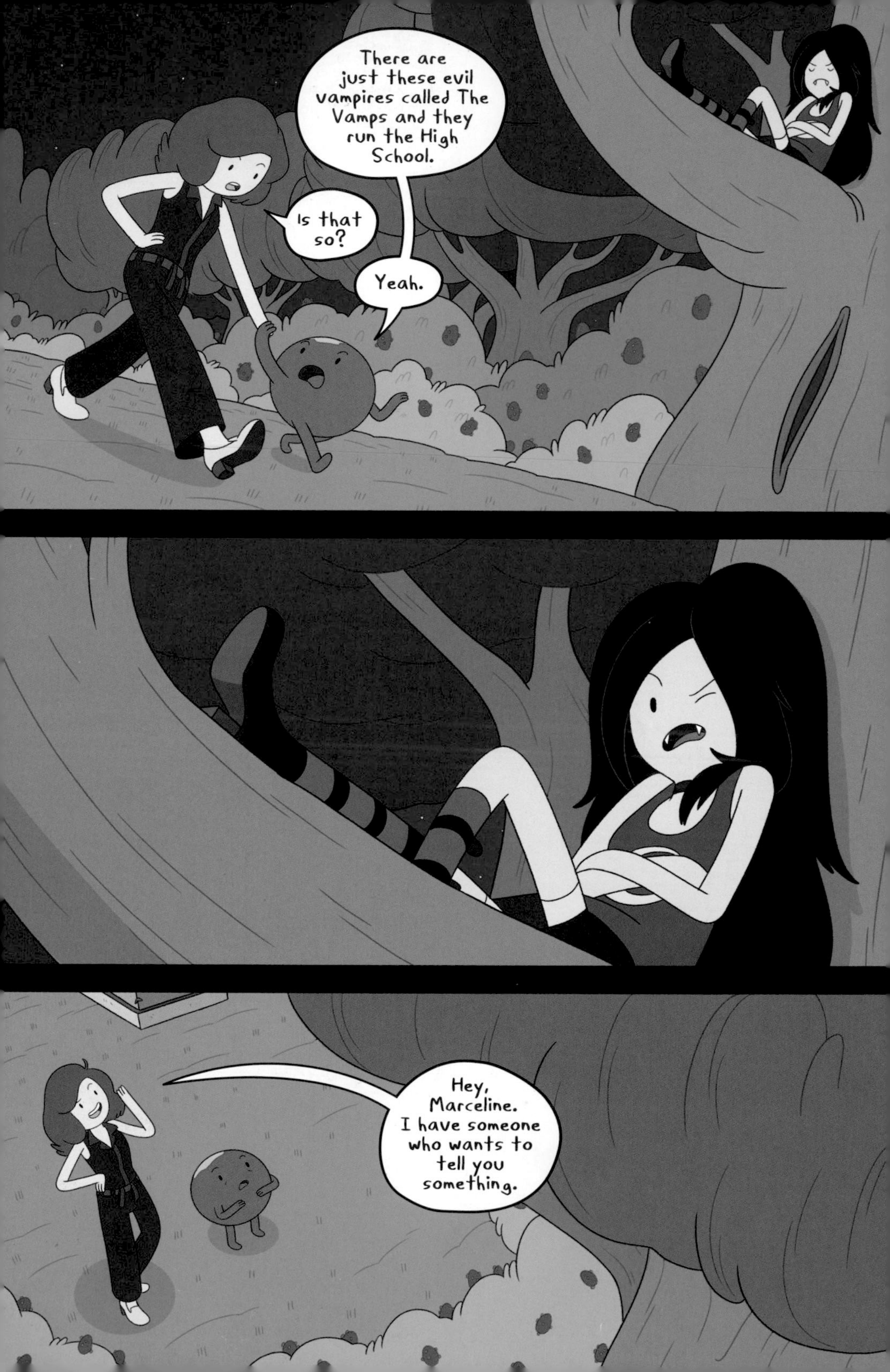
There are just these evil vampires called The Vamps and they run the High School.
Is that so?
Yeah.
Hey, Marceline. I have someone who wants to tell you something.

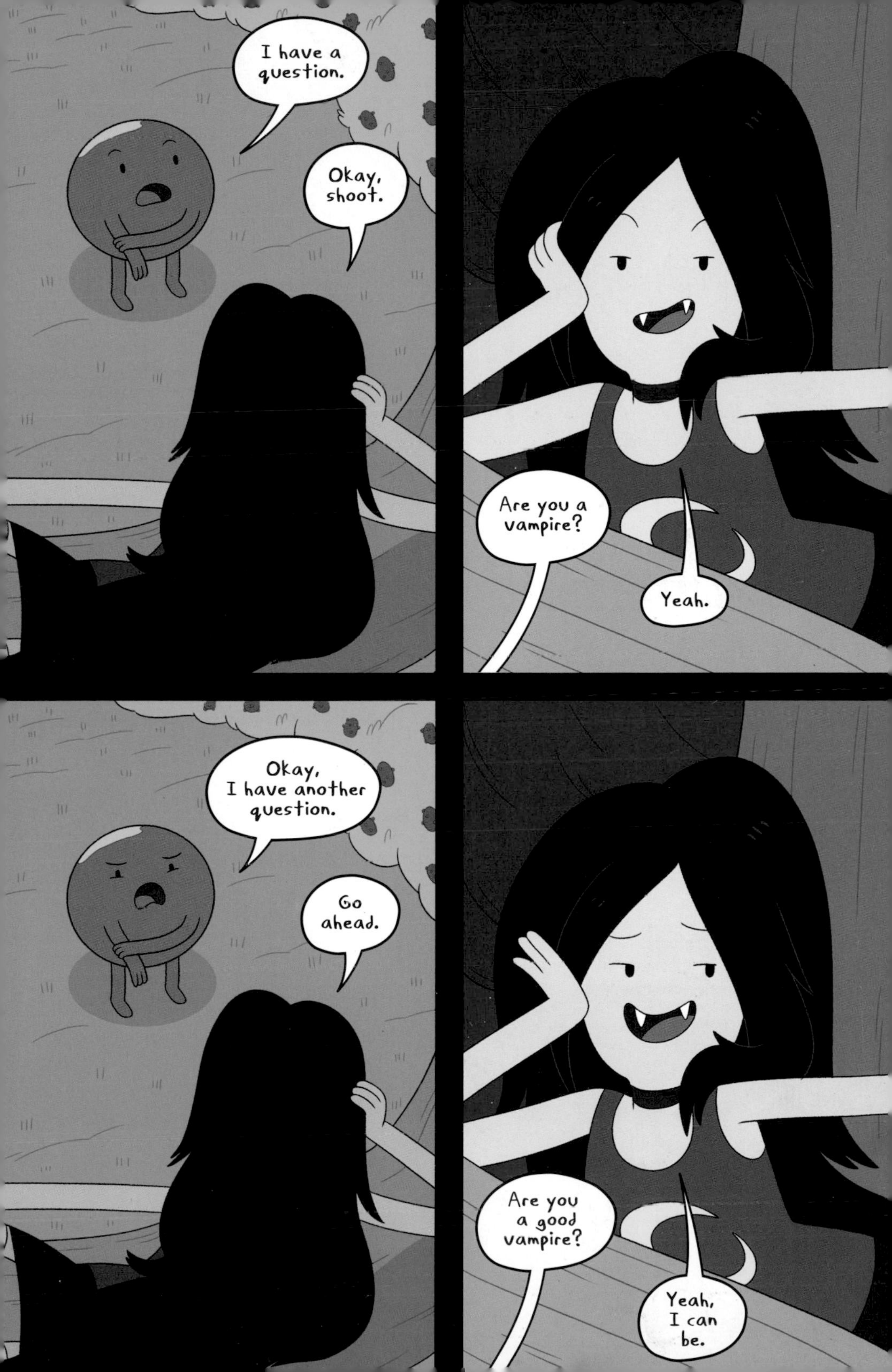
I have a question.
Okay, shoot.
Are you a vampire?
Yeah.
Okay, I have another question.
Go ahead.
Are you a good vampire?
Yeah, I can be.

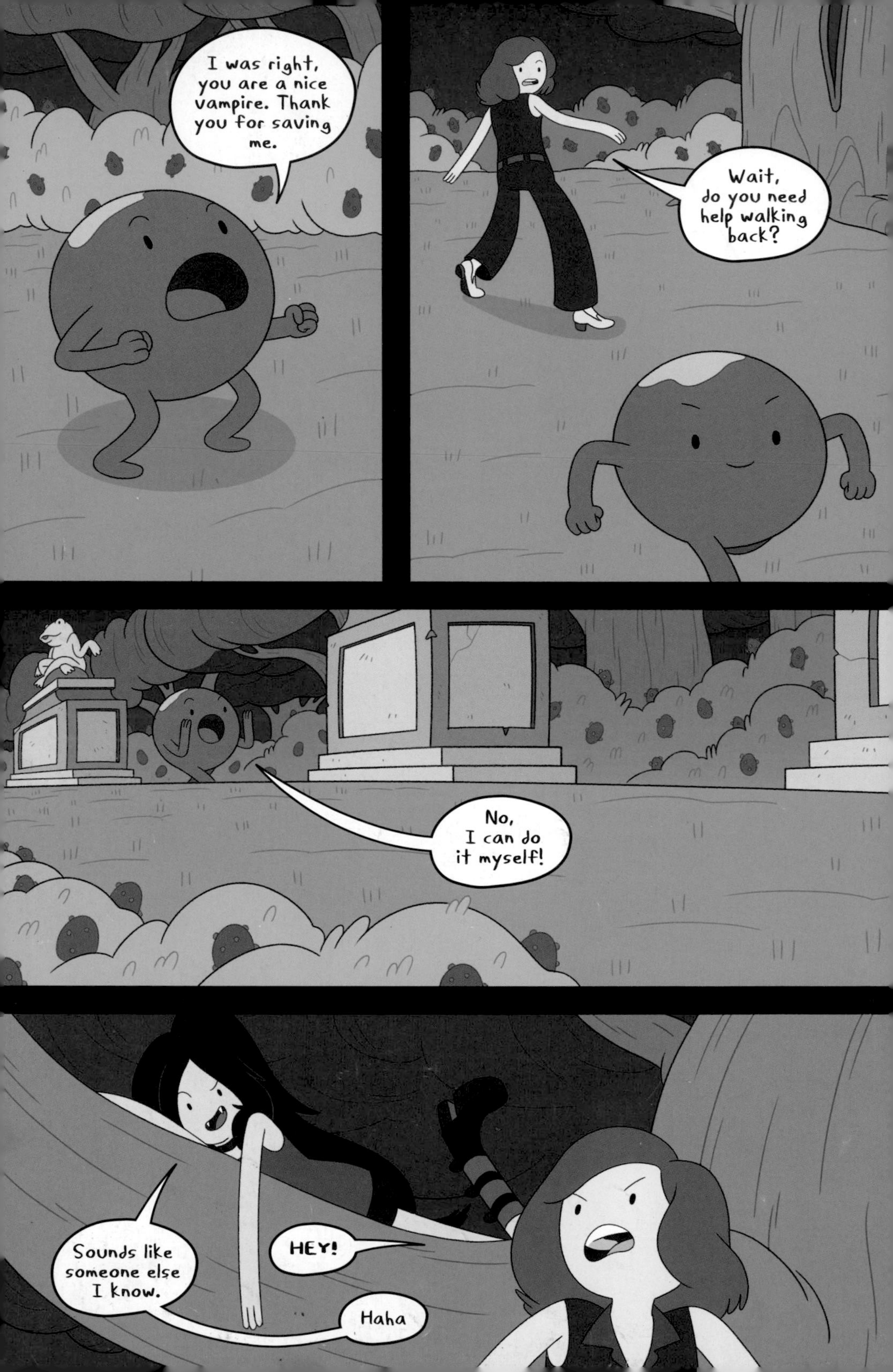
I was right, you are a nice vampire. Thank you for saving me.
Wait, do you need help walking back?
No, I can do it myself!
Sounds like someone else I know.
HEY!
Haha

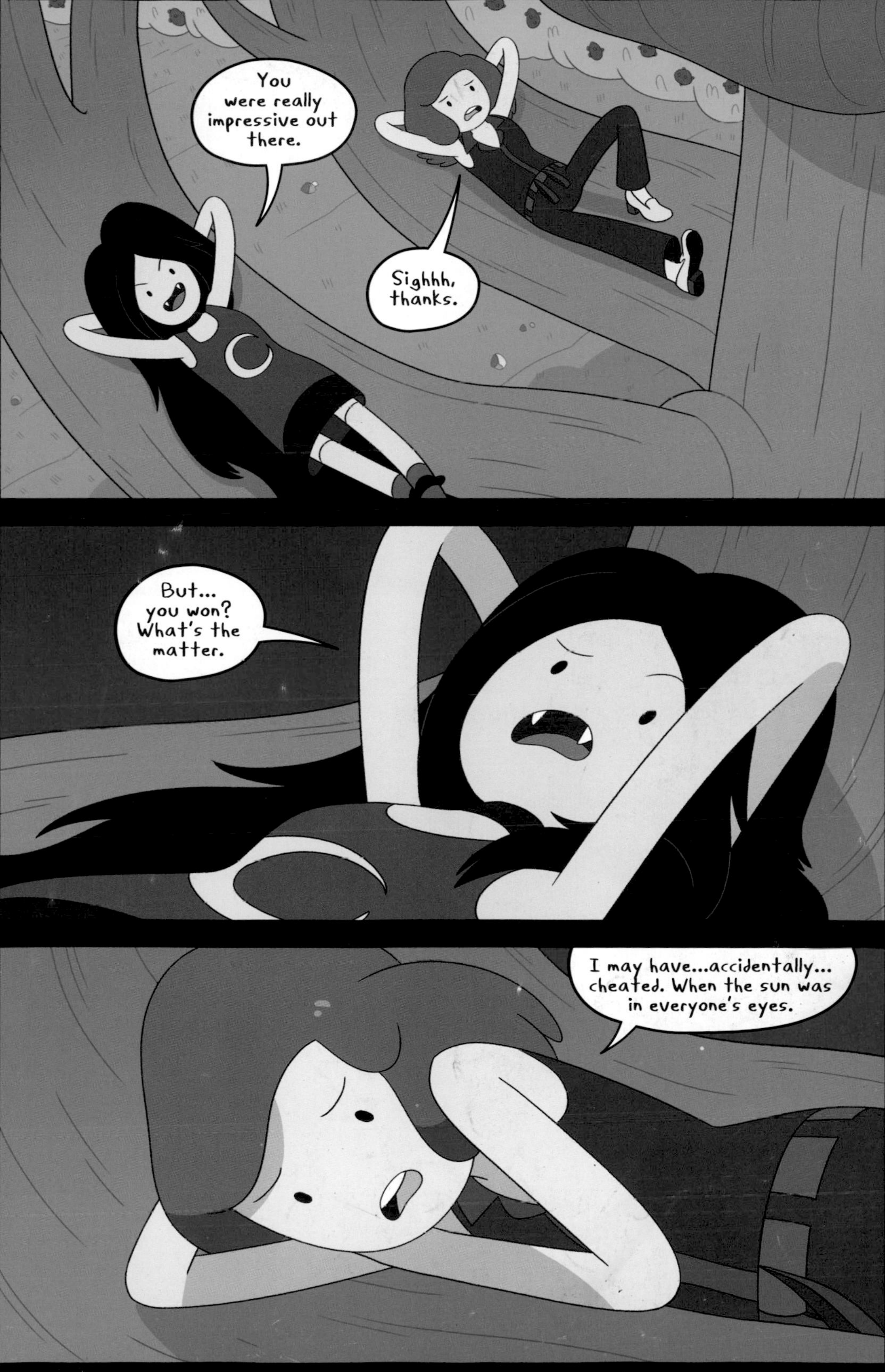
You were really impressive out there.
Sighhh, thanks.
But... you won? What's the matter.
I may have...accidentally... cheated. When the sun was in everyone's eyes.

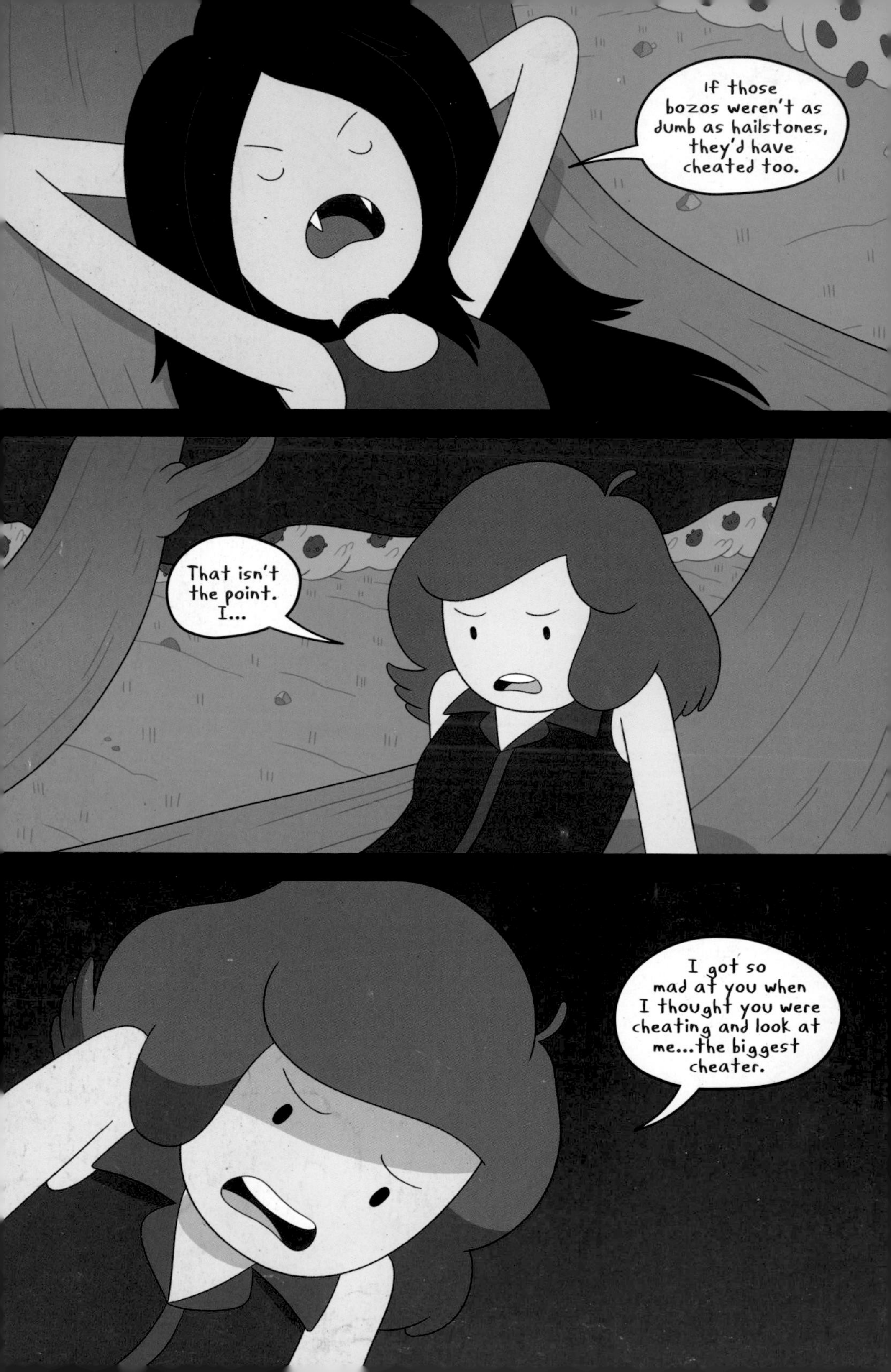
If those bozos weren't as dumb as hailstones, they'd have cheated too.
That isn't the point. I...
I got so mad at you when I thought you were cheating and look at me...the biggest cheater.

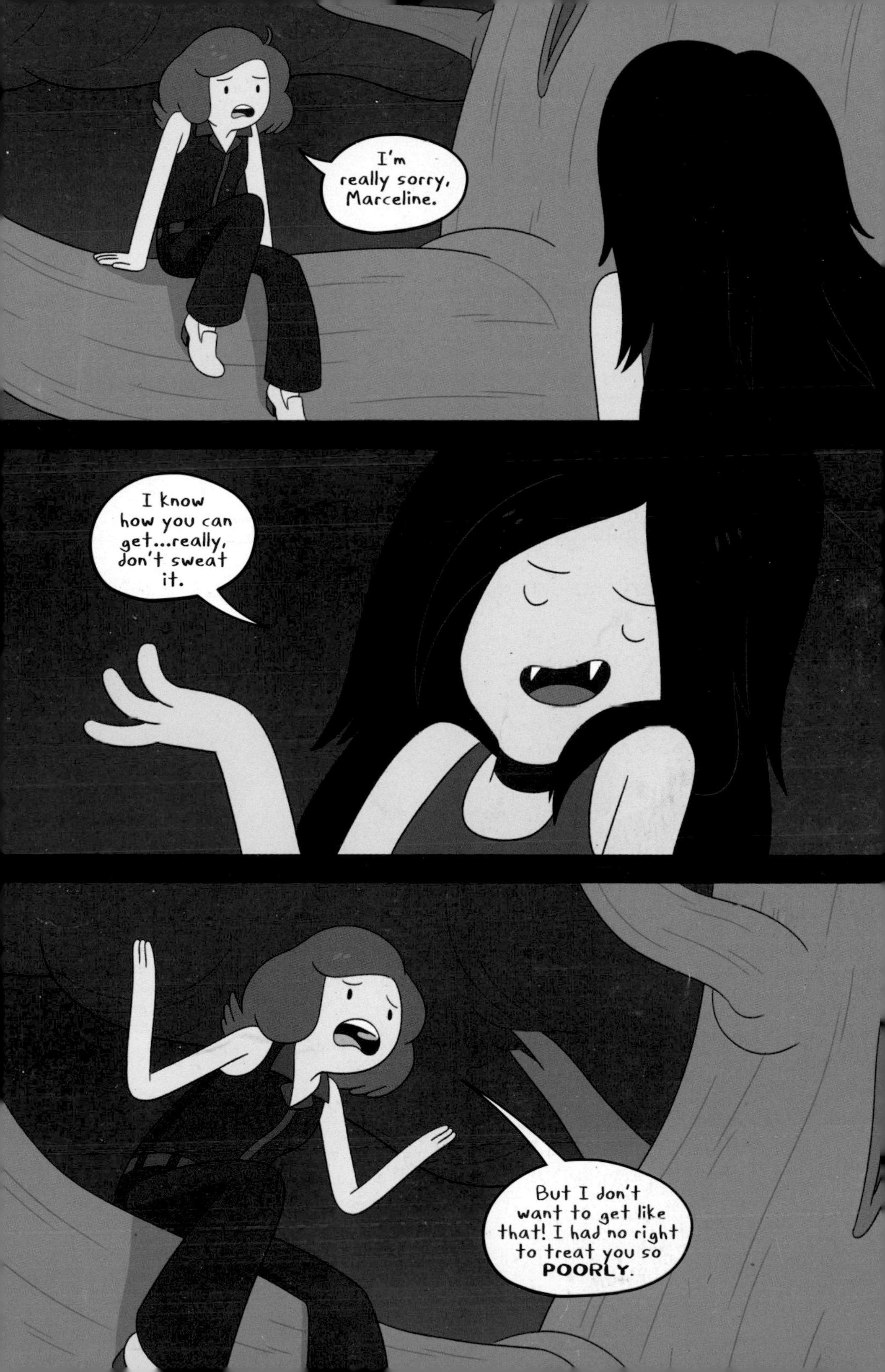
I'm really sorry, Marceline.
I know how you can get...really, don't sweat it.
But I don't want to get like that! I had no right to treat you so **POORLY**.

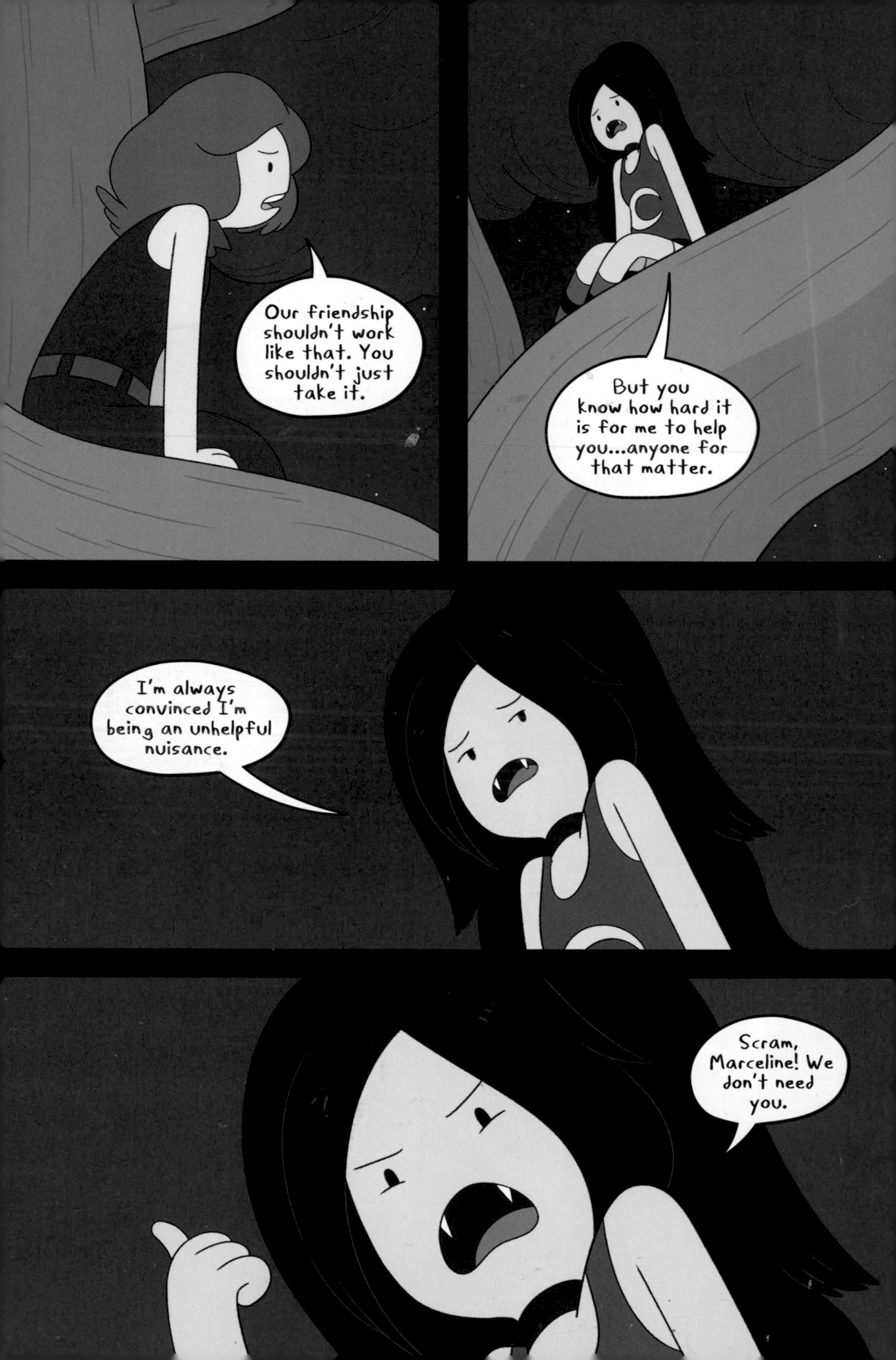
Our friendship shouldn't work like that. You shouldn't just take it.
But you know how hard it is for me to help you...anyone for that matter.
I'm always convinced I'm being an unhelpful nuisance.
Scram, Marceline! We don't need you.

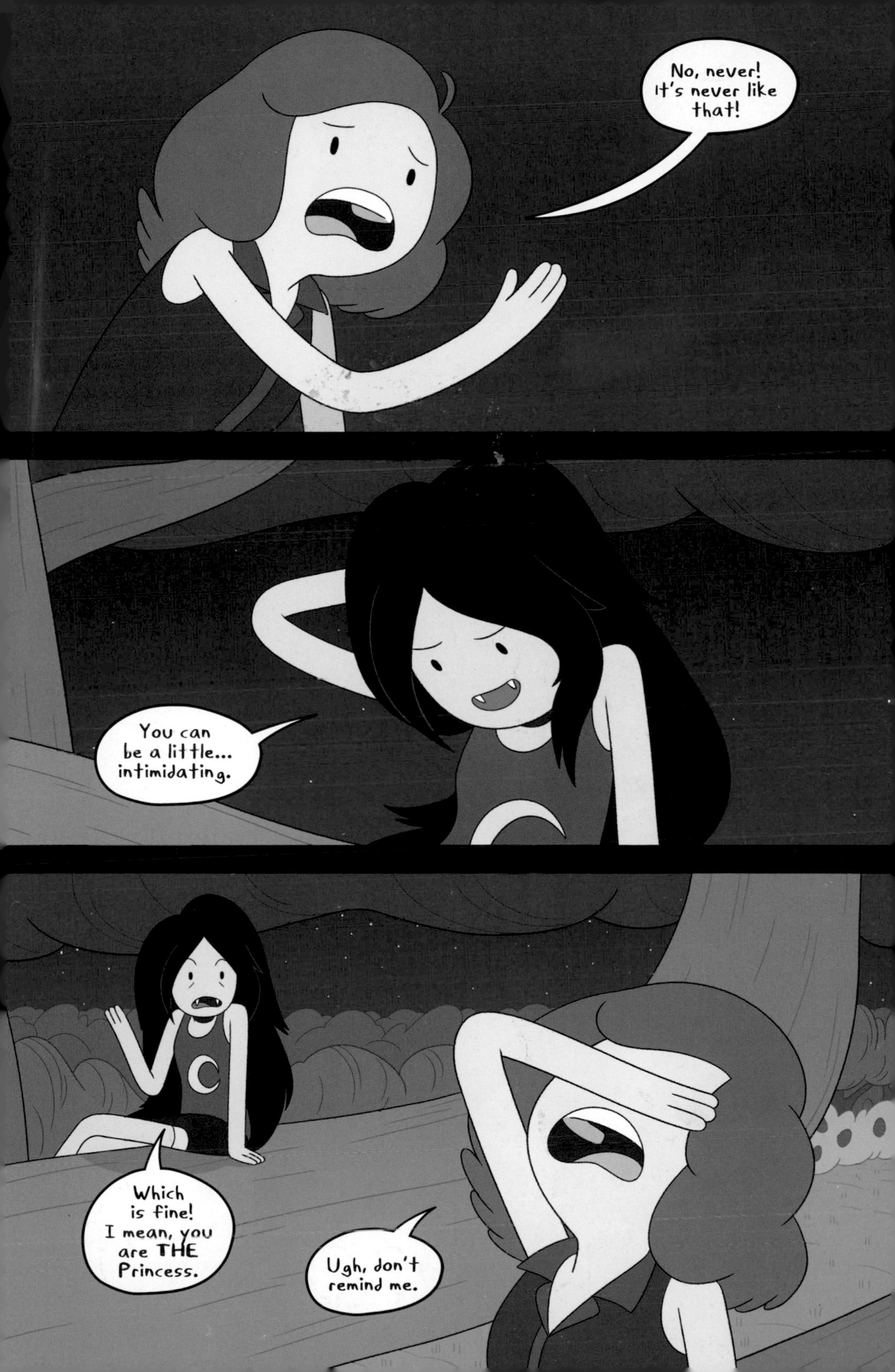
No, never! It's never like that!
You can be a little... intimidating.
Which is fine! I mean, you are THE Princess.
Ugh, don't remind me.

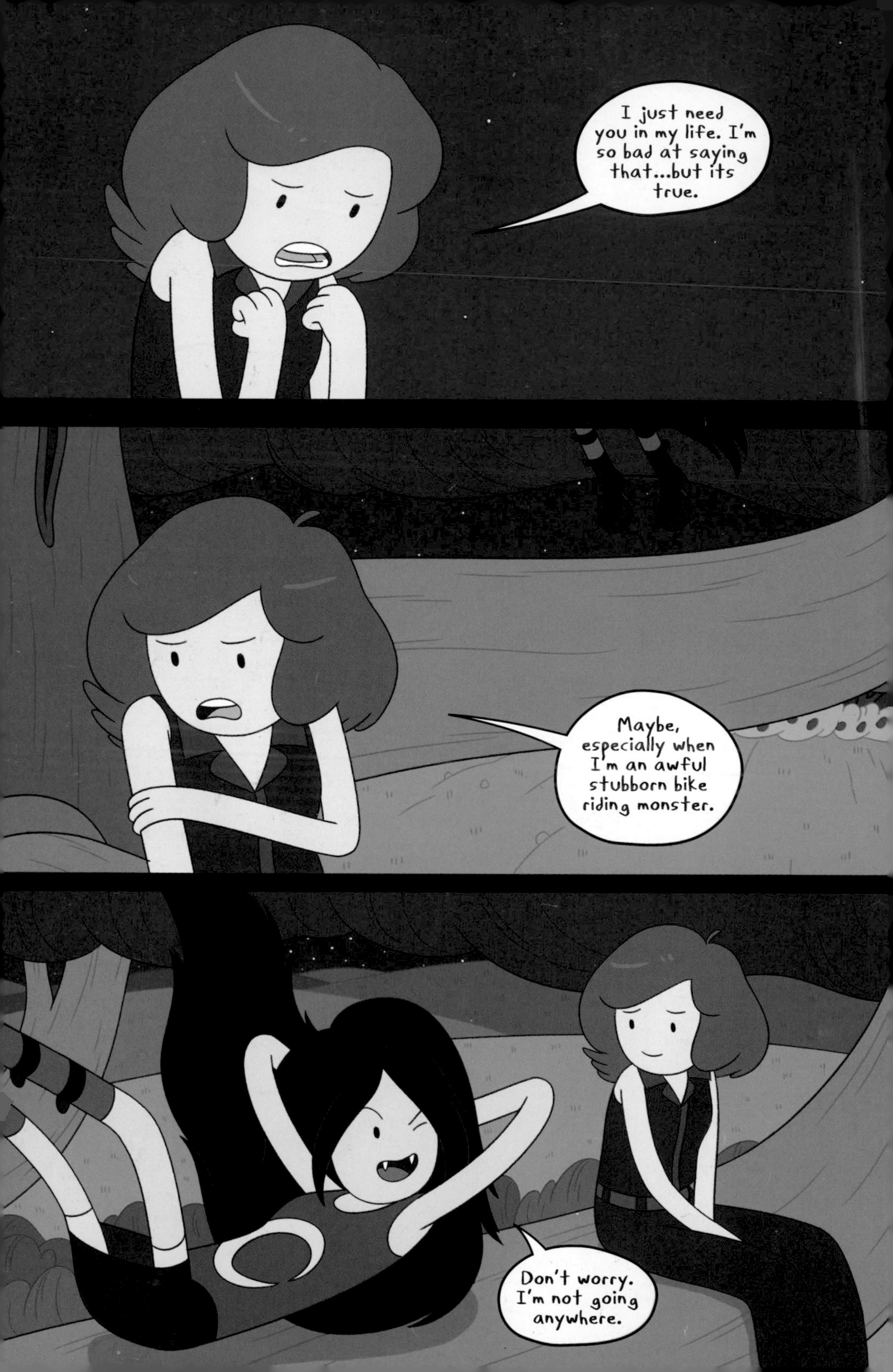
I just need you in my life. I'm so bad at saying that...but its true.
Maybe, especially when I'm an awful stubborn bike riding monster.
Don't worry. I'm not going anywhere.

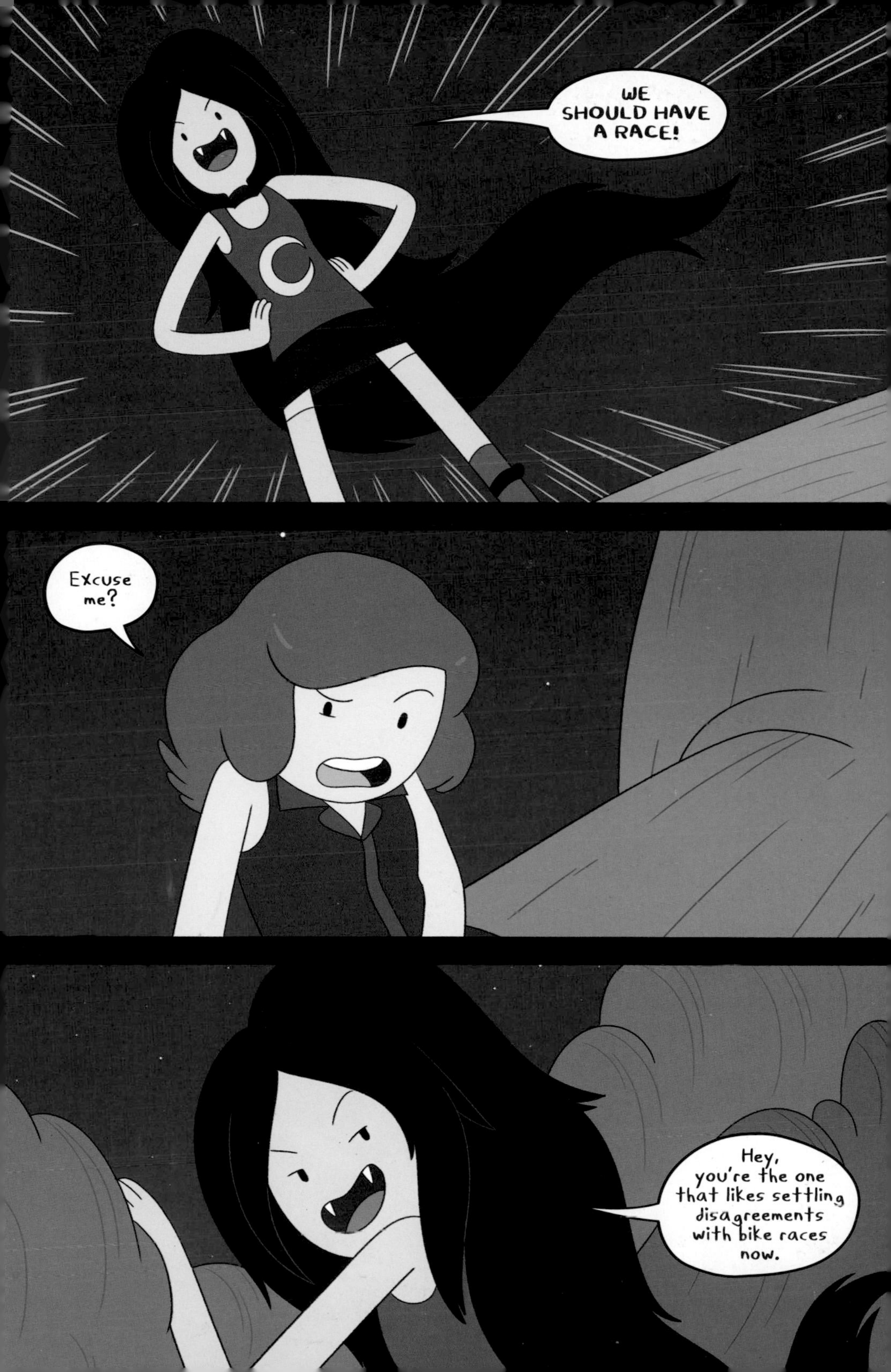
WE SHOULD HAVE A RACE!
Excuse me?
Hey, you're the one that likes settling disagreements with bike races now.

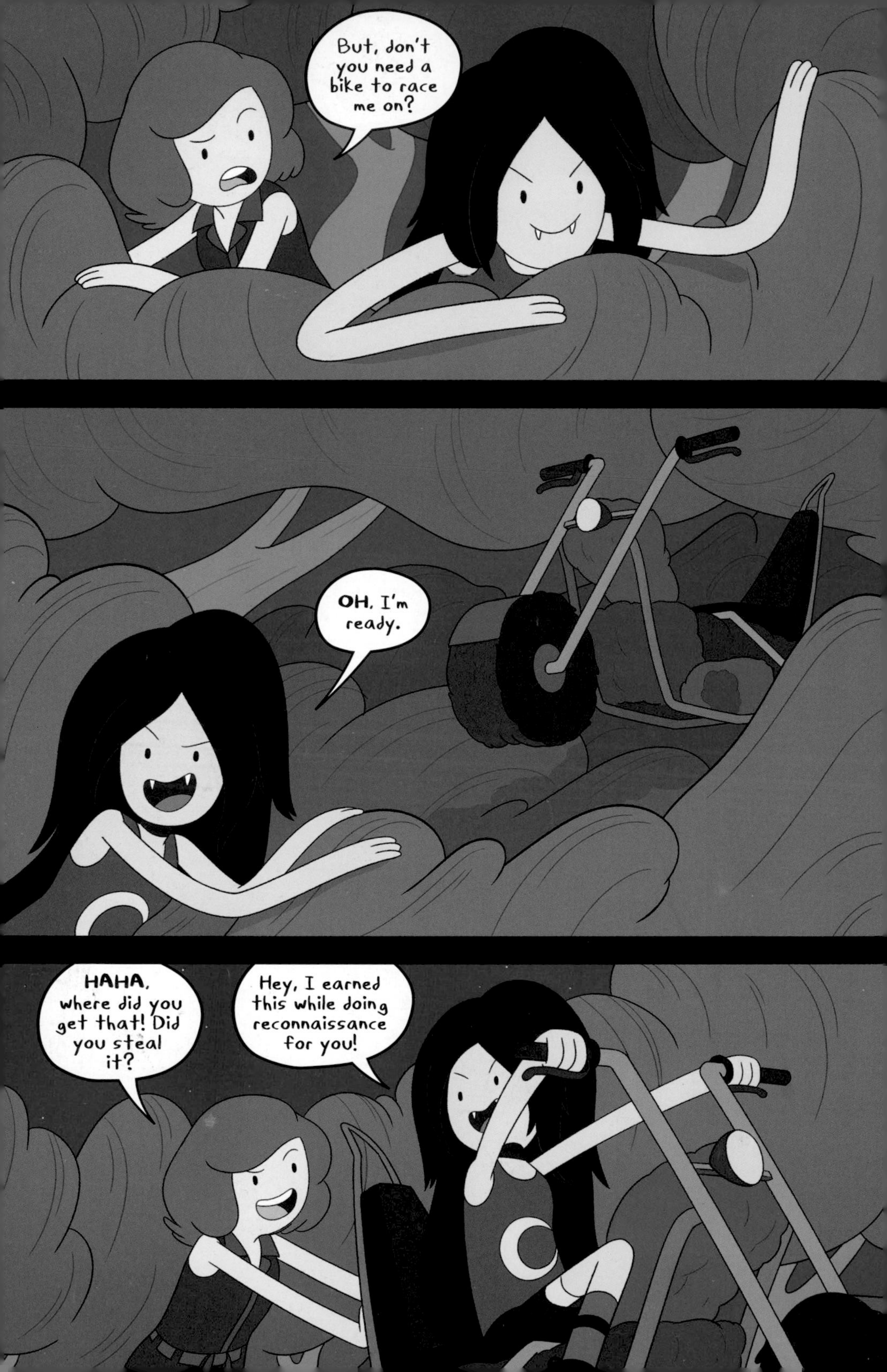

But, don't you need a bike to race me on?
OH, I'm ready.
HAHA, where did you get that! Did you steal it?
Hey, I earned this while doing reconnaissance for you!

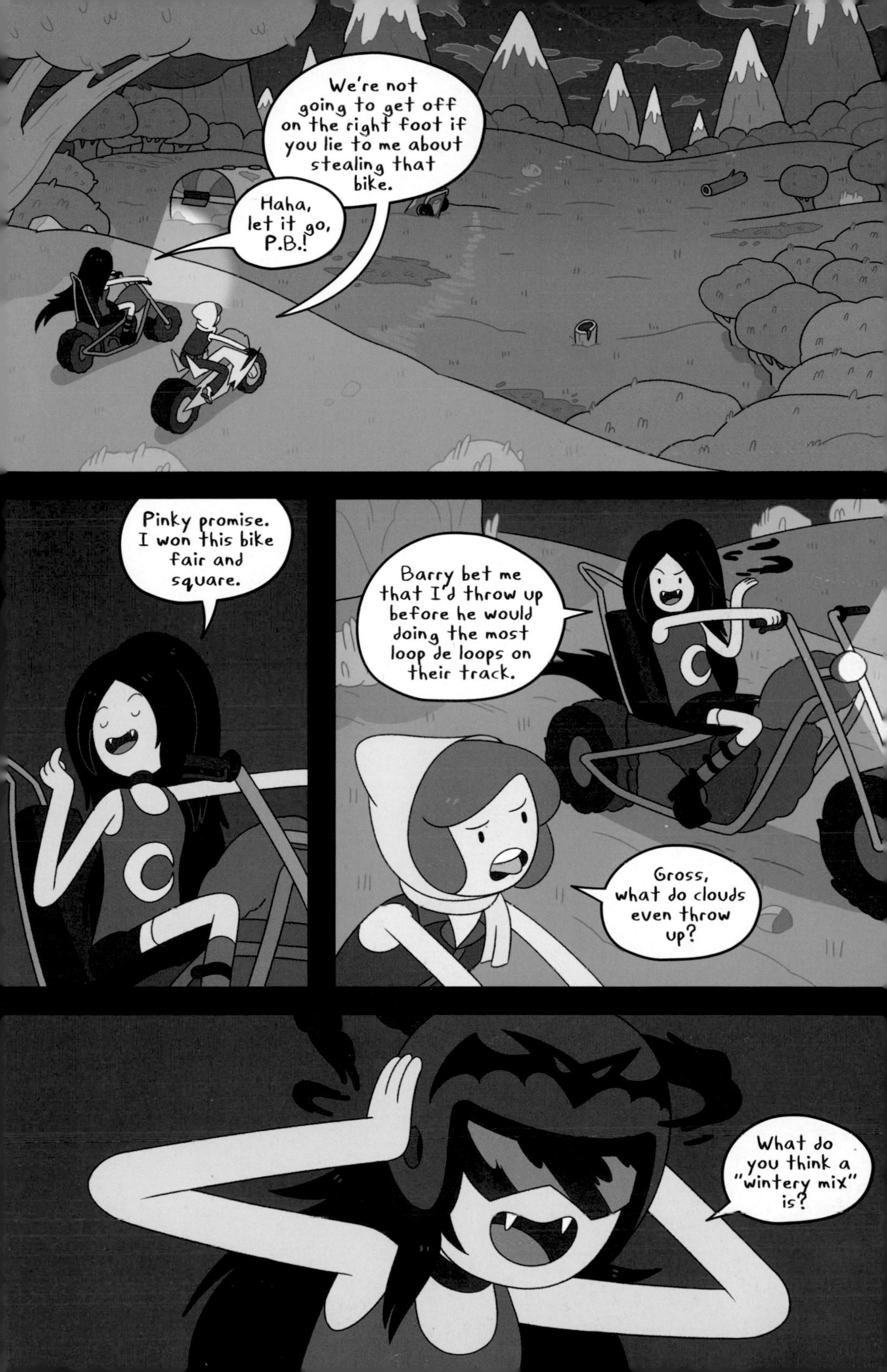
We're not going to get off on the right foot if you lie to me about stealing that bike.
Haha, let it go, P.B.!
Pinky promise. I won this bike fair and square.
Barry bet me that I'd throw up before he would doing the most loop de loops on their track.
Gross, what do clouds even throw up?
What do you think a "wintery mix" is?

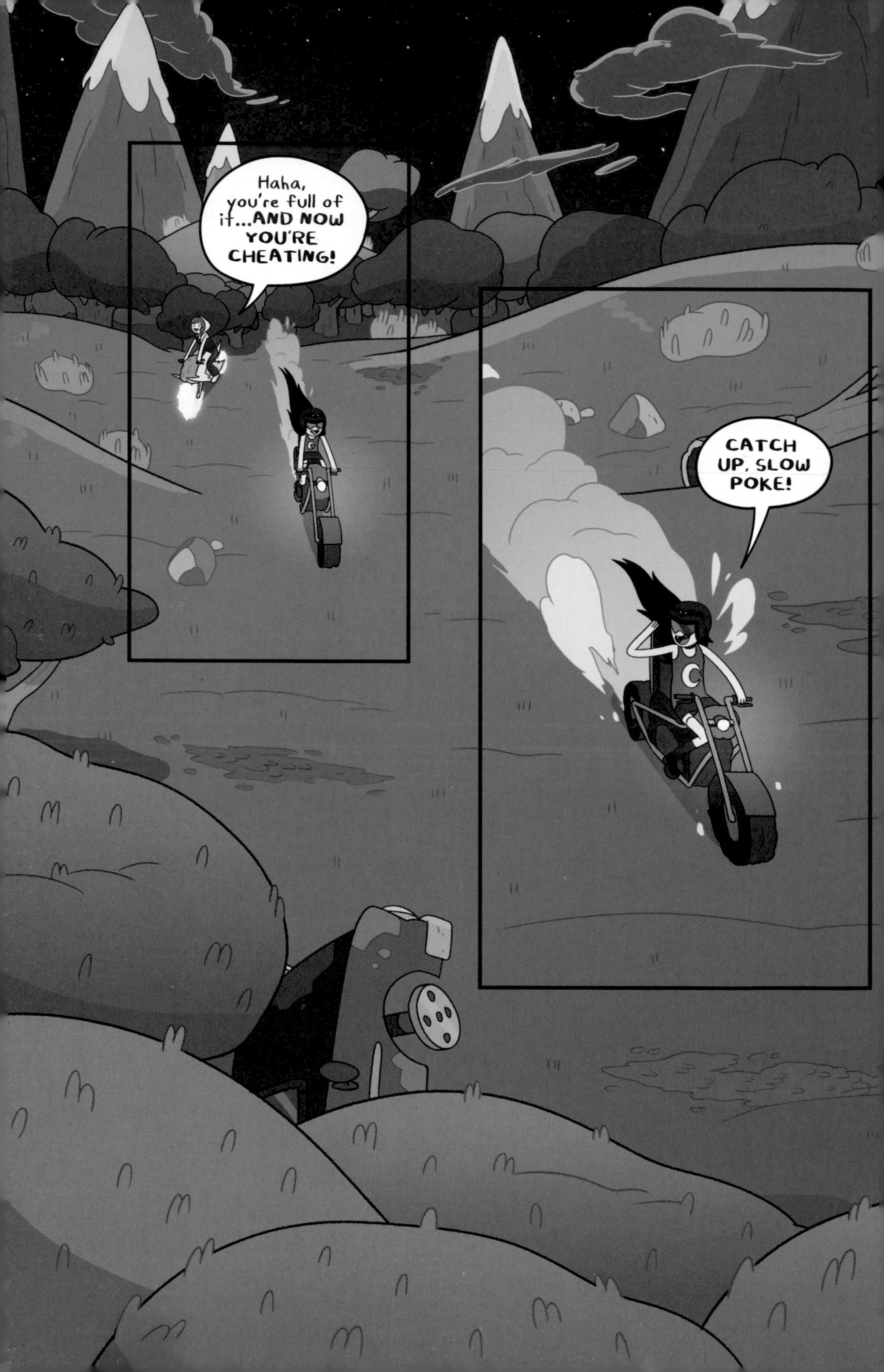
Haha, you're full of it...AND NOW YOU'RE CHEATING!
CATCH UP, SLOW POKE!

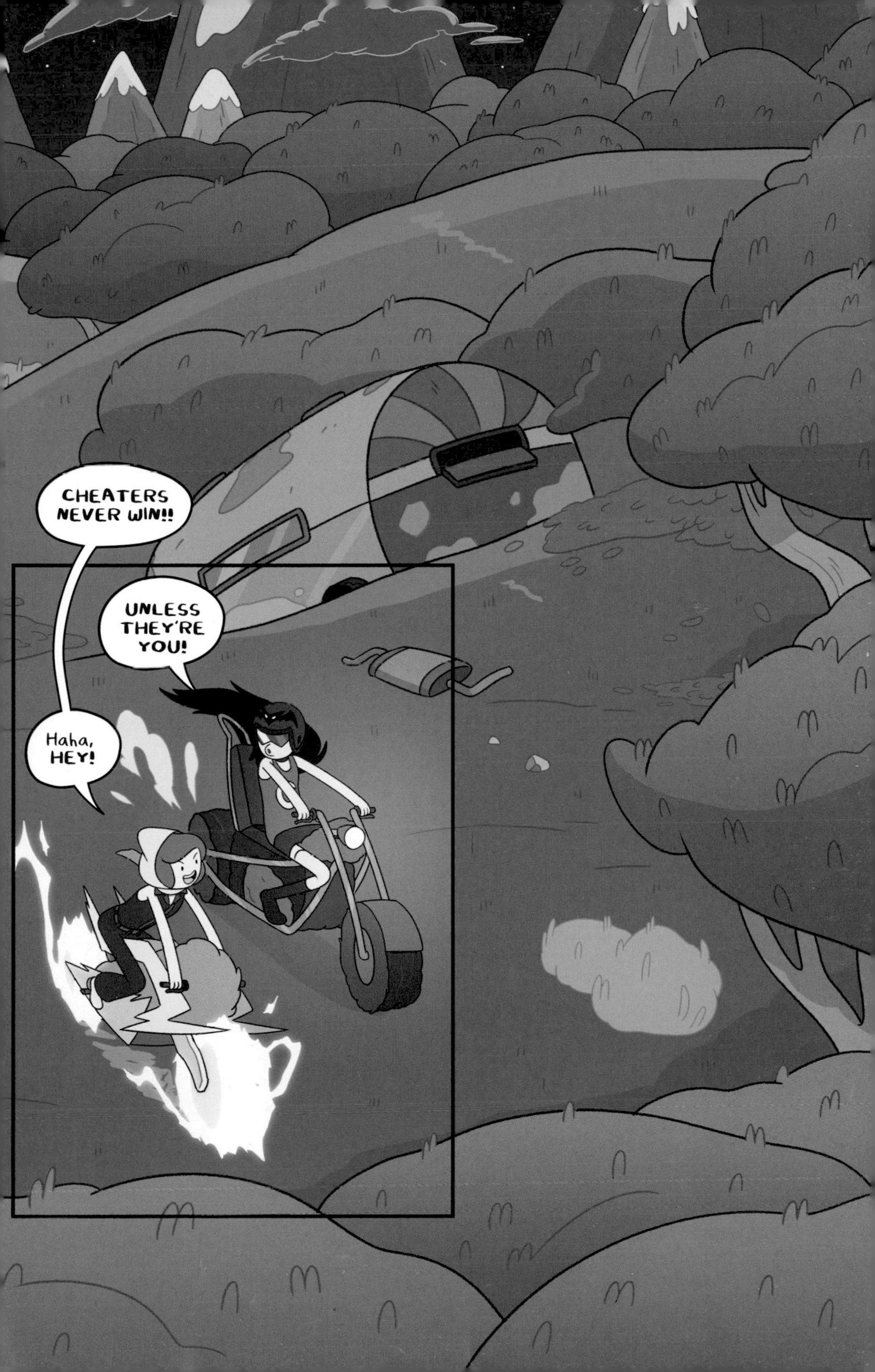
CHEATERS NEVER WIN!!
UNLESS THEY'RE YOU!
Haha, HEY!

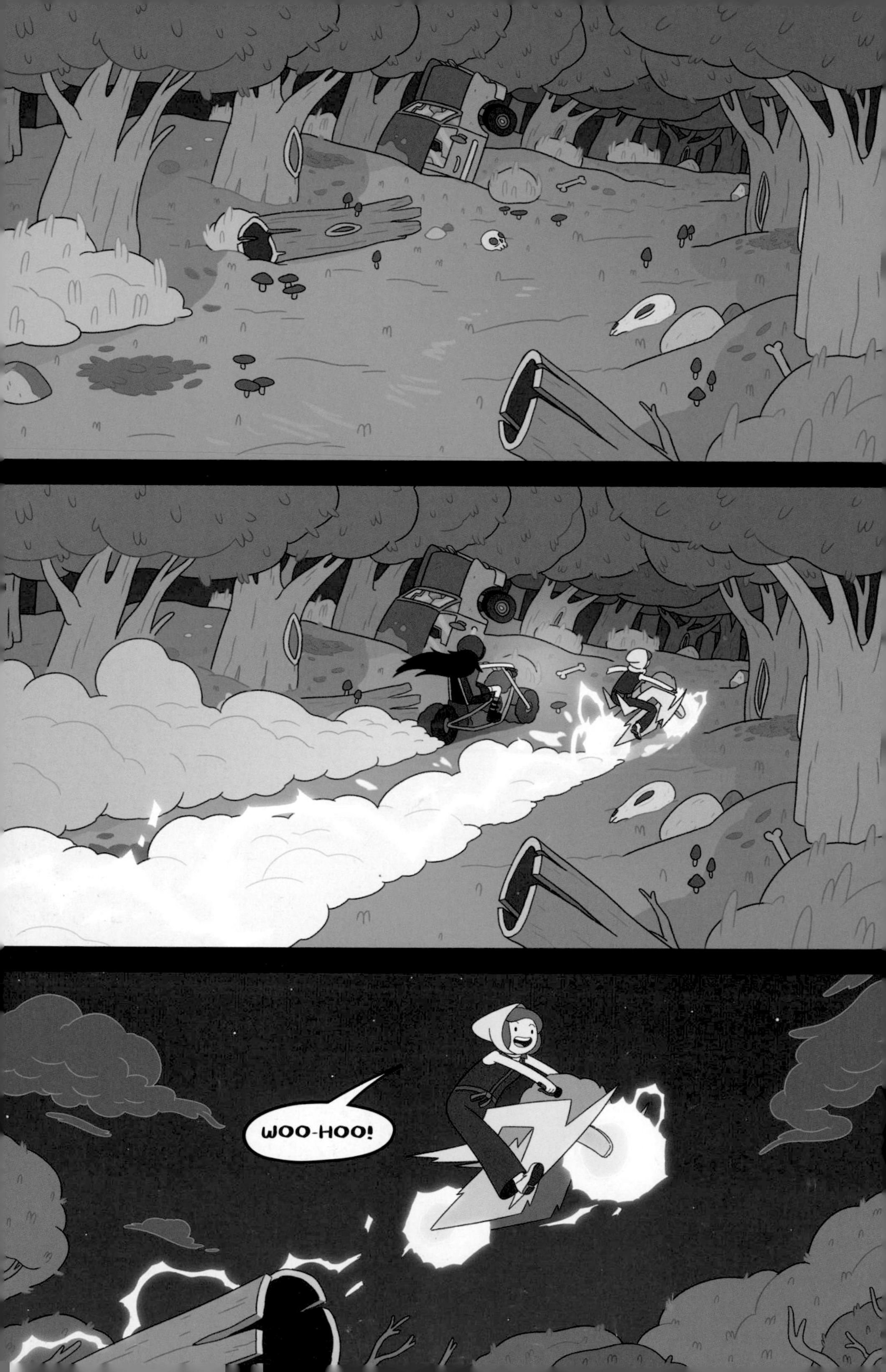
WOO-HOO!

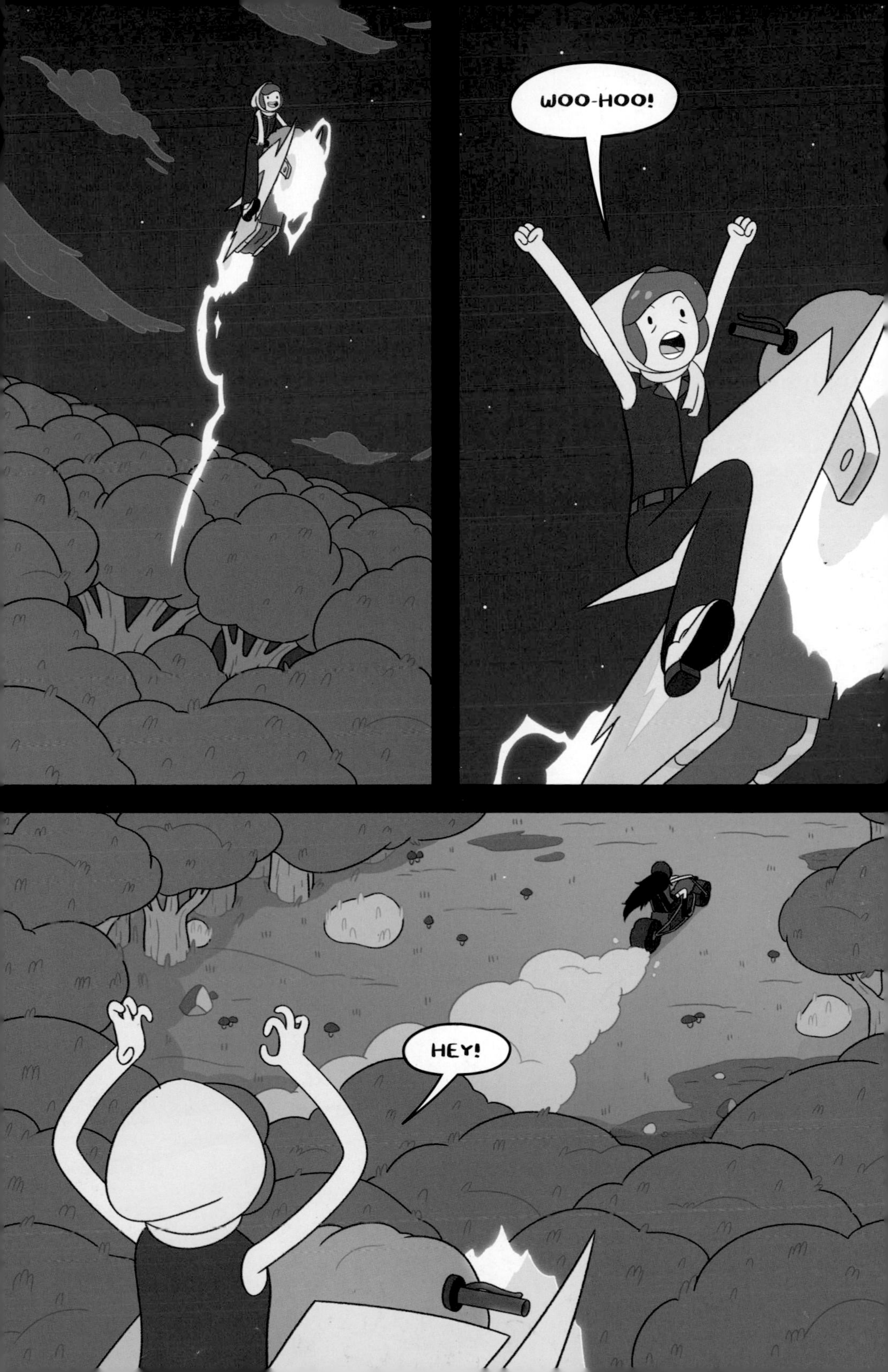
WOO-HOO!
HEY!

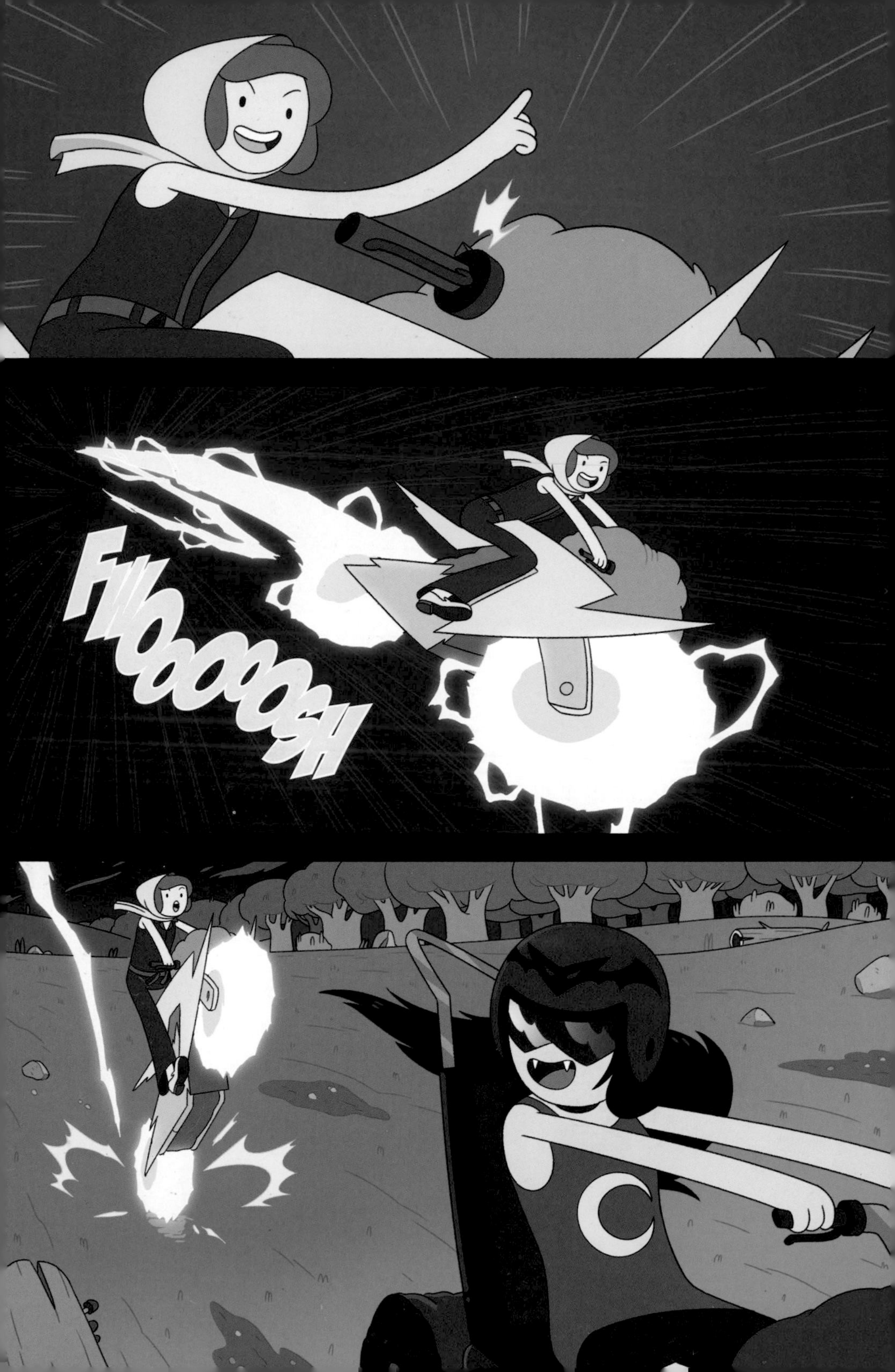
FWOOOOOSH

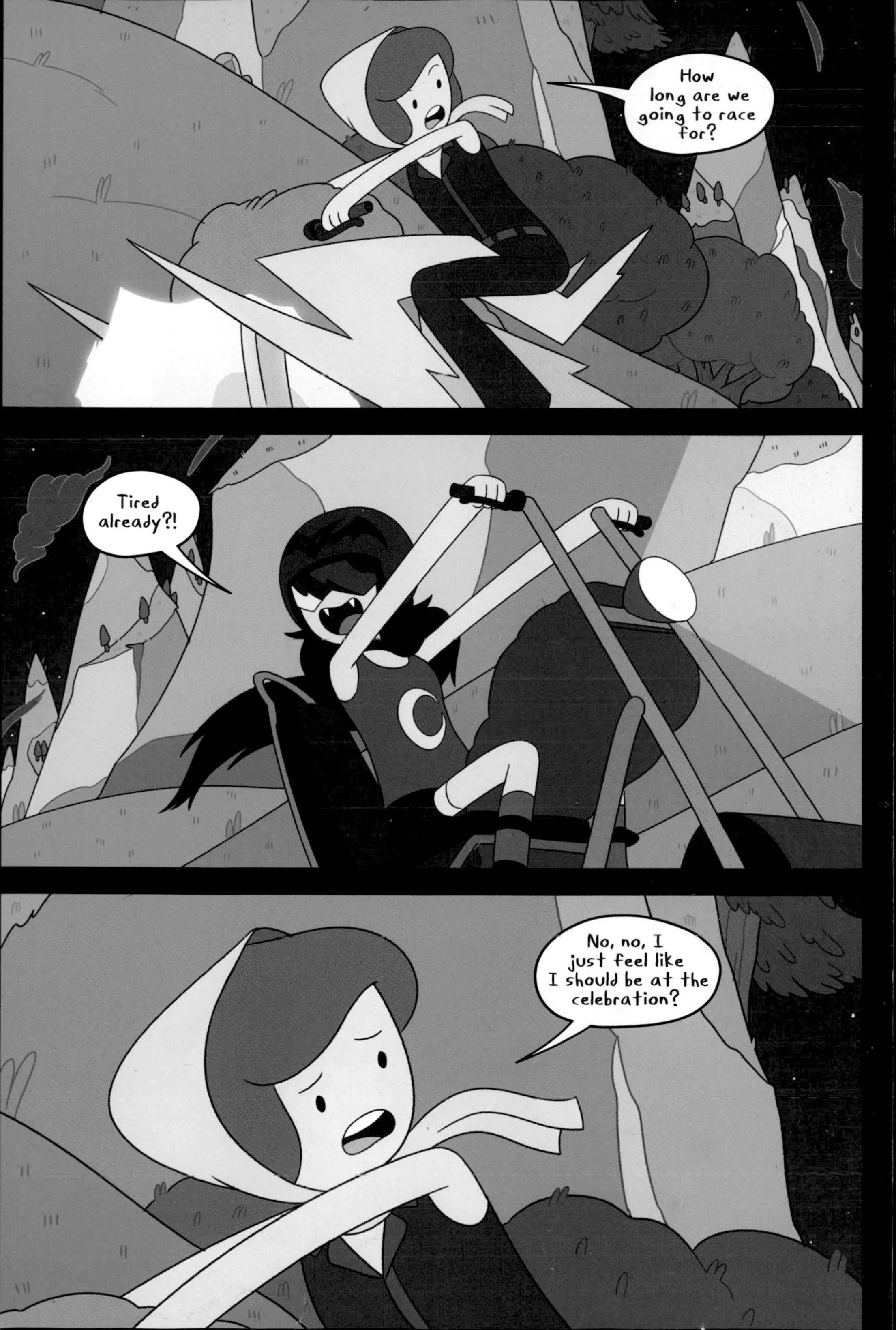
How long are we going to race for?
Tired already?!
No, no, I just feel like I should be at the celebration?

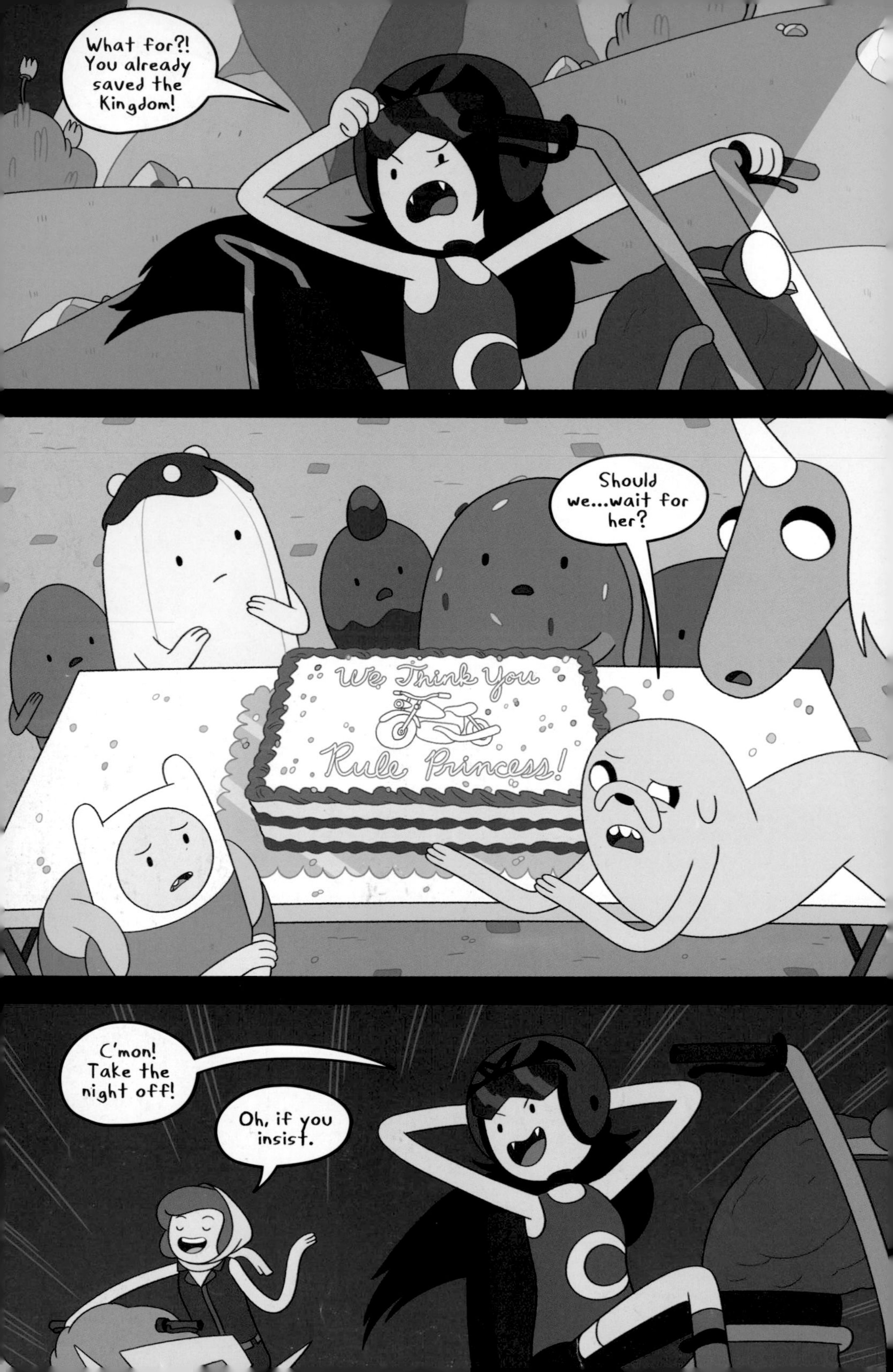
What for?! You already saved the Kingdom!
Should we...wait for her?
We Think You Rule Princess!
C'mon! Take the night off!
Oh, if you insist.

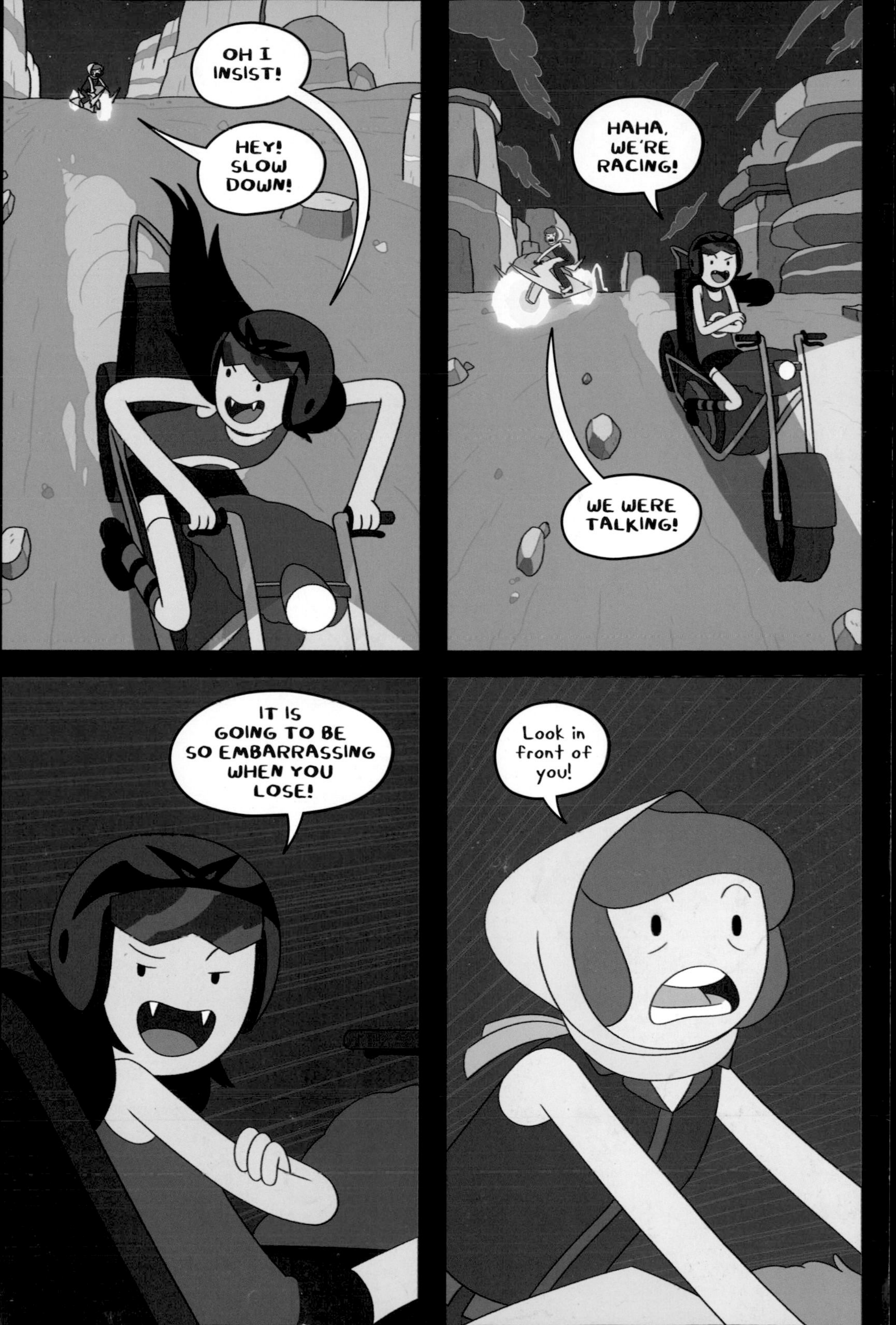
HEY! SLOW DOWN!
OH I INSIST!
HAHA, WE'RE RACING!
WE WERE TALKING!
IT IS GOING TO BE SO EMBARRASSING WHEN YOU LOSE!
Look in front of you!

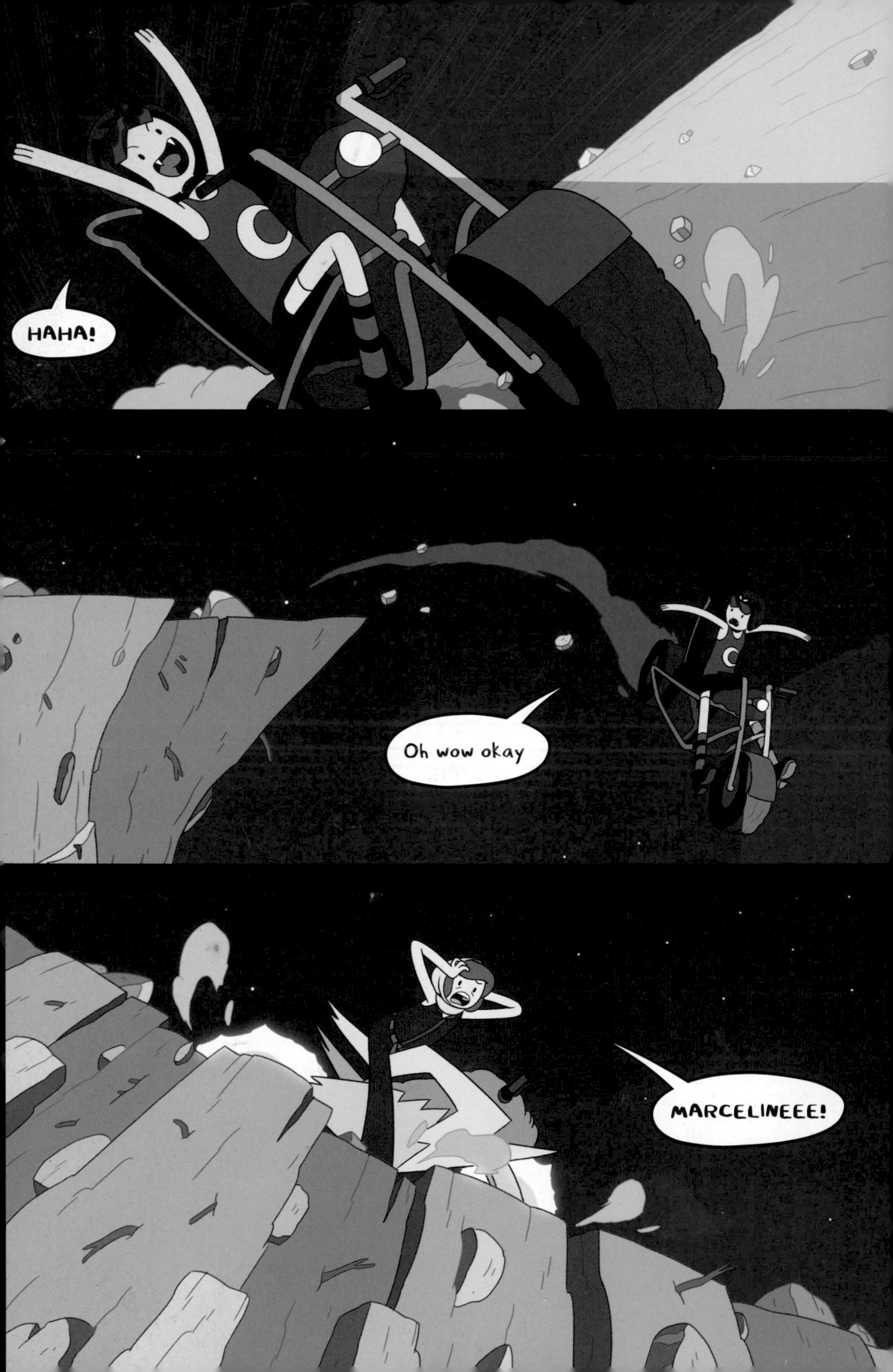
HAHA!
Oh wow okay
MARCELINEEE!

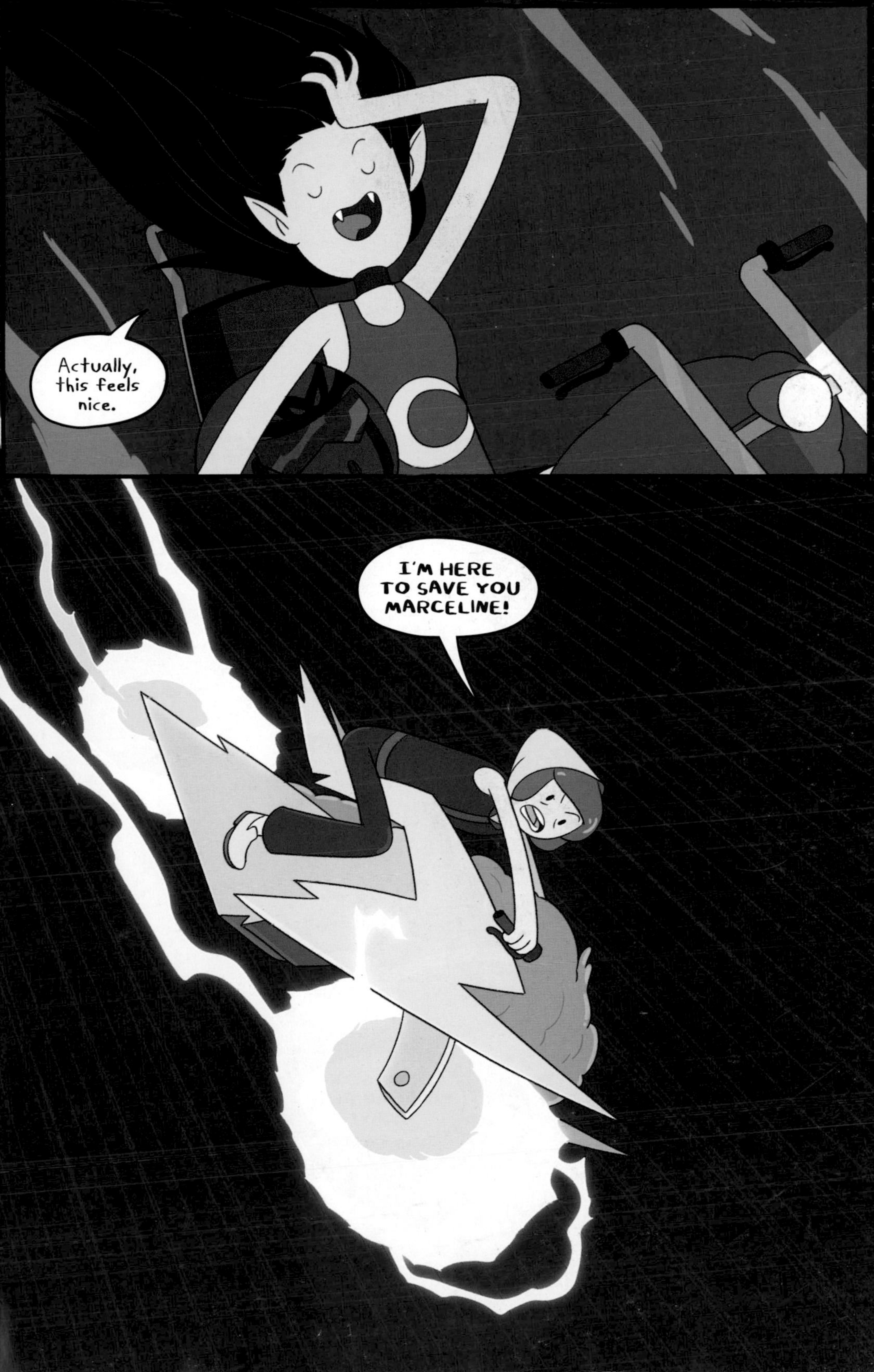
Actually, this feels nice.
I'M HERE TO SAVE YOU MARCELINE!

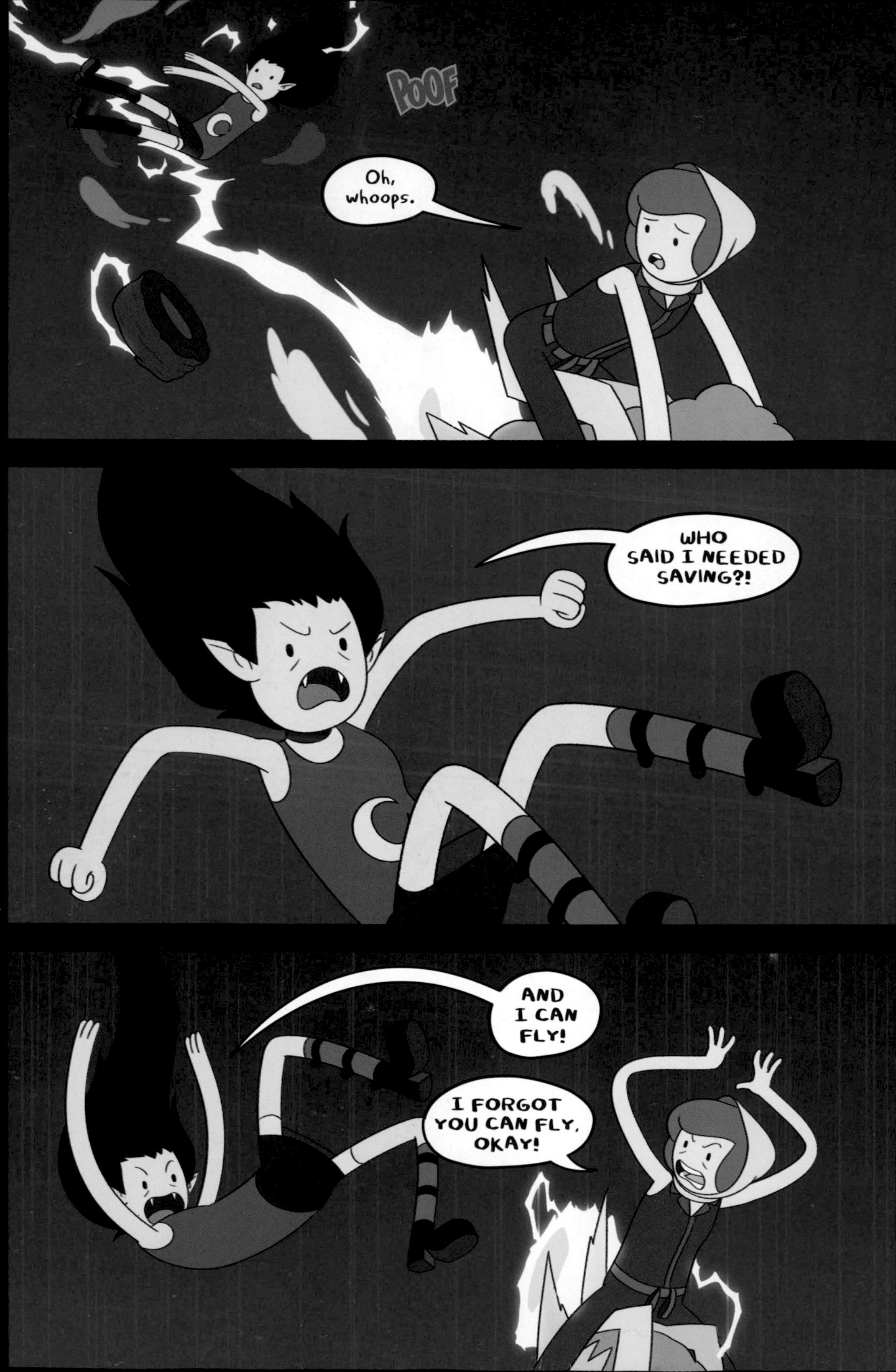
POOF
Oh, whoops.
WHO SAID I NEEDED SAVING?!
AND I CAN FLY!
I FORGOT YOU CAN FLY, OKAY!

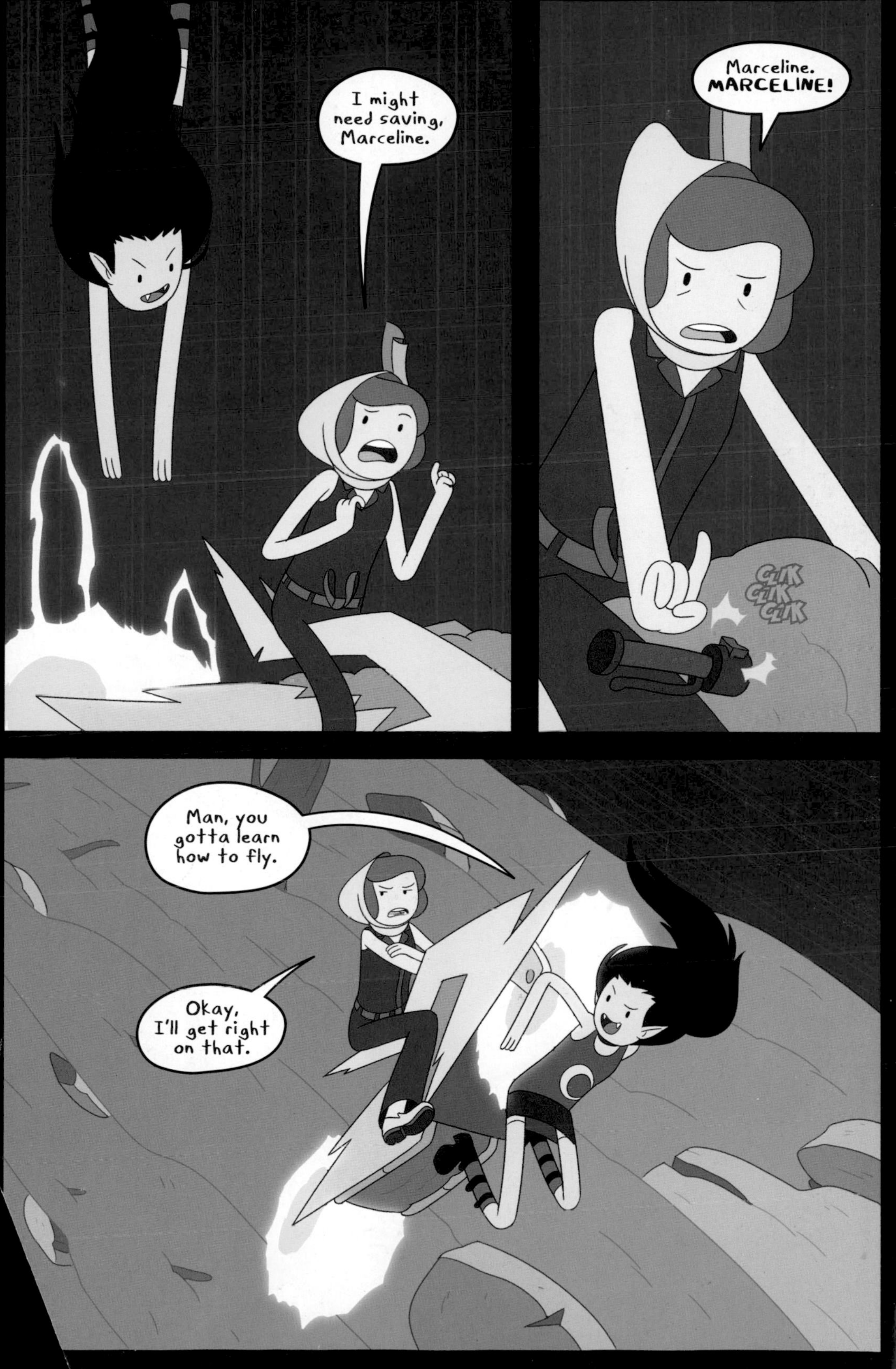
I might need saving, Marceline.
Marceline. MARCELINE!
CLIK CLIK CLIK
Man, you gotta learn how to fly.
Okay, I'll get right on that.

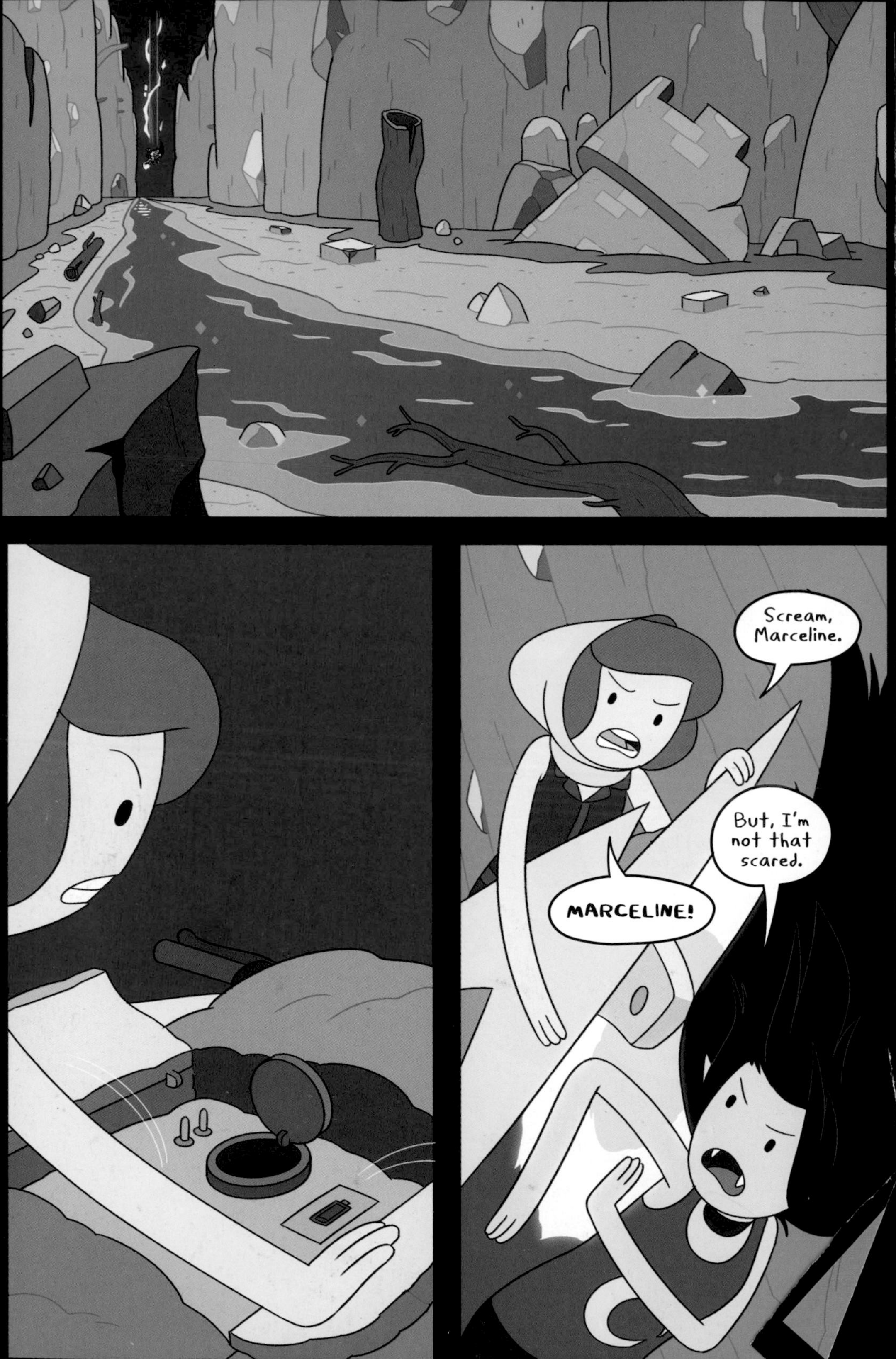
Scream, Marceline.
MARCELINE!
But, I'm not that scared.

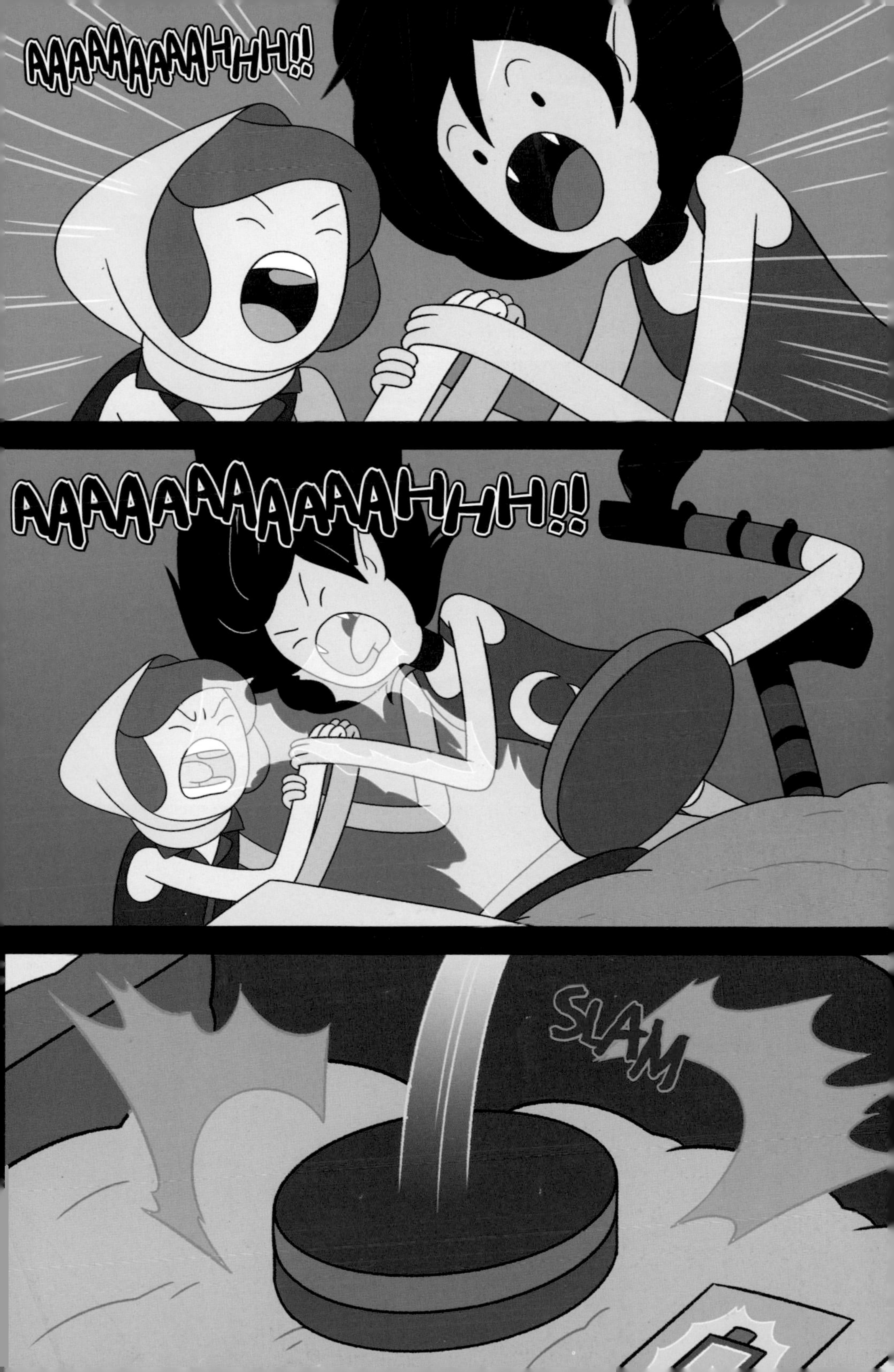
AAAAAAAAAHHH!!
AAAAAAAAAAAHHH!!
SLAM

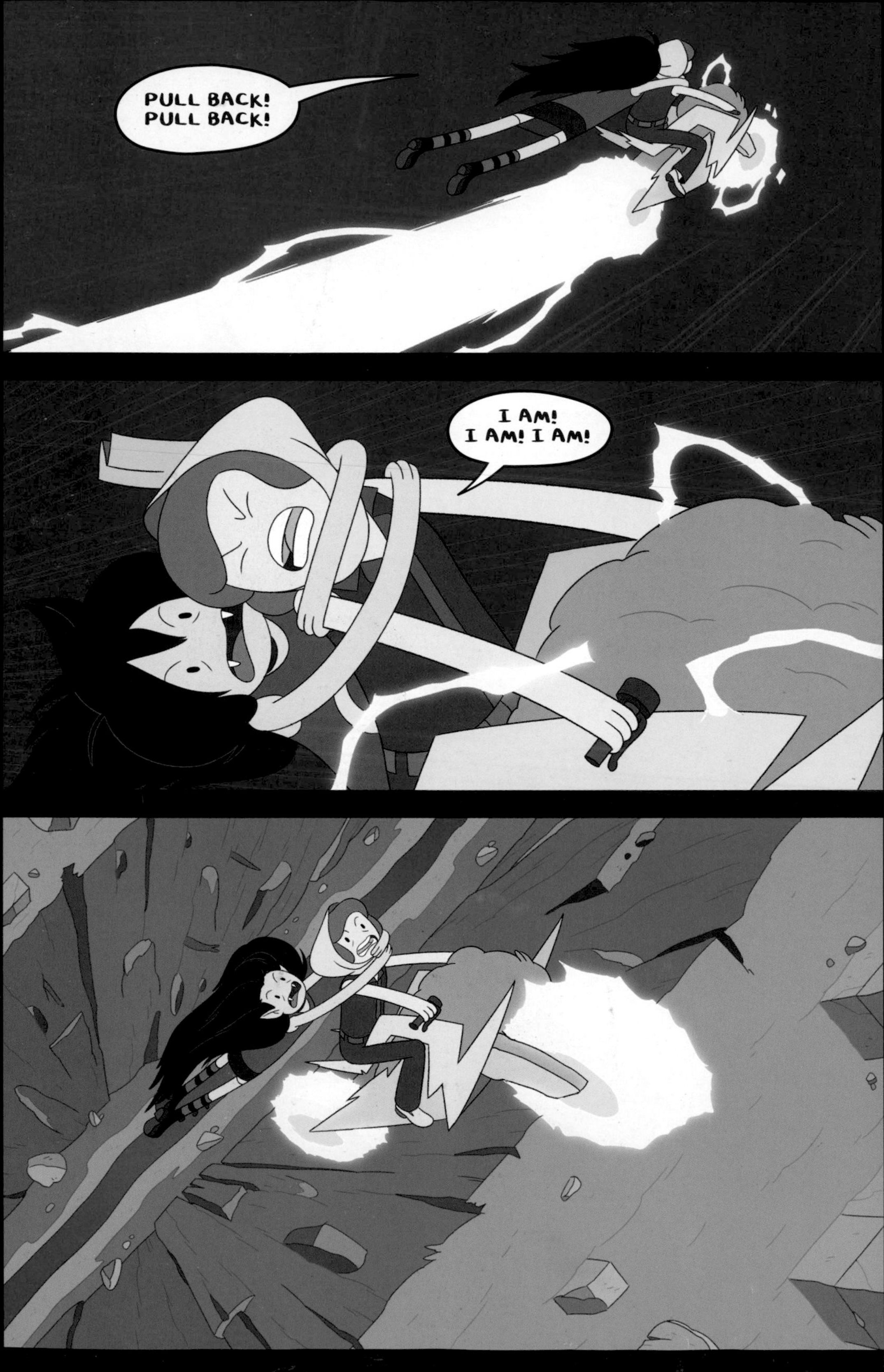
PULL BACK!
PULL BACK!
I AM!
I AM! I AM!

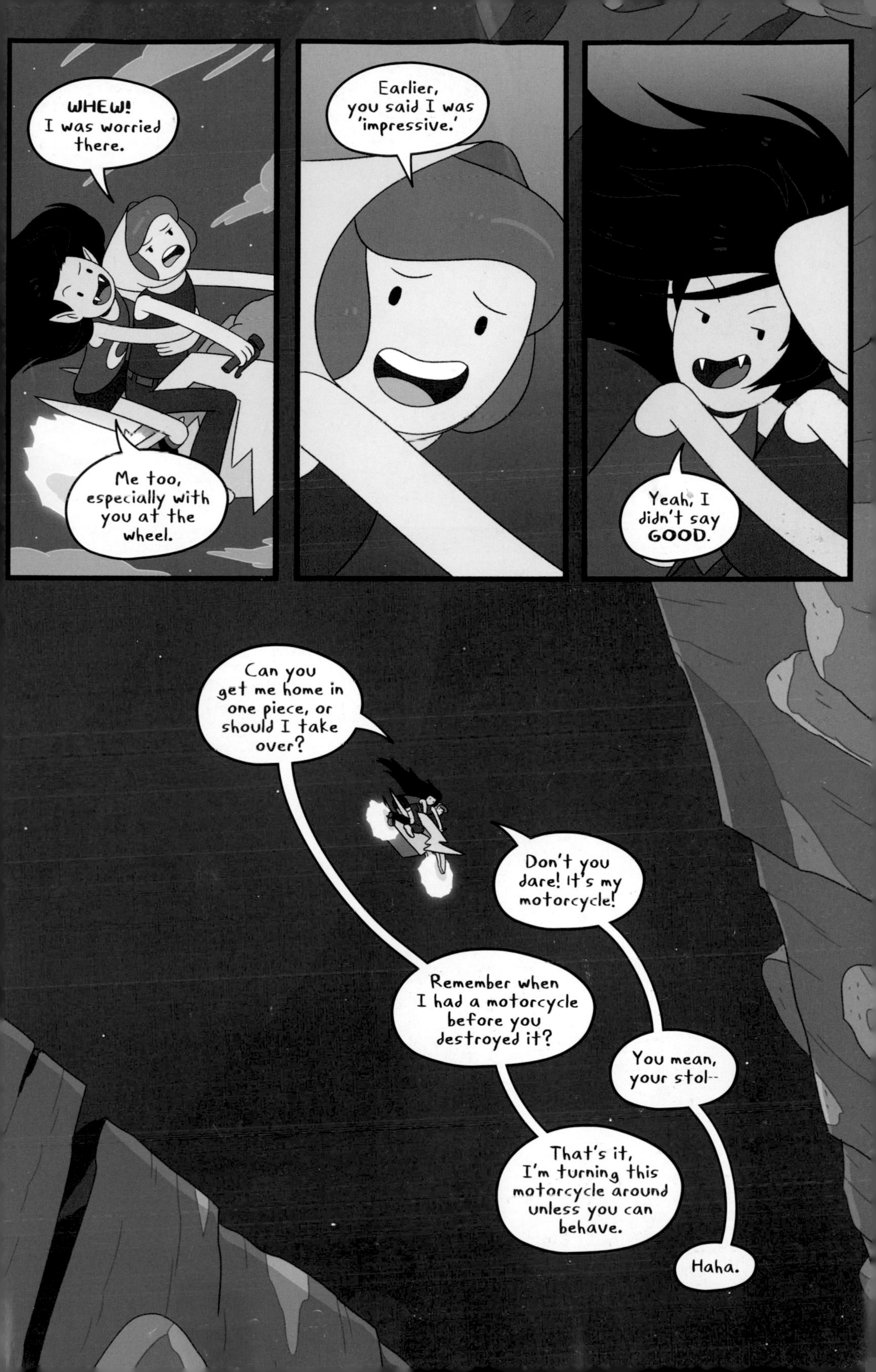
WHEW! I was worried there.
Me too, especially with you at the wheel.
Earlier, you said I was 'impressive.'
Yeah, I didn't say GOOD.
Can you get me home in one piece, or should I take over?
Don't you dare! It's my motorcycle!
Remember when I had a motorcycle before you destroyed it?
You mean, your stol--
That's it, I'm turning this motorcycle around unless you can behave.
Haha.

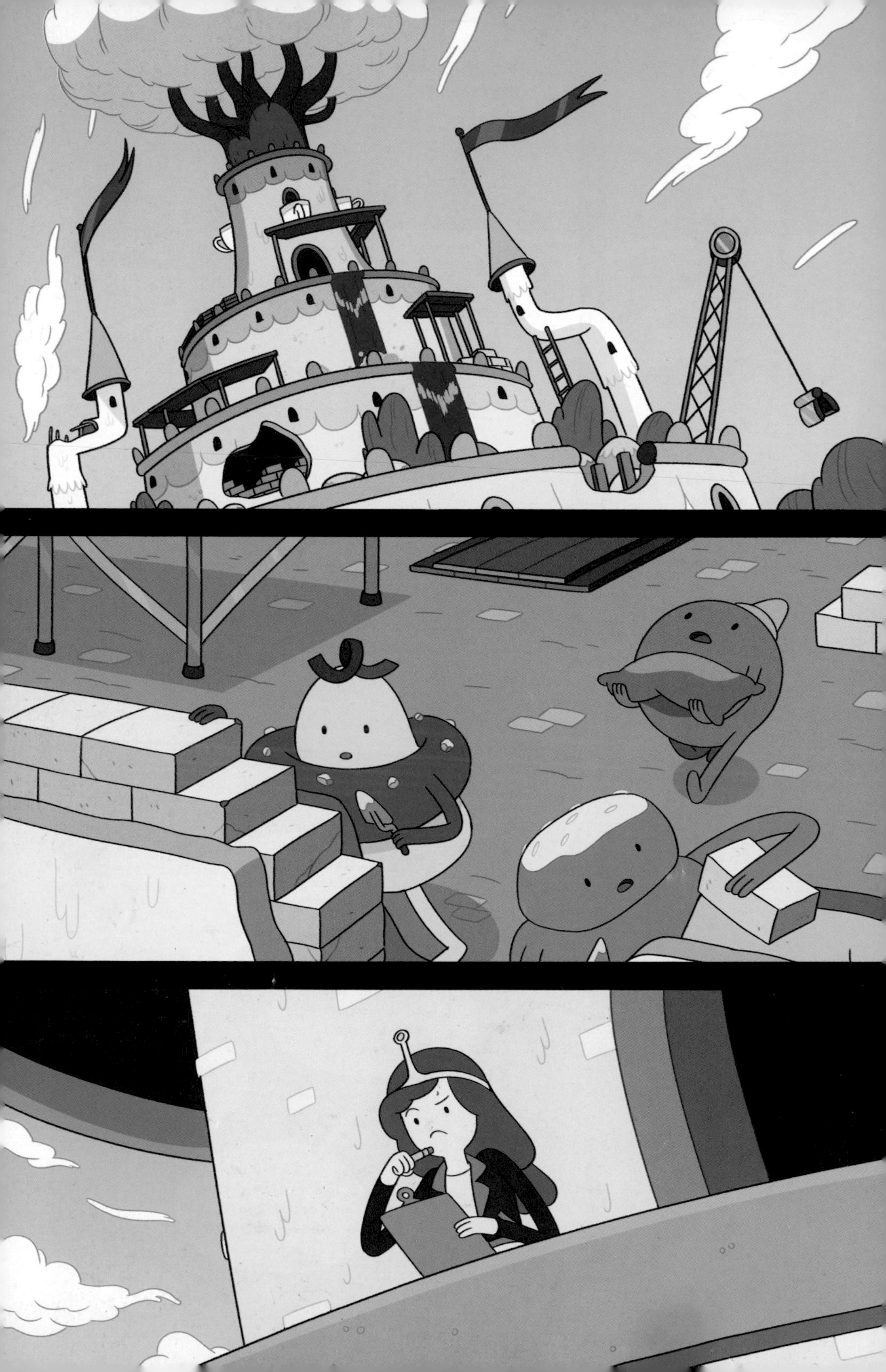

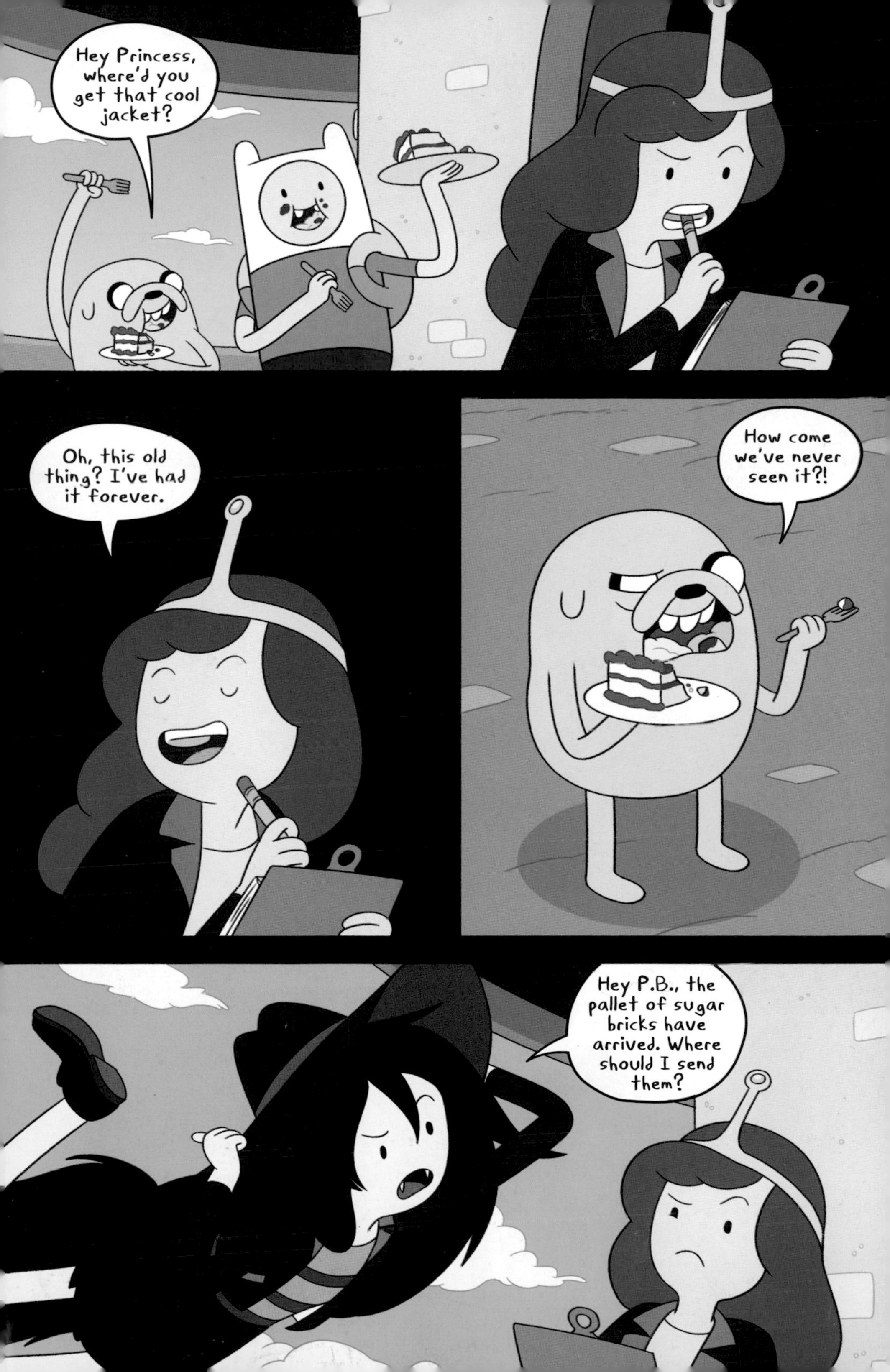
Hey Princess, where'd you get that cool jacket?
Oh, this old thing? I've had it forever.
How come we've never seen it?!
Hey P.B., the pallet of sugar bricks have arrived. Where should I send them?

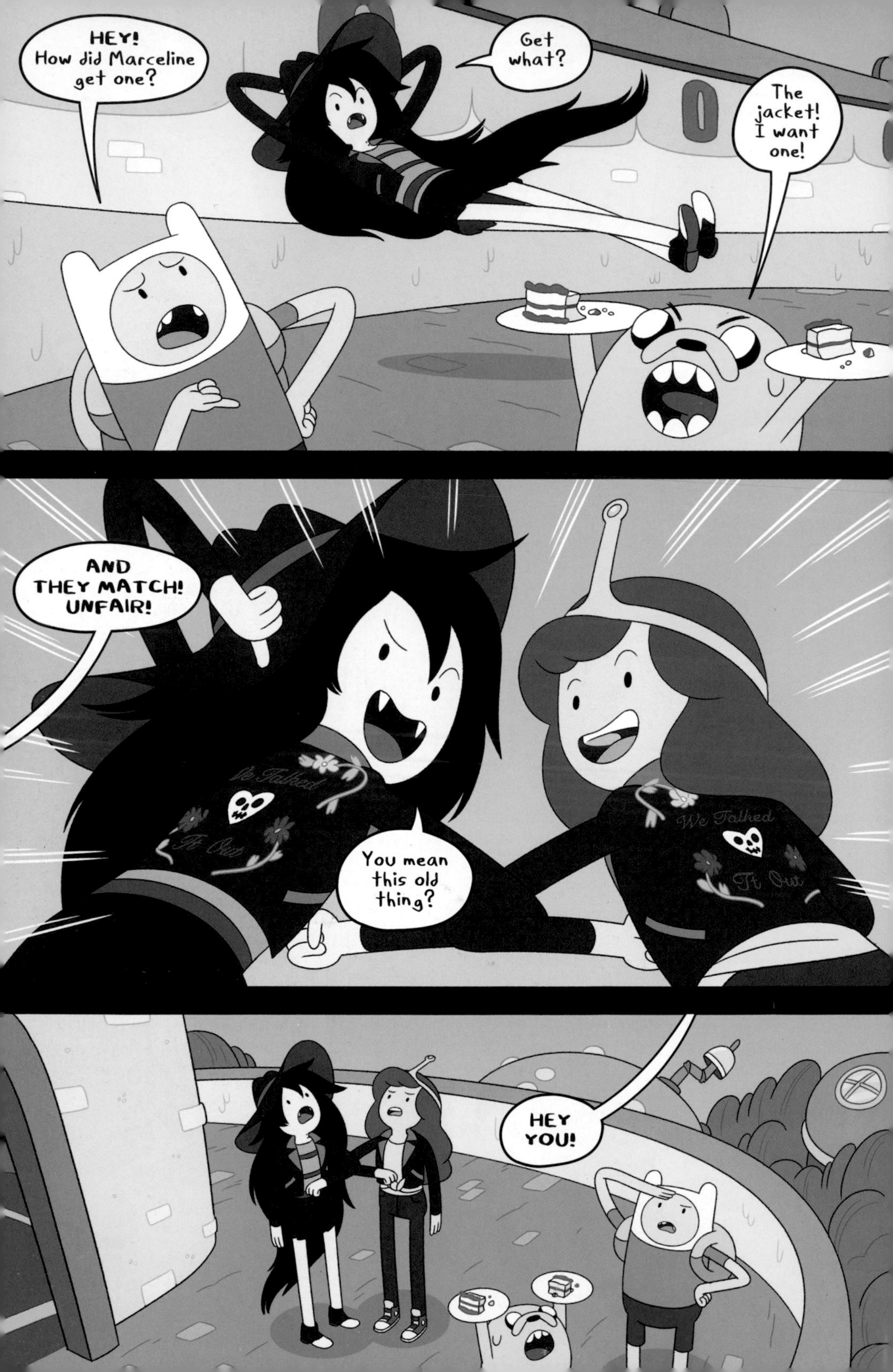
HEY! How did Marceline get one?
Get what?
The jacket! I want one!
AND THEY MATCH! UNFAIR!
You mean this old thing?
We Talked It Out
We Talked It Out
HEY YOU!

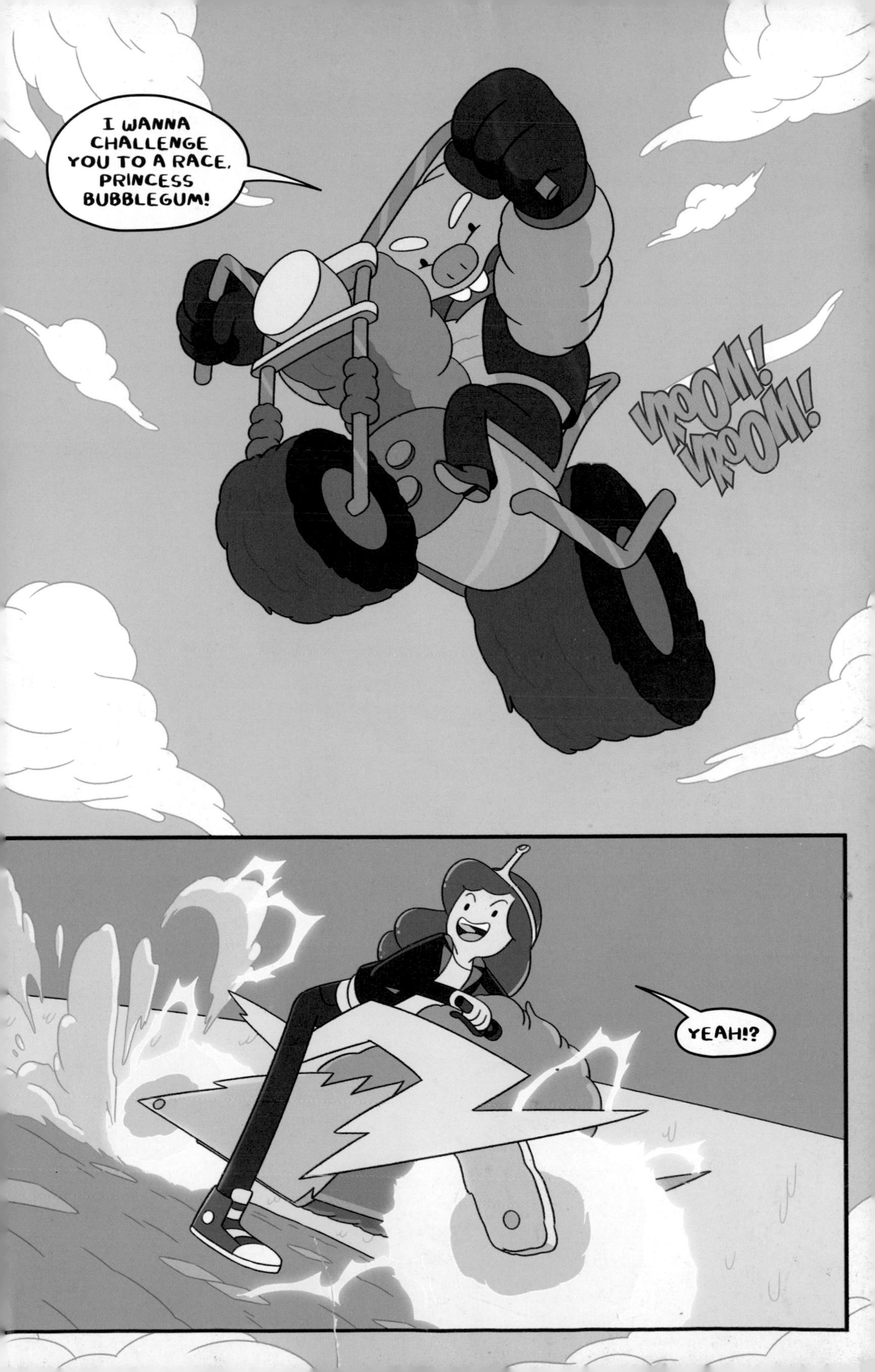
I WANNA CHALLENGE YOU TO A RACE, PRINCESS BUBBLEGUM!
VROOM! VROOM!
YEAH!?

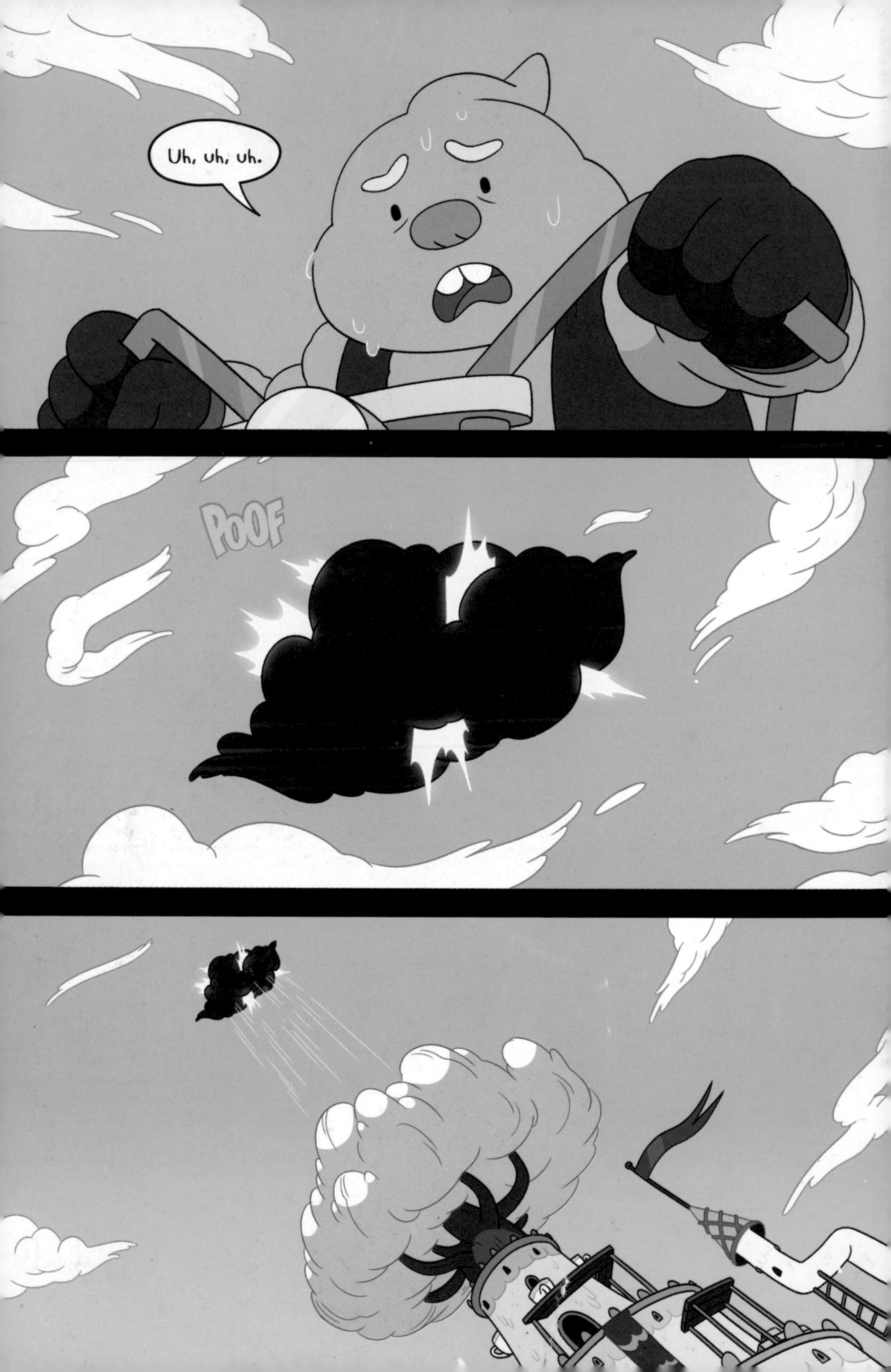
Uh, uh, uh.
POOF

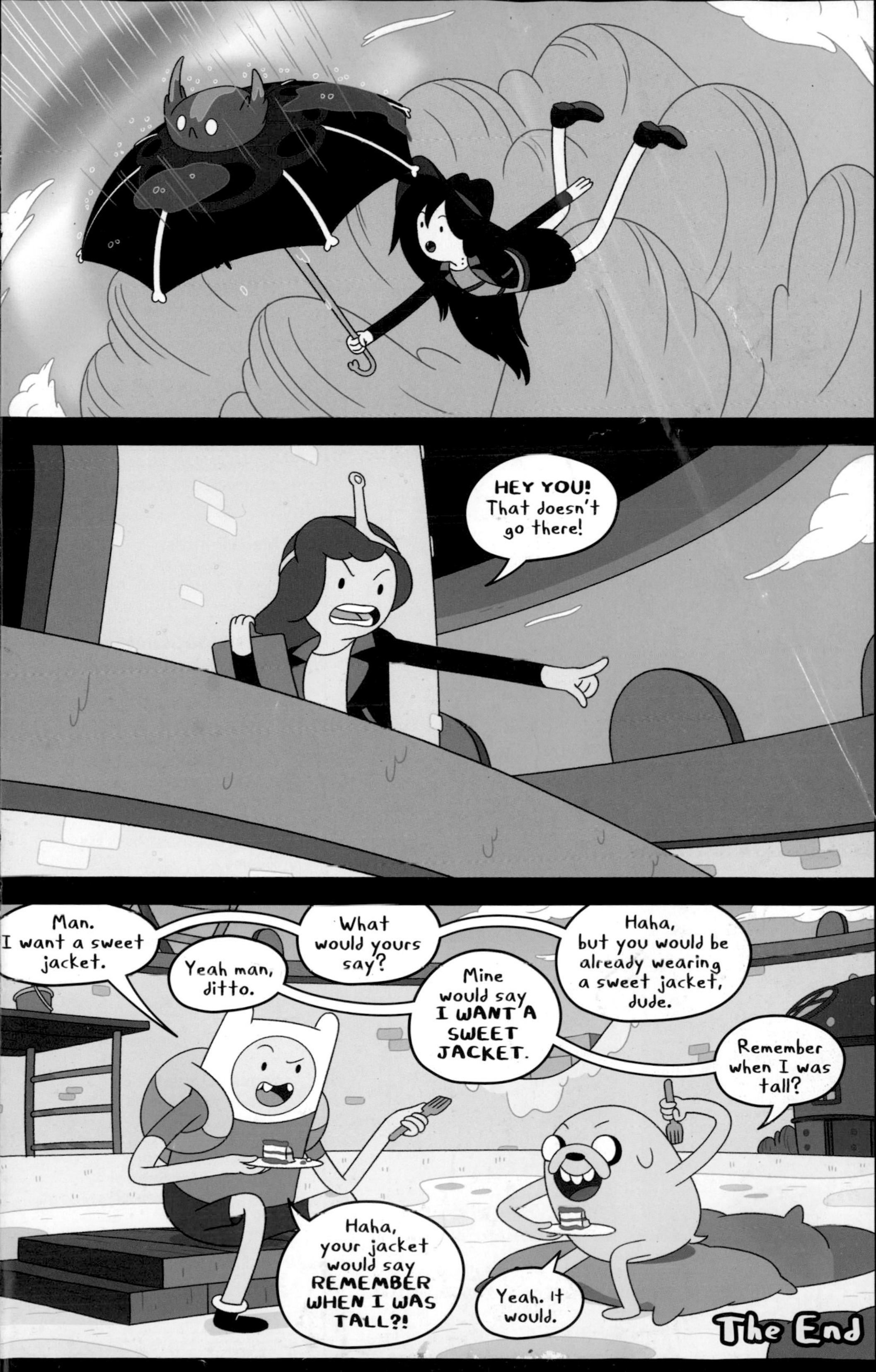
HEY YOU! That doesn't go there!
Man. I want a sweet jacket.
Yeah man, ditto.
What would yours say?
Mine would say I WANT A SWEET JACKET.
Haha, but you would be already wearing a sweet jacket, dude.
Remember when I was tall?
Haha, your jacket would say REMEMBER WHEN I WAS TALL?!
Yeah. It would.
The End

DISCOVER
EXPLOSIVE NEW WORLDS

ADVENTURE TIME

Sam Sykes · Selina Espiritu · Sarah Stern
Brave Chef Brianna

KELLY THOMPSON BRIANNE DROUHARD M. VICTORIA ROBADO
MEGA PRINCESS

THE NOT-SO SECRET SOCIETY
DALEY · CRAFTS · CLARK · BRUNI
KEEP OUT
CAUTION

OVER THE GARDEN WALL

STEVEN UNIVERSE
VOLUME ONE

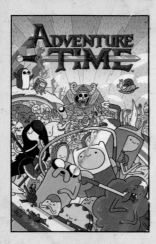

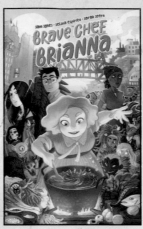

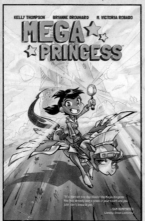

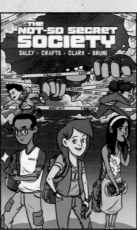

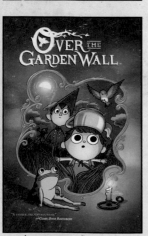

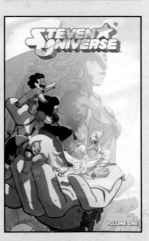

Adventure Time
Pendleton Ward and Others
Volume 1
ISBN: 978-1-60886-280-1 | $14.99 US
Volume 2
ISBN: 978-1-60886-323-5 | $14.99 US
Adventure Time: Islands
ISBN: 978-1-60886-972-5 | $9.99 US

The Amazing World of Gumball
Ben Bocquelet and Others
Volume 1
ISBN: 978-1-60886-488-1 | $14.99 US
Volume 2
ISBN: 978-1-60886-793-6 | $14.99 US

Brave Chef Brianna
Sam Sykes, Selina Espiritu
ISBN: 978-1-68415-050-2 | $14.99 US

Mega Princess
Kelly Thompson, Brianne Drouhard
ISBN: 978-1-68415-007-6 | $14.99 US

The Not-So Secret Society
Matthew Daley, Arlene Daley, Wook Jin Clark
ISBN: 978-1-60886-997-8 | $9.99 US

Over the Garden Wall
Patrick McHale, Jim Campbell and Others
Volume 1
ISBN: 978-1-60886-940-4 | $14.99 US
Volume 2
ISBN: 978-1-68415-006-9 | $14.99 US

Steven Universe
Rebecca Sugar and Others
Volume 1
ISBN: 978-1-60886-706-6 | $14.99 US
Volume 2
ISBN: 978-1-60886-796-7 | $14.99 US

Steven Universe & The Crystal Gems
ISBN: 978-1-60886-921-3 | $14.99 US

Steven Universe: Too Cool for School
ISBN: 978-1-60886-771-4 | $14.99 US

kaboom!™

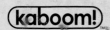

AVAILABLE AT YOUR LOCAL COMICS SHOP AND BOOKSTORE
To find a comics shop in your area, call 1-888-266-4226
WWW.**BOOM-STUDIOS**.COM